I RAN AWAY TO EVIL

BOOK 2

I RAN AWAY TO EVIL

BOOK 2

Mystic Neptune

Cover design by MsArtsy

ISBN: 978-1-0394-5425-5

Published in 2024 by Podium Publishing
www.podiumaudio.com

The
Empire of Sands
Hollow
Nilh
Peldeep
Gren's
Keep

The Untamed Ice Fields
Depths of Despair
North Sumbria
Thistlecrick
Servalt
oria
Kith Bog
Sumbria

I RAN AWAY TO EVIL

BOOK 2

Quests Could Come Later

Madame Potts

[Quest Update: Survive Season Two of Dungeon Delves and Debutantes]
[Welcome to the World of Valaria, an Open-World Battle Otome RPG for the ages.]

[Season Two: Dungeon Delves and Debutantes]
[In Season One, our Heroine Henrietta has worked hard to kill the Dark Overlord, King Monfort, and defeat his minions.]
Error: In Season One, our Heroine Henrietta has worked hard to win the heart of the Dark Lord, King Keith, and his minions.
[After overcoming her traumatic past with the help of her love interests, she finally picked a partner for Grand Duchess Calisto's Spring Ball . . . but is she ready to take the next step?]
Error: After overcoming her traumatic past with the help of her newfound family and friends, she chose to go to the Spring Ball with the Dark Lord.
[Season Two features three new ikemen love interests, new dungeons, access to Servalt and Sumbria, and new crafting material. But beware the threat of revenge from the Dark Enchanted Forest!]
Error: But beware the threats of revenge, for a new power rises in corruption and cruelty.
[Can our Heroine Henrietta complete all of the quests, or will she have even more at stake than she bargained for?]

Season Two Achievements:
0% Scenarios Completed
37% Map Explored
1% Hidden Treasures Found
43% Characters Found

[Come back to your favorite characters with even more Dungeons,
Dragons, and Debutantes!]

The story was changing. The Heroine of Justice was happily living in the Dark Enchanted Forest and *not* traipsing about the continent. She was going to go back home to her dark castle with her Dark Lord husband and live *happily ever after*.

As she deserved.

So what if that meant a lot of quests were going to be unfulfilled? There were others who could be persuaded to fix those problems.

But that was work for another day.

A lizardkin maid rolled in the tea and cake. The wedding cake was a twist on a recipe from the *Out of This World* cookbook, with fresh bimbleberries on hazelnut whipped topping.

Sharing recipes from the real world had been a stroke of genius. Many were enjoying the taste paired with the warm nettle honey brew or the cool elderberry and lime refresher.

Sip.

"Please, everyone, it's time to take your seats."

It'd been *five years* since waking up in this video game, and Part One had successfully ended without half of the continent getting drawn into war with the Dark Enchanted Forest. Happily Ever Afters for all! Even the characters everyone had shipped together had managed to find each other with a little added extra help.

Well, most of them.

Yes, quests could come later; today was a day for *celebration*.

CHAPTER 1

Nobody Managed to Poison the Punch!

Rufus

"I now pronounce you, Dark Lord and Lady!" Their Royal Highness Rowen of Peldeep announced. "You may kiss the bride!"

The pair obliged, and a cheer erupted from the guests as I let out a sigh of relief. Keith was married, and nobody had lit anything on fire!

Of course, that was when the crowd's cheering cut off into a sudden unnatural quiet.

Everyone was looking up in fear. "What?" I stiffened, searching the area for assassins, when an unmistakable green tail with a purple sheen dropped down from above.

Her Eminence Feliwyn the dragon whipped her tail around in her sleep. It landed daintily between the dais and the first row of guests.

Everyone held their breath, readying to run screaming for their lives. The dragon had been asleep for eight years now and not awoken from her proposed decade-long nap.

Luckily, the dragon resettled.

"We invite everyone to the reception," Their Royal Highness Rowen declared loudly, dragging everyone's attention away from the house-size magical lizard, "where there will be music and refreshments."

The tension eased, and I joined the rest of the wedding party as we navigated stage left around the curling tail.

"Getting married beside Her Eminence was *your* idea," I teased Chloe the Necromancer.

"And I told *you* this was going to be a wedding they'll never forget!" She chuckled. "You worry too much, Rufus. Besides, this way she gets to attend."

I scanned the field. We were set up beside Lake Loria, the largest lake in the

Dark Enchanted Forest of Nilheim. Below, in its depths, lay the city of Plittsmouth, home to selkies and kelpies and all other manner of murderous aquatic folk. They were a blast at parties.

After enough time had passed to ensure that Feliwyn wasn't going to wake up—that dragon was *not* a morning person—the lake inhabitants came back to frolic in the waters.

There were no obvious threats, but I activated a perk to be sure.

[You have attempted to use the Perk: **Detect Fake**. You have succeeded.]
[Scanning targets equal to your Perception 30 x **Examine** 6. You have selected all 180 available targets. No Disguise-based abilities detected.]

It didn't work on those individuals who were higher level than me, but not many people on the continent fit that description.

Unfortunately, most of those people were invited to this event.

Sigh.

I checked to make sure my mana could handle another hour of this.

Name:	Rufus Triever		
Occupation:	Commander General		
Level:	54		
Experience Points:	12787/13500		
Hit Points:	616/616		
Mana Points:	540/900		
Class:	Commander		
Titles:			
[Beastfolk], [Protector], [Mediator], [General], [Commander], [Connoisseur]			
Attributes:			
Strength:	26	Intelligence:	30
Dexterity:	19	Perception:	30

Constitution:	24	Charisma:	19
Skills:			
Keen Senses:	2	Leadership:	4
Secure:	6	Bureaucracy:	4
Patient:	6	Examine:	6
Perks:			
Sense Threat, Redirect Blow, Claw Strike, Force Palm, Empathy, Calming Effect, Inspire Honesty, Commanding Voice, Natural Poise, Sense Lies, Personnel, Detect Poison, Detect Fake, Identify Craft.			

I turned my attention to my notifications and finished processing the myriad information en masse.

The headache that accompanied it thrummed in my temples, but I maintained a calm and assured appearance. It was the work of seconds, and I did it every quarter hour. The downside of my abilities was the time it took to comprehend what the system was feeding me, and I'd long ago masked the discomfort with a serene and confident air.

There were almost two hundred guests from around the continent at Keith and Henrietta's wedding, and between my [Examine] skill and my two perks [Sense Threat] and [Sense Lies], I was getting an untenable number of prompts.

I wanted to vomit.

And then, just as my headache was becoming unbearable and my stomach clenched . . . I heard it.

If I had one weakness, it was this. *Her voice.*

> . . . and the battle that she fought was for
> The Dark Lord's Heart she won.

While Minstrel Bronwynn had originally been playing light instrumental music in the background, the Dark Lady had requested a song, and the dulcet tones of the bard's singing carried over the crowd.

They said music tamed the savage beast, so call me savage, because ever since that night I slipped into a tavern in Peldeep and first heard Minstrel Bronwynn perform "The Traveler's Tale," I'd been under her spell.

"Do you think she could be convinced to play at *my* wedding?" Chloe broke me out of my musical revelry. She tapped her chin slowly. Her long, curly blonde hair was done up in intricate braids for the affair, all over with flowers, and while she stood no taller than my bicep . . . she was a *terrifying* force of nature.

"You would have to ask her." I shrugged. "She hasn't announced her summer tour yet, so she might be free."

"Oh, really." Chloe raised an eyebrow at me. "Where is she off to next?"

I took a sip of my drink. "She's going to Servalt for Duke Wyldon's birthday tea party, then she's off to Peldeep for an apple blossom ceremony, and then she promised Henrietta that she'll visit for the Hollow Silver Star Festival, all of which takes place before your wedding at the Summer Masquerade."

Chloe creased her brow in a delicate frown and scrunched up her nose in disgust. "*Whyever* would she agree to visit Servalt after they kidnapped her and broke her instrument? I'm surprised the place hasn't fallen apart already after the whole incident at the Spring Ball."

"Servalt is hunting down the perpetrators," I pointed out. "And they've successfully recovered all of Lieutenant Franni's platoon."

"That still proves my point, doesn't it?" Chloe countered. "If they're still hunting down the villains, then the villains are *still out there*. And there are plenty of reasons to stay away in the meantime."

"You're just saying that because you don't like Servalt." I laughed. "From what the Continental Council has gathered, this mess stretches *everywhere*, and every kingdom is responsible for contributing to the search."

"I *don't* like Servalt," Chloe agreed. "So how is the search going?"

"Duke Wyldon returned to Servalt after the Spring Ball and tore apart every estate associated with Marquess Chadwick. He's done most of my work for me."

"What's left then?"

I sighed, the thought of the previous weeks' overtime a distant nightmare that still wasn't over. "Now that I've finished combing through transit documents from every Servalt merchant going back over the last three years and reviewed every single missing person, and immigration and emigration file, I just need to cross-reference those forms with the other kingdoms border offices."

"Sounds fun," Chloe said dryly. She tried to cheer me up with, "At least it's just paper shuffling? It shouldn't take too long."

"*Do you know how many people have emigrated to North Sumbria in the last year alone?!*" I dragged a hand down my face, dreading the arduous task ahead. It was my fault, though; I'd been teasing my king a lot recently, and vengeance was a dish best served with paperwork. "And that's not everything; I've *also* been tasked to visit our illustrious neighbors to check on those *gifts* our rulers sent them."

Namely, the seventy-five-odd assassins who'd survived the Dark Enchanted Forest and been kindly sent back to the guilds in Servalt and Peldeep. Nobody had bothered to check which assassins went to which guild, but that would be their job to sort out.

I just needed to go and reestablish contracts with both guilds so that it wouldn't happen again. And, under order by my king, figure out how the assassins keep popping up everywhere and getting past the kingdom's golem defenses.

"Now *that* actually sounds fun." A brilliant smile lit up her face as Chloe's fiancée, Countess Julia, walked over to join us.

"Dear, are you bothering Rufus while he's on guard duty?" Julia chastised playfully, winding an arm around the necromancer's shoulders. Julia was a head taller than Chloe, and she took after her mother: tall, dark, and powerful.

"We're *all* on guard duty." Chloe waved a hand over the wedding party. "But it's unlikely anything will happen with Feliwyn so close."

We all turned to the giant sleeping dragon, who remained blissfully oblivious to the celebration going on around her.

"When do you think Her Eminence Feliwyn will wake up?" Julia asked. "I heard King Keith say it was soon, but *how* soon?"

I shrugged. "It's been eight years. . . so any day now?"

"I think she'll nap the whole decade," Chloe said. She finished her drink and wrapped her arms around Julia's forearm. "How about we take a walk? I need to check on *everything*."

"Of course you do, darling." Her soon-to-be wife laughed. "It's almost time to swear fealty, and the unicorns are getting antsy."

"Why didn't you say so?!" Chloe perked up and started for the herds milling about the field away from the celebration. "I'll go speak with Goldenhoof right now."

I finished my drink and headed for the snack table while enjoying the ambiance that Minstrel Bronwynn added to the event. Suddenly, sorting through a few hundred people's emotions didn't seem so hard.

The Dark Enchanted Forest welcomed its new Dark Lady with open arms. No one tried to outright assassinate anyone, even as representatives from around the kingdom offered their allegiance to Queen Henrietta.

And nobody had poisoned the punch!

All in all, the wedding was a great success. And I was ready to get back to the castle for a rest.

CHAPTER 2

It's Better Than Eating Babies

Brownie

"Could you, Brownie?" the queen of the Dark Enchanted Forest pleaded, her huge brown eyes twinkling with evil intent. "Please?"

"Minstrel Bronwynn Lyriel," the king of the Dark Enchanted Forest interrupted, snaking an arm around his wife's shoulders and ordering—nay, begging—"Now is *not* the time."

"Well," Brownie began, glancing at her friend. "It's actually perfect—"

"Ria, tell your friend you've changed your mind," King Keith leaned down and breathed seductively into the queen's ear.

"But I really want to hear it!" Henrietta pouted up at him. "Just this once? As a wedding present?"

There was a forced pause as he held off as long as he could . . . but eventually, the Dark Lord gave in to the whims of his adorable wife. His voice strained against an inner pain that stemmed from embarrassment and uncertainty. "Alright."

Brownie could imagine, since the only other song written about King Keith was anything but *flattering*. Eating babies wasn't the kind of thing you wanted sung about you at your wedding.

"As you will, Your Viciousnesses,"

Henrietta snorted quietly at the address.

Brownie's fingers lightly plucked a melody that she'd spent the better part of a week perfecting. Her new lyre harp, Danielle, had been given to her from *a dragon's hoard*. King Keith had awarded it to her for her part in escaping slave traders with his wife.

She regretted bashing the kidnapper over the head with Suzette, as it'd cost her a lifelong friend. Brownie missed that lyre harp; her cousins in Peldeep had gifted Suzette to her for her tenth birthday, and she'd been playing it for thirteen years now.

Still! She had a new instrument. And the fact that it rarely went out of tune and fit perfectly against the palm of her large hands made the sting of losing sweet Suzette slightly more bearable.

Brownie opened her character sheet. She wanted to make this song a *sensation*.

Name:	Bronwynn Lyriel
Occupation:	Bard
Level:	31
Experience Points:	6360/7750
Hit Points:	221/221
Mana Points:	150/238
Bonded Companion:	Belladonna Windrunner
Condition:	Grimalcat Promise
Class:	Minstrel

Titles:			
[Half Giantess], [Rogue], [Bard], [Minstrel]			

Attributes:			
Strength:	19 (+5 Race Stat)	**Intelligence:**	17
Dexterity:	18	**Perception:**	17
Constitution:	15	**Charisma:**	21

Skills:			
Child of Seven:	2	**Siren Song:**	6
Knife Play:	5	**Inspiration:**	2

Perks:			
Sturdy, Hidden Dagger, Liar's Palace, Piercing Wave, Strength of Sound, Idol, Inspire.			

She activated her bardic skill [Siren Song] to help with this particular performance, allocating the twenty-five mana needed to keep it going for the five minutes.

[**Siren Song** affects targets equal to or lesser than Level 31. Targets affected 31 x 6 = 186. 46 targets selected. For three times the duration of the song, all targets who hear the song gain a +1 modifier to Intelligence and must fight a Perception 21 to break free of the music.]

The notes she plucked were light and whimsical, with a rich cadence that crept through the wedding crowd, drawing attention.

There are many tales in time that tell
Of battles fought between
Heroines of light and villains' evil schemes!
And all would know the Dark Lord
In his castle to the north
Had long been making monsters
To fill in his Dark Horde.

Oh, oh, oh, oh, oh, oh, oh . . .

The king and queen used cruelty,
To raise their princess right.
A sword in hand, to shield the land
From the encroaching night.
They abandoned her to darkness
When they sent her off alone
To battle beasts and monsters there
Who called the Forest home.

Oh, oh, oh, oh, oh, oh, oh . . .

But in the Dark Enchanted Forest,
She found love among the trees,
Where dire wolves howl at the moon
And a troll might offer a cup of tea.
There's laughter in the beastfolk keep,
There's comfort in the selkie song.
And the battle that she fought for

Was the Dark Lord's Heart she won.

Oh, oh, oh, oh, oh, oh, oh . . .

She stormed into the castle
With some bimbleberry scones.
Her blade had never left its sheath
Against the golem stone.
The lizardkin had lunch with her and
Brought her to their Lord
The inner sanctum of his power
To a duel magic and sword.

Oh, oh, oh, oh, oh, oh . . .

But lo His Royal Viciousness
Confused at what he found,
A princess who was sent to him
To die or take his throne.
Instead he took her in and offered her a brand-new start
To live the life she longed for and
To follow her own heart.

Oh, oh, oh, oh, oh, oh, oh . . .

But in the Dark Enchanted Forest,
She found love among the trees,
Where dire wolves howl at the moon
And a troll might offer a cup of tea.
There's laughter in the beastfolk keep,
There's comfort in the selkie song.
And the battle that she fought for
Was the Dark Lord's Heart she won.

Oh, oh, oh, oh, oh, oh, oh . . .

Oh, oh, oh, oh, oh, oh, oh . . .

The princess locked inside her tower
Found family and friend.
The Dark Lord found a treasure

He would hold until the end.
She went to battle life and death
And bring her people peace,
But now she reigns beside the villain
As the Dark Lord's Dark Lady.

Oh, oh, oh, oh, oh, oh . . .

But in the Dark Enchanted Forest,
She found love among the trees,
Where dire wolves howl at the moon
And a troll might offer a cup of tea.
There's laughter in the beastfolk keep,
There's comfort in the selkie song.
And the battle that she fought for was
The Dark Lord's Heart she won.

There was silence from the crowd when she finished. Henrietta wiped a tear from her eye, and King Keith blushed all the way up to his pointed ear tips. Even his horn would've turned crimson if it could.

"Well?" Brownie asked, a touch nervous since it was her first time actually singing that *particular* song in front of an audience.

Hey, she could be fabulous *and* secretly anxious at the same time. She never knew if *this time* she might utterly fail at writing an engaging song. And on the day of her best friend's wedding.

Who'd told Henrietta to go off and marry the Dark Lord, anyway?

Her fears were unfounded, as Henrietta burst into applause and the crowd followed suite. Brownie even caught a nod from King Keith as he composed himself. She read his lips as he mumbled under his breath, "I guess it's better than eating babies . . ."

As far as compliments went, Brownie would take it!

CHAPTER 3

Does Henrietta Know?

Rufus

"What?" My ear twitched, giving away the nervous confusion that gripped me after hearing what my king had said.

"I want you to escort Minstrel Bronwynn to Servalt and keep an eye on her," King Keith ordered. We were alone in Keith's inner sanctum, where I'd been summoned.

I used the opportunity to admire the workshop. Great planetary alignments hung from the ceiling, where a giant guardian snake golem lived. Solar and lunar timekeeping globes circled the dome, mirroring the positions of the heavenly bodies in the sky outside. Along the edge of the room, there was a giant wall of tools that would make any craftsmen weep with envy.

Usually, no one was allowed in here, myself included. The only other time I'd visited in the last decade was to pick up some assassins stuck in a trap.

The Dark Lord stood at his work desk, a masterpiece carved from treant bones. He'd just finished painstakingly inking out a charm for [Enhanced Durability] on a tablecloth when I'd arrived.

I didn't ask why Keith was reinforcing a tablecloth, too overwhelmed with other burning questions. "You want *me* to escort *Minstrel Bronwynn*, the most popular bard on the continent, and keep an eye on her?"

"Yes." Keith lifted a scroll with a broken seal from the Dark Enchanted Forest intelligence unit.

I unrolled it and frowned at the contents. "Does Henrietta know?"

Keith pushed up his glasses and hesitated only a second. "No."

"When are you going to tell her?" I demanded, wondering what Keith had taken from all those relationship books I'd made him read. "Tonight?"

The Dark Lord said nothing. That didn't mean he wasn't going to tell her; Keith stayed silent when he didn't know what he was going to do yet.

"Keith." I dropped the royal title and spoke to my friend. "I'm only going to tell you this once: Henrietta won't leave you if you tell her things she doesn't want to hear, or things that will actively hurt her. And she won't leave you because you have to make choices that she disagrees with."

"You don't—"

I didn't bother letting him finish. "She will leave you because *you didn't trust her or communicate with her.* She will feel hurt and betrayed that you weren't honest. And if you don't trust *her*, then she will stop trusting *you*."

The Dark Lord took a deep breath. "Alright, I'll tell her tomorrow."

I raised an eyebrow.

"Tonight?"

"..."

"Fine!" King Keith waved a hand as he opened a character sheet I couldn't see. The Dark Lord focused off in the distance for a time, and then looked my way again. "I've summoned her."

"Good. I hope you remember my advice while I'm gone—new habits take repetition and reward. I promise you will be rewarded with a happy and healthy marriage if you get your act together and talk to your wife about these things."

With that settled, I looked down at the detailed map comparing the location of molten ash vane poisonings that perfectly coincided with my favorite bard's interkingdom tour over the last year, including an attempt on the Sumbrian royal family, Their Royal Highness of Peldeep, and King Keith himself.

I resisted the sudden urge to rip up the scroll. There was *no way* my favorite musician on the continent was an illegal assassin.

Was there?

"I think it's absolutely a coincidence," Henrietta declared, her finger tracing its way down the scroll as she read the incriminating evidence. "You forget, Brownie was kidnapped and enslaved with the rest of us. *And* she lost her beloved Suzette."

I was pleased to note that Her Viciousness wasn't angry, her aura of calm remaining steady throughout. I also noticed Keith had succeeded in pretending confidence when he'd welcomed Henrietta and motioned me to hand over the scroll.

"Who?" Keith asked.

I replied, "Her lyre harp."

"Exactly. That lyre meant the world to her." The queen held up her finger. "Why would she hit someone over the head with her greatest treasure, *her instrument*, if she was working with them?"

"It doesn't say she is working with Servalt, my love," Keith argued. "It simply says that she's been present every time a molten ash vane poisoning has happened."

Against my better judgment, I agreed, adding, "She doesn't need to be working for Servalt to be a poisoner or assassin . . . and she knew about all of those assassins who were launching a surprise attack on us just before your birthday."

"She was locked up in a carriage with me, battling slave traders, when the molten ash vane was being collected and delivered to your prison," Henrietta reminded us. "And that still begs the question why Marquess Chadwick kidnapped her if he *knew* she was an assassin in his employ. He was clearly getting the poison from someone else."

"You make a compelling argument," Keith surmised, "but that doesn't mean she wasn't involved in other ways. There's also the fact that Marquess Dorset might not have known it *was* her. She's a performer; she could have a disguise."

"As queen of the Dark Enchanted Forest, am I allowed to order Rufus to do things?" Henrietta asked, suddenly changing the direction of the conversation.

I raised an eyebrow at my king and waited to hear the answer to that myself. I'd sworn an oath of fealty when Henrietta was elevated, but it had been multiple generations since there were two rulers of the Dark Enchanted Forest.

"Yes," King Keith monotoned, then he caught my eye, coughed, and amended, "Within reason."

"Rufus!" Queen Henrietta thrust the page back into my arms. "My first official order as queen of the Dark Enchanted Forest is for you to follow Minstrel Brownie Lyriel to Servalt and find proof that she is or is not, in fact, an undercover assassin."

"Yes, Your Viciousness." It was already what Keith had ordered. I took back the scroll, looked it over once more, then did as I desired and ripped it up into tiny pieces. "But I won't go with the evidence on me."

I dropped the remains into a bin beside Keith's filing cabinet before turning back to the pair. They'd been sharing a *look*, but then returned my gaze steadily.

"You should probably have that *conversation* with the Assassin's Guild while you're visiting, too," Keith instructed.

"Of course. If that's all?" I bowed, then left to pack my bags.

This wasn't the first time I'd stalked my favorite bard across two kingdoms . . . and I'd felt equally guilty both times. This *would* be the first time she'd recognize me as I did so, though.

I sighed. If only I could forgo the secrecy and just—

Actually.

We knew each other now. Maybe going the obvious route wouldn't be that hard, and it cost me nothing to try.

I finished packing my things, watered my plants, left instructions with the castle staff, and wandered off to Scowls.

CHAPTER 4

Your Wagon or Mine?

Brownie

Hello, everyone, this is Madame Potts with your last update this spring!

Valaria can welcome their newest queen today after King Keith Monfort of Nilheim married Princess Henrietta, formerly of Drendil. The celebration was in fine form, and nobody died. The tea and cake were especially delicious, if I do say so myself.

Anyone traveling to Sumbria this week will not be able to take the high road. The Sumbrian royals did not heed the words of this humble madame, and poachers successfully caused a stampede of capybara throughout the kingdom. Adventuring parties looking for an easy quest can make their way to the kingdom and help round up the friendly creatures.

The Green Oak Dungeon will have an increase in miner's lettuce encounters. The grass monsters are known to emit Confusion spores from the small white flower on their head, but a rare pink flower miner's lettuce might appear that uses Paralysis spores. Please pack the appropriate antidotes. And note, the monster's cap is edible, and the rare pink one is a highly sought-after delicacy.

Next week, there will be flooding on the eastern road to the Empire of Sands. A storm giant fell into one of the ice lakes on the peak of Mount Arai, sending an overflow to Lake Vayasa. It won't disturb any villages, but travel will be affected.

I am happy to say that Valaria's other newest ruler is making waves. Regent Havork of Drendil swept through the kingdom last week

**arresting many and subjecting others to fines. New laws are being
passed daily, and citizens are advised to go to any of the free herald
posts set up by the regent to explain and answer questions.
The Summer Masquerade invites just went out; did you get one yet?
That's all for today, everyone. Enjoy the nice weather while it lasts.
Madame Potts signing out.**

Brownie listened as everyone at Scowls was talking about the wedding and the announcement from the Crystal Cast two hours after the wedding had ended.

Madame Potts had been announcing portents and news across the continent on the Cast Crystals for five years now, and even if no one knew who she was or how she did it, everyone listened to her because Madame Potts was always right.

Unless, of course, someone took her advice and changed the future. Sumbria was a fool for not acting on her previous warning.

Brownie thought about the contents of the cast as she settled into a chair at Scowls. She wanted to relax after a long day performing at Henrietta's wedding. It'd been a blast, but now she was hungry and tired and ready to spend a quiet evening thinking up lyrics.

Though Brownie had a guest room in the castle, it was attached to the queen's suite. And Henrietta and Keith were very . . . excited to be married. The queen kept her rooms, but she rarely slept in them. Half the time, Henrietta would roll in at breakfast in nothing but a housecoat and some fluffy floofpoof slippers, positively glowing.

It was a bit much even for Brownie's bardic self to handle.

"Great show tonight, Minstrel Bronwynn," a rough voice said to her left as the golden wolf beastman sat down beside her at the bar. They'd met many times since she'd come to the Dark Enchanted Forest to visit Henrietta, though mostly in the dining hall during meals.

He tipped his glass of wine in greeting.

"Thank you, Commander General Rufus." Brownie lifted her raspberry sparkler in return. "I'm glad you enjoyed it."

He was a very fluffy man, and one she'd grown used to speaking with in his half-beast, half-man state. His fur was varying shades of burnished gold to ruddy brown, and his golden eyes complemented his coloring. Rufus had taken off his vest at some point and just wore his white undertunic. It lay open at the top where his collar strained, barely containing his ruff. He wore his suit pants cut at the calf so he could walk around on his partially transformed legs.

He looked like a giant wolven golden retriever walking around in formal wear.

"It was a pleasure." His warm eyes stared at her. "Are you still heading toward Servalt next?"

"Yes." Duke Wyldon had offered Bronwynn a pouch full of gold to show up at his birthday, and she liked the righteous man—and the gold. "Why?"

The beastman hesitated a second, his tail flicking once. "I'm traveling to Servalt for my investigation with the Assassin's Guild next . . . and I was going to offer to accompany you."

Brownie leaned back on her stool to get a full look at Rufus. Something about the way his tail twitched made her think he wasn't telling her everything. But then again, he was the commander general of the Dark Lord's army, and she was a random minstrel from Drendil. She had no reason to pry into his secrets, and it would be nice traveling with an extra pair of paws.

Brownie raised an eyebrow, questioning, "*Going* to offer?"

"I *am* offering," he corrected, this time with conviction. "If you'll have me."

"Then I'd love the company." Her face broke into a large grin, and she thrust out her hand between them. "Let us meet fair weather . . ."

He downed the rest of his drink and put down the empty glass before reaching out and gently wrapping his soft paw pads around her hand and shaking it. He finished the greeting common among caravanners. ". . . and fine luck."

As soon as he finished, he dropped her hand and stood up.

"Then we leave in the morning?" He grabbed his vest and cast a glance around the tavern. Scowls was still rowdy, though the atmosphere wasn't tense. Everyone was in a celebratory mood now that their Dark Magician King had finally settled down.

"Bright and early." She yawned. "Your wagon or mine?"

He contemplated. "Let's take yours. I'll see you tomorrow, Minstrel Bronwynn."

"Goodnight, Commander General."

The beastman left a coin on the table and walked out, his tail wagging. It was amusing how his tail gave away his inner thoughts, often getting the better of him.

It was a shame that their relationship had gotten off to such a rocky start, with assassins and armies at her back.

She'd been surprised when Rufus had stuck up for her back then. He'd told them all she was telling the truth and to let her be. It was unexpected and refreshing, and had immediately endeared the commander general to her. And she *had* been telling the truth; she'd only showed up at the Dark Lord's castle to see if Henrietta was alright and to warn her of the large group of contract killers out for her life.

That, and the fact that he was so fluffy she wanted to pet him. She reminisced on the soft paw pads that'd wrapped around her hands and smiled. She wanted to squish those beanies, but she was a grown woman and could control herself!

Her music often summoned fluffy animals . . . Maybe she could find a willing participant in the forest to let her rub her face on their soft tummy so she could satisfy her urges.

Thoughts of that one time she'd coaxed a unicorn to let her pet his flank played across her mind in a fond memory. Donna didn't like unicorns, so those days were gone.

On that note, Bronwynn decided to turn in early and get a good night's rest before heading out tomorrow.

CHAPTER 5

World Player Indeed!

Rufus

I went to bed, but I didn't go to sleep. Instead, I tossed and turned, both excited for and dreading the travel ahead. My thoughts drifted back to when I'd first met the bard; it was hard to believe that it was only a year ago that my obsession with her music had begun.

One Year Ago

"Rufus!" Chloe Watercress yelled at me from the doorway of my very comfortable dungeon office in the Black Fortress. The enchanted prison cells were partially underground, letting in the sunlight from the outside. The front half remained usable for the prisoners of the Dark Lord—if Keith ever bothered to have prisoners—while the back had been converted into a cozy living space for me after I'd decided to move down here.

"Yes, Chloe?" I didn't look up from my book, knowing that would irritate the necromancer all the more. Also, *The Duchess of North Berkshire* was a very interesting read, and I didn't want to stop midscene. Miss Hana had just been found poisoned, and her knight escort was missing . . . though I highly suspected the butler had something to do with that.

Chloe announced, "I just thought I'd let you know that I'm leaving."

That got my attention.

"Where to?" I sat up quickly, taking the tiny reading glasses off my midsize canine snout. I slotted them as a makeshift bookmark into my romance novel before placing both on the small table beside my reclined daybed. A tinge of worry about where our illustrious king would send her this time crept into my voice. "How many dead?"

It was Chloe's job to [Resurrect], [Revive], or [Raise] those who could be saved around the Dark Enchanted Forest. A flood? She went to fish out the nonsurvivors. A dungeon break? Cleaning up the mess. When the entire forest tended to shift around all the time, travelers never knew if they would wake up in the middle of dire wolf–infested woods or beside the beautiful shores of Lake Loria, where a dragon lay sleeping.

"I'm going to Servalt to enjoy their Annual Spell Script Collegium."

I did a double take, raising one eyebrow. "But . . . why? You get the subscription scrolls every year."

"I'm taking a vacation."

I eyed the woman. Chloe flipped her long blonde curls over her shoulder dramatically, as if nothing bothered her and my opinion didn't actually matter. It must, though, or else she wouldn't be here. In my dungeon. Telling me about it.

"Does Keith—?"

"He approved my leave of absence," she countered. "I'm going for three weeks. I've left two full crates of potions that should last until after I get back."

"Alright." I didn't want to do this, but my notification tabs were going off in the corner of my eye, and I decided I could use the help. I much preferred patience to hitting the problem with a hammer, but judging by the nervous energy and masked uncertainty radiating from my friend, she wasn't likely to open up on her own.

[Passive Skill: **Mediator** has been activated by your **Patient** Chloe Watercress. Primary emotion: Surprise, Startled. Subject may act irrationally. Threat Level: 1]
[Passive Skill: **Patient** has been activated. A **Patient** within the area of your Skill is in need of counsel. Warning: **Patient** Chloe Watercress is under the influence of a **World Player**. Threat Level: 1]

The system blinked with more messages that I ignored. There were always more messages. When I refocused on Chloe, she was pretending to be unaffected, waiting patiently for my verdict.

"Who did you talk to?" While I'd never heard of a World Player before, I could only assume it was a high-level, Rogue-class title. And not someone I wanted influencing my friends—let alone the right hand of the Dark Lord.

Chloe deflated and let out a rare, simple sigh, devoid of her usual dramatic flair. "I received a letter."

Fishing out the scroll, she passed it over. It had a tiny broken seal in the shape of a teacup.

Dear Necromancer Chloe,

Thank you so much for resurrecting me. To return the favor, I would like to pass along this special pass to the Annual Spell Script Collegium. It is a wonderful event held every year that shares all of the latest magical spells and theorems.

I've heard there is even going to be a surprise presentation by the Grand Duchess of North Sumbria on her latest invention, something called an "elevator."

I hope this finds you well, and that you're able to go. And thanks again.
Yours Truly,
Madame Potts

"Wait, wait, wait." I stood and waved the letter between us. "You saved *the* Madame Potts? When?"

Madame Potts was the illusive, elusive, reclusive oracle who told the future on the Crystal Cast Network all around the continent. World Player indeed! Everyone and their human were looking for that woman.

"How am I supposed to know? Do you know how many people I [Resurrect] in a month?" She reached out for the letter and snatched it back. "Anyway, I'm going."

"If Madame Potts thinks you should go, then I'm sure it's where you're meant to be," I mused, retaking my seat on the daybed. "Have fun."

Chloe didn't leave right away. I felt her stare as I picked up my book with every intention of getting back to it. When she still didn't take the hint, I glanced up at her while using the opportunity to clean my reading glasses. "What?"

"I'm not the only one who should get out of here and live a little," Chloe remarked. "When was the last time you left this dungeon—and don't say breakfast!" She knew me so well. "When was the last time you left the Black Fortress?"

"I went to North Sumbria for the Summer Masquerade, and I'm going to Peldeep next month," I argued.

"You went to the Continental Council meetings, sure, but did you go dancing? Did you socialize or do anything fun?" she demanded.

"I have fun reading in silence, and I have no intention of doing anything else, thank you," I replied, placing my glasses back on my face and determinedly shoving my nose into my open book to end the conversation.

Chloe didn't back down. "When I'm back from my trip, it's your turn. We've been stuck in this stupid castle for too long. I can't imagine how many banked holidays you have."

"Need I remind you," I said, "that I am Commander General Rufus Triever, level fifty-four leader of the King's Dogs of the Black Fortress and the First Order of the Dark Lord's army. I don't take holidays!"

"Do you want my advice?"

"No, but I'm sure you will tell me either way."

Chloe stood there with her hands on her hips, the scroll nowhere to be seen. She was eye level with me while I was sitting, and a very terrifying woman who was like a sister to me. "You need a hobby, Rufus."

I lifted my book. "What do you think this is?"

"I know you love reading, but you need something that gets you out of this dungeon. No one knows what your folk form looks like; why don't you use that?" The concern in her eyes actually got to me a little. "You can go out and do something new in Peldeep. Anything! Go to one of the shows or enter a contest or check out the fish market. The Westcoast Shoals Festival should have something interesting."

Imagining myself walking about in my humanlike folk form *at all* was strange, since I'd few reasons to transform fully into a beast or a man. My beast form shed too much, and my folk form was just so . . . furless.

And the thought of any one of those activities, surrounded in a crush of people, left me in a cold sweat. Still, I could see that this meant something to Chloe.

"If I promise to go to *one* show, will you be happy?" I sighed, imagining the horror of being surrounded by an enthusiastic theater crowd . . . Maybe a nice, calm music concert instead. I could do that.

It wouldn't change my life to spend *one* afternoon uncomfortable in the stands.

"That's all I can ask," Chloe agreed. She turned on her heel and walked out of my office, calling out a final farewell before she left for Servalt. I shifted my glasses back into place and resumed reading from where I'd left off.

Now to find out what exactly the butler had done to Miss Hana's knight escort!

CHAPTER 6

Bribing Your Horse

Brownie

Any time she had to travel through the Dark Enchanted Forest, Brownie packed light. More than once, she'd had to abandon her wagon to dire wolves or the odd griffin attack. Once they'd even been attacked by a wandering band of knee-high mushfolk.

Every time, she'd managed to escape harm and track down an adventuring party or members of the Dark Lord's army to come help her retrieve the wagon itself, but the items inside were still subject to being stolen. Or eaten.

Speaking of theft, she'd lost count of the number of times bandits or brigands or worse had captured her. Luckily, her skills as a traveling bard came in handy at such times. For this particular trip, she was using a well-made bright red shoulder bag from a semifamous seamstress. The herringbone weave was popular in North Sumbria these days, and Brownie had bought it as a present to herself after her harrowing ordeal at the Spring Ball.

"You're up earlier than expected."

Brownie looked over her shoulder as she finished checking the lines that secured her wagon to her horse. Rufus stood in the courtyard with a winning smile as bright as the sunrise just cresting the eastern sky. His sharp canines flashed. He wore comfortable adventuring attire: white tunic, soft leather calf-length pants, and a dark brown vest with pockets.

"Good morning to you too," she returned with a grin. Donna, her temperamental roan mare, shot the beastman a suspicious look as he tossed a small travel pack into the back of the wagon. Brownie told her horse, "It's alright. He's my *guest*."

Donna chuffed and stamped her foot before turning away to inspect their surroundings as if she were a mere horse and *not* a fully intelligent bonded companion that could keep pace with a unicorn.

There was a reason Brownie had no qualms bringing her through the Dark Enchanted Forest. Donna could take care of herself, and their Bonded title let them keep tabs on each other even at a distance.

"Who else are we waiting for?" Rufus asked as he walked up to stand beside Donna.

Brownie noted with amusement that Rufus could look her in the eye. She usually stood a head above the crowd, so it was nice traveling with someone she could speak to at the same level. "No one; it's just you, me, and Donna here."

"Really?" Rufus raised an eyebrow but didn't comment further. Instead, he reached out a hand to the horse.

Donna whipped her head around before Brownie could warn him. Instead of the expected yelp, however, the mare stopped and lipped at a lump of apple Rufus held out for her.

"Sorry for bribing your horse," he said, contrite. "I should have checked with you first. I'm just used to animals feeling intimidated by this form and needing all the help I can get."

Rufus rubbed Donna's nose as the mare butted up against his palm, which was better than mauling him, so Brownie considered it a win. "Donna is her own horse, so I'm not worried, but thank you for the apology. You can hop up front or ride in the back as you prefer."

Brownie jumped up and took her usual spot at the reins.

Rufus eyed the wagon. It had four sides to keep everything inside during high-speed bumpy chases and was loaded with a mix of hay for Donna and decoy travel bags. Brownie's new instrument hung on the back of her wagon seat at the ready, and her red shoulder bag was flap open, waterskin at the ready by her side.

"An intelligent horse?" He stared at her horse, who looked like any other normal roan horse. "And you're alright with pulling the cart?"

Donna nickered and tossed her head.

"Yes," Brownie translated. "At the end of every trip, she gets a bushel of high-grade oats and some enchanted carrots."

"Then it's nice to meet you, Donna." The beastman nodded to her horse then walked over to hop in the passenger's seat. His tail stuck comfortably through the long opening between the seat and the elevated backrest.

"Ready? Then we're off!" She sent a mental signal to Donna to head out, gave a flick of the reins for show, and navigated them all out of the Dark Fortress, across the moat, and eastwards to Servalt. When they were free and clear on their way, she noticed Rufus let out a sigh of relief. He must have been itching to get going as much as she was. Brownie let Donna lead and turned to her passenger.

"So, where am I dropping you off in Servalt, Commander General Rufus?"

"Just Rufus is fine," he said. "I'm actually going to Duke Wyldon's birthday party as well. That's why I reached out."

Something felt off, but Brownie knew Rufus was on official business, so didn't press. Instead, she relaxed and set aside the reigns, leaning back and pulling Danielle from her soft leather case. "Then we have a long ride ahead of us! How about a song for the road?"

Rufus, who'd otherwise been awkwardly settling in beside her, gave her the first *real* smile she'd seen on him that day. Genuine and open. "I'd love to hear 'The Traveler's Tale'?"

Brownie nodded and started the familiar melody. She had a few important deliveries to make, and a performance to rock; he had business with a bunch of assassins.

Though their paths might overlap more than he thought . . .

Through deep oaken valleys
In dark mountain passes
Cross river and lake and occasional straight
My feet love the water,
The knee-high wild grasses
Man-made cobble stone is not up to my gait.

I tread the wild places
And know the rock landing,
The hunting trail, country road, highway and track.
I climb the cliff faces,
My world ever standing
On earthen-made floor from the countryside back.

I sleep under starlight
In breath-catching heather
Or sometimes I rest in the deep forest nooks
The burrows and bracken
In rain or cloud weather
The fallen leaf tresses a roof in my crook.

My wandering ways lead
To clearings of hallow
The hill is my country, the road is my home.
The forests and woodlands,
The green pasture fallow,
I find ever peace when the further I roam.

I am the rough weather,
A soft trodden route,
The trail to the backlands, the marchland, the glade
I am the cool water,
The crickling spout
That travels the lost ways through undergrowth shade.

Someday you may meet me
In the gold field of grain
Across the cold deserts or shoreline by night
On sloping wild hill lands
The rooted old by lane
That know the forgotten and carry the right.

And when our paths crossing,
Our eyes meet and catching,
Greet me with a smile and the nod of a friend
For I will know dwellings
And they know my singings
This traveler's tale from beginning to end.

CHAPTER 7

Preventing Keith from Unaliving Himself

Rufus

The farther we traveled from the Black Fortress, the easier I felt.

The knot in my stomach began untangling itself. The worry that accompanied ignoring notifications and the pressure from those constant updates in my head slipped away. All I had to process was one bard and her horse . . . and interestingly enough, the horse was easier to read.

Donna was confident, content, and enjoying the sun.

Granted, I would only be picking up on any strong negative emotions, and it was a beautiful day, sun high in the sky, with a cool breeze. There wasn't much to feel negative about.

It was my job to appear composed at all times; I had an army to lead and a castle full of minions to keep from killing each other every day . . . but my cultivated image paled next to Bronwynn's—she *was* relaxed. It was probably that feeling that'd drawn me to her music.

"So tell me, Commander Rufus," her melodious voice roused me from my thoughts. "How long have you been commander general of the Dark Lord's armies?"

"Officially? A decade."

She raised an eyebrow at me. "Officially?"

"I was chosen by Her Eminence Feliwyn as King Keith's playmate when I was six, and we were expected to grow strong enough from there to win the job." There wasn't much to hide when the entire Dark Enchanted Forest knew. "The year Keith came of age, we all competed. I was eighteen when I won the Winter Solstice Tourney and claimed the title commander general. Keith won Dark Lord, and Her Eminence Feliwyn flew off to go have a nap that very afternoon."

Bronwynn frowned. I waited for her to gather her thoughts until she asked, "What did your parents think of that? Being chosen?"

"It was a great honor." I tried to sound proud, but it came out flat.

"Really?" Her eyes still gave away her displeasure. "Alright then, what was it like being the Dark Lord's playmate?"

"I was tasked with preventing Keith from unaliving himself. I was mostly successful, too." The image of our illustrious king jumping off a building with his untested mechanical wings came to mind. Or that time he jumped into the lake after a selkie because the girl promised to take him treasure hunting.

Patina was now a lieutenant in the Dark Lord's army, and the treasure hunting had been fun once I'd made sure she wasn't just there to assassinate my prince. Keith was always walking into the line of fire, exploding himself or bringing home murderous creatures he'd somehow managed to convince *not* to murder him. His wife included.

My lips quirked at that thought.

"How did you meet our Dark Lady?" The name made me actually smile. The tiny fluffy princess who'd become our queen was about as evil as our distracted paper-shuffling king.

"She was pretending to be a maid, and kept coming to listen to me sing at the castle village fountain," Bronwynn said, fondness in her speech. "It was nice having someone following me around asking for more songs."

Our positions were switched, then.

"How old were you?" I pushed down the slight envy I had for our queen getting to hear Bronwynn's songs from childhood.

"Twelve, I think?" She shook her head. "I always prided myself on figuring people out, but who would've guessed she was a princess with calloused hands like those? And we got busier as I became famous and she took on royal responsibilities . . . Honestly, I just ignored or explained away the signs. She's my best friend, you know? Being a half giantess in Drendil meant I didn't have a lot of friends, as you can imagine."

The kingdom *was* known for being cruel to nonhumans.

"It must have come as quite the shock." For a second, I thought about offering to counsel Bronwynn. It was a perfect opportunity while her guard was down . . . but that would be tricking her into becoming my [Patient].

It would make it easier to complete my task . . . but it would also make the entire trip *unbearable*. And I'd feel awful.

And there was no certainty that she'd even accept the prompt. Not everyone was like Henrietta, who'd shown up in my dungeon and accepted the request unquestioning, and then poured out her heart and soul without much effort on my part.

"I felt less shocked and more . . . I don't know. *Betrayed* is a strong word." The bard shrugged. "Sad that she didn't trust me?"

There was so much to unpack there, and I was standing on the edge of manipulating her into a full session . . . but wallowing in the past on such a nice day was a shame.

And, if I was being honest with myself, I respected the bard too much to use my interrogation skills on her. I would, if needed, but I *didn't* need to. Yet.

I changed the subject. "And now?"

"Now I'm glad she's found happiness." Bronwynn grabbed her waterskin. She unwound the top as she continued. "And it's nice that she's smack-dab in the middle of the Dark Enchanted Forest. I'll be visiting often, since I cross the forest every other week."

On the outside, I nodded politely. On the inside, I was mentally screaming. The idea made my heart race, and at the same time, I could feel my stomach tense. I didn't think I could see Bronwynn at the dinner table every two weeks for the rest of my life without wanting to confess my sins.

Which sins? All of them. That I was an adoring fan. That she already knew me from her concerts. That I was on a mission to spy on her.

The quest to discover if she was, in fact, a top-secret agent bent on illegally assassinating the world leaders with molten ash vane was the *only thing* keeping me from outright sharing my own dark secrets right then and there.

The hair on the back of my neck stood up as three notifications lit up at the edge of my vision.

We were about to have company. And whoever they were, they were not happy.

CHAPTER 8

[Call of the Wombat]

Brownie

In all the years Brownie had been traveling in the Dark Enchanted Forest, she'd only run into a stoneskin wombat three times.

They were cute, cuddly, and the size of a cart. They were deadly when they attacked with rolling rock-hard butt attacks that could break bones and shatter stones.

The stoneskin wombat was technically classified as a monster race, and defeating one would provide experience points. Any creature that could spawn in a dungeon was called a monster, but only a monster that spawned in a dungeon would be subject to dungeon madness.

This was just a regular, enormous, disgruntled wombat monster with a very hard butt. It'd probably been born the old-fashioned way.

Rufus had tensed beside her a second before they'd rounded a corner and found a caravan being affected by a [Call of the Wombat].

It was an intimidation-based attack that made the wombat everyone's focused target.

Rufus made to stand up, but Brownie grabbed his furry arm to stop him.

"Stay calm." The bard reached behind her and pulled out a brown sack from the wagon. She knew from experience that stoneskin wombats didn't like dogs of any shape or size, and that included beastfolk and beastkin.

The caravan, three wagons pulled by alligator-dogs, looked like a branch of the Dark Horde supply chain. A handful of lizardkin were spreading out to protect their goods while two with spears kept the snarling stoneskin wombat at bay.

"Here, now!" Brownie called, jumping down and slowly walking forward. "What's happening?"

The creature didn't appreciate her approach and bared its teeth, digging its front foot in the dirt as if getting ready to roll forward and smack her with its stone behind.

Brownie reached into her sack and pulled out her secret weapon for trips through the Dark Enchanted Forest.

Enchanted carrots.

A small bunch of lovingly grown, sweet farm-fresh enchanted carrots. They were shiny. They were fragrant. And they were instantly of interest to the wombat.

She shook the bunch, letting the creature take in the smell. Wombats, hippogriffs, unicorns, angry humans, and a surprising number of other creatures could be calmed by their delicious scent. "Sorry for any trouble you've had on the Great Road, Mighty Stoneskin Wombat. Obviously, you're a noble creature who didn't deserve to be bothered. I hope this is enough to let us all pass?"

The wombat closed its mouth and stuck its nose out toward her, sniffing curiously. Donna looked utterly affronted, but Brownie sent a feeling of reassurance to her horse. She'd kept some back for Donna.

One lizardkin stared at the bard like she was on fire, and the other covered her face to hold back a laugh. Luckily, the stoneskin wombat was focusing solely on the bard and her carrots.

The monster made its decision and waddled over, grabbing the bundle in its mouth and gently headbutting her hand. It was infinitely superior to it butt-butting her, so she gleefully opened her palm. When the stoneskin wombat leaned in, she gave into temptation and gave the giant hairy monster head scratches. It particularly enjoyed it behind the right ear.

She ignored the "Is this really happening?" comment from direction of the Dark Horde. She had more important matters to attend to.

"Thank you for your understanding, Oh Noble Stoneskin." She lavished adoration on the creature. After being tempted all morning by her travel companion, this was exactly what she'd needed.

There was a moment where everyone waited, watching with bated breath, until the stoneskin wombat decided it had had enough pets. It snorted, rolled away suddenly, and happily waddled into the underbrush with its prize carrots.

Everyone let out a collective breath.

Brownie just smiled. Music and food were both wonderful tools to calm a savage beast, and she armed herself with both while traveling.

The lizardkin stood at attention, and when it was obvious that the stoneskin wombat wasn't coming back, addressed the pair.

"Commander Rufusss!" the one on the left, with short, spiky blue hair and tinted orange scales greeted. "Minstrel Bronwynn. Thank you for your aid."

Rufus nodded, his demeanor firm and commanding. "Core Vandith, report."

The simple word had both soldiers stand up even straighter. Core Vandith stated, "We're returning from a sssupply drop off at Kith Bog for the fire damage repairsss. Two more, and the village will be as good as new. We also loaded up a shipment of peat from the bog and dropped one off in Thistlecrick. Thisss here is bound for the Black Fortresss."

"Good," Rufus acknowledged. "Then we won't keep you."

Brownie regretted the destruction of the village. She'd warned Henrietta and Keith about the assassins, but she couldn't have imagined that they would light the village on fire.

She waved at the Dark Horde as they got everyone back into formation and continued up the road.

Rufus only relaxed again when the army was out of sight. As his eyes flicked slightly, she assumed he was reading a notification.

"Do you think Thistlecrick is still up the road?" Brownie asked a few minutes later, when Rufus was no longer focused on his character sheet. "I'd like to stop by the hot springs if you aren't in a hurry?"

"The only guarantee is that it'll be on the north side of the Great Road." He shrugged. The forest was notorious for moving around. The only constants were the great roads traveling east to west and north to south, and the castle at the center. "And I've no aversion to a stopover. It'll be good to check in with Derilla now that he's out of diapause. We barely exchanged words at the wedding."

The General of the North, Derilla Vane, was an arachne who looked like a pointy-eared, sharp-toothed man above the waist, and a spider below. He came up to Brownie's nose in height.

Brownie smiled. "Then let's hope it's still between us and Kith Bog. I'd love a relaxing soak!"

CHAPTER 9

The Smell of Wet Dog

Rufus

I'd said that I would be alright with a hot spring stopover in Thistlecrick, but I was, in fact, *not* alright.

There was something so unforgettable, so recognizable, so *fragrant* about the smell of a wet dog. And I was that dog—wolf. Whatever.

So when we actually arrived at the hot springs an hour later, I excused myself to go find Derilla Vane while Minstrel Bronwynn headed for the baths.

"I'm surprised to see you this far from your dungeon." Derilla smirked, pouring me a cup of dewdrop petal tea. The Naga clans had escorted me into the deepest part of the estate, to the private dwelling of the arachne general. He sat in his usual spot, overlooking the beautiful mountainous hillside.

I accepted the cup, refusing the offer of cream, and considered how much to tell him. I was technically his superior, but the last time we'd battled was four years ago at the winter solstice, and since then, he'd grown more powerful.

On the years Derilla couldn't attend due to his diapause, the arachne's apprentice Merik of the Naga clan would compete as a proxy. He won the position every time, but dared not claim the title himself. Everyone continued to call Derilla the general even while asleep. The arachne was terrifying, and could probably defeat even *me* in a fair fight.

Not that Derilla ever fought fair.

At this time, he was neither my superior *nor* my king. I ignored the building pressure churning in my stomach from a combination of notifications blinking in the corner of my eye and Derilla's passive [Fear] perk. This was why I hated leaving my dungeon.

I cultivated a calm facade, even going so far as to activate [Natural Poise].

[**Natural Poise**, passive effects: perfect posture and an air of confidence. Effects can be identified by anyone with an equal or higher Charisma. When activated, +1 Charisma for minutes equal to Charisma.]

"I'm on a trip to meet with the new leader of the Servalt Assassin's Guild, and to have a *polite* talk with them about recent events."

"Alongside Minstrel Bronwynn?" Derilla took a sip of his own tea. He was a very relaxed arachne who felt like the silent edge of violence.

Since he had surpassed me in level, I didn't need to check my notifications; they weren't about him. Still, I could see he was hostile even in his hospitality.

I shrugged. "She's going in the same direction, and she is our queen's best friend. I'm watching that she makes it there safely."

Derilla considered, swirling his cup as he stared at one of the many waterfalls in the distance. His rooms, no matter where the city moved, remained overlooking these three stark hills. Hot springs flowed in bubbling pools worn into the mountainside, and all manner of beasts traveled to soak in the waters.

The largest waterfall fell into a pond made of runoff from the hot springs at the bottom of the ravine, which left the peaks shrouded in shifting mists. It had a harsh, ethereal beauty.

"As you say." The arachne nodded, amusement heavy in his voice, but also acceptance. "And how is Her Viciousness settling in?"

"Not much has changed, except Keith is smiling like an idiot and she's helping more with the paperwork." Something any good ruler needed: the ability to file reports. "And I am reminded every day how foolish her parents were for sending her off here to die. What idiot throws away a highly trained administrator?"

Derilla grinned. "A dead one."

"Undead, technically," I corrected. "Now they are haunting the royal cemetery in Drendil, as I've heard."

For that, I was relieved. There'd been jests at the table about tossing the couple in *my* dungeon to get some much-needed counseling. Could I have destroyed them and reformed them into upstanding members of society with the force of my overwhelming mental perks? Maybe. Would it have taken a lot of time? Yes.

And then I'd be stuck in their company.

That wouldn't do. Also, I was not a manipulator by nature. My mediation style revolved around facts and repeat reminders: *Don't lie to your spouse. Don't withhold information from your spouse. Don't not talk to your spouse. Don't ignore the burning passionate fire that dwells in your soul that tells you to be vulnerable and lay bare the feelings of your heart to your spouse. Don't lie to your spouse.* And so forth.

"Speaking of, when *is* your spar?" I asked, finishing my tea and sampling some of the food set out.

The naga were half snake, and the arachne were half spider, and both enjoyed a predominantly carnivorous diet. The platter reflected that; delicate slices of fish were layered into the shape of rose petals, grilled boar bites were skewered with a variety of dipping sauces, and tiny grilled squid were crispy. They all tasted wonderful.

For the first time, Derilla tensed. His devilish grin tightened, and he let loose a bit of his dark intent. As soon as it flared, it was back under control. "We had a quick bout before the wedding, actually. A single pass."

"Oh?" I was surprised they'd chosen to do so in private. Unless Her Viciousness had foreseen the results and chose to spare the general an audience to his defeat.

"I'll be going back into training," the arachne stated. "But I'm not going into diapause this year. You can expect me at the winter solstice."

"I look forward to it." And that was that.

We lapsed into silence, enjoying the scenery.

A second round of trays were brought in. Soy phoenix eggs were served on rice, alongside a warm miso broth with fresh green onion. They were much smaller than the usual floofpoof bird eggs commonly eaten in the Dark Enchanted Forest.

Eventually, we moved to the private hot springs reserved for the General of the North. I transformed, losing the hair and my snout. I did not become human nor elf in this form, but could pass for both with my slightly pointed ears. I attributed my lighter than usual golden-brown tan to the hours spent indoors.

I soaked happily in private, long after Derilla excused himself, and hoped my travel companion was having an equally relaxing venture.

CHAPTER 10

You Court Death!

Brownie

Donna had happily gone for her own horse spa so Brownie was free to spendtime in the hot springs.

The bard was expecting to enjoy her time soaking in a luxurious bath cut into one of the mountains. The resort Clan Melusine had brought her to was a wandering spa path a variety of hot springs, waterfall-mist resting stops, and with cold water pools all found in the harsh beauty of nature. It was almost dinnertime, and the sun was casting shadows through the mountain pass.

Brownie was *not* expecting the waterfall she was meditating beside to light up like the Peldeep Festival of Lights. She also did not anticipate a lizardkin clothed in robes of silver to *burst from the waterfall* and land before her as she sat in nothing more than a cotton bathing robe and fluffy slippers.

At least he wasn't facing her.

He landed in a powerful pose, robes billowing. His blue-gray hair was pulled into a top knot, and his green scales were gray at the tips.

"Ha ha ha!" the man laughed, elated, chest puffed out and his hands in fists on his waist. He managed to feel like an esteemed graceful master and a battle-ready warrior at the same time. Brownie didn't get up; she hadn't finished her meditation cycle yet.

"The Ten Thousand Star Artsss are complete! Nothing shall ssstop me this time in our revenge, Father. I shall defy the heavensss and reclaim my birth-right!" And then, he was talking to himself in a very main character manner that Brownie wished she could pay closer attention to. "Oh, Father, if only you could sssee me now. I will restore our honor! Thisss I swear to you."

He relaxed from his impassioned speech and then stretched one arm over his head and held the position for a few moments before switching to the other. He then cracked his neck before bending into a crouch, one leg extended as he touched his toes.

She was counting her breathing and focused on the feeling of her mana flowing in a calm manner throughout her entire body. When she was ready, she released a long breath and finished. Brownie stood up. For a large and curvy half giantess, she could mute her presence very well; all training from her childhood.

"Good evening," she said calmly so as not to startle the lizardkin.

It didn't work.

"Ack!" He twisted around, and an icicle shattered against the mountainside beside her left shoulder. "You court death, sssneaking up on this master!"

Her heart raced, but she ignored the cloying fear that crawled up her spine. She was *not* a direct-combat type. The man hadn't seemed like the kind to ice now and ask questions later, but apparently, Brownie was mistaken . . .

Still, bluffs were bluffs, and if she didn't walk her way out of this with pretend bluster, then she could at least *fake* it until she got close enough to push him off the side of the mountain.

Brownie had some idea of the identity of the man she was talking to, and asked, "General Knolith, I presume?"

He paused, taking in Brownie's tall, curvaceous stature and partially undressed state. A ruddy hue bloomed on his otherwise green cheeks. The lizardman only came up to her elbow, with a full view. "Do I know you?"

"No," Brownie stated simply, crossing her arms. "But I've heard about a lizardkin who practices the Ten Thousand Star Arts from His Royal Viciousness, King Keith, and I assumed. My name is Minstrel Bronwynn Lyriel."

Good. She praised herself on an excellent name drop—always important when coming across random all-powerful martial generals bursting out of waterfalls on an otherwise quiet day.

"And who are *you* to ssspeak freely with the king of the Dark Enchanted Forest?" he demanded.

"I," Brownie stated, "am the queen of the Dark Enchanted Forest's best friend."

"Wait." He took a step back, a hand going to his chest. "*Who* is your best friend?"

"I am Queen Henrietta's best friend," she repeated. "And traveling with Commander Rufus Triever on our way to Servalt."

"Keith has a *wife*?" General Knolith said, incredulous. "Our Keith? The one who never leavesss his workshop?"

Brownie smiled. "As far as I know, Henrietta met him *in* that workshop, and the rest is history. They got married yesterday."

"He got married and I missed the wedding by *one day?*" The lizardkin spat blood. Literally. Somehow, no droplets managed to get on his clothes as he pulled out a silk kerchief and swiftly wiped. He recovered remarkably quickly, eyes meeting hers. "Wait, you said Rufusss is with you?"

"Yes." She wondered if General Knolith always had a habit of saying "wait" before repeating exactly what had been told to him. "I did."

"Take me to him!" the lizardkin ordered. "I need newsss from a reliable sssource, and better him than that *ssspider.*"

Brownie couldn't help it, she raised one eyebrow and stared at the general. He waited, expectant.

At this point, Brownie's mind was racing, and she settled on two options.

One, she could politely tell the lizardkin general that she was *not* going to leave her relaxing spa day to go traipsing about Thistlecrick wearing nothing but her cozy cottons and fluffy slippers. Explaining to him that she was, *in fact*, not a citizen of Nilheim to be ordered about. Letting him know that she didn't, *in fact*, know where Rufus was. And even if she *did*, why would she lead him there just so he could interrogate a potentially similarly undressed Rufus lounging in some hot spring somewhere trying to relax.

That image made her pause for a second.

Or two, she could lead General Knolith out of the mountain path, take him to the highly private inner quarters of the General of the North's lair, and potentially get to listen in on Dark Enchanted Forest gossip and watch the lizardkin's reactions when Knolith learned that the Heroine of Justice *didn't* mass murder everyone in Nilheim and instead became the Dark Lord's pastry chef and won him over with bimbleberry scones.

Between the two, there was only one real option.

CHAPTER 11

Have You Thought About Joining the Fan Club?

Rufus

I probably should've gotten out of the hot spring a while ago, but I had a high Constitution, and there weren't any tasks demanding my attention. I could take the time to relax for once.

Sitting around in a dungeon all day was hard work.

Or maybe overdoing it for years until I finally slowed down and felt the crushing weight of it all was just making my work *feel* hard. Sigh. I complained a lot for someone with a roof over my head and delicious food on my plate.

This wasn't so difficult until a year ago. I'd been a competent and well-respected member of the Dark Lord's army . . . And now, I was all of that and restless.

My mind turned to the night everything changed.

One Year Ago

"You can sit 'ere at the bar, then," the troll ordered, showing me to what had to be one of the last free seats in the house. "Just don't tell Ol' Malley it were me that let you in."

I thanked the man too quietly to be heard, but he didn't need my words with the pouch full of silver coins in his pocket. It was shockingly expensive to bribe my way into the event. Luckily, it paid well being commander general, and I didn't have much to spend the money on back home.

No one here knew who I was, though, since I'd switched out my primary title from Commander to Connoisseur.

I sat at the end of the long counter, waiting. Tankards clanked and glasses thunked as the crush rushed to grab a drink before the show started. I ordered a red wine myself.

After reaching Constitution twenty, regular alcohol didn't affect me much, but I enjoyed the taste. It was more bitter in this form. Or maybe it was just the quality. I spent so little time in my folk form that it was hard to get used to seeing the light-brown, tan skin of my furless fingers gripping the glass instead of a padded hand with sharp claws. At least my golden-streaked ruddy hair resembled my natural coloring, and my canines were still sharp. I sighed.

In the corner of my vision, my notification tab was signaling more pop-ups for me to review. It was better than usual, since I wasn't in the Dark Enchanted Forest managing updates as well.

I chose to ignore them. Tonight, I was supposed to be *relaxing*.

Hah.

"Fine friends and good gentles." An older tigerkin man in black roguish attire stepped onto the stage, and the crowd started shouting. He smiled, showing sharp teeth. "I would like you all to welcome the one, the only, Bard Bronwynn Lyriel!"

The entire place exploded into cheers as a half giantess walked onto the stage. I sucked in a breath; she was a *vision*.

Bard Bronwynn was a half giantess with long curly hair that caught the flames in the lamplight. She wore a red dress that clung to her curves, and a belt with three knives and a mug clipped to it. She held a custom-made lyre harp that fit into her large palms, and she strummed a chord dramatically.

A skill amplified the sound and made it more powerful, filling the room.

"Who's ready for a good time?" Bard Bronwynn called to the crowd. Everyone shouted affirmation, and then there was a sudden, ethereal *calm* as the entire place stopped to listen to the opening notes of her song.

It was an old song about the knight Sir Eglamore, who took up his new sword and set out to fight a wyvern . . . only to have the grand battle end when the sword got stuck in the beast's teeth before it flew off. The knight, feeling sorry for himself, went to the pub and got drunk, telling anyone asking after his sword that if they fetched it, they could keep it.

I was laughing before I knew it. The music, the lyrics, and the overwhelming beauty of the experience of watching Bronwynn Lyriel perform floored me. Something about the show calmed my overly frayed nerves and left me with a sense of exhilaration. For the first time since I'd taken up the mantle as Commander General, I felt like a person again. She was the most beautiful and incredible woman I'd ever seen.

"Ah, another convert! I haven't seen you before. First time?" A voice broke into my revery. "Isn't she amazing? Have you thought about joining the fan club?"

"A fan club?" I pulled my eyes away from the bard as she took a pause to drink some water.

An older black woman with antlers was sitting beside me. Her hair was twisted into locks and pulled into a half updo. Her deep green eyes were smiling. She was accompanied by a pink pixie no bigger than a fairy godmother's wand sitting on her right shoulder.

"You look how I felt when I first heard Bard Bronwynn!" the pixie piped up, his wings fluttering to keep him poised on the older woman's shoulder. Enthusiastic shock-blue eyes met my golden. "We *all* love Bronwynn's music and keep track of her shows so we don't miss any new songs! I'm Ross, and this is Frida."

Frida looked back at the stage. "She's starting again; we can speak later."

Later, after the show, I was dragged off to spend the rest of the evening talking about the bard. Her history, her likes, her songs. I regretted only finding her music tonight. Years of concerts and shows I could have attended.

For the rest of my week stay, I bought my way into her concerts. I got front-row seats.

The group knew her schedule, and I painstakingly planned to be at all of her major concerts going forward. I wrote her letters. I sent her gifts. I got to know the other members, and we became good friends. It was a lot of work to keep a fan club running; paperwork, missives, newsletters, etc. I was very good at all of those things, and my responsibilities rapidly grew. And after a few months, I was the *leader* of her fan club. Frida and Ross laughed at me when I gave a passionate speech and accepted the position.

The president was in charge of telling everyone the bard's schedule over the club's Cast system, running events, and keeping everyone up to date. The hard work had all been worth it when Bronwynn accepted a request to perform at a dinner party in Sumbria.

I took my job as president very seriously. I rented a tavern, inspected the food, and handmade a gift basket for Bard Bronwynn, complete with chocolate, baked goods, and a spatial ring full of flowers.

It was perfect.

And then it all burned down.

CHAPTER 12

Have You Considered Running Off to Be a Baker?

Brownie

Knolith followed Brownie through the mountain pass. She knew the lizardkin could've taken himself there much quicker than following her relaxed walk, and wondered why he bothered.

He interrupted her thoughts with a rude, "So *you* are the new queen's best friend, hm?"

"*Of course,*" Bronwynn stressed. She knew her worth.

He considered that.

He could doubt her all he wanted, she thought, but what she'd said was true.

In fact, she'd been friends with Henrietta before she knew the girl was a princess, when they were both still naive children.

Many Years Ago

"That was *wonderful.*"

Bronwynn the Bard looked up from playing her lyre harp at the town fountain. A little girl wearing maid clothes stood there, hands clasped together and eyes bright.

"Thank you. I'm Bronwynn." The compliment made Bronwynn blush. She loved playing, and every happy face was a boost to her bardic heart.

"I'm Hen-Henrietta," the girl stuttered.

She had the fluffiest brown hair and softest brown eyes—hard to distinguish from the crowd. Her hands were marked with callouses from weapon use, and her posture was perfect. Bronwynn assumed she was more than just a maid; perhaps a noble lady's guard or spy?

Bronwynn would know; she'd probably met more spies than any other twelve-year-old in Drendil.

The girl looked younger than ten, but since Bronwynn was a half giantess who eclipsed even some human adults . . . well, it was hard to tell.

"Like the princess? Nice." Bronwynn nodded, shoving a short curly lock behind her ear. Her hair was dark brown with reddish tips that always magically colored themselves every morning no matter if she cut off the ends or not. "Do you have any requests?"

The maid's smile faltered. "I don't get to listen to a lot of music . . . What do you like?"

"If you have the time, I can play you *all* of the most popular songs right now!" This was her chance to shine, and Bronwynn jumped to her feet in excitement, placing her foot on the fountain and strumming her instrument with a strong opening chord.

Then Bronwynn paused, realizing she might have let her enthusiasm for performing get the better of her. Most of the people who stopped here didn't have the time to listen to more than one song. And everyone got nervous when they witnessed the full height and bulk of the bard as she loomed over them.

Her momentary anxiety washed away as the maid beamed up at her. "That would be great! I have a few hours before I need to find my way back."

The two enjoyed an afternoon of music, and that was the start of a very important friendship—for both of them.

Especially a few months later . . .

"Brownie!"

The nickname had the bard turning in the streets and smiling at the adorable maid. "Henrietta! Well, aren't *you* free a lot this month?"

"My mom caught me writing down a recipe." The maid sighed and took the bard's arm. They continued walking down the street. "She doesn't want me baking."

Brownie had no idea why getting in trouble left Henrietta free for the day, but she assumed the young maid was sent home and just took her sweet time getting there. Whenever Brownie saw her friend a lot, it was usually followed by the maid being absent for a long month or two. For "training." This happened especially when Henrietta's mother was particularly upset.

As such, Brownie appreciated the time they did get to spend together.

"Have you considered just running off to be a baker?" Brownie half joked. Apprenticeships were important, but if *she were* told to give up being a bard, Bronwynn would do just that: run away, get famous, and then come back in triumph!

Henrietta sighed. "I don't know any bakers. Who would bother teaching a pr—*palace* maid to bake?"

"But you're already familiar with the process?" Brownie asked, suddenly guiding Henrietta in a specific direction in the castle town market.

Henrietta nodded. "I've always wanted to know how the castle pastry chef makes all of those intricate desserts . . . so I've been sneaking into the kitchens to watch. I baked my first batch of cookies at six!"

"Did the castle chef like them?" Brownie asked, weaving them through a short alley and then up another street in the market.

The maid tensed. Looking down, she said sadly, "He got fired for letting me try."

"What?!" Brownie couldn't believe that someone with a prestigious job like castle pastry chef could be fired so easily. "Why?"

"My mother is a very exacting woman . . ."

Brownie had pieced a lot together in the time they'd been friends, and Henrietta's mother sounded both awful and powerful. Maybe even one of the queen's own personal maids. It would explain the strict tasks and the knife wounds on her friend's hands. Or that one time Henrietta had been hiding a limp.

Brownie's Perception wouldn't have missed *that*, and the bard wondered again what Henrietta's actual job was.

"Then we just won't tell her," the bard announced as they arrived at their destination.

Henrietta looked up at her, confused. "Tell her what?"

Brownie gave the girl a huge smile before waving her hand at a cute little bakery bustling with activity. "That you're helping out at Mira's Bakery."

"Wait, what?!" Henrietta stopped dead in the street, and there was a moment, a single small moment, where even *Brownie's* Strength couldn't pull the girl. Then the maid quickly relaxed as if she hadn't just demonstrated Strength over fifteen.

Brownie ignored the revealing moment and continued. "I know a great baker who'd love a part-time assistant to help her and her husband out. Now, let me introduce you!"

Henrietta let Brownie drag her behind the shop to the back door. As the maid stood up straight and professed her desire to bake with a noble finesse, Brownie rubbed her arm. The feeling of overwhelming *solid* Strength lingered in her mind.

More than just a regular palace maid indeed.

And where Brownie had helped her, Henrietta had returned the favor a few years later.

"I got a real gig!" Brownie burst in through the back door of Mira's Bakery, where she knew Henrietta would be working.

Henrietta laughed; her arms covered in flour as she calmly continued kneading a large batch of sourdough. "You've had a bunch of gigs. Didn't Connor start hiring you to play at the tavern since you came of age last year?"

"Not like that!" the bard exclaimed. "I'll be playing for a *noble!*"

"Is the new gig better paying, then?" the maid asked, lifting a hundred-pound bag of flour like it was a cup of tea and pouring it into a giant bowl.

"Yes!" Brownie pretended not to notice—just as Baker Mira and Journeyman Jeff, the had decided not to notice—and replied, "They're offering me a whole silver to play at the Tisbury estate this weekend! They're having a ladies tea party, and *someone* recommended me!"

"That's wonderful." Henrietta smiled, though she didn't meet Brownie's eyes.

"Thank you," Bronwynn said sincerely. "I know you must have mentioned me to someone at the palace."

Henrietta scratched her neck, embarrassed. She got a bit of dough on her collar but didn't seem to notice. "I'm happy to talk about you. I'm proud to have such an amazing bard as a friend. Besides, you got me this job; it's the least I could do to put in a good word."

"When are you finished?"

"She's been done for twenty minutes." Jeff, a burly black-haired human with quiet eyes and a calm temper stuck his head in the back. "So you can stop gossiping in my bakery and go get some fresh air."

"Perfect! Let's go, Henrietta. I want you to hear my song set."

The maid took off her apron and ran to join Bronwynn at the door. The bard reached out and picked the dough off her friend's collar. It was important to hide any and all evidence, Brownie knew, or she might not see her friend for a long time.

She played and Henrietta listened until it was time to go perform her heart out for a bunch of nobles.

This was more than just finding part-time work in a bakery. It was the opportunity of a lifetime, and she wouldn't have gotten it without the tiny maid she'd befriended.

And one day, Brownie swore, she'd repay the favor.

CHAPTER 13

If He Hurt Her

Rufus

The naga had built many different kinds of relaxing atmospheric rooms to cool down in while going between hot springs or massages or cold pools. Some of these rooms were designed to help meditation; others were perfect for napping.

I found myself in the latter. I'd showered to wash off the heavy minerals from the hot springs, and now I was laid out in a reclining chair. The room had gentle mood lighting and one wall made out of rock salt. I'd bought a pair of red-and-white striped shorts for my transformed self, and borrowed a soft, white housecoat to relax in. After nearly a year of running around in this human form, I'd grown more comfortable with it than before.

The air was crisp, and the temperature just right to drift off to sleep.

My nap was cut short by someone approaching and a sharp knock on the door.

"Commander general?"

The yawn was unstoppable, and I stretched, one arm over my head. "Yes?"

Elder Clarissa of Clan Lamia stood outside. "General Knolith has come out of closed-door cultivation and is asking for an audience. We've set him up with tea in the lounge."

That had me up. "He's here?"

"Yes, Minstrel Bronwynn discovered him on her walk."

"Is she alright?" I jumped to my feet, stalking to the door. Knolith made it clear that anyone who disturbed him would suffer the consequences. *If he hurt her—*"

Just before I could rip open the door, an unmistakable voice said, "I'm fine."

Minstrel Bronwynn was standing outside with Elder Clarissa. My hand hovered over the handle.

There was only one thing I *could* do.

I transformed back into my beastman self, my borrowed shorts ripping as I expanded in size. I kicked them off and pulled the housecoat as tight as it could go . . . which still left my majestic chest hair in full view. The arms were tight enough to pinch, but I couldn't go around with just a towel tied around my waist, so it would have to do.

I opened the door.

"You're sure you're alright? He didn't attack you?" I asked.

My idol stood there in a housecoat and fluffy slippers. She was beautiful and vibrant and still wet. Her hair was wet. I needed to calm my racing heart and my swishing tail. Damn this tail!

It was simple *chemistry* that knocked people off their heels in high-stress situations. I was just worried about Bronwynn, and my heart was pounding and my mind racing and getting away from me because of *chemistry*. I'd liked her since the first time I'd watched her perform, and I was maybe a bit obsessive over her music, but I didn't *like* her.

Maybe.

I was getting ahead of myself. She was here, perfectly safe.

"Well . . ." The minstrel eyed my chest and bursting housecoat before dragging her eyes up to meet mine. My tail stopped wagging when I heard the hesitation in her voice at my earlier question.

"Go on." My voice was deeper than I'd planned.

"*Technically*, he shot ice at me when I startled him," she clarified, "but he missed. And then he told me to find you, so here I am."

She shrugged, and I raised an eyebrow. "Here you are . . . How about we leave that pompous lizard to his tea and go put on some real clothes?"

Wandering around in nothing but a housecoat didn't feel the same without my dungeon office, daybed, and glass of wine.

"That would be great," Bronwynn agreed, plucking at her own housecoat. "I miss my knives."

"Then I can escort you both to the changing rooms." Elder Clarissa bowed.

The bard sighed. "It would've been nice to stay longer; I didn't get to finish the meditation walk."

"You're welcome to come again," the snake elder let Bronwynn know as she led us through a short series of hallways. "We could even arrange something if you were willing to stay a night and perform? Our general enjoys fine music with his meals."

"I would love to. Let's work it out the next time I'm passing through," Bronwynn agreed.

Something about Derilla having a private performance by Bronwynn left a knot in my stomach, but it was her profession—and she was good at it.

I wondered if I needed to remind Derilla that he wasn't allowed to eat people anymore . . .

"Here you are, commander general," the naga said, dropping me off at my room and then leading Bronwynn away.

I said my farewells and went inside to get changed. I deliberately took my time, knowing Knolith was waiting for me, and Bronwynn still needed to wash up. The lizardkin could wait even longer after he'd shot ice at one of the most amazing women on the continent and then ordered her around!

As I exited my room, I found Elder Clarissa waiting to guide me.

"Did you *know* where General Knolith was cultivating?" I demanded, asking the question I'd been stewing on. I'd changed back into my calf-length black pants, a white shirt with laces open at the throat, a vest full of pockets, and my belt and pouch.

"We knew, but we were not expecting him to come out so soon." Elder Clarissa shook her head. "We made a mistake."

"I understand." I sighed and ran a hand through my hair. "Why is the General of the East even *here*?"

"He told the master that he required a mountain for his closed-door cultivation."

There were no mountains in the eastern bog. Rufus nodded. "Minstrel Bronwynn was in the mountains for what, an hour?"

"Yes, my lord."

One thing I knew from her stories was that Minstrel Bronwynn always *had* a story. Every performance would include an interlude where she regaled the audience with some tale or other about how she'd overcome the odds to be there. Whether she was beset by thieves or had her wagon stolen or got trapped for three hours at a bridge by a troll riddle, she always had something, and each was an entertaining recount.

Now I was along for the ride, wooing wombats and dodging master cultivators, and it'd only been *one* day.

"Alright, I'm ready," I said. "Lead me to Knolith."

CHAPTER 14

Did Spring Finally Come to the Dark Enchanted Forest?

Brownie

Bronwynn recognized that Rufus was a very strong, capable, and charismatic individual. She knew he was quick to smile and easy to read, with a tail that got away from him. He was sweet and fluffy, but nothing more than her best friend's husband's friend.

She knew that.

Which was why she hadn't expected to feel a flush when the man had growled "*If he hurt her—*" and then burst out of a room in nothing but a housecoat.

For the first time since she'd met the man, Brownie was made *aware* of him.

She didn't know what to make of that, so she decided to ignore it.

It was time to get ready and go enjoy listening in on the Dark Enchanted Forest gossip between two of the kingdom's leaders! She put on a pair of black tights and an extra-long tunic that fell to her thighs. She'd forgone her red shoulder bag for a simple belt pouch and dagger.

Brownie grabbed her instrument bag and slung it over her shoulder. It was time to go.

"Minstrel." A young naga woman waited in the hallway, tail coiled and wringing her hands. She had long pink hair and deep blue eyes. "I am Janet Melusine, heir of Clan Melusine. May I escort you to the lounge?"

"Is that where Rufus is?"

"Clan Lamia is escorting him there now." The snake woman looked at the floor. "I do not know if they've arrived yet."

Bronwynn sighed. It wasn't a *problem* being alone with Knolith; he just treated her like a servant.

"Ah! Bard! You are back," were the first words that greeted Bronwynn as she came into the private meeting room. "Have you not brought me Commander

Rufusss?" General Knolith relaxed on a collection of pillows, seated at a low table laden with traditional hot spring delicacies. The lizardkin happily ate a red bean mochi ball and savored the flavor.

"He is on his way," Brownie replied, wondering if he'd be insulted if she just sat down at his table and joined him; she'd never felt this hesitation back at the castle. She considered her next move.

Then Rufus walked in.

General Knolith slowly stood to his feet and shook out his robe sleeves to hang perfectly in front of him as he gave Rufus a stiff nod. The lizardkin's eyes were fierce and ablaze with hunger. Brownie couldn't tell if Rufus was the object of his touted revenge . . . or if Knolith might be interested in the beastman for other reasons.

"General Knolith," Rufus returned the greeting then turned to Bronwynn. "I see you've met the esteemed Minstrel Bronwynn. Shall we take a seat?"

Brownie smiled and plopped down on the floor. She chose a nice red cushion with embroidered white coy fish and settled in.

"Wait." Knolith remained standing. "I have asked for this meeting to learn about our kingdom'sss internal affairsss. This woman is *not* in a position to sit with us, no matter who her friendsss are."

"You are incorrect." Rufus poured Brownie a cup of tea, who nodded in thanks while adding a splash of milk and honey. "Minstrel Bronwynn might not be a leader in the Dark Lord's army, but she already knows everything I am about to tell you. Besides, I've heard that you *attacked* her unprovoked. I would warn you now that *any such insult will not be allowed to happen again*."

Both Brownie and the lizardkin's eyebrows rose at that. Rufus coughed. "She *is* the queen's best friend, after all."

"That's why I asked you to see me." Knolith crossed his arms. He probably meant to seem imposing, but Bronwynn was tall enough that she wasn't particularly intimidated. Even from a sitting position. "*That* Keith is *married?!*"

"Sit down, and we'll tell you what happened." Rufus waved at Knolith's floor cushion before refilling the lizardkin's cup. "It's actually the reason Minstrel Bronwynn is here. She knows more about the finer details than me, I assume."

The two faced her, and Bronwynn's cheek twitched; she pulled out her lyre and gave it a strum. "Song first, I guess. Then some explanation."

By the time she finished "The Dark Lord's Lady," Knolith was gaping incredulously. Rufus then explained how Drendil had declared war on the Dark Enchanted Forest, but the army had been stopped at a bridge troll crossing—courtesy of Gerda the Bridge Troll—and how Henrietta and Keith had sent them packing.

Then *she* explained the kidnapping and slave trading attempt by a noble in Servalt at the Spring Ball, and how Princess Henrietta had saved Dark Lord

Keith's life with the help of her friends. Finally, Brownie recounted the marriage proposal, which she'd heard from Henrietta in great detail, and explained that Chloe the Necromancer had given up her wedding so that the Dark Lord wouldn't outright elope.

"Chloe's engaged too?!" Knolith slapped a hand to his forehead. "What? Did ssspring finally come to the Dark Enchanted Forest? Where is *my* ssstrong and ferocious mate?!"

"Technically," Rufus quipped, "it *is* spring."

"For at least two weeks," Bronwynn added. Though she only did so because General Knolith looked annoyed. She helped herself to a Lady Green tea mochi.

The lizardkin turned on Rufus. "What about *you*? Are *you* sssuddenly in love and getting married as well?"

Rufus stiffened and slowly lowered his tea, his voice rough. "I'm not getting married anytime soon. Besides, even if I *did* find a partner, Chloe and Julia are next. She would *kill* me if I ran off and got married."

"Alright. I think I understand well enough." Knolith frowned. "I guesss I'd better head to the castle to ssswear fealty."

"You might want to check out Kith Bog first," Rufus recommended. He explained. "Since assassins lit it on fire."

Brownie noted that Rufus neglected to point out that had happened over a month ago, and as far as she knew, the town was already rebuilt, and nobody got hurt.

Except the assassins, but who counted assassins?

Knolith took the bait and jumped to his feet. "What?! Assassinsss lit my home on fire? And you didn't lead with that?!"

"It's fine," Rufus said as he sampled a small bit of fish cake. "No one died."

"Except the assassins," Brownie repeated her thoughts aloud, smiling.

"But who counts assassins?" Rufus chuckled. "Ah, and your house burned down."

"Agh! Then I shall ssstop in to review my domain, *then* head to the castle." Knolith asked after the underwater city below Lake Loria. "There isn't any ill-begotten newsss from Plittsmouth, right?"

"It's moved to the southeast currently." Rufus shrugged. "And Her Eminence Feliwyn is still napping away. Barely moved during the entire ceremony."

"Truly? You held a wedding in my domain without me? I told everyone I'd be out before the sssummer. You couldn't have *waited*?" Knolith complained, his fist clenching on his knee.

"And deny Chloe?" Rufus chuckled, clearly finding the idea ridiculous. "You can tell the necromancer yourself how she should have delayed the wedding of the king of the Dark Enchanted Forest for a mere general."

Bronwynn knew Chloe well enough by now to know how that would go. It was a simple fact, yet Knolith seemed to take personal offense. The air around them dropped a few degrees as the lizardkin struggled to compose himself.

"That bringsss us to the last reason I've requested an audience." Knolith picked up the hot tea Brownie had refilled and downed it. Steamy breath rolled out of his mouth as hot tea met ice-cold cultivator.

Rufus just raised an eyebrow.

"I wish to test my newfound power." The lizardkin slammed his cup onto the table. "I challenge you to a duel!"

CHAPTER 15

Civilized Members of the Dark Army

Rufus

Ever since I'd first crushed Knolith in the Winter Tourney at eighteen and claimed the title of Commander General, the lizardkin had used every excuse to challenge me.

It was usually a chore, but *this time*, I was glad for the excuse.

"Alright." I retained my calm and collected appearance as inside, I warred with the desire to punch Knolith in the face.

The lizardkin gave me a side-eye. "Just like that?"

I stood up. "You've been rude to my . . . friend, and we can settle this like civilized members of the Dark Horde."

So what if I *usually* found a way out of battling every Tom, Rick, and Knolith who challenged me?

Usually, I was busy or not in the mood. The fact that *everywhere* I went, *someone* challenged me, especially since duels had become popular, meant I'd grown tired of it very quickly. I was the right hand to the king, and people wanted to know: Could they hold their own against the commander of the Dark Horde? The most powerful warrior in all the land?

It was exhausting.

And Knolith *always* challenged me. Even before that. From the time I was sent to Keith as a playmate, the lizardkin had taken every opportunity to compete with me. It was hard enough being handed over like some toy, but then, I'd had to protect the future king with my life *and* put up with a very hostile young Knolith.

I thought about this as we made our way to the Thistlecrick training grounds . . . And the more I thought about it, the more I *really* wanted to punch Knolith in the face.

"This is just like how Henrietta and Keith started." Bronwynn chuckled. "Though with less bimbleberry scones. Perhaps spring *has* come for you and Knolith."

She was standing with me as we emerged onto the training plateau. Her flaming red hair caught the last rays of the sun.

"This is not our first duel." I ignored the not-so-subtle romantic subtext and stated the facts simply. "Knolith has always challenged me like this, even before duels became normal. You could say that he did it before it was fashionable."

North Sumbria, the most trendsetting and magically advanced domain on the continent, had started a passion for dueling recently. Though Queen Henrietta had mentioned that some of those trends had been actually started by someone else, and they were using North Sumbria as a scapegoat for their creative liberties. She'd heard it from the ruler herself, Grand Duchess Calisto.

But I digressed.

Knolith walked into the ring and took his stance, waiting, while I prepared. I didn't want him destroying my good vest, and a lot of my skills required preparation.

[Passive Skill: **Mediator** has been activated by your **Patient** Knolith Stardancer. Primary emotion: Anger, Resentment. Subject may act violently. Threat Level: 4]
[You have attempted to use the Skill: **Examine**. You have succeeded. Six targets may be observed. **Knolith Stardancer** selected. Target is under observation. Predictive analysis: 68%. Available predictions: attack trajectory, perk activation, and team-based movements.]

Luckily, there was ample time to activate my abilities on the walk here and while talking to Bronwynn. Even as I stopped to take a sip of water and set aside my vest, the number rose to sixty-nine percent.

"Are you ready, Commander General?" Knolith asked politely, though he bit at the title. He got into position, and my skill took it all in, bringing it up to seventy-two percent.

I nodded; it should be enough. I entered the circle.

The plateau and the stands remained empty; no one had been invited to the bout, and the regular trainees cleared the area for us very quickly. I felt their keen eyes from many observation windows cut into the tunnels of the mount.

Something I was also used to. *Sigh.* I missed my dungeon.

"Ready when you are." I flexed my claws and used my natural born Beastfolk title to shift my nails further toward my full beast form. I cracked my neck.

[Title: Beastfolk. A natural born shifter between folk and fair. Able
to transition between forms, with three natural states: folk, beastfolk, and beast. Mana cost to shift: 12x transition percentage.]

I spent the twenty-four mana without fear; my mana pool had started to refill
from my earlier ability activation.

"Then I shall have the honor of dealing the first blow." Knolith started with
a step toward me. Lines of blue-and-red light that only I could see predicted his
movements. "See if you can dodge *this*."

A blade of ice formed in his hand, and he executed a sharp strike at my face.
I caught the blade, swinging it away, not bothering to use [Redirect Blow].

Skills and perks were useful, but sometimes, regular skill was enough.

The lizardkin completed a fluid motion that repositioned his blade, aiming
for my throat. The red lines showed me where the strike would land, while the
blue lines flared, warning me of his intent to activate a skill or perk.

His powers had leveled up significantly during his closed-door cultivation.
Knolith let out a blast of ice with the swing of his sword that shot eight jagged
shards my way. Each was easily dodged, though one nicked the fabric of my
tunic. As I expected, the garment was compromised and took [Frost] damage.
As quickly as I could, I whipped off my shirt and tossed it aside before I was
encased in ice.

I glanced at Bronwynn, who looked like she was at a show. She'd pulled out
snacks from *somewhere* and was munching away, staring at us.

My [Examine] of Knolith was at seventy-eight percent, but I didn't bother
remaining on the defensive.

It was time to end this.

As the lizardkin raised his sword for another attack, activating another perk,
I stepped forward and executed a palm strike.

[You have attempted to use the Perk: **Force Palm**. You have
succeeded. Knock back 6 paces, dealing 6 x 26 points of
physical damage.]

Knolith tried to reposition his blade to block, but my palm struck his chest. I
regretted the need to remain stalwart in my position that had me drop my hand
down from his face at the last second. Sigh.

I took a cut to the arm as he was flung backward. The martial expert landed
with grace, gently, as if he were not subject to the laws of gravity. It did not matter, though, because he landed with his heel outside the ring.

There was a moment of collective silence before a roar of activity took place
inside the tunnels. Bronwynn joined in with exuberance as she stood and cheered.

Watching her made my heart race. I knew she'd just enjoyed the show, but her cheering me on in the stands left me with a sense of accomplishment unlike any battle I'd won in the past.

Winning was just a necessity to my security; it wasn't something to celebrate.

I turned back to my opponent to politely offer my hand . . . and Knolith was glaring at me with a deeper rage than I'd ever seen. His nostrils flared, and the slits of his lizardlike eyes cast daggers in my direction. But he wasn't staring into my eyes.

He was staring at my wagging tail.

CHAPTER 16

Am I Your Favorite Bard?

Brownie

"You take joy in my defeat! I knew it!"

Brownie felt the rush of vicarious victory fade as General Knolith accused Rufus. The naga watching from the viewing windows also quieted, and many began to whisper among themselves.

"No! I, um . . ." Rufus grabbed his exuberant tail. "I simply enjoyed the fight?"

"If it helps, I think we all enjoyed the fight," Brownie interrupted. No sense watching a rivalry story turn wrong when she could join in and steer everyone in the right direction. "It was a short bout, but your ice sword blast was as beautiful as your footwork! And you both managed to land a hit. Doesn't that make you happy?"

"What? Happy?" Knolith had dragged his fierce eyes away from Rufus and stared, confused, at her.

"You literally froze the clothes off of Rufus." Brownie pointed to the fluffy bare chest of the beastman, his sleek muscles covered only by his neutral golden coat.

"She's right." Rufus nodded. "It was a close call. And I might not be so lucky next time."

The tunic he'd sported earlier was a frozen, rumpled sheet lying on the other side of the ring.

Knolith looked between it and the beastman.

"I told myself that I would defeat you, and I will. No matter how long it takesss," the lizardkin declared. His robes gently swayed without any discernible breeze. Brownie wondered if there was a perk for that. "This was just the beginning. Be prepared for the winter sssolstice. I *will* inherit my rightful place as commander general!"

"I thought the Dark Enchanted Forest was a meritocracy?" Brownie interrupted. Both men faced her again, and she shrugged. "Was I wrong?"

"You're not wrong, Bard," Knolith said. "But I *am* destined to be the commander general!"

"Did Madame Potts say so?" Brownie asked, still confused where the certainty came from. "Was there a prophecy?"

Rufus was the one who actually answered. "It's not like that, so far as I'm aware. He just wants the job."

"*Wantsss the job?*" Knolith repeated, incredulous. "My father was the commander general, as was his mother before him. Our family has been the right hand of the ruling house of Nilheim for *thirteen generationsss!*"

"The point of a meritocracy is to let everyone have the opportunity to compete. It prevents more deaths in the long run," Rufus said gently.

"My father died of *shame* that I did not inherit his title, and I sssswore on his *deathbed* that I would defeat you. You know this!"

"Your father died of shame?" Brownie interrupted again. "I'm sorry for your loss."

Rufus frowned. "His father died of a heart attack—and he's not dead *now*. Old Dame Julith got to him in time with a Revival potion. I saw him at the St. Veralyn's Day Tourney last month."

St. Veralyn's Day was a holiday celebrating Dragon Veralyn the Green, who'd defeated an evil knight named Sir George of Lindale. Brownie knew many songs featuring the knight's evil deeds—primarily his well-known dislike for dogs and horses. And the one time he'd kidnapped a dragon's princess and tried to marry her. Luckily, Veralyn went after the poor girl. Imagine the audacity!

Arranged marriages were stressful enough. Look at Henrietta's. Her parents had tried to marry her off to an idiot marquess who couldn't tell the difference between a lyre and a lute! At least the System controlled title contracts for things like marriage or having children. Such things required both parties to select [Yes].

Knolith raised his hand dramatically then made a cutting motion between them, his martial sleeves elegantly flowing with the movement. "I *will* reclaim my rightful place. And I *will* defeat you at this Winter Solstice Tourney."

"I'll accept your challenge *then*." Rufus waved a hand dismissively and went to retrieve his frozen tunic. "Now, if you'll excuse me, I have to go find a new shirt." The commander general walked over to Brownie. He slipped on his vest and offered her his free arm. "Shall we?"

She waved goodbye to the lizardkin as she followed Rufus off the plateau and into a cavern stairwell.

"Where're we going?"

"Have you had a chance to see the city yet? There's a restaurant with live music overlooking the Carn Waterfall," Rufus offered. "My treat after getting attacked by one of my generals?"

Ambient sunset light from the many small window holes carved into the stone blended with the magical lanterns overhead, casting shadows on the stairs.

"That sounds nice . . . but . . ." Brownie felt the soft golden fur beneath her hands.

"But?" he asked, his voice soft.

"Shouldn't we get you a new shirt?"

He chuckled. "Probably."

"I mean"—she gave him an obvious appraising look—"you look nice without a shirt, but the restaurant might insist?"

Or not. This was the Dark Enchanted Forest. Brownie couldn't see there being a "No shirt, no pants, no service" rule when half-snake or half-spider or half-horse people commonly wandered about. It would be insulting.

"Then I should *definitely* put on a shirt," Rufus joked. "I don't know how many compliments I can take from my favorite bard."

"Am I your favorite bard?" The way he said it, so matter of fact like that, didn't sound like a simple platitude. Brownie took a step forward, now looking up at him from the lower staircase. She was beaming.

Rufus must not have meant to say it that way, by the nervous look on his face, but then, a genuine smile that showed off his canines took over. "Yes. I love your music. You're incredibly talented, and I can honestly say you're my favorite performer on the entire continent—and I've been to a *lot* of shows."

"Thank you." The admission was more than she expected from the leader of the Dark Lord's armies. Her cheeks burned, but she didn't mind. "Then I'm happy to go to dinner, your treat."

CHAPTER 17

So Why Don't You Just Not?

Rufus

Thistlecrick was a village etched into the mountain leading down from the plateau. It wound through connecting hills, and while they weren't as tall as the mountains to the west, the valleys and peaks were still impressive. The naga and other residents of Thistlecrick all lived sprawled over the slopes or inside the many caves, but the marketplace and businesses were front and center by the town gates. Bronwynn and I had passed through here the previous day when we'd ridden up the winding path to the city from the Great Road.

The restaurant was called Knobbinson, and had been owned by the Knobbin family for some three hundred years. They were a family of preela—brown-haired, floppy-eared, thin-winged, faelike people on the taller side. The preela were originally from the Empire of Sands, but a few had traveled across Valaria and set up businesses here and about.

The owner, Mrs. Ellie Knobbin, greeted us at the door. "Rufus, my boy! Just look at you! Still commander general, I see?"

"That is correct." And she could see. It was an effect of the title that made everyone in Nilheim recognize their commander general on sight.

"Excellent." She nodded approvingly. "Come this way."

The woman was an old friend of Her Eminence Feliwyn, as anyone could tell by her no-nonsense attitude. She had us escorted in and sitting at a table in good time. She'd found us a spot overlooking the mountains with a clear view of three waterfalls.

"It's good to see you again, Mrs. Ellie. May I introduce you to Minstrel Bronwynn Lyriel?" I said as soon as we were settled.

"A pleasure." The preela eyed Bronwynn appraisingly. "And is *this* pleasure, business, or company?"

"Company," we both answered at the same time.

"I'll bring you water to start." Then she was off.

Brownie chuckled. "I do like how *straightforward* everyone is."

"It took a lot of work," I said, proud. "But it was worth the effort."

"What does *that* mean?" she asked, then smiled at her own straightforward question.

I tried not to let my passion run away with me, and tentatively explained, "Culture is one of the first things that can change when a new ruler takes the throne, and when Keith stepped up, he wanted to promote a happy, logically minded, efficient Dark Enchanted Forest."

"Hence the four-day workweek? And the free unlife care?" Brownie asked.

I nodded. "A well-rested and confident Dark Horde will be more self-sufficient . . . And why spend so much time and resources on people we don't take care of physically? It's a waste. That's why we have free healers, health potions, and a necromancer whose job it is to [Raise], [Resurrect], or [Revive] the masses."

"And the straightforwardness?"

"I've spent the last eight years offering mandatory counseling for most of the Dark Enchanted Forest."

"You can't have privately met with *everyone* in the Dark Enchanted Forest, though." Bronwynn started to laugh, then cut herself off. "Can you?"

"I didn't need to see *everyone*. Just the leaders, and some of the army troops." I picked up the menu and looked it over, deciding on the orange-glazed and crispy-breaded floofpoof bird served on a bed of wild greens with a side of long-grain rice.

"Suspend my disbelief; how was that possible?" The minstrel took my cue and also perused the menu.

"There are only about forty thousand people in the Dark Enchanted Forest, and most of them work in the army, in business, or in caregiving. I visited each military point and screened the eight thousand minions in the Dark Lord's army over four years," I explained.

"On a four-day workweek?" Brownie raised an eyebrow. "That's . . . *forty* people a day?"

"A lot of the problems were solved with training management, so even less. And I didn't really take days off back then," I admitted, reminiscing. It had actually been one of my favorite parts of my new job. "My skills make it easy to read people. I would wander through the Dark Army units and each town and get a feel for things pretty quickly. A few interviews and a day or so issuing quests, and things were mostly settled."

That was back when I'd ignored my own labor laws and worked every day. Even just six people a day, three hundred and sixty days out of the year—give or take days for travel—meant I'd easily assessed two thousand people a year. And four years later, I'd seen most of the army and villages. I didn't need to personally visit *everyone* in the forest—just the people in charge and the people who were struggling. And by that point I'd trained The King's Dogs, twenty other mediators who could aid in my work across the Dark Enchanted Forest.

"It helps that there are so many different types of people living in the forest," I mused. The actual culture of each region changed drastically, but one thing remained. "Once it became normal to ask and answer questions, everyone started doing it."

The residents were all cutthroat and used to telling it straight, which meant there wasn't a lot of push back.

"So you drilled all of the soldiers, and then wandered the forest like a wiseman offering wisdom to anyone your stats told you needed guidance?" Bronwynn joked. "How old *were* you when you started?"

"Eighteen?" I set the menu aside to show Mrs. Ellie I was ready to order. Brownie did the same. "I should mention I'd already had ample time to practice on everyone in the Black Fortress long before then. I was given to Keith shortly after I turned seven, and leveled up enough to be useful by the age of ten."

The bard tilted her head, eyeing me. Her curly hair fell over her shoulder, distracting me for a moment. She was beautiful, and her dark eyes shone with red flecks in the candlelight. "You keep saying that."

"What?"

"Are we ready to order?" Mrs. Ellie appeared at Bronwynn's shoulder, interrupting my chance to question her statement. The preela placed a glass of water in front of each of us. "I should also let you know our soup of the day is a vegetarian slow-simmered caramelized squash soup with homemade dumplings."

"Ooh, may I have that with a side of the house bread selection?" Bronwynn chose a platter of different local breads, with whipped honey butter, apple butter, and chive butter for dipping. "And a glowing nettle citrus fitzer."

I placed my own order, with the addition of a cold golden ale, and the preela left us. I asked Bronwynn, "What did you mean? About what you said before?"

"It's just that you keep saying you were *given* to Keith. Like a pet."

"Because I *was*." The words were out before I realized how they'd sound. Her Eminence Feliwyn was tyrannical in her rule. When she'd told the Dark Enchanted Forest that her ward required playmates, playmates were sent. I was chosen, and so I went.

Sure, I could go back to Gren's Keep now; I had a sister who remained there still. But my family had *chosen* to send me away.

It was a great honor to live in the Black Fortress . . . and if I wanted to *stay* in the Black Fortress, in my rooms, then I had to be the commander general.

Bronwynn still looked confused, so I took a sip of water, deciding on what to say. "I was sent to play with and protect our king in his childhood, like a pet. Many were sent as an option, but dogs make great companions."

The indignity that followed me from that day had fueled the actions that had brought me to where I was as an adult. And the woman sitting across from me, sipping her water with neither pity nor pride in her eyes, was one of my few sources of relief.

It was unhealthy. It was toxic. But a small part of me had come to rely on her music to grant me any sort of distraction from my life.

Bronwynn quirked an eyebrow. "So why did you stay? Why don't you just *not?*"

I stiffened. "Not be the commander general?"

"You don't sound like you enjoy it," she stated simply. "I mean, the *being* a commander general part. Advising people is great, but there are a lot of different ways you can do that . . . So if you don't feel empowered by your work, you could do something else?"

"I enjoy—" I cut myself off.

Did I, though? What was it I'd told Queen Henrietta that first day we'd met? *Look at what you want instead of what's expected of you.*

The minstrel was as good at this as I was.

"I don't think King Keith sees you as a pet," she remarked. "I think he admires you. And what about Chloe? Is she also a pet?"

Chloe was . . . an enigma. Someone Feliwyn had brought home one day who was smarter than she ought to be and overpowered from the start. The fact that she had no ambition at all had let her join in the political mess of the Dark Enchanted Forest with minimal trouble.

"Chloe is more like . . . a sister?" Closer than his own blood sister.

"Then why can't you be a sworn brother?" Bronwynn crossed her arms. "Do you think that if Knolith beats you and takes your job, you won't be welcome back?"

CHAPTER 18

Very Cute

Brownie

Brownie kicked herself for her insensitive questions, but Rufus just seemed so *empty* when he spoke about his circumstances. It was a far cry from his animated explanation recounting his community engagement plan for promoting a healthy, happy Dark Horde.

"My rooms in the Black Fortress," Rufus said quietly, "are reserved for the commander general."

The implications of his response were matter of fact.

"And the dungeon?"

He hesitated. "I don't know."

"Maybe you should ask King Keith when you get back?" Brownie took another sip of her water. "If I lived in a trial-by-combat meritocracy, I'd have a backup plan. Maybe buy a house?"

Rufus stared at her for a long moment, making Brownie feel awkward. She stumbled over a quick placating, "Or not! What do I know? I'm just a nobody bard wandering through."

"You are *not* a nobody," Rufus countered firmly. "You're *the* Minstrel Bronwynn Lyriel."

Again, heat burned her cheeks, and Brownie found herself caught by his intense golden eyes. She straightened. "You're right. I am fabulous. But I still went too far. I'm sorry."

"They were words I needed to hear, so thank you." Rufus smiled and Brownie smiled, and then their food arrived.

Silence settled comfortably as they ate, both enjoying their meal. As promised, a live performance started about halfway through dinner. An elderly naga played a zither and sang soft lounge music, his voice soothing. Brownie found herself closing her eyes and truly relaxing for the first time since General Knolith had burst out of that waterfall.

"I hope you enjoyed the meal," Mrs. Ellie came by at the end. She eyed Rufus, taking on the tone of a shameless aunt. "And do send my love to Chloe and Keith. No one visits anymore, and I didn't get *nearly* enough time with any of you at the wedding."

Brownie didn't recall seeing the woman at the wedding, but she'd been focused on performing, and there had been *a lot* of magical guests.

"I will, Mrs. Ellie," Rufus assured the preela. He paid for both meals at the front desk; Mrs. Ellie raised an eyebrow at *that*, but only shot them a knowing smile.

"You two have a good night." She waved. "I'll come visit when Feliwyn wakes up. It won't be long now. Lovely to officially meet you, Minstrel Bronwynn."

"Likewise," Brownie replied as Rufus offered her his arm. She happily took it, and they wandered into the marketplace. The sun had set long ago, and lanterns illuminated the night market. It was bustling, and if anything, it was *busier* than during the day. Especially with the arachne.

"I am so happy I'm not afraid of spiders," Brownie stated, watching the street full of half-spider, half-human monsters. They bartered and traded just like anyone else. Laughed the same, too.

Honestly, classifying any race that spawned in dungeons as "monsters" was not very nice. Dungeon madness only affected *spawned* monsters, and all of the regular people Brownie had met in the real world were perfectly lovely.

Or they were criminals. Or they were both.

Her family *was* very eclectic, so who was she to talk?

"Have you met many arachne?" Rufus asked. They were walking with the flow of foot traffic, and stopped to peek at stalls as they went.

"My uncle married one four years ago," she told him. That particular older aunt-in-law lived in Peldeep. Brownie's family had welcomed the tall and powerful spider woman into their fold with open arms. Aunt Larraina Stannard had even given up some of her silk to Brownie on St. Veralyn's Day. She'd surprised the bard with a thin silk strap for her instrument that could survive almost anything.

Danielle sported that very strap now.

". . . Is your uncle human?" he asked. "Or giant?"

"Human. My grandfather was human, and my grandmother was a storm giant. They had seven sons. Three humans, three storm giants, and my father, who is half giant and the youngest." Brownie smiled. "My mother's parents were both human from Drendil. They had seven daughters, and every single one married a nonhuman. Mom is also the youngest."

"I thought Drendil was . . ." He trailed off, trying to find a delicate way to say terribly narrow-minded xenophobes.

"They are," she stated. "That's why most of my family moved to Peldeep."

It made for big and confusing family reunions.

On her father's side, her fourth uncle, Faren Stannard, had been the last to get married. She hadn't seen them in some years, after Larraina had laid a clutch. She'd taken the two hatchlings into seclusion, and would stay there until the children could control their powers well enough to not accidentally murder anyone. Uncle Faren had gone into hiding until Larraina's urge to kill and eat him abated. That was usually around the same time the children reached level ten and got their first title. Most children leveled up once every year naturally, but arachne hunted with their young to speed up the process.

Brownie pulled Rufus to look at a small pottery table with a variety of earthenware. Five pendant flutes with different gems set in the front caught her eye.

"Oooh, these are beautiful!" Her bardic heart melted looking over the adorable palm-size instruments. They were oval, with a circular chamber and finger holes front and back that got bigger with each note.

"Thank you, miss." A young naga boy with lime-green hair and pink eyes smiled warmly. "Ma cast them with the essence of gladeroot, so they have a bonus to carrying sound outdoors. I have them in the three tones. Also, one for the pitch-perception races, and one that only dungeon monsters can detect."

Rufus raised an eyebrow when Brownie picked up the pendant flute with a yellow teardrop-cut stone in the front. A soft cord necklace was attached to the top.

"That's a lemon quartz," the boy told her. "I used [Cleanse] on it, so feel free to try playing—though you'll need a skill to detect the pitch."

Brownie blew gently into the mouthpiece, her fingers playing the chorus for the song "Minstrel Fine." She heard nothing.

Rufus, however, nodded along to the music. She smiled and handed over two silver pieces. "I'll take this one. No need to wrap it."

She slid the necklace over her head and tucked the pendant instrument under her dress.

"I'm impressed that you managed to hear that," Rufus commented as they resumed their walk. "Is it a skill, or do giants have pitch perception?"

"I can't hear it." Brownie smiled up at her traveling companion. "I bought it because *you* can hear it."

"I don't understand."

Brownie fiddled with a curly red lock. "We aren't in a party, so we can't use the communication interface. I'm always getting kidnapped or robbed or lost . . . I thought it would be great to have a way to contact you without anyone else knowing."

"That was a lot of money for a one-trip convenience." Rufus frowned.

He was right; a few silver coins could feed a family for a month.

"I also wanted it, and this gave me the perfect excuse!" Brownie was a musician . . . and she might have a terrible habit of collecting instruments. Of course *this* instrument had a purpose, so she could definitely justify buying it. Brownie lifted the oval instrument to dangle in front of her. "It's so cute! Look at it!"

Rufus stared at the instrument, and then his eyes met hers. "Very cute."

He didn't look away, and every flirtatious bone in her body let her accept the attention for what it was—until Rufus broke eye contact suddenly. He took a deep breath and offered his arm to the bard.

Brownie took it.

They ambled together through the market and back to the clan house. Brownie almost, *almost* asked Rufus if he was interested in being more than simple traveling companions . . . but she hesitated.

He was her best friend's husband's best friend. They would be seeing each other often.

She had a hard time getting to sleep, her mind filled with a pair of golden glowing eyes.

CHAPTER 19

Wait Until We Get Kidnapped

Rufus

I started the day with a splash in the ice baths.

I'd woken up early and ready. Too ready. An ice bath was in order. The feeling of cold on my skin, not covered in a golden coat, was exhilarating. It cleared my mind and let me get back to planning the rest of our trip.

We would depart Thistlecrick this morning, grab lunch or dinner at Kith Bog—depending on where the village was today—and then be on the road again. Donna was a very agile and speedy horse, so we might even reach the border tonight.

I activated my birth title Beastfolk and changed back into my normal self.

Technically, my hairless folk form, all the way to my giant beast form, was all my "normal self," but I'd been living in my semitransformed state for so long, it felt the most natural. Many beastfolk picked one look and stuck with it.

Bronwynn was waiting for me at breakfast, her usual chipper expression sleepy and wan.

"Morning," she said, yawning and sinking into her steaming cup of tea. My nose detected Lady Green leaves, extra caffeinated.

"Morning," I returned, pouring myself a cup from a teapot at the table. We'd been given a private room for breakfast. Everything was set up on a spinning wooden circle in the middle of a round table designed for floor seating. I liked sitting on the floor. I liked the tea. And I liked the company.

Stop it, tail.

Two days journeying with my favorite bard wasn't good for my heart. Seeing her sleepy eyed and slightly rumpled wasn't helping either.

"Are we ready to head out after breakfast?" I asked.

She nodded. "Yep, ready to go whenever."

The unigoat yogurt parfait with bimbleberries and markle berry spread tasted delightful, and I happily ate a floofpoof sausage baked in flaky pastry. There was also a fruit and vegetable platter that caught my eye. I was done quickly, while Bronwynn still had a full plate and was nursing her mug.

Derilla Vane wouldn't be awake for some hours, so I'd bid our host goodbye before going to bed. That meant I could sit around watching my idol slowly eat her breakfast without seeming weird. It wasn't weird.

I refilled my cup to have something to hold.

She didn't seem to mind the company, silent as it was, and we eventually headed up.

Donna looked *majestic*, with a lovingly brushed coat and braided flowers in her hair. She butted her head against my hand when I reached out to rub her nose— and almost bit off the hand when she realized there were no treats waiting for her.

I dodged and placed my fingers under her chin, giving it a scratch.

"Here you are," I said, bringing up my other hand, which *did* hold some apples I'd purloined at breakfast. I ran my hands over her coat and pet her to my heart's content. "You're beautiful."

"That she is," a voice said from the wagon seat. Bronwynn was ready, reins in hand. "Nice dodge, by the way."

"You don't become commander general of the Dark Lord's army without recognizing when someone wants to bite you." I smiled at the horse and gave her one last pat before joining the minstrel on the passenger side.

Bronwynn nodded. "Just be careful—she's going easy on you."

I raised an eyebrow and got comfortable. My bags were already stored in my spatial ring. It would be nice to leave the village; my notification tab was getting overwhelmed again, and I didn't have the want or care to check the logs.

Donna whinnied and stamped one foot, then we were off.

"And I've told *you* that you can't go around *biting* my passengers," Bronwynn mused. "Wait until we get kidnapped or someone tries to steal the wagon."

The horse didn't sigh dramatically because Donna was a horse . . . but she did do the horse equivalent and huffed.

"Do you expect those things to happen to us?" I felt bad cutting in between a woman and her horse, but I wanted to know.

"It's the usual way of things." The minstrel shrugged. "I'm a child of seven, and a traveling bard."

I just stared at her.

"My parents were both seven of seven, and I inherited their passive skill [Child of Seven]; it's the skill responsible for creating encounters." She waved up and down at herself. "*And I'm a bard, who travels every day.* Ever since I came of age, I've had to pass three trials to get *anywhere*. Luckily, a kung fu lizardkin burst out of a waterfall at me yesterday, and I'm counting that."

"And the stoneskin wombat?" I asked, intrigued.

She smiled. "Two down, one to go. I should prepare!"

Bronwynn dropped the reins and let Donna drive herself—or should I say, the minstrel gave up the *appearance* of driving. Donna seemed perfectly capable of getting wherever we needed to go, and we all knew it. Meanwhile, the bard took off her red bag and placed it beside her, then she slung her instrument forward on its shoulder strap, ready to play.

The beautiful lyre harp strummed a perfect note under the skilled minstrel's fingers. Bronwynn and I both appreciated the sound. She sang the opening to one of her more popular pieces, "One More Song to Go":

The leaves are changing color and
The river's running cold
And there's hearth that's waiting for me.
Somewhere down this road
There's rhythm in my footsteps
And there's music in my soul
And I've at least, one more song to go.

"I miss Suzette every day," she confessed. I'd been there at the breakfast table when Henrietta and Keith presented her with the new instrument. "But Danielle has a lovely sound. And she rarely goes out of tune, which is a blessing. I still like to keep a tuning key on me at all times, though . . . just in case."

"It sounds lovely," I said, trying to hide my excitement.

"Thank you." She smiled, and then considered. "Alright, so after a monster encounter and a powerful person seeking aid, my third encounter will probably include someone with ulterior motives, nefarious intent, or something equally unsavory. Or maybe we'll just run into Gerda and have to answer a riddle!"

The gates of Thistlecrick were guarded by two armored naga warriors holding halberds. They waved us through, and the road outside was free of traffic. We had a short distance to go to descend through the winding path to the Great Road.

"I've never crossed Gerda's troll bridge. I admit I've been portaling around the Dark Enchanted Forest more than I've been taking the roads," I said. There was no way I'd make it to Bronwynn's performances if I ran all day to the border. It was a few days by alligator-dog if I went with the army, which also didn't work.

Luckily, Gimtak the imp had a high-level teleport skill and a love for money. I suspected he *also* loved the sight of me on my hands and knees crawling through an imp-size portal.

"You've never crossed a troll bridge?" Bronwynn asked, a touch incredulous. She plucked a light ayre on the instrument. "Even growing up in the Dark Enchanted Forest?"

I shrugged. "I traveled with a dragon. There used to be one on the bridge up the north road, but Larry the Bridge Troll only had the *one* riddle."

She stared at me expectantly.

I coughed, trying to remember it correctly.

"When I am forward,
I'm heavy, a lot.
But when I am backward,
You know I'm not."

CHAPTER 20

It Was a Spectacle!

Brownie

Brownie's brows squished in deep thought. She even momentarily stopped playing a tune to tap her chin twice.

"The trick is if the riddle contains a silent *k*," she mused, "making it a type of knot, or it's a heavy backwards *not* . . . I think . . . the second. So my answer would be 'a ton'?"

Rufus grinned, showing his canines. "You're brilliant. That's exactly right."

One of the things that Bronwynn was beginning to realize about the commander general was that the man didn't hesitate to praise. Sometimes overly much so.

It was nice.

"Which is good," Rufus continued, leaning back and sweeping the forest with his eyes, "because I'm *terrible* at riddles."

His ears twitched. She'd noticed this about him when they first left the city; his heightened senses made him seem on edge.

"Wait, really?" Brownie stared openly at the beastman.

"I'm great at figuring out *people*, not a random series of statements designed to test factual ingenuity." Rufus coughed. "If I wanted an intellectual challenge, I would prefer to test the bounds of *emotional* intelligence."

He waved his hands animatedly. "What is the focus point between each topic? How long can I look in a person's eyes before discomfort sets in, and what does that say about them? What part of someone's childhood left inherent values that aren't being recognized by their partner—" He stopped and ran a hand through his hair. "Sorry, I've gone off topic. I'm terrible at riddles."

"Unless those riddles are people." Brownie nodded.

"What can I say"—he gave her a wolfish grin—"I like people watching."

"Then as your sole traveling companion, I will try to be interesting," she said. "Actually, I think I spend a lot of time people watching myself."

The minstrel plucked her strings, once, twice, and thrice. An arpeggio. It sounded beautiful, but somber.

"It's not the same, but I think I spend half of my time reading the crowd, and the other half hoping I've read the crowd right." Brownie had a history of wonderful concerts because she was a good performer and she recognized that . . . But there had been a few shows that had turned into disasters. "This one time, I sang the wrong song, and someone burned down the stage."

Rufus stiffened beside her.

"It was a *spectacle*!" She pushed down the embarrassment and recounted the tale. "I was invited to perform at a luncheon in Sumbria by my fan club, and everything started out great . . . But near the end of my set, I started taking requests. Someone called for 'The Tragedy of Magicians.'"

"And?" Rufus stared at her with a pained expression. He must not be a fan of that particular song. It was a pretty dark song about the history of King Simon of Drendil—Henrietta's father, actually—killing off the magicians in Drendil twenty years back.

The Drendil court astronomer had made a terrible prophecy: that a magician would end the royal line of Drendil. In fear and frustration, the king had gathered up the five practicing magicians in his kingdom and ordered them put to death. That had proved his undoing, because one of them had managed to free himself at the last minute and [Curse] the king with his dying breath.

It never would've been possible to commit such atrocities if the Mages Tower hadn't been dealing with the aftermath of the Sumbrian revolution at the time. But it *had* happened, and Mykal Kell the Bard had written an amazing ballad capturing the story.

Brownie laughed. "So this young mage was unsuspectingly eating his lunch—and heard the story for the first time. The boy was so overwhelmed, he miscast and hit the stage with a fireball!"

Rufus choked. He gathered himself. "And how did that make you feel?"

The man was a walking counselor, she knew, and watching him slip into habits when he got concerned was cute. Brownie reached out and patted his furry arm. It was very soft. "Don't worry, I was fine! And one of my patrons paid for the damages."

It was a generous donation. She was amazed at how her life had turned out.

She was still amazed that she even *had* a fan club!

"And you weren't *upset* that the entire show was *ruined* because of *someone's* song request?" Rufus asked.

Brownie shook her head. "Don't overthink it. Burning down the place isn't even that bad. It's better than the time I sang at a banquet for Duke Francis, and he wouldn't take no for an answer. I lost so many knives that night."

She sighed sadly, mourning the loss. She'd had to beg her mother to send her replacements as an early birthday present.

The hair on the beastman beside her *shivered* to attention. His eyebrows dropped, and shadows darkened his eyes. His forced calm fell away to reveal a very angry Rufus. "What did he do to you?"

Not that it was his *business*, but Brownie considered the question. "Honestly?"

His golden eyes burned into hers, and she returned his grim look with a sudden, vicious smile.

"I'll tell you the whole thing. Let's start at the beginning." They had a while until they reached civilization, and she loved a good story. "It was just last summer, and I'd gotten a letter from Queen Thalia saying she wanted to hire me for her nephew's birthday. Who was *I* to deny a *queen*? I learned my mistake almost as soon as I arrived at the duke's castle . . ."

Her audience of one listened, captivated.

"The newly elevated Duke Francis was an idiot—and didn't realize that a pretty face like *mine* wasn't the birthday gift."

CHAPTER 21

Bronwynn's Third Encounter

Rufus

I knew that the first thing Knight Commander Havork had done when he'd stepped up as the regent of Drendil was to throw Duke Francis into a dungeon . . . but that didn't stop me from wanting to go to Drendil and personally drag the young duke back to *my* dungeon.

And not the one with the comfy chairs.

Maybe it was my upbringing, but I took freedom and consent *very* personally. And the lack thereof was a sure way to raise my hackles. Literally. The hairs on my spine stood against my tunic, and only [Natural Poise] kept me from bristling about the edges.

"I'm just glad you were alright in the end," I told the minstrel after she regaled me with a tale that included her leaping over a table, drinking a tankard of ale, jumping through a window onto the outer stairs, tripping three knights down that flight of stairs, pinning Francis to a wall with five daggers, and then riding off into the sunset on her trusty companion, Donna.

In fact, Donna had come out with a much higher take down number as she broke out of the stable and crossed the castle to get her bard. My respect for the horse, already high, rose even higher.

Bronwynn shrugged. "All in a day's work for a minstrel."

"I don't think escaping out of castle windows is normal for most musicians," I stated. We'd turned onto the main road a while ago and were happily moseying along.

"If the need arises," Bronwynn assured me, "I'm very good at throwing myself or others out of windows. If defenestration were a skill, I'd be at expert rank."

Her enthusiasm worried me, but I was sure that on *this* trip, there would be *no* defenestration needed . . . and if it was, I'd trust her to handle herself.

Bards always landed on their feet.

The sun rose over the Dark Enchanted Forest as we trudged forward. Donna was tireless, though sometimes, she would wander off to the side of the road and inspect something.

The trip was peaceful. We passed three catkin female adventurers on their way to Green Oak, and a giant wild boar the size of the wagon. The boar snarfed and snorted when it saw us, but Donna actually saved us from any confrontation. When she saw the boar wasn't moving out of her way, the mare raised her head elegantly, chin in the air. She looked down her nose at the creature and *whinnied.*

She sounded like a princess dressing down the staff for getting dirt on her horseshoe.

The boar's eyebrows shot up comedically high, and he chuffed. He was making excuses.

Donna stamped her foot and started walking straight for the beast, who promptly got out of her way. The mare didn't even look at the boar again, simply passing it by and continuing down the road.

Bronwynn didn't think anything of it, acting like a rabbit had just crossed our path.

She was the same when we rode past a group of tiny mice wearing jackets and wielding swords fighting a hawk in a field later that afternoon. And the time we saw two elves ride by on unicorns, heading back the way we'd come.

Finally, I asked, "How often do you travel the woods?"

Bronwynn opened her eyes; she'd been relaxing in the sun. Her red-tipped hair caught the light beautifully. "Depends on the year. I don't really *like* sailing, so if I have the time, I'll choose the extra few days it takes going through the forest. I prefer encounters here than on the ocean."

"So it's not always in the Dark Enchanted Forest? It could happen in Servalt?" I did a Perception check, finding nothing. The forest had its own magic and its own personality. It would probably delight in sending encounters to a bard.

"Anytime, anywhere. From the moment I 'start the quest'"—she made air quotations around the last part—"which in this case was the second I left Henrietta's wedding."

"So we have until you arrive at Heatherfeld?"

"Yep." She glanced around and sighed. "I think Gerda's bridge *and* Kith Bog have moved, so we'll see what comes our way."

"The boar didn't count?" We'd certainly come across a number of things already, and it was barely midafternoon.

"Donna handled that." The minstrel shrugged.

"I see." I prepared my skills and switched to the defensive. I had high stats, and anything that messed with Bronwynn would have to go through me.

Then, we *did* come to a bridge. Brownie quickly parked the wagon off to the side and jumped down.

"This is perfect!" She laughed. Her smile was so bright it caught my breath. I got down and walked with her to the bridge.

"What if we don't know the answer to the riddle?" I asked, unsure. "Should I fight her?"

"She also accepts coin," Brownie told me. "But I'm sure we'll be *fine*. You're in for a treat—literally, if Gerda's baked anything new today. She's as good as Henrietta in the kitchen."

We walked forward, and I steeled myself for the bridge troll to jump out at us . . . but nothing happened. Brownie looked around the bridge in mixed confusion and disappointment.

"What now?" I asked.

"I guess we cross?" With trepidation, Bronwynn went back to the wagon and took Donna's reins. The horse butted her head against the bard but let herself be led along. Bronwynn came up beside me and took a deep breath.

"Ready?"

I nodded.

We set off across the bridge.

And nothing happened.

"Does that mean she doesn't control that bridge?" I wondered.

"I'll go check."

Donna nickered and pulled her reins free.

"That's fine." Bronwynn nodded. "But we shouldn't stop longer than half an hour."

Her horse pulled the wagon off to the side of the road ahead of them, then Donna shook herself lightly, magically divesting herself of the wagon. She wandered off into the woods while Bronwynn went to inspect the bridge. She stuck her head over the side before popping back up a second later. "No, her door is right there. Maybe she's just busy?"

"She can't be on every bridge all the time," I reasoned. "I'm just impressed she can keep the bridge after we crossed it without any penalty . . ."

The half giantess shrugged. "You'll have to ask her."

We stretched our legs, ate a snack, and took the opportunity to step away for a few minutes for a reprieve. Then we just sat around while Donna did whatever a horse did in the dark woods.

Bronwynn was surprisingly quiet during the wait for her horse. She looked like she was distracted by something, and worried.

"Is Donna alright?" I asked, wondering after the horse who'd just traipsed off into the Dark Enchanted Forest.

A forest that sometimes ate people.

"She's fine." Bronwynn looked at me, and she must have seen my concern because she sighed and explained, "I'm just not used to going on an adventure without a bridge troll riddle. That means my third encounter could be *anything*."

"I'm sure it'll be *fine*. Maybe we'll meet some bandits around the next corner?" I tried to cheer her up, and it looked like it was working.

She shot me a forced half smile. "Maybe?"

At that point, I switched to distraction tactics, pointing at her new necklace. "Are you comfortable with the new instrument?"

Her hand came up and gripped the oval pendant. "Wanna hear?"

"I'd love to."

Bronwynn performed beautifully, and it distracted her until Donna returned. We packed up and set off.

She was still on edge when we crossed the border of the Dark Enchanted Forest and into Servalt. The tree line thinned out, and gentle green fields stretched toward a small town close to the border. Our last stop before arriving at the party tomorrow morning.

The minstrel was frowning. "I was *sure* we'd meet someone in the forest . . ."

I didn't know what to say. We'd made great time, and had plenty of opportunities to find an inn, settle in, and grab dinner.

"Maybe whoever was going to approach us saw me and decided otherwise?" I offered.

"I traveled with the Heroine of Justice once. Our boat was attacked by Elder Greg the Kraken, the Dancing Blade pirates, and we rescued a shipwrecked prince of Peldeep," Bronwynn explained. "I was expecting to meet at *least* a talking squirrel!"

"Maybe there'll be a bar fight here before we go to bed?" I looked around the peaceful dining area, grasping at straws, hoping to find something to make her feel better. "Or someone will try and steal Donna tomorrow morning?"

She actually brightened up at that. "You're probably right. Let's wait and see."

There wasn't anything else I could do, so I bought her a drink and enjoyed listening to more of her adventures while she explained to me some of the different kinds of "encounters" she'd faced on her past adventures. Even as I enjoyed the tales, a small feeling of discomfort crept into my heart. My favorite musician on the continent was out there getting kidnapped or stranded every other adventure. She could use a bodyguard.

I pushed down the sudden, strong, all-consuming desire to be that bodyguard.

There was a perfectly comfy dungeon with a daybed, lurid romance novels, and a full wine cellar waiting for me back home. And an important job.

Somebody had to keep King Keith alive. Although, he *did* now have a high level, competent wife . . .

Was my job even necessary anymore?

Sigh.

As I was lying in the small bed at the inn that evening, I realized something important about Bronwynn's third encounter.

Bronwynn had said she'd meet someone with ulterior motives, nefarious intent, or something equally unsavory.

I slapped a paw pad against my face.

She *had* already faced three encounters on this journey.

You!

Brownie

It took a while for Brownie to get to sleep, worrying that her final encounter might happen that evening. But it didn't. She had an uneventful night and woke up to a beautiful but windy June morning.

She was nervous all the way to Heatherfeld, the castle village ruled by Duke Wyldon of Servalt.

They'd arrived a day earlier than she'd anticipated, but instead of finding room at an inn and waiting until the morrow, Rufus had convinced her to join him at the castle.

"It will be fine," he assured her as they rode up to the front gate of the estate.

"You know I'm the entertainment, right?" Brownie reminded him. "I'm supposed to use the side door."

"So? I'm the commander general of the Dark Lord's armies, and you are my guest." Rufus jumped down and offered her his paw. "Shall we?"

"Alright." Brownie couldn't resist the urge to hold those squishy paw pads and accepted his escort, jumping down beside him. The beanies were just as soft as she'd imagined.

She reminded herself to focus on the *rest* of the beastman holding her hand.

Two castle attendants hurried out to greet them. One took Donna's reins and led the mare off to the stables while Brownie sent her horse a small plea to behave herself. The other attendant accepted Rufus's letter of invite and led them inside.

"Please wait here while I inform the duke of your arrival," the woman said, bowing them into a comfortable sitting room off the castle entry. She was mid-size for an elf, with pointed ears and a greenish tinge to her otherwise pale skin. Her hair was honey brown in a tight bun with some strays. "I'll have the kitchen prepare a light refreshment."

The attendant paused, giving them time to declare any preferences or allergies, but the only thing Brownie had trouble with was watermelon, and that just made her tummy gurgle.

When they said nothing, the attendant bowed and backed out of the room, leaving the door open.

Brownie took off her instrument case and delicately leaned it up against the chair before settling into the very comfy seat. She'd left behind everything else—red shoulder bag, belt pouch, and knife—for this meeting.

Rufus leaned in across the space between the two chairs and whispered, "Actually, I may have been given a small side mission while visiting this particular event."

Brownie raised an eyebrow.

"Keith is miffed with Duke Wyldon at the moment," Rufus confided. "And I'm to make it known that the king of the Dark Enchanted Forest is *displeased*."

"Ah." Brownie knew there *must* have been a reason for Rufus to travel to this particular event. It didn't make sense when Servalt and Nilheim weren't close allies, and she'd rarely seen anyone from the Dark Horde at any of the events she'd performed here previously.

Excepting the Servalt queen's Milestone celebration three years ago, of course, when King Keith himself had made an appearance.

But that was different.

The queen had further cause to celebrate her birthday then because she had held on to a magical amethyst Milestone for the full year. It had granted her a permanent +1 to any attribute. The queen had chosen Constitution, a great choice for her Royal Barbarian class.

Brownie had been humbled to get to play at the birthday banquet.

"Do you know *why* King Keith is angry at Duke Wyldon?" Brownie eyed the innocent-looking Rufus, who was patiently waiting for their host.

"Apparently," Rufus said, stretching out his legs and crossing one over the other, "Duke Wyldon propositioned Henrietta."

Brownie gasped. "No?!"

"I most certainly did *no such thing*!" Duke Wyldon declared, standing in the doorway. His face contorted in an affronted frown. "I *proposed* to the princess. It's not the same thing *at all*."

"Your Grace." Brownie jumped to her feet and bowed while Rufus took his sweet time standing up. Brownie was certain that Rufus had already known that the duke had arrived.

"Wyldon." Rufus nodded. He raised an eyebrow at the man. "As I understand it, Henrietta was happily engaged when you *proposed* marriage. And you didn't believe her like a reasonable adult when she said as much, ignoring her opinions and going as far as to announce *publicly* that she must be under mind magic."

Duke Wyldon stiffened. "I was *worried* for her."

The duke was a half elf, with an ashen gray complexion and raven black hair that he kept in a low ponytail. He was clean-shaven with a stern disposition, and a pair of scholarly glasses on his nose. Proper, sophisticated, and well respected.

Brownie was almost surprised that he had chosen *her* for the entertainment. Currently, she was trying to not appear entertained herself.

"And my king found your worry insulting," Rufus stated, matter-of-factly.

"He's *the Dark Lord*," Duke Wyldon said through clenched teeth. "He should be *pleased* that people consider him dangerous."

Too bad the duke had joined them before the tea service. Brownie wished she could sit back down in the comfortable armchair and watch the proceedings with a snack and a glass.

"So?" Rufus shrugged. "Servalt was caught in kidnapping and trading slaves. I can't see why being the ruler of a Dark Enchanted Forest is any worse?"

The duke sighed. "Must we discuss this now? If you are fishing for information on the investigation, then you can just *ask*."

Suddenly, the duke turned to Brownie. She stood straighter and gave him a polite smile. He surprised her by saying, "If anything, *you* should be the one I explain this to. On behalf of my countrymen, I *do* apologize, Minstrel Bronwynn. Again."

"Think nothing of it, Your Grace," she told the man. Of course, if King Keith hadn't gifted her a new instrument, then she would have had *much more to say on the matter*.

As it was, she was just happy everyone was safe.

"I've had spies within the Assassin's Guild, and I've ordered them to do everything in their power to find the responsible parties," he tried to assure her, and Brownie felt her smile strain against her cheeks.

"Thank you, Your Grace."

"One of my operatives is actually here for this event. I wanted you to meet them in my presence so that there will be no . . . misunderstandings." Duke Wyldon looked over his shoulder toward the door. "Jack?"

An all too familiar face stepped through the door. His clothing was tasteful, a tunic and vest and tight leather pants. His face was clean-shaven and attractive, and his hair swooshed to the side with a very manly swoosh.

Brownie immediately recognized the man. "*You!*"

CHAPTER 23

The Only Slave Trader Who Ran Away

Rufus

I unconsciously moved between Jack and Minstrel Bronwynn when I heard the worry in her voice.

"*I* am Jack Laverick." The well-dressed man bowed in greeting. "It's nice to meet you."

"We've already met," the minstrel said dryly. "When you kidnapped me."

"No helping it, but I *do* apologize to Minstrel Bronwynn." He ran a hand through his sideswept ear-length hair. "If it helps, Jacques was just my undercover persona, and I would have rescued you when we reached the drop-off."

"That *does* help," she stated blandly. "And it explains why you were the only slave trader who *ran away*. Here I thought you were just a coward."

Jack countered with a confident smile. "I am very good at running, thank you. It is hard to perfect a well-timed retreat, and I'm one of the best! You had rescued yourselves, so there wasn't much to do except return and report to Duke Wyldon."

"Furthermore," the duke coughed, "I would like to add that we had no idea *who* they were planning to kidnap, only that Marquess Chadwick was up to something nefarious. It was a rare opportunity to get proof of his crimes in action."

I crossed my arms and cut in. "At least the man is in the mines now."

"My other operative, Jess, made it to the mansion where they locked up the Dark Lord." The duke nodded. "We were gathering proof when the princess burst in and saved him."

"I'm surprised, actually," I said. "I thought Servalt's *nobility* were highly respected for their honor, while your merchants were corrupt. I guess the times are changing."

There was a quiet moment as they all stared at me with mixed looks: Bronwynn pleased, Jack surprised, and Wyldon exasperated. Provoking the duke was on the list of small tasks my king had given me while traveling, but it was proving a very enjoyable chore.

"I do not think that *you* have any right to judge our entire noble class on the actions of one," Duke Wyldon finally retorted. "You have an arachne general. They are *literal* cann—"

"Ah, ah, ah!" I interrupted. "I thought you were *just* saying how we shouldn't base the actions of one on the many? At least take a breath before you lead into hypocrisy."

Bronwynn was gaping with unfettered glee. I was glad to see she was enjoying herself.

Jack, a true master of his craft, had silently moved toward the door. He bore no noticeable weapons except a small dagger that poked out of his boot, so if our heated words came to blows, he was probably aiming to run out and summon the guards.

"You've gone too far!" The duke's complexion had turned grayer as I spoke, and I could almost *see* the man's blood pressure spiking. I'd finally broken through his defenses. "I—"

A knock interrupted my victory, and we all turned to see the female attendant from before wheeling in a trolley. She looked about innocently. "Tea?"

"For my *guests*," Duke Wyldon ground out. "I have more important matters to attend to. Jack, come with me."

It looked like Jack wasn't the only one who had skill in a well-timed retreat.

"That was *impressive!*" Bronwynn plopped herself back down in her chosen armchair and slouched into the seat. "I'm impressed."

"Thank you." I rejoined her in the other armchair and turned to the waiting attendant. "And thank you. For the tea."

She passed me a cup of steeped honeybush tea, a gentle drink with a slight citrus scent. She looked a little worried. "My pleasure. Though I hope I didn't interrupt anything *too* important . . . I've never seen the duke leave like that."

"He's not angry at you." Bronwynn piped up from her chair. She happily accepted her tea as well. "We might have been discussing heavy politics, and emotions were running high."

An excellent way to put it. I approved.

The minstrel continued, "Which is why some calming tea will do us all some good. What are those?" She pointed to a few pastries stacked on a tray next to the teapot.

"Huckleberry tarts and some garlic scones." The attendant smiled. "Please enjoy, and when you are ready, I can show you to your room!"

There was a second while the words registered. I was the first to speak. "We will be needing two rooms."

"We aren't . . ." Bronwynn began, then changed it to, "We simply traveled here together. But we aren't *together* together."

The attendant looked between us and then met my eyes, her expression pained. "But you only brought *one* invitation."

At that, Bronwynn balanced the scone plate she'd just received on her knee, reached out, and picked up her instrument case. She unlatched the opening, pulling out her contract. She explained, "I'm the bard for Duke Wyldon's party."

"*The entertainment?*" The woman stared at Bronwynn like she'd suddenly grown two heads, then she looked between the bard and the tea trolley like she couldn't believe she was serving a fellow staff member, and a lowly bard at that.

"Pardon our early arrival," I said, and the attendant's polite-but-dead-inside eyes met mine. "Minstrel Bronwynn is my queen's greatest companion, so I, *the Commander General of the Dark Lord's army*, was asked to escort her here safely."

That had the woman stiffen and straighten to attention. Her professional smile returned, and she managed to gather her thoughts. "I will go prepare a second room, then. If you'll excuse me."

There was a heartbeat where we were left alone before Bronwynn burst into unrestrained laughter.

"I can't believe you just said that!" Bronwynn exclaimed, leaning back into her chair.

"What?" I feigned ignorance and picked up my own scone, buttery with a rich garlic that smelled overly strong.

I was greeted with a very warm smile. "Seriously, though, thank you."

"*Anytime.*" I tried to hide the conviction in my voice and play it off as casual camaraderie. I'd even say I succeeded.

CHAPTER 24

My Horse Picked That Lock?

Brownie

Donna was *not* happy, and Brownie could tell.

One minute, the bard was relaxing in companionable scone-chewing silence with Rufus, and the next, she was getting a *very* affronted message from her horse.

The level one bond wasn't strong enough to actually send verbal messages, but it was strong enough to let Brownie know that if she didn't get to the stables *now*, then someone might lose a finger—or worse.

"I have to go." Brownie jumped up from her plush chair. It was only thanks to her Dexterity eighteen that she placed the tea on the tea trolley without spilling.

"Why? What's wrong?" Rufus was on his feet almost faster than she was; level difference made a difference. He also expertly divested his snacks.

There was a brief moment where she was tempted to jump out the window to save time . . . but the windows were glass and latched.

"I have to check on Donna!" she said, already running out the door with Rufus hot on her heels.

The room they were waiting in was literally just inside the doors to the castle, and the stables were outside. The second they exited the main door, they *heard* the problem.

"Blasted horse!" A young man, pale and human, was trying to put a muzzle on her mare. He wore the duke's livery, as well as boots and gloves that marked him as a stable hand.

Donna was having *none of that nonsense*. She reared up, kicking out at the man. One hoof clipped his shoulder, and he cursed again. Donna wrenched her face out of the offending accessory, and the muzzle was sent flying.

"*Excuse me.*" Brownie's voice was stern and loud, startling the young man into distraction.

She flinched as Donna whipped her head around to bite flesh. Instead of the expected agonizing scream, Rufus was suddenly standing there, catching the mare's chin and petting her nose. He pulled out a sugar cube he must have swiped from the tea trolley earlier and offered the treat to the horse.

"Shh, beautiful. Bronwynn and I are here," he spoke softly to the mare. Brownie was surprised Donna let him. "You were *magnificent*. And we are unworthy."

Granted, his low voice was smooth and comforting. That beastman knew how to talk to a woman—*horse*. *Female*. Of the equestrian variety. He knew how to talk to *mares*.

Brownie turned her attention back to the stable hand, crossing her arms and glaring at him.

When Rufus had appeared in the spot between Donna and the unfortunate stable hand, the stable hand had been forced to vacate the space to somewhere else.

Which was just a nice way of saying he'd been laid on his rear.

"Are you the owner of that *beast*?" the stable hand demanded, climbing to his feet and rubbing his shoulder.

"She isn't my owner, no," Rufus quipped. Bronwynn let out a very unbecoming snort. "Do you always call the duke's guests by their race?"

The man's head snapped back like he'd been struck.

"That is *my* horse," Brownie interjected, knowing the words would irritate Donna but accepting her fate. She stepped forward and demanded, "What gave you the right to treat *my* mare like some pack animal to be muzzled?"

"If she's your animal, then you probably already know," the stable hand accused, his voice acidic. "She's a *terror*, and she ate our Bensen's prized oats!" He waved wildly at a container deeper in the stable hall with its lid open and the oats in question pilfered. An open lock dangled from the lid latch.

Brownie resisted the urge to glare at her horse, instead activating [Liar's Palace].

[You have attempted to use the Perk: **Liar's Palace**. You have succeeded. +2 Charisma. Anyone with a Rogue Skill equal to or greater than yours may see through your lie. Anyone with a Perception equal to or higher than your Level 31 + **Informant** 6 Skill will be able to see through your fabrication. All others will recognize that you believe what you are saying. This Perk is in effect for Charisma 23 x Level 31.]

[**Liar's Palace** remaining time 00:11:56]

[**Liar's Palace** remaining time 00:11:55]

Brownie scoffed, pointing at the box. "So you are punishing *my horse* because *you* didn't lock up the expensive oats?"

"What?! Of course I locked that box. Your horse must've . . ." He trailed off. After a look of sheer frustration played across his features, he decided to push through. "Your horse picked the lock while I wasn't looking!"

"I'm confused." Brownie crossed her arms and stared down at the young man. "You are telling me that *my horse* picked *that lock*."

The stable hand turned red—from anger or embarrassment, she knew not— but before he could say anything, a loud voice called out, "Here now, Jimmie, what's happening?"

Everyone turned to the servants' entrance and found seven liveried attendants all dressed in the same black tunic and dark gray pants that the man Brownie was arguing with sported.

"Mister Ling!" Jimmie bobbed a quick bow to the older man standing at the front of the group. His next words came out in a jumble, and the stable hand's cheeks burned even redder. "You see, I, uh, I'm . . ."

"This esteemed gentleman," Brownie stressed politely as she inwardly regret- ted having to throw the man under Donna's metaphorical carriage, "claims that my *horse* picked that lock."

The eyes of everyone standing there turned to Donna, and Rufus kindly coaxed the mare out of the way so the empty wooden oat container was in full view. The lid was slung up and back, with a metal padlock ring open and dan- gling precariously from the lid ring.

"She must've!" Jimmie exclaimed, panicking as his fellow hostlers started to give him strange looks. "I locked the box myself after feeding Bensen. Then I tied the mare in the hall while I finished getting clean water, and I come out to find *this one* eating the good oats!"

"Jimmie." Mister Ling looked like he had some mix of fae and fair about him. Old but ageless, his voice soft and firm.

The young stable hand let out a breath and made an exasperated sound. Qui- eter, rebellious, he mumbled, "It's *true*."

"Mister Ling?" Brownie stepped forward to the senior attendant. "I don't want there to be any trouble, so I will pay for the oats. Jimmie was injured by my horse and might just need some time to rest."

Mister Ling raised a single eyebrow, appraising her and her horse. "Are you sure, miss?"

"I'm sure." She pulled out a silver coin, more than enough to cover for high- quality feed, and used her thumb to flick the coin. Mister Ling caught it in the air. Brownie turned to Jimmie and pulled out one of her low-grade healing potions then handed it to the startled stable hand.

She kept her few potions and most of her wealth in the spatial storage ring on her right pinkie finger. It wasn't the kind of thing a regular bard would have—the ring cost more than her house back in Drendil. A fan she'd met in Servalt gave it to her, and it was a very impressive thing to show off to the castle staff. It wasn't the kind of thing she revealed often; not to anyone who might get *ideas*. Of course, she wasn't worried about Rufus—he probably had a chest full of these back home.

The beastman was still distracting Donna with pets and adoration, for which she was immensely grateful. The mare, for her part, was decidedly ignoring Brownie's eyes.

Donna was a horse, yes, but she was a *magical horse*. Like a pegasus or a unicorn. Just because she couldn't talk didn't mean she wasn't intelligent. At the same time, she had been raised in the Dark Enchanted Forest and often ignored the rules. The stable had prize oats, and so she would eat the prize oats. If the elves had a problem with that, then it was an elf problem.

Brownie was more surprised that Donna had gotten caught. She resisted the urge to glare at her horse or send pokes through their bond, giving up on wasting the energy. It wasn't the first time, and it wouldn't be the last.

"As you say, miss, there's no trouble at all." There was a subtle edge to Mister Ling's words that broached no argument. The other stable hands, who'd quietly stayed back until now, jumped to action with seamless efficiency at his next words. "We'll clean up here and take care of your horse properly. Jimmie."

The young stable hand's head snapped up from where he'd been gaping at the health potion. "Ah, yes?"

"Take the evening off and heal up," Mister Ling ordered. "I want you in proper form for the guests tomorrow. Laurence can fill you in on the schedule tomorrow morning. You're to work with him."

"Yes, Mister Ling—"

"*Found you!*"

Brownie looked up at the pinched frown of the tea attendant. The woman looked about as happy as she sounded.

Which was to say, not at all.

CHAPTER 25

My Bard

Rufus

As one of the more powerful people on the continent, I'd been a representative of Nilheim at Continental Councils hosted around the, well, *continent*. I'd stayed at inns, palaces, and even the Mages Tower. And I'd never experienced so much adventure as I had in just a few days travel with Minstrel Bronwynn.

People did not look at me the way a simple attendant—no disrespect to the profession intended—was looking at my bard.

Cough. My favorite bard.

"Does this mean our rooms are ready?" I demanded, stepping out from behind Donna. I gave the horse one final scratch behind the ear before handing her reins off to a ready stable hand.

"Ah, yes, Commander General." The attendant took a small step back, and I made the effort to relax my face. Baring one's teeth was never good form, so I slipped into a partial smile as I walked over to Bronwynn and offered my arm. "Shall we?"

"Alright." The minstrel took it, amusement crinkling her eyes. She cast a wary eye at her horse, holding it for a few seconds, and then turned back to me. "Let's get settled in."

As we approached the attendant in the castle doorway, I told her, "I will keep my things in the wagon for now."

Everything in my bag was for traveling, and anything important was in my storage ring.

"I just need everything that is red," Bronwynn said. "I can come get my things after we've settled in."

"You can't settle in without your things," I told her, then ordered the staff present, "See that someone delivers Minstrel Bronwynn's red luggage to her room. Now, lead on."

"Right this way." The woman bowed. I worried that the antagonism would continue, so I thought deeply as we were led to a small room on the first floor to drop off Bronwynn. It was obviously a servant's quarters, but the minstrel was pleased, and it looked clean and serviceable.

I resisted the urge to offer to switch rooms with whichever they gave me. Bronwynn had been hired for this event, and if she wanted to sleep somewhere fancier, she was her own person and would say so. Her room also overlooked the stables, and that was perfect if Donna needed aid.

Besides, her window had a perfectly safe landing spot below it.

I asked if she would like to have dinner with me that evening, but Bronwynn surprised me with a rejection, following it up with how she was going to practice until the morrow. As such, I left her to her own devices and followed the attendant to my own rooms on the second floor.

We were en route when I decided that it was an opportune time to ask the woman my questions directly. The straightforward approach was usually the correct approach.

And it was my favorite.

"Miss, is there something I should know about my companion? I've been sent to guard her, but was not given much detail on Minstrel Bronwynn." The words gave her the chance to explain, and showed my eagerness for her opinion.

"My name is Claire." She stopped on the way up the stairs and looked down at me, uncertain. Making up her mind, she continued. "You might not know, Commander, but common bards are a very untrustworthy lot!"

"Truly?" I held back an eye roll. That was like saying all assassins were killers. Or all rogues were thieves.

Who was going to open a lock if you lost the key? Who better to run customs checks and find fraud than a Rogue class with a high Perception and a mastery at finding hidden compartments?

Who better to track lost children in the Dark Enchanted Forest or solo monsters, or put up banners along rooftops during festivals than an Assassin class?

"The duke is usually very picky about whom he hires, and only qualified royal musicians have been brought in on previous special occasions." Claire continued up the stairs until we arrived on the landing.

The second floor hosted many portraits of the duke's family. I admired the art that consumed every spare inch of the walls in front of me. It was eclectic, with many different branches arranged neatly for inspection. He even had a preela cousin, the long furry ears with little black tufts matching the other aspen coloring of the duke's family.

I turned from inspecting the paintings and asked, "But Minstrel Bronwynn is an acclaimed international minstrel; does that not make her on par with a royal musician?"

"A traveling bard is a traveling bard, and known to steal the silverware or"—Claire shook her head, her hands gripping together in front of her stomach as she leaned forward slightly—"your heart!"

Of course, anyone who *heard* the minstrel would have their heart stolen by her music, but I didn't think that was what she meant.

"The wild and untamable roaming bard is known for *wooing*," she said quietly, as if it were a great secret.

"I see," was all I could ground out before I took a deep breath. This couldn't be good for my blood pressure. "You are saying that *Minstrel Bronwynn* is known for this? You have been told stories? Personally?"

"Well, no. But she's a *bard*."

The sentiment was ridiculous and so offensive that I stood affixed while the woman simply raised her eyebrows as if inviting me to *agree*.

It occurred to me that I had the entire rest of the day free . . . I wondered if Duke Wyldon had a dungeon? Somewhere with a locked door to unpack a lot of toxic baggage. With a comfortable couch.

"Miss Claire," I began, deciding that getting all of that ready was too much of a hassle. There were two sure-fireball ways to convince someone to change their world view, however: by making them think they'd thought of the idea themselves, or . . . the hard way.

"I am confused. Minstrel Bronwynn is an acclaimed and *credited* musician who is internationally famous. She has performed for *royalty*, and is highly spoken of among the well-to-do. Her songs are sung by adventurers and kings, and you are saying she is loose because of her musical title? Without any proof?" It took every nerve in my body to keep a light tone in my voice. Incredulous, not angry.

The attendant's pointed ears turned red, and she must have realized the error of her ways because she took a step back, startled. "No! I've just heard—"

"I'm also curious why you would speak against the wishes of His Grace," I stated calmly. I took a step forward and bent down to look at her more closely. My tail twitched, but she wasn't paying attention to my tail. Her wide eyes held mine. "Openly criticizing his choice of performer when he *personally* requested her for her professional caliber."

"That's not it! I only—"

"I understand." I dropped my voice into a soft lull and stood up straight again, bobbing my head in acknowledgement. "It must have been a mistake when you repeated vicious gossip. You would *never* speak ill of your master's guest."

"Of-of course not!" She grabbed the rope I threw at her and looked relieved.

I smiled a too-wide smile. "Which is why I'm sure you'll be the *first* to tell everyone how exciting it is to have a famous bard like Minstrel Bronwynn here. You wouldn't want to *embarrass* Duke Wyldon."

"As you say, Commander General." She nodded vigorously, and I left her still sweating outside my guest suite.

Hopefully, that would be the end of that.

CHAPTER 26

If You Counted Not Getting Caught As Behaving

Brownie

The day dawned clear and bright and perfect. Bronwynn refused to acknowledge it and rolled over to go back to sleep.

When she *did* wake, the sun was warm, the wind was cool, and breakfast was romancing lunch. She didn't worry about missing either, grabbing a honey oat bar with dried bimbleberries and almonds from her ring. Then she whiled away an hour thinking about the afternoon to come.

It was a surprise how much time she could waste just thinking about lyrics or practicing on her instrument. Her cousins used to tease her about it, though it turned out it wasn't a *waste* when it let her achieve her dream.

"Time to show them why I'm a *Minstrel.*" She smiled and picked out one of her favorite dresses, designed for exactly this type of event. It was a darker red bordering on black, with tiny glittering garnets sewn into the fabric. It clung to her waist and smoothed her curves as it accentuated her figure. She wore soft black tights and heeled boots that gave her even more height.

She'd have to remember to duck at the servants' door. Remembering to duck was a lifelong struggle.

Brownie finished with a light glitter on the cheeks and red lipstick, then she grabbed her red shoulder bag with its fancy herringbone weave and her lyre harp case.

"Minstrel Bronwynn!" A page girl ran up to Brownie when she stepped into the servants' hall. The girl had tussled short light-purple curls and big blue eyes. She had the same ashy skin color as the duke, and Brownie wondered if they were related.

"Yes?"

The girl bobbed a slight bow and then smiled a gap-toothed grin. "I'm Page Saryl, at your service. May I show you around?"

The smile was welcoming, and Brownie found herself taking a liking to the girl. "Thank you, I would love that."

"We've moved the entire event to the garden." Saryl led Brownie through a maze of back doors and onto a stunningly colorful path full of flowers in bloom. "It's been months of rain, and everyone was excited to finally get the chance to enjoy the sun. I can't *tell you* how dreary it's been. Was it raining in other kingdoms? What about in the Dark Enchanted Forest? Fenn, from housekeeping, said you played for the Dark Lord *himself*. Is that true?"

The girl's breath ran out, and Brownie resisted the urge to laugh out loud. "I've performed for every crown royal this side of the Empire of Sands. And no, it's not raining anywhere else. At least, no more than usual."

"Wow! Oh, just through here, Minstrel Bronwynn. We've set up a place for you in the corner."

The performance area was perfect; a small chair surrounded by a flowerful circle of pink hydrangeas. She was only a few paces from the head table, which itself was at the bottom of a short staircase leading to a stone patio with closed double doors. Servants came and went from side doors at either end of the large patio.

She admired the two griffin statues at the base of the staircase.

She could tell it was the head table because it was long and rectangular with chairs on one side, while the rest of the garden green was covered in smaller intimate round tables.

"May I take your things?" Saryl asked, seeing my instrument case and bag sitting on the grass.

"Yes, please." Brownie handed over everything.

"Of course, Minstrel Bronwynn. I can put them with the rest of the staff's belongings." Saryl bobbed her head.

"Actually, could you put them back in my room?" Brownie asked, debating taking the bag back to grab her spare tuning peg inside. She decided it would be fine to leave it.She kept a tuning peg in both her red bag and her lyre case. And her wagon. And her cloak pocket. Even the ring on her finger contained one, along with any other *important* things, like snacks, rope, a change of clothes, and an antidote potion.

"Of course!" The page bowed again.

She settled in and started to play warm-ups. The castle staff were still setting up, laying out cutlery and carefully folded napkins that looked like cute swans. They brought out cut flowers and salt and pepper, all while Brownie happily played. The atmosphere was pleasant.

And her horse was behaving herself—if you counted *not getting caught* as *behaving*.

Brownie did. Her crate of carrots and rutabagas was lighter, but it kept Donna happy.

Then the first guest arrived.

She assumed he was a guest because he strutted in with his chin held high and his tail higher. Not that it even reached Brownie's knee, given that the guest was the size of a large cat.

He was a grimalcat.

Brownie had only ever met one other, when she was seven and running from bullies through a back alley in Fallstaff Harbor. She had been in pretty bad shape. Just when she'd thought she'd get caught, a grimalcat had wandered by and saved her. She would never forget his fluffy brown fur with little gold horns and yellow eyes.

That was the day she made a promise to give up her old life and step on the path to becoming a bard.

This grimalcat was black, with glowing green eyes and two tiny little green horns between his pointy ears. The creature sported batlike wings that he currently had tucked at his sides.

"Greetings, Adventurer Slake." An attendant bowed low to the grimalcat, as low as one was expected to bow before a visiting duke. "As you are the first to enter, may I show you to your seat?"

The grimalcat nonchalantly rubbed his paw against his face. Brownie had to focus harder on her song and not on the thought of squishing the little beanies. She had a problem.

"Right this way."

The grimalcat was shown to the head table, where a fresh bowl of cream was presented to the creature with a flourish. He eyed the dish, then daintily stuck out a tiny pink tongue and lapped at the cream, satisfied. He didn't move from his chair.

"Announcing, Mage Lina of Colwood."

And so it went until the entire garden was full of well-to-dos. Rufus arrived midway through, looking a little irritated if she read his slightly lowered tail and drooped left ear tip correctly. The man hid it well with his powerful demeanor, but she could tell he wasn't enjoying himself.

She slipped into an instrumental version of "Traveler's Anthem," which she knew he loved. His eyes caught hers from across the garden, and he sent her a small smile. It warmed her all the way to her tummy, and she had to catch herself.

Finally, the guest of honor arrived. The head attendant's voice rang loud and clear, drawing everyone's attention, and I rounded off the chord, coming to a clean stop. "Presenting Duke Wyldon Holst of Servalt."

There was a polite round of applause for the duke . . .

And then someone threw a bottle of bright red liquid with little black flecks at the man.

CHAPTER 27

And Head Scratches?

Rufus

A Few Minutes Earlier

"Are you planning on visiting the capital during your stay, Commander?" a pale human with short curly hair asked me.

The man, Lord Peter Ainsworth, was *very* excited to meet someone from the Dark Enchanted Forest. He had been standing with me since shortly after I'd arrived.

"I will be, yes." I was glad for the mild distraction from the otherwise well-mannered guests. Servalt had come about when the northern nobles had stood up against the elite classism of Sumbria, and as much as I'd teased Duke Wyldon the previous evening, they really were an admirable crowd.

And then there was Peter.

"I can show you around the town. A cultured beastman like yourself must have finer tastes . . ." Peter gave me a knowing smile that was not accurately knowing *at all.*

I resisted the urge to sigh, simply looking down on the man with a passive glance before sweeping the crowd. "Perhaps. I have a few kingdom-level quests to complete first." Unless Bronwynn was set on added company, at which point I would do the one meeting with the Assassin's Guild and then ignore the rest.

I didn't openly stare at her, but knowing she was there made the disaster that was me standing at a birthday party with no social acquaintances to speak of bearable.

"Ah, a working man. I get it. When you've finished your business, then." Peter nodded and took a glass of sparkling enchanted mistwine from a server. The beverage gave off beautiful swirls of red smoke and tasted like sweet strawberries.

I selected a dry pear cider with hints of citrus and enjoyed a slow sip.

"Presenting Duke Wyldon Holst of Servalt." The voice carried over the crowd, and we all turned to face the duke as he entered from a private set of double doors that had been previously closed on the veranda. The half elf strode in with confidence, and he nodded a polite greeting to his guests from the top of the stairs.

The corner of my eye blinked with a new notification as unease settled in my gut and my entire body felt [Sense Threat] activate. My heart beat faster, the hair on my body bristled, and my head whipped around to Bronwynn, artfully finishing her note.

"[Imbue] [Haste]." That's when someone, an elven young lady wearing a light pink dress, knocked Peter toward me. I caught the human and watched in horror as she threw a bottle of molten ash vane.

The bottle sailed through the air toward the duke while my Perception thirty allowed me to watch everything unfold in slow motion.

There were shouts as people activated their abilities. The vial hit the [Shield] spell, slowed, glowed, and then rebound forward. Duke Wyldon whipped up his arms and yelled, "[Force Wall]!"

The still glowing vial hit the gray shimmering [Force Wall] and slowed again—but again, it kept going. A look of shock and horror fixed on the duke's face. A guard, who had activated her own version of [Haste], launched herself from her spot beside the griffin statue.

But she wouldn't make it.

I shoved Peter back into the elf assassin, knocking them both to the ground, then I spent mana to pop my claws. I'd need them to handle the duke. We would have to remove any poisoned parts as quickly as possible if he was going to survive. Worst case, I could save an ear or foot and use my high-level potion to bring him back. If there was time.

Wyldon would lose his Duke title upon death, as was the norm with kingdoms outside the Dark Enchanted Forest, but he would *survive*. He was lucky a member of the Dark Horde was in attendance. He wouldn't even be undead, since I got to it so quickly . . . assuming I got to it quickly.

And of course, I would absolutely hold it against Wyldon to further annoy him. If there was enough left of him to save, that was.

All of this flashed in my mind as a black cat leapt from a nearby chair and caught the vial with its mouth midair, landing proudly on its feet.

Excuse me, a *grimalcat* leapt to catch it. No one should ever mistake the two, or the grimalcat would seek vengeance for the slight. They were proud; they were majestic . . . And they carried a grudge forever.

The creature spat the bottle of highly dangerous potion onto the ground and lay down beside it, batting it playfully with soft paws. The poison swished around inside, a beautiful swirl of red with black flecks.

The guard landed with a brutal *thud* in front of the duke, rolling down two stairs before catching herself. The duke lowered his arms, staring at the grimalcat.

"Lord Peter, secure the assassin!" I yelled, tossing my one and only pair of Veralyn's Enchanted Restraint Manacles at the human. He was partially straddling the elf, who'd pulled a knife from somewhere.

"Get off me, you knave!" she screeched. She wasn't going down without a fight and stabbed at Peter. My instincts were correct, and the awkward young man dodged the knife while making a strangled *eep* sound. He whacked the elf in the wrist, yelling a panicked, "[Disarm]."

At that point, three guards had their swords pointed at her throat, five martial guests had acquired weapons and encircled the assassin, and one young Lord Peter was cuffing her with Veralyn's Enchanted Restraint Manacles.

"Thank you, everyone." The duke shoved his glasses back up his nose and brushed off invisible dust from one sleeve. "And thank *you,* Lady Tate. If you really *are* Lady Tate, maybe we will finally have some answers."

According to my skill [Detect Fake], the lady wasn't using any abilities to change her appearance or voice or otherwise disguising herself. She was either a very good look alike, or the real thing.

"I'm just the beginning." The assassin *pouted,* so I was leaning toward this being the real Lady Tate. "The boss won't let you live."

"Take her away," Duke Wyldon said coldly. He reached up and smoothed out his pinched brow. "I'll see about getting information out of you to take down your boss before she has a chance to succeed. Happy birthday to *me.*"

She clamped her mouth shut at that and glared, saying nothing more as the guards dragged her off.

I noticed the grimalcat had returned to the head table; the molten ash vane was nowhere to be seen. He sat on a higher-than-normal chair near the middle of the table, and his vibrant green eyes blinked slowly at me when our gazes met.

He broke eye contact when Duke Wyldon swept down the stairs and up to the grimalcat, bowing low before the creature.

"Thank you, Slake; I don't know what I would have done without you." The duke smiled, and his face lit up with appreciation and a rare softness. "I owe you one."

Slake raised his eyebrows and sniffed.

"It was just an assassin, my friend." The grimalcat spoke with the accent of the Empire of Sands, with its drawn-out vowels. His delicate black wings flared a bit and settled down; a subtle wing shrug. "Who counts assassins? I have a new interesting sample; that is payment enough. Ah . . . and head scratches?"

"Of course, but let me address my other guests first," the duke said with all seriousness before turning to us. Duke Wyldon coughed. "Welcome to my humble celebration, friends and family. Please, find your seats, and we can have lunch."

As if on cue, Bronwynn began playing again, her music light and upbeat. The summer sun shone down on her sparkling dress, and I stared at her longer than I should have. I was one of the last to take my seat, which happened to be directly beside the grimalcat at the head table.

Even the novelty of sitting beside a grimalcat couldn't drag my attention away from the beautiful minstrel playing in her corner. I wasn't in the mood for the lavish food being carried out. My stomach churned even as the usual lyre filling my ears would have otherwise soothed me. This was *another* event with the bard and an assassination attempt using molten ash vane.

The thought filled my mind so much that I didn't notice when the grimalcat turned his attention to me.

"Commander General Rufus?"

The voice drew me out of my head. "Yes . . . I'm sorry, I do not know your title?"

The grimalcat's little green horns and green eyes were the only thing of color on the inky black creature, until he smiled and showed off his sharp white teeth. "Adventurer Slake Drakeford. A pleasure to meet you."

Wait.

How did I not know that one of the most successful and powerful people on the continent, Slake Drakeford, Dungeon-Conquering Adventurer Extraordinaire, with more loot than a kingdom . . . was a grimalcat?

CHAPTER 28

You Can't Judge an Assassin by Their Dress

Brownie

This always happened. The duke had almost died, and here Brownie was, playing away the afternoon with some lighthearted string music.

At least the experience points were good.

The rest of the afternoon was an excited murmur of contemplations among the guests. Duke Wyldon was an upstanding member of the royal court, nephew to the king, and he kept good company. As such, the conversations available for eavesdropping were of excellent quality.

Brownie turned her attention to the young man that had been talking to Rufus at the start of the party. Lord Peter. From what she knew, he was the second son of the minister of foreign affairs, and set to inherit a barony on the northern coastline.

"I finally got to witness one of those blasted assassins everyone's been on about!" Lord Peter sat at a table with a blue selkie count, a black human nobleman, and a calico catkin miss.

Brownie wouldn't look too closely at anyone—she was supposed to be background noise—but after a few sweeping glances, she'd placed most of the guests. The catkin, one Miss Cara Sassafras, actually growled, "I'm sure that is the real Lady Tate. That woman is a *menace*."

"You're only saying that because she punched you in the eye during morning training last week," the human, Lord Owen Law, said.

"No," Miss Cara snapped. "I'm saying that because she is constantly wearing *ruffles*. The dress she wore today should be *burned*."

Lord Peter chided, "You can't judge an assassin by their dress, Cara!"

"Watch me." Miss Cara sniffed, dramatically looking up and left with her eyes closed, crossing her arms haughtily.

"We don't even know if that *was* Lady Tate Terpenlily. The Terpenlily's have been a loyal and proud noble family since the revolution," Lord Peter said.

"It might, actually," Count Cypress, the selkie with short blue bangs that covered his eyes and a blue vest, rebuked. "We all know she was hoping to marry Marquess Chadwick—"

"That old man?" Lord Peter blurted, not hiding his shock. "*Ow!*"

"Shh!" Miss Cara mumbled something Brownie couldn't hear, and the table quieted for a moment. Finally, Peter grumbled, "If her family owed that much money, then they should have tried something else."

Brownie pocketed that bit of information and turned her ear to other conversations.

"You should come to the Dark Enchanted Forest sometime," Rufus was telling a purring grimalcat. "We have a few hidden dungeons."

Brownie chanced a glance and smiled to herself. The beastman was scratching the grimalcat below his chin as the creature lay curled in the commander general's lap.

"I always enjoy a new challenge." The grimalcat headbutted Rufus's paw when the beastman paused in his administrations, and Rufus continued his pets. "Maybe I *will* visit after this. When are you returning, Commander?"

"If I may," the duke interrupted from further down the table. "Why does the Dark Enchanted Forest have hidden dungeons? Isn't it better for trade to spread that information?"

His eyes were practically shooting daggers between the commander general and his lap companion. Brownie didn't blame the duke; both the grimalcat and the lap he rested on were very desirable.

She pushed away the inappropriate thought and turned her attention to the guard from earlier.

A maid had just hurried out from inside the hall and stopped beside the guard at the top of the stairs. She was standing politely at attention, ready to collect plates or serve tea with the other maids at any second . . . but in actuality, she was shooting barbs and concerned comments at the guard.

Both women were whispering, but Brownie could read lips, and she didn't worry about staring openly at a guard.

"Tina, I'm fine, love! It's just a bit of armor bite at my side where I landed wrong." The guard wore light plate from head to toe. She had a short helmet with an open face, a gorget at the neck, chest plate, upper arm guards, gauntlets, a tasset belt over black leggings, and greaves. Brownie winced; pinched armor was the worse. "I'll be right as rain by tomorrow."

The maid swatted the guard on the arm even as a single tear fell down her cheek. "You're *not* fine; you almost *died*."

Brownie left them to their own devices. At this point, her music was cut off by a loud trumpeted fanfare near the garden path entrance. The minstrel finished her arpeggio and put down her lyre.

"All rise for His Highness, Prince Zachary Servalt," a woman in palace liveries announced, and everyone in attendance quickly stood to welcome the royal.

Except Rufus, of course. He had a grimalcat on his lap.

Prince Zachary was an eighteen-year-old half elf; his mother an elf and his father a selkie. While he had the usual features of a half elf, with slightly pointed ears and sharper nose, as well as multiple shades of brown hair that resembled tree bark, his dark teal coloring and slit-pupil eyes were testament to his selkie heritage.

"Cousin!" The prince smiled at the duke, who was pushing up his glasses and hiding a neutral expression behind the sun reflected on the lens.

The duke bowed and addressed his surprise guest. "Prince Zachary, welcome. I thought I wasn't going to see you until this evening?"

The prince frowned, and Bronwynn would have sworn it bordered a pout before the man took a breath and airily waved away the question. "That is the formal dinner; I wanted to wish you a normal happy birthday like everyone else."

"I'll have a seat prepared." Duke Wyldon nodded stiffly. Brownie felt pity for the duke; the tension in the man's shoulders couldn't be good for his back. As a musician bent over an instrument for hours, she could attest.

The smile that bloomed on the prince's face would have melted butter. "Really?! I mean"—cough—"of course, thank you."

Duke Wyldon raised his eyebrows and swept a look at his guests, still standing. The prince quickly caught on and loudly declared. "You may be seated."

His royal voice was strong and confident, belying the actual appearance of the eager young man joining the head table.

The grimalcat was *not* amused when the prince took his seemingly empty high chair. Of course, the prince apologized and returned the seat to the creature.

Which was followed by obligatory pets.

CHAPTER 29

With a Hi-Ya and a Swoosh!

Rufus

I absentmindedly watched Slake Drakeford, Adventurer Extraordinaire, napping in a sunny spot on the lawn.

We were running past when the lunch should have come to its conclusion, but someone was keeping everyone in their seat.

"Then I slew the kraken with a *hi-ya* and a *swoosh!*" The royal sitting one seat away from me was regaling his cousin with his new spear form and his last trip to the Depths of Despair Dungeon. The duke patiently listened to the excited prince, nodding every so often.

The grimalcat flicked his tail in his sleep, and it inspired me to move. I was the only person here, aside from Slake, of course, high enough in the order of precedence to directly greet royalty without reserve. I waited for a natural pause—difficult to spot, but I was a master of communication—and stood up to draw attention.

"Prince Zachary, Duke Wyldon," I spoke firmly, bobbing a shallow bow. "As the luncheon draws to a close, I would like to thank you on behalf of Nilheim and my king for your gracious hospitality. A toast, and happy birthday."

The garden clinked with glasses as everyone hurriedly toasted, many eyes alight with relief.

"Happy birthday, Cousin!" The prince joined in the toast with an easy smile.

"Thank you, Commander General." The duke nodded, his otherwise stoic shoulders visibly relaxing under my keen senses. His eyes sharpened as we locked gazes, and he continued. "I'll be escorting Prince Zachary for the rest of the evening. I hope you have the opportunity to relax, and maybe keep my *other guest* company while I'm away."

His eyes snapped to the house and back to me.

"Of course." I smiled, flashing my teeth. I was sure it frustrated the man to allow me the opportunity to investigate Lady Tate *first*, but our kingdoms had an agreement to work together on the molten ash vane assassinations. "Send my regards to Their Majesties."

The prince drew himself up and gave a well-trained regal nod that seemed out of place on the young man. He adopted a neutral and dignified frown as he said, "I shall convey your message, Commander General."

The prince's show of regal poise was broken when he promptly looked to his cousin for approval. I resisted the urge to smile and pretended I didn't see.

With that, Duke Wyldon stood. "Then I would like to thank everyone for coming."

Prince Zachary and the duke left via the stairwell and through the double doors.

I shook my head as they left. For some reason, the duke hadn't informed the prince that he'd been attacked by an assassin moments before Prince Zachary showed up.

That was going to bite him in the family bonding later, but that wasn't my business . . . as much as I wanted to intervene for no other reason than I was nosy.

I sent Brownie a smile as everyone packed up and left the gardens. She was still playing gentle background music, and would continue until every guest left.

Lord Peter waved and called out that he'd hopefully see me tomorrow in the capital as the guardswoman who'd taken a fall during the attack stepped forward to bring me to the prisoner.

She led me through a side door.

The duke's estate had a holding cell that seconded as a pantry, and I could see Lady Tate inside the room through the barred windows on the hallway door. Outside the door stood two guards and a man of unknown race dressed in clothes favored by underwater inhabitants, with thin flexible woven tights that only came to the low calf, and a skintight, high-neck tunic without sleeves. The man looked like he wasn't wearing any shoes, but in fact, he simply had on a flat leather pad held onto each foot by a loop around the big toe.

"We were expecting you. Do not worry, the room is barred against sound— she cannot hear us." The man nodded a greeting, meeting my golden eyes with murky greenish-gray orbs. His silver hair fell to his shoulder on the right side; the left had been clean shaven. His skin had a gray-blue tint. "My name is Pjori Galr. I'm a Soothfinder from Tevl."

I smiled and returned his greeting. "Commander General Rufus, but you may call me Rufus. I did not realize that Duke Wyldon was working with the Coraldark."

Tevl was an underwater ocean city in the bay of Norn Island, a large island off the southeast coast of Servalt. The people there were hostile to land dwellers, and prone to raid the Sumbrian coastal villages. Anyone seeking their city without an invitation was found beneath the steep island cliffs. At least, their *bodies* were found there, washed ashore after their ships were dashed against the rocks.

"As much as he is working with the Dark Enchanted Forest," Pjori mused, looking through the bars in the door to the awaiting Lady Tate. "I'm enjoying my stay here so far; Servalt is not one to judge where you came from."

It was true. The place was no meritocracy, but the monarchs were adamant on fairness between its upper and lower echelons. And many were accepted into bureaucratic positions or trades based on skill. They didn't make just *anyone* a noble, but some people could earn the title through merit or great deed.

"Is there something you are looking to find out specifically?" I asked, crossing my arms.

Pjori shook his head. "My princess is going to be attacked soon, and I've been sent to find out more before it happens."

"Did you receive a message from Madame Potts?"

"No." He didn't explain further even after a pause, so I would assume it came from Pjori's soothsaying or another Clairvoyant class in the Coraldark.

I cracked my neck and rolled up my tunic sleeves. "Then, between a Sooth-finder and my Mediator, I'm sure we will find something. It's too bad the duke is otherwise engaged."

Pjori smiled, and I noticed his teeth were just the tiniest bit pointy. "He's going to miss all the fun."

CHAPTER 30

Basking in the Afterglow

Brownie

Eventually, every guest had left except the grimalcat. Brownie didn't mind him and continued playing for the staff as they tidied up.

Music always made cleaning go faster.

Then Page Saryl showed up, her lyre harp case in her hands. "Minstrel Bronwynn!"

"Let me just put away Danielle, and I'll be ready to go," Brownie said, accepting the case and carefully packing the lyre harp away. The case was a hard, stiff, layered canvas with a long shoulder strap. It had a pocket sewn on the front for her tuning tools and a few spare coins.

"Who?" Saryl obviously didn't know whom she was talking about, but her mind was elsewhere. "No! Please, Minstrel Bronwynn. Something terrible has happened."

That made the bard pause. "Go on?"

Page Saryl's blue eyes were near watering, and she bowed very low. "I can't find your bag!"

"The red one?" Brownie immediately regretted leaving that tuning key in her bag. She wanted to let out an aggrieved sigh, but the crushed look on the page girl's face stopped her. "Did you drop it on the way here?"

A violent headshake of those short purple curls refuted her suggestion. "No, I put it on your bed with your music case, b-but it isn't there anymore! We should tell the duke!"

The page looked ready to burst into tears on the spot.

"Page Saryl, it's *fine*. I promise." Bronwynn stood up and slung her case over her shoulder. "Besides, I'm sure the duke is a little busy right now, what with the prince visiting."

"It's *not* fine." Saryl was really taking this hard, her ashen skin even paler than before. Brownie bent down and put a comforting hand on the girl's shoulders.

"Why don't we backtrack together and take another look?"

"Alright."

The servant's staircase on the left led into a mudroom before continuing into the castle workrooms: kitchen, laundry, and servant's quarters. Brownie swept the mudroom with one long glance. There were a few packs and cloaks and shoes, but no familiar red bag.

"I took the shortcut to your room through here." Page Saryl brought Brownie through a small servants' door on the other side of the mudroom and into a tight-fitting hall. The cramped space was obviously meant for staff to wander around the castle without going through the main hall. Brownie just barely fit in the passage; she *was* half giant, not half elf. The path arched in a circle, and luckily, it was a short distance to another set of tight doors.

The bending down to not hit the ceiling was manageable for that short time, but it left a bit of a crick in her neck. She'd also had to slump her shoulders awkwardly to keep Danielle safe from hitting the wall.

Needless to say, she was happy when they came out into the regular hallway, just down the way from her room.

It was a very quick search to determine that the red bag was, in fact, gone.

Brownie turned back to Saryl, bending down on one knee to be at eye level with the page girl.

"Listen, Saryl." Her voice was soft and her face calm. "This is not your fault. Things go walking at events like this all the time, and you did the right thing telling me right away. The duke should be proud to have such an honest page."

In fact, this was exactly why Brownie kept her red bag to begin with.

A blush creeped into the distraught girl's cheeks. She looked down at the ground. "But it *is* my fault. I was supposed to make sure you and Mister Moray were properly attended."

"Mister Moray?" Brownie asked, hoping to distract the girl from the threatening tears.

Saryl nodded. "He's the baker His Grace hired for today's cake. Mister Moray is really nice."

"How about this; I'll stay here, and you can inform the housekeeper about what happened?" Brownie worried that if she left the girl to her own devices she'd actually go and tell the duke. The bard wanted Duke Wyldon to remember her as an excellent musician, not as the contract worker blaming his staff for losing a small bag.

"Alright, I'll tell Madam Brillabelle. But it might take a while . . . she is *very* busy."

"I'm not going anywhere for quite some time, especially since I'm Commander General Rufus Triever's ride, and his next appointment isn't until tomorrow. I'm just going to get changed into something more comfortable." Brownie carefully hung her lyre harp in its case on the coat hook.

The page bowed again, sniffed once, and quietly excused herself.

Brownie changed into comfortable leggings and a long tunic, belt and pouch, and comfy shoes. She reapplied a bit of makeup around her eyes and some glitter on her cheeks, and was thinking about going out to visit Donna to make sure the mare hadn't gotten into any more trouble when there was a knock at her door.

She opened it to find a very, very short human, his brown skin weathered, and his salt and pepper black hair tied back in a low ponytail. He looked up at her, and his eyebrow twitched. "Minstrel Bronwynn?"

"Yes?"

The man shoved a small silver platter with a domed cover toward her. Brownie took it, but just stood there holding it, confused. "I didn't ask—"

"Saryl was in the kitchen earlier. Upset," the man started. He scratched his cheek and looked uncomfortable. "She told me what happened, so I promised I'd bring you a treat. These are just some leftover pastries from the party, and I know they won't replace your stolen bag, but I hope—"

It was Brownie's turn to interrupt. "Oh! Are you Mister Moray? This really isn't necessary, but I wouldn't say no to a snack."

"I am, and take it. There was plenty of extra for the staff to enjoy." Mister Moray nodded. "I'm sure the duke will reimburse you for whatever was taken. There's no excuse for something like that happening."

"It's really alright. It was just a bag," she protested.

"Still . . ." He looked like he wanted to say more, but trailed off into silence. They stood there a moment longer until Mister Moray coughed. "Well, have a nice day, Minstrel Bronwynn."

"Thank you." With Mister Moray gone, Bronwynn sat down on her bed, lifting the cover off the silver plate. There were two markle berries stuffed with caramel, a roasted pistachio cream pudding, and a palm-size slab of crunchy peanut brittle.

"Wow." The food tasted as good as it looked. Brownie made appreciative noises and savored each dessert slowly. Saryl was *absolutely* correct; Mister Moray was *really* nice.

She was basking in the afterglow—and a little sad that she'd finished everything—when another knock sounded at the door. This time, they didn't wait for her to open it. She was barely off the bed and standing presentably by the time her room was full of knights.

Three knights to be precise, all in full armor. The first one to enter, an elf with darker hair and skin, asked, "Minstrel Bronwynn?"

"Yes?" Brownie raised her hands in the air. "If this is about the stolen bag, I'm serious! It'll be alright. If you want to pay me for a replacement, that's fine, but—"

"You are under investigation for the attempted poisoning of Duke Wyldon Holst," the elf interrupted. "We are to escort you to the holding cell for questioning. Please come quietly."

CHAPTER 31

Assassins Have Rights Too, You Know!

Rufus

Pjori leaned against the wall behind Lady Tate and stared at me with a hint of amusement mixed with shock.

"And then Mama told me I had to follow *that woman* around for an entire week and do whatever she said—no ifs, ands, or buts about it." Lady Tate was crying into a delicate pink kerchief with floral embroidery that she'd pulled from her décolletage.

"That's terrible." I nodded sympathetically. "What did she make you do?"

Lady Tate clenched the kerchief in a tight fist. "You don't understand, Rufus! She made me stand in a corner for six hours after she told me to wait for her to come back from a meeting with Duke Lector. *Six hours.* I missed Lady Genevie's sword fighting practice bout, and for what? To wait around for a summons. It was so embarrassing!"

"This was from 'the boss'? How rude." I reached out and poured a bit more tea into the young woman's teacup.

She nodded, hiccupped, and then sipped her glass. "That's what everyone calls her. It's not even an interesting title."

"Does she even *look* the part of a fearsome leader, or were you forced to cater to a nobody?" I raised an eyebrow. My inner thoughts were racing while my face remained calm. I even tilted my head slightly to appear more curious and less like what I'd just asked was highly coveted information.

Lady Tate scrunched up her nose in contempt. "She's barely worth noticing. Plain brown hair. Even her eyes were brown."

"She obviously doesn't compare to you," I said, ignoring the eye roll *that* garnered from Pjori.

"The boss is bent on attacking the duke." *Sniffle.* "She said something about him closing in on something."

"That's what you told the duke when they escorted you here." I smoothly leaned my elbow onto my armchair and stuck my chin onto my clenched hand. My other fist rested on my hips, elbow out. I tried to look pensive. "You know, I think that was why they brought you here instead of to a more civilized waiting room. Of course, you were just trying to warn them, and nobody even listened to you. They should feel ashamed."

After walking into the room, I'd made a royal huff about the care of a noble and how uncivilized it was to leave the lovely Lady Tate without so much as tea. When the shock had worn off, the guards had jumped to attention and brought in everything I'd demanded: a table, two comfortable chairs, and a trolley. My [Detect Fake] perk had been critical in this instance.

Snacks were still on the way. I'd spent less time *eating* during the luncheon and more time *petting*. No regrets, but I was still hoping for some of that cream pudding.

"It was *awful.* I just threw a Greendeath potion at Duke Wyldon—approved by the Assassin's Guild, no less. I don't know why they locked me up like this." Lady Tate glared at the guards. "Assassins have rights too, you know!"

Even without my abilities, I could tell she was telling the truth. She honestly had no idea she'd been carrying molten ash vane. I wasn't going to be the one to tell her.

She didn't see the sudden dark look overtake Pjori behind her. A good thing, because that would've detracted from my work so far. The man must have soothed *something* with [Soothfinder], because he was reading over a notification.

"This 'boss' has been pretty busy since she took over the Assassin's Guild." I nodded. "I'm sure the paperwork will be filed properly. But, as of this morning . . . I'm afraid it wasn't."

"Wait! What? No, I *saw* the order myself!" For the first time since I'd been coaxing Lady Tate, I gave her cause to worry. I prodded. It was open-ended, letting her come to her own conclusions. I knew she wasn't high enough in level to gauge whether I was lying, and while I didn't know for a fact if the Assassin's Guild had properly registered their targets as was law—people needed to know who was and wasn't eligible to inherit—I could guess that this particular report had probably gone unapproved.

Seeing as Duke Wyldon was currently in charge of processing those reports.

"Your assassination attempt wasn't legally registered," I repeated, shooting her a concerned look. "Maybe they were busy. Is there something we could use to defend you? A *reason* it could be late?"

Lady Tate was not an idiot. I could tell she'd only gone through with everything was because she would be protected by an assassination order and the boss of the Servalt Assassin's Guild . . . but without that order, she'd just attacked one of the most powerful people in the kingdom without cause.

"I-I . . . Well." She stumbled for a second, and her eyebrows scrunched up in concentration. Finally, she gave us exactly what we'd been hoping for. "Oh! I overheard her say that she was going out to meet with an international agent when I last saw her. I haven't actually *seen* her since. Another guild member handed over the potion."

"That must be it. When did she leave?" I nodded, convinced.

"Day before last." Lady Tate smiled in relief. She dabbed her eyes one final time then stuffed the kerchief back where it'd come from. I wondered absent-mindedly if Brownie also kept things tucked away in . . . unorthodox places.

Suddenly, Lady Tate was smiling knowingly. I cursed; my tail was giving away my thoughts again.

Sigh.

"Thank you, Lady Tate." I stood quickly. "I'm sure after the duke hears about my findings, he'll do the right thing."

I didn't know what "the right thing" was in Servalt. In Nilheim, she would be stripped of her rank and forced to spend a year serving in the Dark Horde while myself or one of my agents counseled her. She could do with a habitual rehabili-tation plan and narcissistic thought pattern recognition therapy. Since she had no idea that she'd had a permadeath weapon, Nilheim would provide education and source material for that, too.

"Soothfinder Pjori." A new guard stood outside the door, peering through the bars.

Pjori opened the door to a crowd. His voice sharp, he ordered, "Report."

"We've got another suspect." The guard stepped aside, and Brownie stood there, looking confused and embarrassed, one arm held behind her back by the guard.

She waved at us with her unrestrained arm. "Hello."

CHAPTER 32

He Politely Recaptured Her

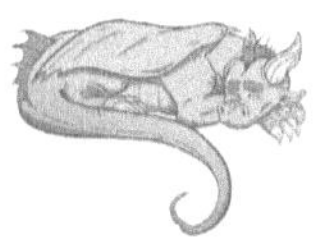

Brownie

Sir Thistlewick, as the lead elf had introduced himself, ushered us all into the room before bowing. "One more for you, gentlemen. I'll leave her in your capable hands and continue our search."

He slipped out, closing the door behind him.

Brownie heard the latch lock, trapping her in here. But she wasn't fazed. This wasn't the worst situation she'd found herself in. *Cool and calm* meant she was ready to *cut and run* when the time was right.

And Rufus being here gave her an extra sense of security. Not to mention he was giving her that reassuring smile. He had a very nice smile.

They were in a cellar of sorts, with two comfortable chairs set up in the middle. The assassin from earlier was quietly assessing the situation from her seat. A storm kelpie in land form leaned against the back wall, his murky eyes watching everything with a controlled demeanor.

"And *why* is Minstrel Bronwynn here?" Rufus stood, facing her guards. Something about the way the beastman's tail stiffened made her think he wasn't as calm as his neutral expression let on.

Brownie wondered if she could get away with puling out snacks from her spatial ring, but decided against it. She didn't want to draw attention to it. They'd already searched her tiny pouch and determined she could keep it; there were just a few decoy coins in there.

"We found *this* in Lady Tate's room." A shorter human with bushy eyebrows fumbled a bit before pulling out Brownie's missing red shoulder bag. He waved his findings triumphantly and announced dramatically, "The bard's bag!"

The front flap flipped back from his enthusiasm, and something fell out.

"Oh, good, my tuning peg," Bronwynn said, smiling. Now she wouldn't need to worry about replacing it.

Rufus bent down to pick it up and flipped it over in his hand twice.

"Here you go, Minstrel Bronwynn." Rufus handed it to her.

The beastman knight that held her arm released her. Brownie accepted the tool and tucked it into her belt pouch, where it stuck out a bit since it was too long to fit in a regular coin pouch. Once that was done, she gave her arm back to the knight to hold.

He politely recaptured her.

"Why did you give it back?!" the bushy-eyebrow human knight demanded. "That was evidence."

He was less polite.

Instead of replying, Rufus raised an eyebrow at the human. "And *who* are *you*?"

"My name is Sir Norman Harth," he replied, puffing out his chest.

Rufus stared at the man. Sir Norman didn't say anything else. Rufus stared harder. An awkward silence filled the room until Rufus stated, "That wasn't what I wanted to know, Sir Norman."

"It wasn't?" A confused pinch furrowed Sir Norman's bushy eyebrows together.

"No," Rufus explained, his voice deep and fierce. "The question is, *who* are *you* to question *me*?"

The storm kelpie snorted. Brownie felt her heartbeat quicken; Rufus had a very smooth voice when he hit those lower tones. She imagined what it would sound like if he sang a ballad with that voice.

Sir Norman huffed. "I've been a knight of this estate for nigh on fifteen years! I know the protocol. All effects of a captured individual are to be stored for evidence until the person in question is, um, questioned."

"I have a question." A high-pitched lady's voice came from behind Rufus. Everyone turned to stare at Lady Tate, who had her arms crossed and her chin stuck out. The ruffles of her skirts were voluminous, and she looked like a proud and angry pink puff pastry to Brownie.

"Go on," the kelpie urged.

Lady Tate looked Brownie up and down and then pointed to the red bag. "Why did you find *that* in my room? I've never seen it before—and I don't care for people going into my room without warning just to leave things. It's *rude*."

"But you don't mind that they were searching your room when they found it?" Brownie asked before she could help herself. Rufus was tapping his chin in thought.

"Of course," Lady Tate stated, waving her hand elegantly in the air as if to brush away Brownie's concerns. "They told me they were going to search my room, and it is a perfectly proper thing to do in this case. *That,*" she sniffed, "is not mine, and is false evidence planted against the bard. I would expect better of the duke."

"Sir Norman." Rufus turned on the knight so quickly that the human took a step back, startled.

"Yes?"

"Do you know a castle attendant named Claire?"

Sir Norman frowned. "Why? She's got nothing to do with you."

"We'll see about that." Rufus suddenly smiled. He turned to Lady Tate. "You are certain that you've never seen this bag before?"

"Of course not." Lady Tate crossed her arms and somehow managed to look down her nose from her sitting position. "I have *class.*"

The idea that Lady Tate didn't like Brownie's style only reassured Brownie of her own taste; she would've been worried otherwise. Also, it went to show that Lady Tate wasn't as fashionable as she seemed—herringbone weave was all the rage in North Sumbria, and it was spreading like wildfire amongst the other kingdoms even as they spoke.

"How did you get the *poison* for today's assassination?" Rufus inquired.

Lady Tate shrugged. "A guild member met me at a carriage stop outside Heatherfeld and gave me the bottle."

"Thank you for answering my questions, Lady Tate; it's been a pleasure." Rufus bowed and offered her his hand.

"This was the nicest interrogation I've ever had, Commander General." Lady Tate allowed Rufus to help her to her feet.

Brownie was confused by the hint of dark emotion that gripped her when the elf placed a hand on those soft beanies and stood beside the beastman. They momentarily looked like a picture out of a fairytale. A tall golden beast prince and the pink ruffle dress lady.

Then the commander general let go and swept his arm toward the door. "A knight will accompany you to your room, and you can take a nice rest until the duke returns tomorrow. I'll let him know about *everything* you've had to suffer."

"Thank you. It really was awful." Lady Tate shuddered. Brownie scoffed; the elf still had both her ears, so it couldn't have been that bad. She spotted the kelpie in the corner rolling his eyes. It looked like he was thinking the same thing.

Rufus ordered, "Now, everyone out while we interrogate Minstrel Bronwynn."

CHAPTER 33

I Had a Problem

Rufus

I was not the beastman for this job. And the longer I spent with Minstrel Bronwynn, the more I realized that I was a *terrible* choice for discovering if the woman was actually an illegal international spy and assassin bent on unleashing permadeath on her unsuspecting victims.

Just look at her! She was sitting in the chair across from me with a relaxed smile on her face. The second the guards had left us, she'd even pulled a bag of cookies from the storage ring I'd gifted her all that time ago and put them out with the tea. She looked like she was *excited* to get interrogated; like it was a game because obviously it *wasn't* her, and she was just here for the ride.

I resisted a sigh.

"So, you think this 'Claire' set me up?" Bronwynn asked as I poured her a cup of tea. Pjori, for his part, had moved to a new spot against the wall where the minstrel could actually see him. She even smiled and nodded at him when he did so.

I ignored all of the spiraling emotions in my chest, opened my notification tab, and dropped into my activity logs. So far, I'd not been the recipient of any failed skill or perk, and my [Inspire Honesty] was on cooldown. Not that I needed it. [Inspire Honesty] didn't make the target tell me the truth; it made them realize the truth and be honest with *themselves*. They had every freedom to not share their thoughts and retain agency.

"I'm also intrigued," Pjori cut in. I contemplated getting him his own chair, but he seemed perfectly content.

"She was the attendant who treated you so poorly yesterday."

"But why would she go so far?" Brownie tilted her head, confused. "She doesn't even know me?"

"That's the problem. She *doesn't* know you. Instead, she judged you based on nothing except your profession." I clenched my hand until I felt my nails starting to dig in.

Pjori shrugged. "Her prejudice is not grounds for interrogation, only the deliberate misguidance and alteration to evidence in an investigation is. *If* she did it."

The man eyed Brownie with suspicion, and for some reason, that made me feel better. *Someone* needed to be sensible in this room, and it certainly wasn't going to be *me*.

I'd felt overwhelming embarrassment and apology when they'd escorted Bronwynn into the room, despite the fact that even now she was *still* the leading suspect in the molten ash vane smuggling. It was natural to return her tuning peg and offer her a seat . . . and not because I wanted to manipulate her into a false sense of security.

I honestly felt like she wasn't to blame. That there was just no way that *Minstrel Bronwynn* was the murderer. If I hadn't felt this passion for the woman for a year already, I'd think I was under some sort of mind magic or love spell. No. Of her many listeners, I was just one of the more intense fans . . . and getting to know her on this trip wasn't helping me knock her off that pedestal. If anything, it was making me like her all the more.

Yes, I had a problem.

"A good lead into questioning," I acknowledged Pjori's pointed message to start. "Minstrel Bronwynn, can you tell us everything you did leading up to Lady Tate's assassination attempt?"

Bronwynn's face lit up in that way it did when she was ready to tell an elaborate tale. Her arms came up to animatedly accompany the story, and she happily went into minute detail on her wake up, morning routine, and performance practice. I found myself nodding along, enraptured; she could turn brushing her teeth into an interesting adventure.

Pjori, luckily, had taken over taking notes.

We were at the part where the grimalcat had arrived when a hurried set of footsteps sounded down the hall. Pjori was at the door ready to open it when the flurry of panicked knocks hit its rough wooden surface.

A young page girl stood there, her cheeks cherry red from the run. She had the fluffiest curly purple hair I'd ever seen, and big fearful eyes that were hardened with an inner courage.

"It's my fault!" she exclaimed.

"Page Saryl, you may come in." Pjori motioned her inside. Rufus didn't know if he had already met the girl previously while staying in the castle, or if he'd pieced two and two together from the minstrel's testimony so far.

The page girl fit Bronwynn's description of her perfectly.

When the door clicked close behind Page Saryl, the girl jumped and glanced back, but otherwise held her shoulders stiff and her back straight. She looked like she was waiting to be sentenced to the gallows.

"Page Saryl here did *nothing wrong*," Bronwynn said, coming to her feet. The minstrel was a large and tall woman who loomed over Pjori and the child in the tight space. For the first time that evening, she didn't seem like she was playing audience to a great show or performing her part in the story.

"I understand, Minstrel Bronwynn," Pjori replied. "But we still need to ask her a few questions."

I put out a hand and placed it reassuringly on Brownie's arm. "We won't jump to any conclusions without discussing it first, I promise."

"Alright." She relaxed and resumed her seat. She looked like she wanted to remain standing guard beside the page, eyeing her with a regretful expression, but the holding room wasn't big enough for everyone to just stand around two empty chairs. Pjori also took a step back, giving the young girl space to talk.

Page Saryl took a deep breath through her nose and then exploded in an unending cacophony of word torrent. "It was me! Minstrel Bronwynn entrusted me with her red bag. I brought it to her room, and I left it on her bed. The bag was so pretty and fashionable and-and someone must have snuck in after m-me."

The idea that someone in the mansion had actually stolen the bag seemed difficult for the page girl to even voice, and she had to force it out. She took another breath and continued. "I don't know how it got into Lady Tate's rooms, but it wasn't Minstrel Bronwynn's fault. It can't be!"

I liked the page; she had a good sense for these things. "Thank you, Page Saryl. We will do everything we can to find the true culprit. Now, we might want to start questioning everyone else that Lady Tate and Minstrel Bronwynn spoke to. Could you go and tell Sir Thistlewick to round up Hostler Jimmie, Attendant Claire, and Jack—"

We all started as the door suddenly opened and a man casually leaned against the frame. It was none other than the duke's man himself, Jack Laverick.

"Did somebody call my name?"

Red Herringbone Bag

Brownie

"Master Jack!" Page Saryl bowed low to the man who'd just interrupted.

Brownie was almost pleased to see the man, if only because he was a suspect and about to be subject to interrogation.

It wasn't like she held a *grudge* against him for his part in her kidnapping. She knew that he had been undercover and actually working for Duke Wyldon; she just missed Suzette, and he reminded her of the destroyed lyre harp.

Jack nodded at the page girl and smiled a sunny half smile. His teeth almost shone with a sparkling light. The man must have at least Charisma thirty to be that suave. "Saryl, I'd like to ask you to hold off summoning anyone."

Rufus was not amused, cutting in. "Why?"

"I know who did it."

The whole room held their breath, but Jack didn't continue. Instead, he made a shooing motion to the page. "So you can rest easy that Minstrel Bronwynn is innocent. Just don't tell anyone, alright? We are still investigating, and it's important to keep what you know close to heart until everyone is caught."

"Really? Phew." The page girl released a really long breath, and then nodded vigorously. "Alright, Master Jack! I won't say anything, promise!"

"Lovely." Jack waved the page out and down the hallway before stepping inside and closing the door.

Brownie wasn't getting up to greet him, and she wasn't going to relinquish her comfy chair for questioning. He'd have to stand.

Rufus crossed his arms from his armchair and demanded, "Alright, Jack, out with it. Who stole Minstrel Bronwynn's red bag and moved it into Lady Tate's room?"

"I did."

Brownie was the first to reply. "What?! Why?"

Jack shrugged, stuffing his hands in his pockets. "How else was I going to get you past all of the guards and into the holding cell to talk about the incident?"

"Minstrel Bronwynn has *nothing* to do with this investigation," Rufus almost growled. His voice rumbled, and Brownie felt a tingle in her spine. It was actually really sweet how angry he got on her behalf.

Wait, she was supposed to be concentrating on the traitor who'd stolen her beautiful custom-made red herringbone bag. It was a bag she carried as a distraction, but it was still *pretty*. And expensive.

Jack turned to Brownie. "Duke Wyldon wanted your report and opinion on the whole affair. But he didn't want you to be labeled as one of us, an official investigator, in case someone from the castle is reporting to the Assassin's Guild."

"She could still be placed in unnecessary danger by your antics," Rufus said. He linked his fingers and leaned forward to rest his elbows on his knees.

Jack waved away the commander general's concern with a flippant hand gesture. "Minstrel Bronwynn is an esteemed world-traveling bard who's tougher than you think. I should know; I've seen her fight."

"Does this mean I get my bag back?" Brownie cut in. "Because if not, you're going to need to replace it."

"It's technically evidence, though it's not like we haven't returned other things already." Pjori snarkily looked at Rufus, speaking for the first time in a while. The man was the quiet type.

"She needs her tuning tools for her job," Rufus countered. "That would be like taking a bard's instrument as evidence and not giving it back. Or a knight's sword."

Pjori, obviously teasing Rufus now, retorted, "Until properly investigated, all evidence should be—"

"I *have* been properly investigated, so return my bag, thank you." Brownie didn't let him finish. No one was allowed to tease Rufus on her watch.

"Here you are, Minstrel Bronwynn." Jack pulled her bag from out of nowhere. "I took the liberty of liberating your bag for you."

Brownie let a tiny little bit of the hostility she held toward the man go. Just a bit. "Thank you."

She took the bag and slung it over her head, then opened the flap to see if anything else had gone missing.

"If you are wondering," Jack said before she had the chance to ask, "your money was still in the bag when I left it in Lady Tate's room. And it went walking between there and here."

"Looks like there are a few *other* rogues in the duke's employ," Rufus said dryly. Brownie noticed he too had relaxed when Jack handed over the bag.

"You say that like it's a bad thing." Jack smiled and flicked his head so his hair wouldn't fall in front of his face.

"The duke will replace the stolen money, I'm sure," Pjori cut in. "So let us get this over and done with, shall we?"

Jack and Rufus both made to reply, but Brownie was faster and louder. "Rufus and Pjori both heard my testimony. I don't know anything about Lady Tate other than she has questionable taste in fashion and a job to melt Duke Wyldon. She didn't. The end."

Rufus covered his smile with a paw, and Pjori snorted. Jack nodded seriously, as if everything she'd said was of extreme importance. "Perfect. I'll accompany these two to the capital to report to the duke. You may join us or remain here until your performance request expires."

"Why do you want Minstrel Bronwynn to join us?" Rufus demanded.

He stood up and offered Brownie a paw. As she took it, she remembered him doing the same for Lady Tate, and Brownie held it longer than she needed to.

They were such soft and tempting paws.

"Because she knows enough about the slave trade, the Assassin's Guild, and what its members look like that she might be able to recognize someone. I only stayed with the actual transport crew; Minstrel Bronwynn here could recognize the undercover agents in Duchess Calisto's employ, or in town, or—"

"The only person I know who got away that I could recognize is *you*," Brownie retorted.

"I'm easily recognizable, it's true," Jack shot back, "but we didn't capture *everyone* that night. An extra set of eyes would go a long way. I heard the young spy that Marquess Dorset captured escaped as well."

"He wasn't working for the slave traders or the Servalt Assassin's Guild. He was a Blackfog spy," Brownie pointed out.

"Still—"

"Minstrel Bronwynn," Pjori cut in. "Are you coming or not?"

Rufus looked like he wanted to say something, but he held his tongue. She had originally been planning on joining him in the capital anyway. She wanted to go shopping and maybe start a sudden citywide musical number or two.

Servalt's capital had some very on-key shopkeepers.

This sounded as good as a sudden citywide musical number . . . and who said she couldn't still fit one in on the new timetable?

Brownie smiled. "Of course I'm coming."

CHAPTER 35

Bramblebriar

Rufus

I was going to *throttle* Jack Laverick.

The man had happily invited *my* bard—ahem, *travel companion* to accompany us on a highly dangerous trip . . . and Bronwynn was a civilian, no less. Seeing how friendly Jack was being to Bronwynn, I was starting to suspect that maybe, just *maybe*, the duke was also having suspicions about her.

He wasn't an idiot. And despite how certain I was that she was innocent, Bronwynn was consistently at or around every molten ash vane sighting. It wasn't advanced mythical magery.

"Are you sure?" I spoke as gently as my turbulent thoughts allowed. This could be a set up. Or dangerous. Or—

"I'm sure." Bronwynn smiled at me, and my worries faded. They were still there, but they were insignificant and small when faced with her enthusiasm. She was going to have a blast; I could already tell. My stomach flipped in anxious spasms, but I pushed away the feeling.

Bronwynn was her own person and could make her own decisions, I reminded myself for what felt like the thousandth time. "Then we need to have a plan before we go."

Up until this point my plan had been to go to the Assassin's Guild, shake down the "boss," get her to sign a new treaty, and maybe find out something about the molten ash vane. And of course, watch Bronwynn from afar to see if she had any shady dealings about the capital. Now, she'd be coming to *our* shady dealings. Sigh.

"I can be ready to go within the hour," Bronwynn offered.

"I'll make my own way to the capital and meet you there," Pjori said.

Jack nodded. "Likewise. I still have a few things to finish up here before I leave. I've heard that one of our staff was unkind to Minstrel Bronwynn?"

"It wasn't that bad." Bronwynn shrugged, and as much as I wanted to unleash my frustrations about the staff . . . it wasn't my place to do that. It was Bronwynn's.

Jack raised an eyebrow. "Then I'm sure a simple talk will suffice."

"If we're all meeting in the capital"—I crossed my arms—"How will you find us?"

It was only a few hours' ride to Servalt's palace city, but if we weren't traveling together, then we needed a meeting point.

Pjori and Bronwynn turned to Jack. The human returned their gaze confidently. "We can meet at the Wistful Cup Inn. I know the owners, so just say Jack sent you, and we can use one of their private rooms going forward."

With that, we all left to get ready.

The trip from Heatherfeld to Calis, the capital of Servalt, was short and sweet.

Calis was near the eastern coast, and the crisp seawater breeze carried the unmistakable hint of algae and ocean. I sneezed a few times when it hit me, but it wasn't an unpleasant smell. The city itself had walls that dwarfed the tallest dwarf; even one with the highest-level [Control: Size] skill that could become larger than the trees of the Dark Enchanted Forest.

Brambles with thorns as long as my palm grew on the city walls.

Queen Delia's mother, the Countess Bloom, had been cursed with a sleeping sickness in her youth. The only way to break the curse was to prick her finger with the thorn of the bramblebriar—a rare magical vine that was only found in ancient dragon lairs. Luckily, Her Eminence Feliwyn had hoarded a few seeds she was willing to trade for a very special deal. If Countess Bloom's family allocated a portion of their printing paper for the dragon's use, they could have the magical plant that would break the curse.

I myself had read many of the lurid romance novels written and published by that dragon; they were works of literary genius! Full of dread pirates and outlaw dukes and fae queens. Perfection.

And so, the walls had been used to grow the bramblebriar, and Bloom had awoken with a gentle stab to the finger, and everyone had lived happily ever after.

The plant had even proven pivotal to the war efforts during the revolution, keeping Queen Delia and King Astor safe during the long siege until reinforcements from North Sumbria could arrive.

But that was in the past, and today, we rolled into town through open gates.

"This place is beautiful." Bronwynn sighed, admiring the thousands of colorful pennants strung above the streets. All of the buildings were painted in a mix of two or more vibrant colors, and the cobblestones were actually made of rusty red bricks that clinked under the wagon wheels. The majority of the residents were of elven descent, but many half elves and other races walked the streets. People were smiling, and the late afternoon sunshine was bright and welcoming.

I nodded, lifting one paw to cover my eyes as I peered down the road. The Wistful Cup Inn wasn't within sight of the city gate, so we'd need to hail a guard for directions. We'd want to be settled in before dinner.

Good afternoon, all!

Suddenly, the crystal towers for the Cast Network flashed, and a familiar voice rang out over the crowds. Donna stopped as everyone came to a standstill to listen to the announcement.

> **This is Madame Potts, back with the latest news.**
> **Gerald the Grey is looking for his hat. It was last seen in Colwood, but he lost it on his way to Calis, poor man. If anyone sees the magical flying hat, they might bring it to any Mages Tower representative or magical guild for a hefty reward. Be careful! It bites.**
> **The Dungeon Valley Deep is suffering a glitch on the sixth floor, so don't bother hunting rover rolls. Until further notice, they aren't able to be looted properly and provide no instant drops. You can still gain experience points from the hunt, though.**
> **I saw that Slake Drakeford, Adventurer Extraordinaire, will be in the Dark Enchanted Forest tomorrow, so if you are on the roads, you might catch a peek of the legend himself. Pets are always appreciated, but be sure to ask first.**
> **The wedding for Countess Peregrine and Knight Commander Bastian is set to create a political connection between Sumbria and Peldeep for the first time in over a century. A special announcement for all involved: Anyone living in Peldeep should be warned that Sumbrian nobles are all a bunch of pompous and ruthless idiots ready to try and flog you in the street if you so much as look at them. The delegations from Sumbria should be warned that if they actually try it, their bodies will never be recovered. Merfolk make the most amazing arts and crafts out of elf bones that I've ever seen.**
> **The sixth prince, Lucial Neftor from the Empire of Sands, visited Peldeep on his way home from Grand Duchess Calisto's Spring Ball, and hasn't left yet. This madame thinks love is in the air and he is courting one of Their Royal Highness Rowen's children. No word yet as to who has caught the prince's eye, but he's going to find himself in trouble this weekend if he doesn't go after his lover. You need to overcome your doubts, or you'll lose everything, Lucial.**
> **If anyone is looking for blue ore, they can travel to Drendil's west coast in three days. Two pirate ship's containing the material are in**

a battle on the open seas right as I speak. Their ships are going to sink, and the cargo will start washing ashore by the end of the week.
That's everything, folks.
Yours truly, Madame Potts

CHAPTER 36

Who Do You Think is Madame Potts?

Brownie

Even before the Crystal Cast ended, Bronwynn was looking up along with everyone else. Brownie craned her head around and shaded her eyes with one hand, but found only clear blue skies.

"Any hat in sight?" Rufus asked. When Brownie met his eyes, she wondered if he'd joined in the search at all. He was staring at her so comfortably, with a gentle smile that made her heart beat faster.

"Nothing," she got out, trying to ignore her awareness of the beastman sitting inches from her. If she leaned over, she could . . . "We should get going. I think there's a city guard station a few stores down."

Rufus nodded. "Lead on."

Donna didn't need any more encouragement, trekking through the still distracted crowd. Wonders upon wonders, she didn't step on anyone.

"So," Brownie said. She needed to get the idea of hugging Rufus's fluffy arms and petting his soft fur while he smiled at her like earlier out of her head. To do so, she picked the most interesting topic on the continent. "Who do *you* think is Madame Potts?"

Rufus hesitated, his brows furrowed in thought. "I mean, I shouldn't say this . . ."

"What?"

She was immediately very interested in what Rufus Triever *shouldn't* say about Madame Potts. Brownie even leaned toward him with enthusiasm. "Tell me!"

"The Black Fortress . . . Well, the castle staff have a bet going on in the break room. It's been up for a few years now," Rufus explained, reaching up and massaging his neck awkwardly. "And the leading guess was tied with . . . you."

"Really?!" Brownie burst into laughter at that absurd thought. "*Me?* As Madame Potts?"

"Of course, *I've* never thought that." Rufus slapped his hand against his chest.

"Oh?" She appreciated the sentiment, and at the same time, basked in the idea that people out there thought that Minstrel Bronwynn Lyriel was *the* Madame Potts. Madame Potts was a *legend*.

"I always assumed it must be Duchess Calisto." Rufus shrugged. "But I'm told that's not the case."

"I always thought it was Their Royal Highness," Brownie confessed.

That got a chuckle out of her travel partner. "The ruler of Peldeep? Rowen *is* dramatic enough for it, I suppose."

"And from what I've heard, they've never questioned Madame Potts's predictions!" Brownie waved her hands dramatically. "Not from the very beginning!"

"Good thing too. Do you remember the first serious prophecy involving Peldeep?" Rufus asked, sounding amused.

Brownie, in fact, did not remember. She shook her head.

"That Their Royal Highness would get assassinated in their bathtub," Rufus stated dryly. "Apparently, some alchemist assassin got molten ash vane into the bathwater."

Brownie whistled softly, wrapping her arms around herself at the thought. It was not a pleasant way to die. "I see."

Rufus added, "I don't think Their Royal Highness sounds like the woman, though."

"Who says that Madame Potts is a woman?" Brownie countered. "She could be anyone with a voice-changing amulet."

Rufus hailed the city guard as they approached. "Excuse me, but where can we find the Wistful Cup?"

"Two streets up and turn left. You can't miss it!" the guard replied, pointing them in the right direction. Rufus nodded a thank you while Donna followed the new directions on her own. Having a smart horse was wonderful . . . most of the time.

"Honestly, it's lucky Their Royal Highness heard the Cast and trusted it." Brownie continued the conversation as they moseyed up the street.

"Technically, Knight Commander Bastian heard it and burst in on the ruler before they'd set foot in the royal tub." Rufus shivered. "Bastian was elevated to his current position because he risked his life to do so."

"Then wouldn't it *not* be Their Royal Highness?" Brownie frowned, her mind racing. "Who Crystal Casts a premonition about their own demise while preparing to get into a tub of permadeath?"

"To see who was willing to stop you?" Rufus reasoned. "And Their Royal Highness is exceptional about their privacy, so no one knows much about them in their private life."

"So they might or might *not* be Madame Potts." Brownie nodded. This conversation didn't disprove her original theory, but it did give her more to think about. "Whoever she is, she was at the Dark Lord and Heroine's wedding. We were standing in a field with *the* Madame Potts."

Rufus chuckled. "Apparently, Chloe [Resurrected] the madame once."

"What?!"

"Yes, Madame Potts sent Chloe a letter as thanks."

"No! That's amazing!" Brownie dropped the pretense of driving the carriage entirely as she let go of the reins to clap with excitement. "Does she remember the people she'd saved right before that ?"

Rufus shook his head sadly. "There'd been a bunch of natural disasters and floods that month; it could've been one out of a hundred."

"Then does that mean that Madame Potts lives in the Dark Enchanted Forest? Wait, hold that thought." Brownie loved discussing the enigmatic, reclusive woman, but Donna had come to a stop in front of the Wistful Cup. It was time to dismount and get to sorting out stabling.

The inn was sprawling, with white-and-blue outer walls and a quaint slanted brown roof. The capital city buildings were full of whimsy, and this was also the case with the Wistful Cup. Wooden cutout teacups had been placed in decorative circles on the outer walls, and the ledges had alternating blue and white panels carved to look like waves.

Each room had its own peaked window, shutters open, and fresh pink-and-white flowers hung from the windowsills.

"You got room for us?" Brownie called out, waving to a stable hand carrying a pitchfork and a bucket.

The stable hand, a short older lady with long ears which pointed straight upward and sharp eyes, raised an eyebrow at them. Her pale face was spotted with blemishes that stood out against her flushed cheeks, and her long white hair was braided with a few wisps framing her face. "Aye. But you're gonna need to store that wagon elsewhere."

The beastwoman, for I assumed she was a beastfolk who preferred walking around in her folk form, clapped her hands together loudly.

"Yes, Mistress May?" A troll poked his head up from one of the horse stalls behind her. He was a darker green than Gerda, with short, cropped hair and thin eyebrows.

"Can you help our customers bring their wagon over to Trader Tulip's?" Mistress May leaned against her pitchfork. Brownie considered storing the wagon in her ring for only a second before deciding against it. She didn't trust any establishment that was friendly with Jack Laverick.

"Right away, Mistress!" The troll came out to help unhitch Donna. Brownie let them do the heavy work—she preferred not risking her fingers to manual jobs as often as possible. There had been this one time, before she'd become famous, that she'd broken her wrist while helping her neighbor in Drendil carry water the morning before a show; that had *not* been a fun night. At least when she'd sprained her finger cleaning out the dungeon with her cousins in Peldeep, they'd had potions to spare.

It's why she paid to carry around a healing potion and antidote! You never knew when you'd be forced to play before a visiting duchess with one arm in a cast.

"Thank you." Brownie and Rufus grabbed their things and hopped down, letting the green fellow lift the wagon and roll it away. The troll nodded at her before heading out.

"No need to worry about your wagon," Mistress May stated, swinging her pitchfork up and over her shoulder gracefully. "Trader Tulip is well and above board, and has a guarded storage lot for her merchants. It'll be four copper a night to leave it there, and I'll add it to your account. A room and stable board is six copper."

"Make that two rooms, please," Rufus interjected. He adjusted his bag on his shoulder and looked up at the inn, then back at Brownie. "Are we staying just the one night?"

"I thought you were going to meet Jack and then continue on to the castle?" Brownie shrugged. She loved his company and wasn't in a hurry to get rid of the attractive beastman.

"You're here to see Jack, are you?" Mistress May stuck a finger toward the entrance. "Make sure to tell Amber that when you check in. She'll get you all settled. I'll take care of your mare here." Donna, who up until this point had been side-eyeing and investigating her temporary home, turned to Mistress May. The mare let out a huff before wandering over to greet the old woman.

"It's nice to meet you too, Donna." Mistress May smiled for the first time as Donna butted her head gently against the woman's shoulder. "I have just the right stall for you. Come this way."

Brownie stared on in disbelief as her horse affectionately followed Mistress May into the back of the stable. That woman must have a skill. It was the only way.

"Shall we?" Rufus drew her back to the present, nodding toward the door.

They walked into the Wistful Cup just in time to watch a drakin half transform in the lobby and breathe out a burst of fire.

CHAPTER 37

Singed Fur Is No Joke

Rufus

I was impressed by the control the drakin woman showed as she carefully adjusted her flames, bringing the large hearth back up to a roaring happy fire. A great cauldron hung over the flames, full of bubbling water.

"One," *cough*, "moment." She let out a puff of smoke and then transformed from a large, scaled, winged, fire-breathing dragon woman to a petite human-looking creature with flaming red hair, bright red eyes, and black skin.

We waited as the young woman shook herself a bit and then greeted us politely. "I'm Amber! Welcome to the Wistful Cup! Where every room comes with a complimentary tea service. How may I help you today?"

Bronwynn stepped forward. "We'd like two rooms, and Mistress May is dealing with our horse and wagon."

"All right, follow me to the counter and we can check you in." Amber bobbed a polite curtsy and led us to a large wooden desk with ledgers laid out.

"We're also supposed to mention," I added, "that Jack sent us." I didn't enjoy saying it, but business was business. The man was insufferable, and I wasn't glad to be associated with him, but Amber didn't seem to share my dislike; she immediately beamed a huge smile at us. "Wonderful! I'll let you know when he is here and ready to see you. Any friend of Jack's is a friend of ours. Here are your keys. I've got you two top-floor rooms facing the street. If you have any questions or concerns, let me know."

"Thank you, Amber," Bronwynn said. "What did you say about complimentary tea?"

Amber reached down and pulled out a thin wooden slat beautifully carved with a list of teas and tea accessories. "You have one of these in your rooms," Amber explained. "Anytime, once a day, you may place an order for tea at no charge. After that, the usual costs apply. All of our teas are sourced directly from the Pixie Prim, and we pride ourselves on an excellent cup."

As a connoisseur of fine beverages, the Pixie Prim was one of my favorites—and not just because they were from the Dark Enchanted Forest. The pixies really knew how to care for plants, and their tea was no exception. Ignoring Jack, this inn was proving to be a perfect choice.

"Alright. I look forward to it." Bronwynn lifted her bags, and we headed for the open spiral staircase. On the left-hand side of the stair, there was a doorway that said "Tea Room," and to the right, "First Floor Rooms." The lobby itself opened up all the way to the third floor.

We found our rooms easily and settled our things before agreeing to meet in the Tea Room after.

I didn't have much to unpack, so I paced a bit to pass the time before heading back down. Nothing like a good pacing.

Before I could walk into the Tea Room, Amber headed me off and let me know that Jack was waiting in a private room. Bronwynn still hadn't come down.

That might actually be a good thing; I wanted to get a chance to talk to Pjori and Jack without Bronwynn. It was time to clear up a few things.

The two were waiting for me, drinking tea in a meeting room on the first floor.

"Well met, Rufus," Pjori greeted from his chair farthest from the cozy fire. He was nursing a cold cup of chai, by the smell, and Jack was sitting next to him drinking Lady Green.

Jack leaned back in his large armchair. "I told you this place was the best."

"You told me this place was safe to talk business," Pjori countered, but it was obvious he wasn't too committed to arguing as he happily sipped from his glass.

"Are we getting straight to business, then?" I asked, taking the third out of the four chairs set up for this meeting. I sat across from Pjori so I wasn't right beside the fire. I didn't want to be; singed fur was no joke.

"You could order tea first," Jack suggested.

"*Or* I can say that I don't appreciate your choice to drag Minstrel Bronwynn into this mess and *kindly* ask you to explain your employer's plan for her," I said, crossing my arms and leaning back into my own chair. It was very comfortable, with good lower-back support and a small blue-and-white pillow.

Pjori and Jack shared a look, and Jack finally looked serious. "The bard is a suspect."

"Of course she is," I countered, stating the obvious. "She's been at multiple molten ash vane sightings, and you can confirm yourself she was at the last two. You also know that she probably wasn't working for your assassin employer if she also got kidnapped."

Hearing about that day, and the trials my favorite bard—er, and my queen—had suffered still made my stomach clench and churn.

"So you know . . . Is that the reason you're traveling with her? To test her?" Pjori asked.

"Among other reasons," I admitted. "But so far, I haven't seen anything at all that relates to the assassination cases or her involvement. The only lead was a false lead you yourself planted, Jack."

"It was *perfection*. A proper excuse to question the bard without giving anything away. I wasn't expecting you and Page Saryl to defend her so adamantly. Luckily, I am very smart and came up with another excuse on the fly." Jack puffed out his chest.

Pjori added, "It *was* a good idea. I didn't know any of this and was ready to properly investigate her at the party."

"You"—Jack waved a hand at me—"are making it hard to follow through with my questioning. Stop getting in the way."

"All of that just to get her alone today?"

"Yes." Jack smiled. "Today, you're going to let us do our job. Ah, and here she is now."

CHAPTER 38

His Golden Eyes Locked on Her Tongue

Brownie

Brownie decided to make use of the tepid water basin to wash off a bit of the road. Before she went downstairs, she did a basic check on the doors, the windows, and the exits. If she jumped from her window, which conveniently opened wide enough for her to clear with ease, then she would land mere feet from her horse at the front of the inn.

The hallway ended in a big window overlooking the side of the building opposite the horse stable. It was a narrow section just big enough to walk single file along, and it would make a great escape route—especially if she could clear the jump onto the next-door roof, which was only two levels.

With a kick in her step and her instrument slung over her shoulder, Brownie wandered downstairs.

"The others are waiting for you this way!" Amber smiled at her and showed her to a private room. When Brownie walked inside, she noted that Pjori, Jack, and Rufus were already seated. Rufus was perusing the tea menu in the chair closest to her.

He looked up and gave her a pained smile. "The waitress will be back in just a second, want to share a menu?"

"That sounds great."

The other two were happily sipping their own drinks as Brownie leaned over the beastman to stare at the menu. She was surprisingly conscious that her hair tickled his shoulder and he flinched, but the two of them ignored it. At least, she tried to ignore it.

She had just finished dragging her eyes over the menu when the waitress came to take their order and she took her seat.

"It's good to have you here with us, Minstrel Bronwynn," Jack started, putting his cup aside and leaning back into his chair, crossing his legs. She noticed that Pjori, too, put his cup aside.

"Honestly, I'm happy to be of help." She slapped a fist into her open palm. "Just point me in their direction, and I'll tell you if I recognize anyone who might have gotten away. I got a good look at the undercover castle staff and the other slave traders—not that *you* should need help identifying the slave traders."

She couldn't resist the jab.

Jack didn't seem to mind, however, and nodded encouragingly. "That's all we can ask. I'm also wondering if you can tell me about some of the assassination attempts you've seen? I wasn't at the party today, but I understand this wasn't your first time witnessing a hit?"

Brownie tapped her chin in contemplation while her mind raced with possible answers. Finally, she settled on, "Yes, I've performed for a lot of very powerful people. I've seen a couple assassination attempts in my time, including today. There was this one time in Sumbria, a rebel attacked the royals in their theater box. And of course, I was at the Spring Ball. But only the attacks by Marquess Chadwick and Lady Tate were made by Servalt assassins . . . The Sumbrian royal's were attacked by other Sumbrians."

"I should point out," Rufus added, "that Peldeep also had that molten ash vane assassination attempt, but the maid found guilty was from the Empire of Sands."

Jack frowned. "They could still be working with Servalt."

"Aren't you going to the Assassin's Guild?" Brownie turned to Rufus. "Why don't you just ask?"

"You're going to the Assassin's Guild?" Pjori asked. He raised an eyebrow at the commander general.

"After this." Rufus shrugged. "I'm going to negotiate terms with the new guild leader."

"You can't," Jack stated, matter of fact. "Now, if we could—"

Rufus cut him off. "And why not?"

Brownie wondered how Jack planned on stopping a high-level commander general of the Dark Lord's army from carrying out his quest, and hoped her Mint O' Mile tea came soon. And snacks.

"Because 'the boss' isn't like Gloria," Jack said. He nursed the last bit of his tea in his hands, resting it on his lap. "She doesn't accept meetings, and she will ambush anyone who is dumb enough to fall for one. Now, can we get *back to the matter at hand?*"

Oh, that was interesting. Brownie noticed how Rufus awkwardly glanced between her and Jack before giving in. "Alright, but we need to talk about this 'boss' later. I have a quest to meet with her, and my king won't take kindly to excuses."

Brownie wondered if Jack realized that Rufus was leading him on. If he turned around and went home right now because it was too dangerous to proceed once Rufus had learned that the meeting was actually a trap, King Keith wouldn't bat an eyelash. He'd just take Rufus's word at face value, and they would make a new plan. Henrietta's husband didn't have a micromanaging bone in his whole body, and he carried an unnatural trust in his subordinates . . . Maybe it was a skill?

"Minstrel Bronwynn—"

"Brownie," she interrupted Jack. "Everyone can just call me Brownie. Unless you're hiring my musical services, I'm here to help as just myself. And calling out 'Minstrel Bronwynn' all the time is getting a bit old."

Pjori nodded approval from his chair, and Jack gave her a long-suffering expression from constantly being interrupted.

She had no sympathy.

"As I was saying," Jack said, firmly. "If you could just tell us more about the assassin from Sumbria? I'd like to know what they looked like?"

"There were actually four assassins at the Sumbrian Royal Theater." Brownie tapped her chin.

A knock sounded three times on the door. At Pjori's acknowledgement, the waitress opened it to bring in a trolley with Rufus and Brownie's tea, and a collection of baked snacks. She also brought in two teapots full of steeped tea refills for Pjori and Jack.

Jack was strangely quiet, but his hands shook slightly as they gripped his cup.

Maybe he had a thing about being interrupted? Her Aunt Luna, a Celestial Maiden, would positively glow in the dark when people interrupted her. Sometimes, she even emitted [Light] damage in an area of effect if she wasn't properly respected. Luckily, Uncle Gordon worshiped the ground she walked on and was ever in her favor.

Brownie thanked the waitress and accepted her teacup of aromatic meadowmint and early-spring chamomile blend. She closed her eyes, appreciating the full experience as she took her first sip of the high-quality beverage.

"Ooh, hot!"

Rufus laughed. Watching her blow on her drink, he set his teacup aside and opted to sample a cookie instead. Brownie stuck her tongue out at the beastman. His golden eyes locked on her tongue, and he flushed a bit, looking away.

"SO! Back to the questioning! You said there were *four* assassins?" Jack got her attention again. He spoke slowly and with purpose . . . so much so that her years as a Rogue told her that maybe, just maybe, he was hiding something.

"Yes . . ." Brownie looked around. Pjori was quietly sipping his tea and eyeing the entire affair just as he'd done in the holding cell. Rufus had looked *sheepish* when she arrived . . . and Jack was Jack.

Ah.

[You have attempted to activate the Perk: **Liar's Palace**. You have succeeded.]

CHAPTER 39

I Would've Noticed a Bunch of Elves Running Around

Rufus

I knew that Jack had failed the interrogation the second the words had left his mouth.

Sure, Bronwynn . . . Brownie? He liked the name Bronwynn. It was beautiful, just like her. Maybe he could get away with just calling her Bronwynn. It irked him that she had told all of them to call her so casually. It would have been nice to have it naturally play out between the two of them.

Another reason to make this harder on Jack.

"They were all elves from Sumbria, and only one of them had an enchanted dagger with molten ash vane," Brownie said. She was telling the truth. My Perception thirty would have caught on, especially since I knew her so well. "I tackled the leader from the stage and prevented him from succeeding in the attack."

"You *what*?!" My blood pressure rose so fast that I was worried I'd see red. I whipped my head around to stare at the half giantess across from me. "You tackled a man carrying molten ash vane?"

She shrugged like she hadn't almost dissolved into nothingness, leaving me— leaving the world without her in it.

I had to calm down and retract my claws from the armchair. One was stuck, distracting me for a moment, since I didn't want to absolutely shred the blasted upholstery freeing it.

"I'm fine," Brownie replied. "Anyway, the four elves wearing purple fichu were carted away; purple accessories are the symbol of the rebellion forces that still live in Sumbria today, or so I learned. No one got hurt, and the royals were ungrateful and left without so much as a thank you. Can you believe it?" She tsked, obviously unimpressed. I was still trying to calm my fast-beating heart.

Jack nodded. "I see."

"Anything else you wanna know?" The slight lilt in her voice made me pain-fully aware that she knew. I knew she knew, but Jack didn't seem to catch on.

The man picked up a tart but didn't eat it. He was fiddling with it in his hands. I wondered if he knew he was getting crumbs on his leather pants.

"Have you ever been in the same city as other molten ash vane attacks that you could tell us the gossip for?" Jack asked innocently. "You travel a lot."

"Technically, I was visiting my cousins when Madame Potts foretold that Their Royal Highness was going to be assassinated. But I only found out the whole story when Rufus told me about it on the way here." She shrugged. No lie detected; another truth.

Jack looked at me askance, and I nodded. He turned back to Bronwynn and took a sip of his tea. "And Duke Francis?"

"What about Duke Francis?" Bronwynn tilted her head, sending her curls tumbling over her shoulder. I loved her curls; they were playful and wild, but controlled in bouncing loose ringlets that came down to her collarbone. She sounded as confused as she looked.

Jack raised an eyebrow. "Did you see any Servalt or Sumbrian elves at Duke Francis's birthday celebration? I heard you performed for the man before his attempted assassination."

"Wait, what?" Bronwynn frowned and leaned forward in her chair. "Duke Francis was targeted?"

"Yes," Jack said. "Unfortunately, the Drendil royalty kept the entire thing as secure as a dragon's hoard. We've been unable to gain any details on the entire affair, not even if molten ash vane was used . . . But from the carpentry order, it seems like something burned a giant hole in the floorboards."

Bronwynn leaned back in her chair, her hand raised to her chin, and the other supporting her elbow. She was deep in thought, and no one pushed further until she had a chance to think.

"Alright," she started; I felt my stomach drop out from under me. She couldn't be admitting—"I'll recount the day as best I can."

Ah. Well, I was an idiot.

The minstrel told everyone the tale, repeating everything she'd told me plus a few extra details for the investigation notes: Where the duke was sitting. Who he was sitting with. What time it was when she rode off into the sunset. Jack nodded politely along to the story, and Pjori took notes.

"And that's all?" Jack pressed. I noted that he was gripping his cup very tight . . . It would be amazing if the vessel broke. I could only hope.

"That's all."

There was a newfound strained silence in the room. Jack downed the rest of his cup and placed it on the side table.

And then there was a knock on the door. The waitress came in and offered to refill our tea from the teapots. Everyone agreed, and the waitress left again.

Jack regained some of his earlier composure. He blew on his now third cup of tea. "So you have no idea if Sumbria or Servalt had anything to do with Duke Francis's assassination attempt?"

She shrugged. "Drendil is almost entirely human. I would have noticed if a bunch of elves were running around. I think I might have even been the only nonehuman there."

"I see."

At that point, Pjori tapped his small booklet with his parchment pen. "Thank you, Minstrel Bronwynn; you've been an incredible help to our investigation."

"You're welcome." She bobbed a nod over her own tea where she had her cup nestled in both hands in front of her. She turned to stare at me. "If that is all, should we finish and get going to the Assassin's Guild?"

"Hold on," I said. "What do you mean, *we?*"

CHAPTER 40

The Bad Side of the Pixie Prim

Brownie

Watching Rufus get flustered was surprisingly enjoyable, and Brownie happily explained to the beastman why she had decided to go with him.

"You don't need me in the guild with you. You need me on standby when the boss betrays your meeting and tries to take advantage of you." Brownie waved at Jack. "He's already said you shouldn't go and it's a trap. Besides, I can look for our runaway slave trader if they show up at the Guild."

Rufus was glaring daggers at Jack. When his golden eyes caught hers, she paused.

"If you follow me," he said, staring at her so intently that she felt the hair rise at the nape of her neck. His voice was low. "You will be needlessly put in harm's way."

"I don't think they will care if I hang around outside . . ." She trailed off.

Rufus stood up and put his tea aside. He sounded like it was pulling teeth to get the words out of him. "I am not going to stop you from doing what you think is best. But I am a delegate from the kingdom of Nilheim, with all the power and security that allows me. I am also over level fifty."

He didn't say that she was none of these things, but Brownie felt the weight of his words nonetheless. She hesitated.

Then Pjori cut in. "Have neither of you *been* to the Assassin's Guild?"

"Shh!" Jack was sipping his tea, amusement written clearly on his face. "Don't tell them."

The two turned on Pjori. The storm kelpie coughed. "The Assassin's Guild is the building next door."

"What?" Rufus crossed his arms, still the only one standing at this point. Brownie thought about joining him in a show of solidarity against Jack . . . but she hadn't finished her dessert.

"That's why we chose to make the Wistful Cup our base of operations," Jack explained. "One eye on the enemy. And if Miss Brownie is staying here, then she'll have ample opportunity to notice any familiar faces on the street."

"I am scheduled to meet with a representative of the Assassin's Guild outside the Artful Acorn in one hour's time." Rufus looked between Jack and Brownie.

"That is two doors down, past the guild," Jack informed helpfully.

Brownie took a bite of tart. The cherries were simmered in sugar beforehand, and the entire treat was a slowly savored delight. If only a handsome beastman weren't staring at her while she ate that tart. There were so many crumbs.

"I'm leaving now," Rufus told her, and she hurriedly took another bite.

Brownie had barely finished, but she stood up and brushed off her outfit. "Then I guess I'll wander upstairs to keep watch? How long do you think it should take?"

"An hour." Rufus looked like he wanted to say something more but chose otherwise.

Brownie hummed. "Then if it's longer, I'll start to worry."

He stiffened but nodded. Then he turned to the two still seated. "I hope that now that you've invited us here, you will be sure to keep this building secure in my absence. I'll be leaving my things upstairs."

Jack waved away his concern. "The Wistful Cup is neutral ground and under the protection of many different parties."

"Nobody wants to get on the bad side of the Pixie Prim," Pjori added, shaking his head. "Even I know that, and I'm not from here."

Rufus nodded and walked to the door, opening it up politely for Brownie. She glanced over her shoulder at him and said, "Goodbye," then walked out of the interrogation room with her head held high . . . and forty-nine seconds remaining on her [Liar's Palace].

Following Rufus to the Assassin's Guild was the perfect excuse to follow Rufus out of that room. She'd noticed around the same time he did that there was more to her being there than just as an accessory to her previous experiences with the slave traders . . . and she was giving Rufus the benefit of the doubt that he wasn't in on the entire thing.

His outright anger at Jack made her feel slightly reassured.

The unfortunate thing about the Assassin's Guild being right next door, and the meeting place for Rufus two doors down from that, was that she couldn't just sit in a chair and watch at the window. She had to crane her neck to stare down the street while Rufus set up kicking his heels outside a shop down the way.

At least he was as tall as she was, which was to say very tall, and easily spotted.

The assassins discovered as much; three approached him earlier than his appointed time. Technically, two approached him, and the third hovered close by, pretending to be interested in something that was on display in a storefront window. Brownie knew immediately they were Assassins. Once you picked up the signs, it was easy to tell most of the Rogue classes apart.

The generic signs were obvious; [Silent Steps], [Soft Foot], [Hide Tracks], [Shadowstep]. There were so many different perks that came with a Rogue-based class. They all had the same thing in common: that the person moving left no trace of their passage. And not just sound, but the stylized way they moved just screamed "don't look at me" and "I'm not here." It gave away the class to anyone who knew what they were looking for.

Brownie had grown up surrounded by family members who specialized in obfuscation. She even had Rogue as her coming-of-age class, not that she told people that. Don't get her started; Brownie loved her family, she just loved music more. She was very lucky that her family's training in the [Rogue] class gave her improved dexterity that helped her play her instrument, but she was equally lucky that her family her decision to become a bard since it brought her joy.

Maybe she would swing by and visit her cousins when she got home; she didn't always stay long enough to see everyone between her trips.

Or not. What with everyone up in arms over the molten ash vane, it would be better to lay low.

Rufus and the two assassins finished talking. Sure enough, they walked back toward the Wistful Cup, and into the building next door.

Now it was just hoping Jack was wrong, and Rufus made it out again in one piece.

CHAPTER 41

At No Point Did I Break Jack's Nose

Rufus

I was a calm beastman, usually.

The only thing that got me excited was a romance novel or a Minstrel Bronwynn concert, so I wasn't in the practice of needing to hold back my temper. After today, I felt that I'd been tried and tested, and had come out admirably.

At no point did I break Jack's nose. And while the man was a competent attendant and an excellent spy, he was also directly responsible for Bronwynn sitting in a window watching me being led into danger.

Bronwynn, who was excellent at jumping out of windows.

Jack had put a civilian in danger. Sure, she wasn't from the Dark Enchanted Forest, and she wasn't my responsibility. But by the gods, I was the leader of her fan club, and it was my duty to . . . I don't know. Prevent her from breaking her fingers going up against a bunch of assassins late on a weeknight.

"This way, Commander General," the young man wearing a casual white tunic and button-up trousers said, opening the door to the Assassin's Guild. His companion remained outside, leaning against the wall of the building. We walked down a short hallway that ended in a reception room where an elf woman leaned back in a chair behind a desk; her feet were up on it and crossed over nonchalantly. A piece of paper lay on her face, blotting out the light. When the door closed behind us with an audible *click*, I realized how otherwise quiet the entire place had been up until that point.

"Aren't you supposed to—" The elf lifted the sheet of paper with one hand before stopping when she saw the two of us. A huge smile bloomed on her face as she promptly dropped her feet to the floor and stood up. "Well, hello!"

"It is nice to meet you. I am Commander General Rufus Triever." I noticed with interest that the woman looked like a Barbarian class. Her light brown arms were as thick as my legs, and her long brown hair trailed to her hips. Tufts of fur stuck out of her lightweight chest plate. She came up to my chin.

Her smile got bigger as she reached out a hand and I shook it.

"Eva Lina, at your service. You're early, and things aren't ready yet, but I'm sure we can find *something* to do in the meantime."

All of the hair rose on my arm, and I had a feeling that whatever Eva Lina wanted to do . . . I wouldn't like it one bit.

I didn't drop her hand like a hot salamander, as much as I wanted to. Instead, I finished the handshake then politely released it in a casual manner. The hardest part, actually, was not wiping my hand on my pants when we were done. I hid my unease behind a confident smile and my passive skills. "It is good to meet you, Miss Eva. You needn't concern yourself; I was the one who arrived early. I can wait until the appointed time."

"You're no fun." Eva pouted, putting her now free hand on her stuck-out hip. She thumped herself back down in her seat and put her feet back up on the table.

The human who brought me inside let out a quiet sigh. He stood in front of the desk, grimacing at the pile of documents haphazardly fallen on its otherwise clean surface. For some reason, I had a feeling Miss Eva wasn't sitting at her own desk. I felt for the poor man.

"Jimothy, go tell Susan that our *guest* is here early." Eva leveraged the chair backward, from four legs on the floor to precariously balancing on only the back two. She linked her hands behind her head.

"Right away," *cough*, "Miss Eva." Jimothy straightened and nodded at me before leaving through a door on the other wall that led deeper into the guild.

I stood there for some time, but instead of letting the quiet go on comfortably, I said, "So, how is it working for the Assassin Guild?"

Eva's mouth quirked into a small half smile as she eyed me. "It's not so bad, actually."

"I imagine it helps that you have underlings like Jimothy who can file all the paperwork." I nodded. "Most of my staff are field workers, so I end up having to write the reports myself."

The elf looked at me with a bit more interest. "How many people do you have?"

"Twenty army personnel trained to mediate the Dark Horde, and another twenty to manage the civilian residents." I crossed my arms, hiding my hands and popping my claws as I did so. "All trained personally by myself, of course."

"Of course." The words were dry. "I've had to retrain a bunch of people in a short time, and I think that your way is better; if you can teach them from the beginning, then you don't have to beat out the bad habits."

"I'm not in the habit of beating people," I retorted. "So I wouldn't know."

Before she could say more, I asked, "Who's Susan?"

All my research read that physical discipline was an unmitigated disaster which bred hostility and fear with no real positive outcome . . . unless you counted the inevitable stab in the back as a good thing.

The Dark Enchanted Forest assassins were trained with proper combat scenarios, educated through study and debate, and granted excellent resources for survival. Skills were all well and good, but training to be skilled when you were in Veralyn's Enchanted Restraint Manacles and didn't have access to your stats made for highly trained combat units that were more than just a class title.

Short of getting eaten or molten ash vaned, death would just be a minor inconvenience. We didn't want to lose people or have to train more. Also, because they were so well trained, we didn't need a *hundred* of them to try and get the job done. If His Viciousness ever decided to actually *use* one of his assassins . . . one would be enough.

Eva thumped the chair back on the floor, plopping her legs down. She leaned forward and rested her elbows on the table. The elf was rather fidgety. "Susan is the one who handled Marquess Chadwick's requests and will be able to answer your questions."

My eyebrow shot up at that. "Have the Servalt authorities already had a chance to investigate her?"

I'd have assumed Pjori would've let me know that bit of information and what they'd found, even if Jack chose not to.

"Those idiots?" Eva let out a harsh but genuine chuckle. "The knights raided this place under the duke's authority, and they found *nothing.*"

"Oh?" I smiled a little at that, and for the first time since I'd had my suspicions about the elf, I let my guard relax slightly.

Eva's lips tugged back into a half smile, her fingers tapping across the desk. "They were very rude."

There was a knock at the door, and Jimothy came back with a fluffy white catkin. Susan wore a blue tunic and black tights, and stared up at him with big blue eyes that were just a shade lighter than her tunic. She had a pair of tiny half-moon eyeglasses perched on her pink nose.

"I'm here, boss," the catkin spoke, rolling her *R*s. Susan looked me up and down, and I could tell she was still unsure of me when she said, "Alright, Commander General. What would you like to know?"

CHAPTER 42

My Date

Brownie

Brownie was running down the hall, instrument over her shoulder.

It'd been one hour and three minutes since Rufus had walked into the building next door, and for an hour and two minutes, she'd simply gotten comfortable and practiced plucking songs in the window, staring outside every once in a while and craning her head awkwardly to see the Assassin's Guild entrance below.

"Jack!" Brownie reached the spiral staircase and saw the human leaning on the counter and talking with the dragonborn. For an instant, she was torn, but then went for it and hopped the balustrade. The two below were the only witnesses to her exhilarating descent. Brownie landed on the floor and felt a creak. She waited a second to make sure, then stood up.

"Minstrel Bronwynn!" Amber gasped. Brownie couldn't tell if she was impressed or offended.

Jack simply stood straighter and raised an eyebrow.

"You will never guess who I just saw walk into the Assassin's Guild!" Brownie declared, adjusting her instrument on her shoulder.

The man couldn't contain his curiosity anymore and broached, "Who?"

"Slake Drakeford, Adventurer Extraordinaire!"

Jack looked confused. "The grimalcat?"

"That's right. I'm going to go—"

"*Slake Drakeford is next door*?!" Amber slammed her clawed palms on the desk, drawing their attention.

"That's enough, Amber," an aged voice spoke up from behind Brownie. The minstrel whipped around and stared at the elderly stable hand from earlier.

The drakin looked at Mistress May with pleading eyes. "I'm allowed to go look, right? I'll just be outside. I could manage the inn and keep watch for Slake outside at the same time!"

"You can't go running off every time a famous adventurer comes to town," Mistress May chided. Her sharp eyes turned to Bronwynn. "And *you* should be careful of my inn!"

"Ah, sorry." Brownie had the grace to blush. The old woman only came up to her elbows, but she was a force to be reckoned with.

"Now, run along to whatever spy business you all have. You're taking up space in my lobby," Mistress May announced before she tut-tutted and wandered down the hallway and out of sight.

"So," Jack stated. He tapped a finger on his chin. "You're sure it was the grimalcat?"

"Yes." Brownie held back her annoyance at having to repeat herself.

"While I understand the excitement, I don't understand why that had you racing down here," Jack pointed out.

"He inspired me," Brownie said, "and I've decided. It's been over an hour; that's too long. I'm going next door."

"Lucky," Amber sighed, partially slumped on the counter. She was taking not getting to catch a glimpse of the grimalcat pretty hard.

Jack frowned. "We have no reason to interfere in Dark Enchanted Forest business. If Commander Rufus required backup for his appointment, he would have asked—or sent a signal by now."

"*You* don't have a reason," Brownie countered, picking out a particularly perfect excuse. "But my dinner date is running late, and I'm going to go pick him up."

Both of Jack's eyebrows shot up, his eyes staring up at Brownie with a mix of amusement and understanding. "I see . . . Still. It's not a great idea."

Brownie walked toward the front door. Over her shoulder, she said, "It doesn't have to be a *great* idea. It just has to work."

"Your funeral," Jack mumbled.

Brownie resisted the urge to stick her tongue out at the man, instead turning back and delivering a broad smile in the doorway. "Amber, just for you, I'll ask Slake to wander by."

The happy noise behind her gave Brownie courage as she walked next door.

The Assassin's Guild was two stories high and looked like an adorable laundering shop with a decorative oval hanging sign that read "Lucia's Linens." Delicate white lace curtains were drawn, blocking a surprising amount of the inside of the building when Brownie walked past the large storefront window. It was a bright and welcoming building, and not anything like the Assassin Assembly fortress in Peldeep.

"Are you here for shopping, miss?" the assassin, an elf with dark-green skin and rusty-brown short hair asked. He'd not moved from his place beside the door, simply running his eyes up and up at the half giantess as she approached.

Brownie smiled. "Actually, I'm here for a pickup."

That got the elf's attention, and he took a step from the wall. His hands were stuffed in his pant pockets, and she noticed his tunic was of high quality with some embroidery on the collar. Even when he came to his full height, which was slightly taller than your average elf, he was still only to her chin.

"And what, pray tell, are you here to pick up?" The cutting edge to his voice made Brownie's heartbeat quicken . . . with excitement. This was the kind of setup she *lived* for.

"My date."

"What?"

"He was supposed to be done in there almost ten minutes ago!" Brownie stuck out her hip and rested her hand on it, holding the strap of her instrument bag with the other. "And I am not a woman to be kept waiting."

Of course, all of this was happening outside on a busy street. A few elves paused to watch the drama, while most continued on their business.

The elf assassin sighed. "You here for the beastman?"

"Yes."

"I don't think the boss is done with him yet." He glanced at the door to the shop and back at Brownie. "If you were smart, you'd come back later."

"Any later," she stressed, "and we'll be late."

There was a long pause, and Brownie was tempted for a second—just a second, mind—to give up the pretense. There was more than one way to get into an assassin's guild, and Brownie was uniquely skilled for the task.

The elf opened his mouth to reply, "Meow?"

Brownie stared at the elf in confusion, but he seemed equally lost.

Suddenly, a voice drew Brownie and the elf's attention to the shop, where Slake Drakeford sat at the threshold of the open door. He eyed the two of them, then reached up to rub his own ear with a paw. "Are you coming in or not?"

CHAPTER 43

Meow

Rufus

Ten Minutes Earlier

"Thank you, Susan," I said, nodding my head in respect to the well-organized feline. "You've been very helpful."

The last hour had been over and above what I could've expected.

Susan lifted a stack of papers and tapped them once, twice, thrice to make the pages line up straight. I already had a rolled waterproof case with my own copies of the treaties safely tucked away in my storage ring.

"Oh! No need for that, Commander." The fluffy white catkin stood up from the desk she'd taken over and dipped a happy curtsy. She pushed up her glasses and smiled at the compliment. "It was a pleasure."

Susan bowed low to her boss, and Jimothy escorted Susan out of the room.

Leaving Eva and myself alone again. An interesting choice on the guild master's part, as I was many levels higher than she was and could have made this a very bad day for the guild. I couldn't understand why she would put herself in danger, especially when I knew for a fact that she aimed for obfuscation and specialized in illegal dealings.

What was I missing?

"I'm impressed," Eva said dryly. The elf pushed off from where she was leaning against the wall nearby. "You didn't seem all that surprised to learn I'm the new guild master."

What was it with assassins always leaning against walls? I was more comfortable standing at attention myself. Maybe I should try it? Or maybe I should just consider storing a chair in my storage ring. I was surprised I hadn't thought about that sooner . . . so many occasions I could have been lounging comfortably instead of making do with hard benches or wooden inn sleeping cots.

And it would be a real power move to whip out a plush chaise and sit during conversations.

"I know a leader when I meet one," I replied. She was self-assured and confident in a relaxed and standoffish kind of way. She didn't interrupt even once during the negotiations. It was actually refreshing. "Congratulations on the new position."

A wicked gleam crossed her face then, and she smiled a vicious smile. "Thank you."

"My only surprise is that I got to actually meet the elf who managed to survive Duke Wyldon's investigation and get past my king's border guards with a battalion of assassins," I said pointedly.

"It wasn't that hard." She waved away my concern, walking back to Jimothy's desk and reclaiming the seat.

"You can be assured that moving forward, we won't assassinate any of your civilians."

I didn't let the barb get under my skin, but I knew what she was implying.

"Our kingdom is technically leaving the merchants' kidnapping ordeal in the hands of the Servalt authorities, but . . ." I paused for effect, drawing to my full height and stature imposingly, hackles raised, "should we feel that the matter did not end with the marquess, then Nilheim will act accordingly. And if I recall what happened the last time our necromancer visited Servalt . . . Well, nobody wants a repeat performance."

Ever since Chloe had met and fallen in love with Julia during an entertainingly epic trip to Servalt last winter, Servalt had asked Nilheim to consider sending other representatives on official business. For the foreseeable future, or at least until they rebuilt the Grand Collegium.

"I don't see how that has anything to do with *me*." Guild Master Eva smiled innocently. "I'm an assassin, not a merchant. And I have it on the best authority that Servalt merchants deal primarily with mercenaries."

"We both know that one of your men was contracted to Marquess Chadwick and the slave traders."

Guild Master Eva opened her mouth to retort, "Meow."

We both looked down in time to watch a grimalcat press up against Eva's legs and purr softly.

"Slake!" The elf swooped down and picked up the creature in both arms. She rubbed her face against his fur until the grimalcat made protest and gently swatted at her cheek.

"Eva." Slake stretched upward and deftly climbed onto the elf's shoulders, wrapping around her neck so that only his tail hung down in the front. It curled gently against the fluffy armor Eva was wearing. "Have you finished your discussion with the commander general?"

"Almost . . ." The elf drew out the words, suspicion in her tone. "Why?"

Slake flicked his wings a bit to straighten himself on her shoulder. "There was a chance you might kill Rufus, so I'm here to say that just won't do."

"I appreciate that," I said. "It is nice to see you again so soon, Slake."

"Of course it is."

"I hadn't planned on attacking the commander general." Eva reached out and scratched under Slake's chin. "He's here on official business with the guild. But I'm curious; why *shouldn't* I?"

He rubbed his face on Eva's cheek. "The Dark Enchanted Forest doesn't have useless hereditary laws. And killing Rufus will only annoy the Dark Lord."

"It's true. The only reason I'm even visiting is because of your impressive raid."

When Eva looked at me like she didn't believe that was the only reason, I stressed, "We never had to deal with Gloria directly, since she understood that our people in power are targetable—but our citizens are *not*."

"Gloria," Eva spat out vehemently, emotion thick in her voice, "was past her prime. She was so easy to overthrow that I'm surprised she lasted that long."

"Eva, darling, you've outlived your enemies." Slake swished his tail. "You don't need to make new ones. Now tell me where you got the molten ash vane."

The guild master frowned, casting me a side-glance. "I don't have to answer that here."

"Of course you don't." Slake stood, balanced, and then hopped to the floor. He walked a few paces toward the door, where he sat and turned to face us. "But you will. And you are going to tell Commander General Rufus, or I'll be most *disappointed* in you." The grimalcat's eyes glowed slightly green. "I won't sit around waiting for months until everyone gathers the clues to some grand scheme by your benefactor. I was your benefactor first, and you will do me the courtesy of telling the nice beastman here what you know before I get back so that he can go and arrest the duke and be done with it. This entire exercise is *annoying*."

Slake rose on all fours and stretched. "And stop pretending like you're involved more than you are; you're digging yourself into a hole. Now, if you'll excuse me, I'll be right back."

He walked out. I turned to the guild master, who was furious but definitely considering.

No one really wanted to deny a grimalcat.

"Fine," she spat out. "I owed Duke Lector three favors. I approved assassins to North Sumbria, and I participated in that gods-awful mess that was an assault on your queen. Duke Wyldon was the last. If anyone else is using molten ash vane in Servalt, it didn't originate *here*."

I raised an eyebrow, wondering if Slake wanted to join me in my trip to visit the Peldeep Assassin Assembly next.

"The way to bypass your borders was figured out by Guild Master Derek Stannard, so ask him." She said. "If you have questions about molten ash vane, you'll have to take it up with Duke Lector. He supplied all of the materials for his quests, and we purely accepted the hit."

I tried to speak, but she cut me off. "I'm not finished. Before anything else, everyone should know that I have no idea *who* is making it. The poisoner is anonymous and supplies poisons to *both* assassin guilds. We get a drop-off every month or so, and starting last year, molten ash vane was added in."

She pulled out a bag from nowhere. It clinked. "I'm swimming in the stuff. Whoever's making so much of it must be crazy."

I instinctively took a fighting stance, claws out. At least now I knew why she wasn't afraid of me.

"I have absolutely no intention of using any," she assured me, sending it back into storage. "I'm going to use it to negotiate with Duke Wyldon during the investigation. I have a record of how many bottles we received from an independent trustworthy source, and as long as I keep the same number of bottles, I can be assured that Duke Lector will take the blame for supply."

Every sense and skill told me she was telling the truth, though I was hesitant to relax my guard. I asked anyway. "But you tried to use molten ash vane on Duke Wyldon?"

"Again, incorrect. I merely filed the paperwork and picked the assassin; all effects to the case were handled by Duke Lector." She crossed her arms. "That was my final hit. I was hoping it wouldn't work, which was why I called in the Terpenlily family to attack Duke Wyldon. Their daughter is skilled enough to show I made an effort . . . but not skilled enough to be likely to succeed."

"It was closer than you think," I told her. "So you've just thrown Lady Tate to the wolves? She will face the full weight of the law for her illegal assassination attempt."

Eva smiled then, a wide vicious smile. "I have registered the paperwork. All of my assassinations are approved—"

"I hardly believe that Duke Wyldon would approve his own assassination attempt," I interrupted.

"Well, he did." The elf picked up the piece of paper she'd had resting on her face when I first arrived and waved it under my nose.

It was, in fact, an approved hit on Duke Wyldon Holst. And it was stamped with that very duke's own personal seal.

Things had just gotten more complicated. Again.

CHAPTER 44

You Managed to Get Out Alive!

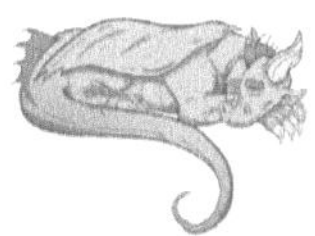

Brownie

"So, what are you doing here?" Brownie asked Slake. Grimalcats liked common sense and straightforwardness above all else . . . from others. It was their job to be mysterious.

At least that was what the other grimalcat she'd met was like.

Slake flicked his tail as he walked ahead of her down the hall. "I know the guild master, and I was interested in where she got molten ash vane."

"As far as I can tell, she has an endless supply," Brownie joked. The rare potion that used to show up once every hundred years was being handed out like candy these days.

That made the grimalcat pause in the hallway and squint his green eyes up at the bard. "I do not think that Servalt has the ingredients to make molten ash vane in endless supply."

"What are the ingredients?"

Slake resumed walking. "Broomlanding pollen, treant tears, griffin eggshell, and mushfolk mycena root, to list just a few that I know of."

Brownie whistled softly.

"None of the key ingredients are found in Servalt, so the person making it is either traveling the world or wealthy enough to get others to find the ingredients for them. But they aren't cheap." Slake slowed as they approached a door at the end of the hall. "The majority can be found in the Dark Enchanted Forest if one is *lucky*, but broomlanding pollen is harvested in Peldeep."

Slake reached the closed door, and after sniffing it twice, it opened for him.

"I hope you two had a good chat." He ran up to the pair and jumped onto a desk piled with papers.

"We did." Rufus sounded stressed. When she entered the room, she found him wearing a tiny set of reading glasses and reviewing a sheet of paper.

An elf, sitting at the desk in front of Rufus, scoffed. "Speak for yourself."

Rufus ignored her. "Slake, thank you. You've been a great help. Any chance you want to go to the castle with me? I have some questions for our birthday boy."

"That can wait," Slake stated. "You have another date already."

Rufus turned and found her standing there. "Brownie?"

She waved at him. "I came for our dinner date."

Rufus looked like he had no idea what she was talking about. Which was fair, since she'd made it up. The beastman was no fool, though, and he caught on quickly. "Ah, yes. Our date."

The elf looked like she was going to say something, but then her eyes lingered on Rufus, who was blushing. She turned to Brownie and sighed. "We were just finishing. Also, it's nice to officially meet you, Minstrel Bronwynn. I am Guild Master Eva Lina. Please give my regards to your uncle."

"I will." Brownie stiffened but nodded. She purposefully didn't look at Rufus. To redirect the conversation, she told Slake, "Also, you have a fan at the Wistful Cup who would love it if you stopped by later."

"I'll think about it." Slake stretched, flexing his claws on the desk and getting a paper stuck on the end of one paw. He batted it off then glanced at us, nonchalantly pretending like it never happened. "Now off you go, you two. I need to speak with Eva about the bottle of molten ash vane I caught."

"YOU WHAT?" Eva was out of her chair and hovering over the grimalcat in an instant. "Slake, you can't just play with—You could die!"

The grimalcat lay on the desk. "It's not the first dangerous thing I've caught at a celebration."

Brownie reached out and pulled Rufus toward the door. His soft arms were fluffy and sturdy and very huggable.

"Did you really get everything you needed done?" Brownie asked while they headed back the way she'd come.

Rufus nodded. "Just in time for our *date*, too."

Brownie had the grace to blush. "You were in here for over an hour! And the grimalcat, *with a vial of molten ash vane*, suddenly waltzed into the place! What if they were in cahoots to murder the commander general of the Dark Lord's army?"

"We *are* lucky it turned out as well as it did, thanks to Slake," Rufus replied. "He has rightful claim to the poison, and will hoard it fiercer than a dragon. And his involvement with the Assassin's Guild master means that I'm more inclined to look for clues elsewhere. Speaking of clues. Did you know that Duke Wyldon approved the assassination attempt today?"

"What?" Brownie would never have guessed.

"Which is why I think I should go talk to him."

There was a moment of final tension before the two exited the Assassin's Guild and found themselves back out on the streets. Brownie didn't realize how nervous she was on behalf of the commander general until she'd safely escorted him out of the building. She blamed Jack, for making it seem like the entire place was full of cutthroat murderous assassins who would unalive first and ask questions later.

Actually, from Brownie's own experience, that's probably exactly who worked in Lucia's Linens.

Speaking of Jack . . .

"I hate to say this," Brownie broached, "but you have two people next door you could ask instead."

Rufus glanced at the Wistful Cup and sighed. "You're right, and that would leave us more time for dinner."

Brownie decided to just go for it. "You know, I might not know my way around this part of the city, but I did find this amazing barbeque house the last time I was visiting."

"Sounds perfect."

They walked back into the Wistful Cup arm in arm. Jack was hanging around at the counter. He didn't look like he was doing anything, though, simply leaning on his elbow, waiting.

"You managed to get out alive!" the human called, actually looking impressed.

Rufus frowned. "Yes, and with valuable information. But first, did Duke Wyldon approve his own assassination order?"

"Yes?" Jack shrugged.

"Explain."

"He's trying to witness the assassination attempts and catch a molten ash vane case as it happens; what better to inspire an international criminal assassin than the hit on the leader of the investigation?"

"I did notice," Brownie pointed out, "that Duke Wyldon had shields prepared and powerful protectors on standby. He presumably had a [Revive] handy as well. And he *did* catch Lady Tate in the act."

Jack nodded. "Exactly. Though I don't think he was ready for whatever magic let that bottle pass through the shields. Or that one of his own family friends would throw the bottle in his face . . ."

Assassins were usually stealthier than that. Sometimes. Maybe.

"Speaking of family, the real perpetrator for the assaults in Servalt is Duke Lector. Of the royal family. I wouldn't put it past simple inheritance schemes for the throne, but that doesn't explain the international activity. I'll inform the Continental Council at the meeting in Peldeep, and you can tell Duke Wyldon.

We only ask that when you have custody of your queen's younger brother, that you keep the council in mind."

The drakin saw them as she entered the lobby. "You're back! Did you—"

"We did," Brownie said. "He said he'd think about it."

The girl let out a very happy squeal.

"And with that." Rufus faced Brownie and gently placed a hand on hers where their arms were still linked. She found the way he tucked her hand into the crook of his arm and then held it endearing. "Let's go."

It seemed like Rufus had successfully completed his mission in Servalt, and Brownie decided it was time to celebrate.

"Next stop, The Tan Tan Flames!" Brownie raised her free hand in a fist, excited for their next adventure:

Grilled meat.

CHAPTER 45

And Fine Luck

Rufus

When Bronwynn told me she was taking me out to dinner, I couldn't have imagined the glorious all-you-can-eat buffet before me.

She had excellent taste that matched mine perfectly. I wasn't saying we were a perfect match; we just enjoyed the same things. And honestly, everything was better with good company.

And she was the best company.

I coughed at my own wandering thoughts.

Bronwynn grinned, her face full of contentment from a delicious meal. "I'm sorry I butted into your meeting with a fake dinner date, but I don't regret it."

"Me neither." A warmth filled my chest, and it wasn't from the rogue pepper grilled boar. "Thank you for the invite."

The other members of her fan club would go to great lengths to see Minstrel Bronwynn for just a few minutes after a show, and here I was spending every waking minute with the half giantess. I didn't know what I was going to tell them, but I knew there was no way I could keep this a secret . . . I'd simply say that Commander General Rufus Triever had been seen traveling with her. I might even do a quick update this evening.

The next stop for Bronwynn was the Peldeep Apple Blossom Festival, while I was headed to the Peldeep Assassin Assembly.

"So!" Brownie eyed me across the table, a conspiratorial look on her face. "What did you learn? Anything I am allowed to know? I understand that you are on an official quest and it's none of my business, but I just can't help asking."

"It's fine," I reassured her. "I learned that the guild master isn't the mastermind, but is still working closely with the person who's been causing all the molten ash vane cases . . . And the person who actually makes the potion is probably in Peldeep."

"No!" The vehemence in the bard's voice startled me. She set down her cup of rosehip iced tea, her next words more controlled. "Really? I thought that Servalt was definitely the prime suspect? I mean, they kidnapped *me* . . ."

I shook my head. "It's not that simple. I'm going to report back to Keith and Henrietta on my findings, and then head straight for Peldeep. Are you, um, are you still headed there next?"

Bronwynn fiddled with the handle of her glass, distracted, but after a second, she said, "Yes. I'm going to need to head out pretty soon if I'm to get past those three encounters before I make it to Vitol. Their Royal Highness has commissioned a live show."

"Would you like to go together? Or are you already tired of me?"

"What? No! I'd love that!" Bronwynn looked at me, and I could tell that whatever had crossed her mind, be it the kidnapping or something else, was behind her. "Are you really done here? Can we head out tomorrow?"

"Let's enjoy one last sleep in a real bed before we hit the road." I picked up my own glass, a sparkling peach tea with frozen blueberries floating on top. "To fair weather?"

She clinked her glass with mine. "And fine luck!"

We finished and headed back to the Wistful Cup. Bronwynn left me to go check in on Donna, and I went up to my room to finish my reports.

I opened my window when I heard the unmistakable sound of a city-wide musical starting in the street outside.

After the song and dance, I finished sending an update to my fellow bardic lovers. Then I pulled out a small trinket golem linked to the Dark Lord. Even with minimal magical theory, I could tell the connection was faint, and it would take a great deal of mana to use it at this distance . . . I was tempted to activate it anyway; Keith had an almost endless supply of mana.

Still, anything I had to say could wait until I crossed the threshold of the Dark Enchanted Forest. If we hurried tomorrow, we might make it across the border, and if Keith was in a hurry, he could send Gimtak to collect the treaties with the imp's [Teleportation] skill.

Then I could sit back and enjoy a lovely trip with Minstrel Bronwynn.

I went to sleep with thoughts of the redhaired half giantess on my mind. I also woke up with dreams of the redhaired half giantess on my mind.

I definitely had a problem.

"I'm ready! And I've got the workings of a new song I'd love to practice . . . if listening to me on repeat for a few hours won't drive you absolutely up the wall?"

"No, that sounds wonderful." And it was.

We packed up and headed back the way we came—faster, since we wouldn't need to detour off the main road to visit Duke Wyldon's castle.

I didn't have a [Patient] connection to the thousands of people in Servalt's capital city . . . but it didn't matter; the information from my passive skills still fed me information from [Empathy] and [Keen Senses]. The moment we were good and clear of the walls, the constant hit on my notifications tab started to show.

And the light music playing beside me made it easier than ever to leaf through them.

For some reason, when the last notification had been processed, and I was sitting there surrounded by the sound of soft lyre harp music, I had to resist the urge to laugh. Or cry. The relief of completing my task, the sheer weight of everything, just fell away as we rolled over hills on a steady road.

I was happier in that moment than I'd been in a very, very long time.

It didn't hurt that I was getting to hear Bronwynn create a new song, one that even Henrietta hadn't heard yet. I knew; I'd asked. The song she was working on was a love story. A lively piece with a catchy chorus.

> Thia of Foxgrove was pretty and sweet,
> she kept the herb garden; she kept the ferns neat.
> And any who traveled through Ironhold pass
> would stop for a poultice, a cream, or liltgrass.

"So? How do you like it?" The voice of the minstrel beside me dragged me from my thoughts. She must have seen that I wasn't immersed in my character sheet and logs any longer and was finally free to talk again.

"It's beautiful," I said, meeting her eyes. She was blushing a bit but had a wide and confident grin. I added, "But I love all of your music, so maybe I'm not the right person to ask?"

"You are the perfect person to ask!" Bronwynn shook her head at my supposed nonsense. "So—Oh, here it comes."

"What?" I followed her gaze ahead of us. We were a few hours out before we reached the next town, and the countryside was a mix of tiny farms and rolling fields with a patch of forest here and there. The Sumbrian Empire had spread from their thick forests in the south, claiming these lands for agriculture many centuries past, and it was still a major exporter of berries and vegetables to the rest of the continent.

Which meant the hooded figures ahead of us probably weren't simple down-on-their-luck farmers who'd turned to highway robbery.

CHAPTER 46

Fluffy and Soft and Wonderful

Brownie

"And here we go again," Brownie muttered.

Rufus growled beside her, claws springing from his paws, long and vicious looking. His hackles raised, and she was about to tell him it was alright to let her handle things when he stood up in the wagon and announced, "I am no mere merchant but Commander General Rufus of the Dark Enchanted Forest. If you wish to walk away with your lives, you should do so *now*."

Brownie counted seven masked and hooded figures on the actual road, and three with some sort of [Obfuscate] skill off to the right. There were no bushes, no trees, and no buildings to hide behind, but they did stand in some overgrown grass, which was more than enough to activate most hiding skills.

She sighed.

"We know who you are," a raspy voice called out from the middle of the group as a single tall figure stepped forward, pointing a long pike at them. Donna did *not* like spears or pikes, and the mare shifted a couple times on her feet. Brownie sent as much calm as she could to the horse through their bond . . . but Brownie also knew that nothing was going to save that man if Donna decided to act.

"Then you also know I'm one of the strongest fighters in the entire Dark Horde. So." The beastman tilted his head. "Why aren't you running?"

There was a bit of hesitation in the bunch, but the leader of the group only laughed. "We came prepared!"

With that, another man threw a bottle to the ground, and a billowing plume of acrid smoke shot out of the ball as it hit the ground.

The first pointed. "Now, attack!"

Donna had had enough. She whinnied and rose up on her hind legs, kicking in front of her. A cry rent the air, and Brownie felt satisfaction through her link with the horse.

[Your bonded companion has defeated a **Blackfog Spy (Level 28).**
You have gained +14 EXP from Donna's **Shared Experience** Perk.]

Rufus shouted, "Stay here! I'll be right back."
"Wait!"
Rufus wasn't expecting Brownie to reach out and grab his arm before he could make the jump down from their wagon. She stored her lyre harp and then activated [Sturdy] to leverage herself as an anchor and prevent him from going anywhere as she sent a message to Donna in her mind and yelled, "Ride!"

[**Sturdy**: Your body is as immovable as the mountain and as force-
ful as the storm. When holding your ground, you add your Constitution 15 to your Strength 19 stat. Current total: 34]

Donna landed on all fours from her second attack and activated [Charge]. She broke the earth beneath her hooves as she launched forward. And as Brownie had anticipated, there was no one in the group powerful enough to hold their own against the stampeding horse.

They burst through the other side of the acrid smoke just in time for Rufus to get flung back into Brownie's awaiting arms. Her ability allowed her to catch him without getting pushed back, which was important because Danielle was still slung over her shoulder. He fell gracefully, turning to try and brace himself, and she was suddenly holding a very soft and fluffy beastman.

He whipped a hand up and over her shoulder, palm to their enemies. "[Protector]."

A great shield formed overhead. It blocked the volley of arrows raining down on them, sending the missiles ricocheting off in all directions.

Brownie was impressed; it was a huge shield, covering the entire wagon and then some. Unfortunately, it didn't last.

"Ugh, the smoke. Let go, I need an—" The beastman coughed, struggling to rise. Then his eyes rolled up into his head, and he went limp, his extended arm sliding off her shoulder. He collapsed fully on top of her, and the shield flickered out.

Even before he collapsed his body had begun to *change*, morphing into a giant golden beast that resembled a cross between a golden retriever and a wolf. His head rested on her lap.

Rufus had defended against the first attack, but a second round of arrows was headed their way. Brownie fumbled for the pendant at her neck, thankful that Rufus in beast form had slid to the floor at her feet. It gave her room to leverage her arm free and grab the small circle flute.

She gave a silent apology to Rufus as she blew as hard as she could.

[You have attempted to activate the Perk: **Piercing Wave**. You have succeeded. The area of effect attack hits targets equal to **Siren Song**, dealing piercing damage. Targets available: 6.]

The seventh arrow fell, hitting the seat. The other six arrows splintered in the air and blew backward from the wave of sound that hit them while Donna nickered in irritation. She could hear the sound of the pendant flute just fine and didn't appreciate the awful ear-piercing noise. The bard sent her apologies to her horse.

Just before they crested a hill and finally made it out of sight of their attackers, a single skill-powered arrow landed in the back of the wagon. It tore through one of Donna's feed bags, and oats spilled out around the jutting-up black arrow.

For a moment, Brownie worried her horse was going to turn around and go destroy the band of brigands for their insolence . . . but Donna knew that Brownie wasn't built for combat. The horse kept running.

The wagon was rolling down the lane at breakneck speed, much faster than a normal horse could have pulled off, and within seconds, they had escaped. She had an antidote for him as soon as she was sure they were in the clear, but in the meantime, Brownie dropped her pendant flute and wrapped both arms around the unconscious Rufus. She told herself it was because she was worried about the bumpy ride . . . and not because he felt wonderful to hold. Fluffy and soft and wonderful.

She had a problem.

CHAPTER 47

On My Knees at Her Feet

Rufus

Someone poured an antidote down my throat.

The tart apple flavor filled my mouth, and I marveled at the high-grade potion. They were expensive, since they were designed to cure most everything, with some small exceptions. My low-grade Wolfsbane antidote would have sufficed; Bronwynn probably didn't have any grade Wolfsbane antidote on hand like I did.

The rare poison had a continuing damage effect, and critical success rate against canine beastfolk. My notification logs could attest to that.

> [You have taken 14 points of Critical Damage. Health 602/616.]
> [Warning! You have been poisoned by **Wolfsbane**. You will lose consciousness in 00:00:10]
> [Unique Effect **Wolfsbane** triggered: **Beast Form**. Spend mana to maintain current form or revert to **Beast Form**.]
> [You have taken 14 points of Critical Damage. Health 588/616.]
> [Warning! You will lose consciousness in 00:00:09]
> [You have been immobilized by **Sturdy**. Duration remaining 00:00:34]
> [You have taken 14 points of Critical Damage. Health 574/616.]

At that rate, I would've been dead in two minutes. While I was particularly susceptible to the poison, at least with wolfsbane I could still [Revive]. That was why wolfsbane, while being incredibly rare and expensive, wasn't illegal like molten ash vane.

My original plan had been to jump off the carriage, clear the wolfsbane smoke, pop an antidote, and then fight off the assassins. I was *not* expecting to get grabbed and stumble into Bronwynn's awaiting arms. I'd barely caught myself as my body had landed on top of hers, which had been strangely immovable and soft and—

I shook my head and groaned.

The antidote was working, and I could feel the last vestiges of poison fade away, but I still felt a slight headache and a touch weak from my depleted health. I'd need to pop a health potion soon.

I realized at this point that I was transformed into my full beast form. It was as natural to me as any other form, though it came with the freedom of not wearing pants. Luckily, my clothes were tailored to go into my storage ring when I transformed.

Dreading what I'd find, I opened my eyes.

Curly hair tipped with red as rich as flames and warm eyes filled my gaze. My chin was in Minstrel Bronwynn's lap as I lay on the floor, my tail hanging over the edge.

We were traveling at an unnaturally fast pace.

"We're safe. Just take your time getting oriented," her soft voice soothed as one of her hands pet me. "They're long gone behind us."

The feeling of her hands running over my body felt amazing; so amazing that I quickly lifted my head out of her reach to escape.

I immediately missed her touch, but fought my base urges until I could convince myself to change back to my usual beastfolk self: short beast ears, mixed ruddy brown and golden fur, muscular chest, folk-shaped arms and legs with canine feet. My paws were similar to my beast shape, simply smaller and upgraded to an opposable thumb.

When I finished, I was on my knees at her feet, leaning against her left leg and looking up at her. Gods, I wanted to change back for more pets. Or kiss her. Or . . . This was probably the heightened adrenaline that I'd read about. After battle or any stressful encounter, the body's physiological symptoms could be mistaken for lust or love or even hatred. I needed to drag my eyes away from her lips and get myself together.

My heart raced as I scrambled back to my seat. "Sorry, um, how long was I out?" I asked, ignoring my pounding heartbeat and feverish disposition.

"Not long, maybe a minute? *I'm* sorry for grabbing you like that; I'm not used to having other people along on my adventures. I know you can handle yourself, but I didn't want to leave you behind . . ." Bronwynn's hands flexed once before she grabbed and handed over her waterskin.

"It's fine. Just . . . don't do it again?" I took a swig and almost choked when my thoughts caught up with me. In the span of fifteen minutes, I'd received a lap pillow, pets, and an indirect kiss from *the* Minstrel Bronwynn. Then told her *not to do it again!*

I told myself I was being ridiculous and took a second drink. It helped. *Stop it, tail.*

"What happened after I was out?" I asked.

"They shot at us; two arrows hit the wagon, but nobody got hurt in the exchange," Bronwynn said. Donna interrupted with a gruff whinny, and the bard added, "Well, technically, Donna took out one of them, and they hit our bag of oats. We're going to need to stop somewhere and buy her a fresh bag—the arrows were laced with poison."

I looked over the back of the seat and found an arrow pointing out of the backrest close to Bronwynn, and another, as she'd described, in a bag of oats. I leaned closer to the arrow next to Bronwynn and gave it a sniff. It was also coated in wolfsbane. Between the smoke bomb and all the arrows, this attack had to have cost a fortune in the rare herb alone.

"I've never run across the Blackfog on an encounter before. Unless you count getting kidnapped alongside one of them at the Spring Ball," Bronwynn said.

"I was the target; they were prepared to fight me." I frowned in thought. It might have been related to the current case, or someone might've just seen an opportunity to go after the commander general of the Dark Enchanted Forest in an isolated location.

"I'm still counting it as an encounter." She reached up and fiddled with the pendant flute at her throat. "How are your ears?"

"Nothing a health potion can't fix." That explained the slight headache. My impressive Constitution was the only thing that'd allowed me to remain conscious as long as I had after breathing in the wolfsbane. Still, I wasn't healing near fast enough, so I pulled out a medium health potion and downed it.

Brownie's shoulders relaxed, and she gave me a relieved smile. "Thank goodness. I was worried, since I blew it right next to your ear."

I flinched and thanked the gods I'd been knocked out. "I can't complain if it saved us. Speaking of, I owe you an antidote potion."

"I wouldn't say no to a replacement," Bronwynn said. "I only had the one."

I didn't have a high-grade potion on hand to compensate her, so I just nodded. I wasn't going to offer her anything less than what she'd given me.

"Since it looks like they were after me, I'll also replace the oats." Donna's ears flicked at that, and I hoped that the mare wouldn't hold the attack against me. "And I'll have the wagon repaired. Do you know when we're going to reach the next town?"

"We passed it already," she said. "I didn't want to stop and give them the opportunity to catch up."

"At this speed?" The wagon was blowing past other travelers on the road at breakneck speeds.

"Donna is a Windrunner," Bronwynn explained. Donna neighed loudly, starting to slow down. "She's very fast; she just doesn't like to run very much."

"I see." Nothing much surprised me about that horse at this point.

When Donna had gone back to a reasonable trot, Bronwynn leaned back into the seat and retrieved Danielle from her storage ring. She caught me staring and gave me a casual shrug. "If Donna thinks we are far in the clear, then we're fine. She's really good about that kind of thing."

"Donna," I addressed the mare. "Thank you for saving us. You are an absolutely wonderful horse, and we are lucky to have you. I promise to buy you the nicest oats money can buy when we stop for the night."

The horse continued on, but she stood straighter, and her tail flicked with pleasure at the compliment.

Bronwynn was staring at me.

"What?"

"You are really good at that," she told me.

"At what?" I repeated.

"Compliments." There was something in the way she said it that made me think she wanted me to lavish *her* with compliments as well. But she was Minstrel Bronwynn, a confident and self-assured famous musician that played for kings and made the common man weep at her song.

Still, just in case I'd heard correctly, I said, "You are very astute, Minstrel Bronwynn. I enjoy showing people my thanks for their hard work, and I find it best to do so with honest praise. I've spent my life trying to build up people's self-worth and let them know they are seen and appreciated . . . It's almost a habit at this point."

Bronwynn stared at me for a long moment, and I wondered if I'd said something to offend her. She was frowning.

Then she said, "Does anyone let *you* know that you're seen and appreciated?"

CHAPTER 48

A Thing for the Beastman

Brownie

"I—" Rufus coughed lightly. "My position is usually the one giving counsel . . . so it's not expected. No."

Of course, Brownie hadn't meant to bring up the conversation from their first dinner date, but it seemed like such perfect timing to do so. She still remembered the way he'd seemed so lost when he'd talked about his place in the world. That his friends and family, his entire *life*, was predicated on his job title . . . a title that he could lose any time someone beat him at the winter solstice.

A title that General Knolith and a myriad of others were *desperate* for.

Brownie wondered what the previous commander general of the Dark Lord's army had done in his day-to-day life. She was *pretty sure* it didn't involve coaching the entire Dark Enchanted Forest through their marital struggles . . .

"Well, *I* think you're incredible," Brownie said. She noted with pleasure his tail was wagging even as he turned to look at her with his usual calm facade. Her fingers itched to pet him again, but she resisted. "You're great at your job, you're honest and kind and friendly, and always trying to make the world a better place everywhere you go . . . and I admire you."

She didn't mean the last to sound like a confession, and she blushed as she realized it could be interpreted that way. Before he could reply, she continued. "Anyways, that's why I think you should give yourself more credit."

Donna chuffed in agreement. The mare turned her long neck to eye the beastman and blew out of her nostrils at Rufus before returning to face the front. Rufus closed his mouth, holding back the reply he'd been about to give. Instead, he said, "As always, you're right. Thank you."

His tail was still giving away the effect her words had had on him, and Brownie let the following silence build between them as they carried on down the road. It was a slightly awkward quiet, but it wasn't bad. What was bad was how close she'd come to complimenting her way into confessing, to outright telling Rufus she had a thing for him . . . Worse, that she now realized she *definitely* had a thing for the beastman.

Irrevocably. It was there.

And based on everything so far, she thought he might like her back. But she wasn't sure. Yet.

Maybe he was just being nice to her. Maybe he took *all* his travel companions out for dinner. Or not. She already knew he complimented everyone equally, so what if she was his favorite bard? That just meant he liked her *music*.

A memory flashed. *If he hurt her.* The words Rufus had so vehemently spoken in Thistlecrick. The words that made her toes curl and her heartbeat quicken. The words that had made her start thinking about him as something *more*. He was handsome, his voice was smooth and lovely, and they shared so much in common. But even so . . . their dates so far had been circumstantial. Their entire situation was circumstantial.

Some small part of her mind told her she should throw caution to the wind and just ask the beastman then and there. If Rufus was traveling with her all the way to Peldeep, they were bound to run into her family—and her cousins would see right through her in a heartbeat.

That gave her a good point of reference. Peldeep. If she hadn't outright asked the beastman to court her by the time they reached Peldeep, then the least she could do was ask him to let her lavish glorious pets on his soft fur. Maybe he could be persuaded to turn into full beast form again so she could rub his tummy.

The inappropriate thoughts kept her distracted until Donna interrupted her with a loud snort. There, up in the sky high above, was a hat.

Neither Brownie nor Rufus could fly, so they simply watched the accessory bob about in the air until it crested a hill out of sight.

They shared a look, and Rufus offered, "I bet if we . . ."

Brownie shook her head. Even one so usually ready for adventure knew that chasing flying hats was an effort in *time*. "That sounds like a lot of work, and we are coming up on the border soon."

Just a quarter hour at Donna's breakneck horsepower speed had taken them across most of Servalt. Her horse raced faster than the wind when she wanted to. Usually, Donna insisted on traveling at their current slow pace. When her bonded horse wasn't being chased by ruffians, she enjoyed a nice casual saunter.

A few minutes later, Donna sent Brownie another nudge through their bond. Something was up ahead. The bard immediately spotted the reason her horse wanted her attention, and it wasn't the hat or anything else she was expecting to see on a quiet Servalt county road.

A familiar figure was standing in a triumphant pose on the road. They were facing the opposite direction to the wagon, but Brownie would know those long strands of braided green hair anywhere.

"Rufus?"

"Yes?" The beastman was obviously distracted with his own thoughts and not paying attention to the road ahead.

"I found out where Gerda the Bridge Troll went."

CHAPTER 49

Nothing to See Here

Rufus

Gerda the Bridge Troll had become a common castle name in recent months.

The woman had come out of nowhere, conquered all of the bridges in the Dark Enchanted Forest, and become a powerful monstress in her own right.

Seemingly overnight.

In all honesty, I'd thought that everyone was just too busy and not paying attention, leaving her many years to wander around mastering her bridge magic. There weren't even that many bridges in the Dark Enchanted Forest that I knew of. The Great Road going east to west had a bridge on either end, and the Great Road going north to south had a bridge on either end as well. So, at least four.

"What I want to know," I told Bronwynn as we slowly approached the troll, "is what she's doing at *this* bridge . . . I don't think she has the permit to make troll bridges outside of the Dark Enchanted Forest."

In fact, Gerda had recently been audited because she didn't have permits for most of the bridges she controlled *inside* the Dark Enchanted Forest. She was completely out of hand. Keith had raised concerns about the troll on more than one occasion, and I was still confused how Gerda had managed to slip an enchantment onto the drawbridge of the Black Fortress without anyone noticing.

If Gerda weren't one of Henrietta's closest friends, I had a feeling things would've gone a lot worse for the troll.

Donna's hooves and the rattling of the wagon weren't exactly quiet, and the second we were within earshot, Gerda spun to face us. Her small tusks peeked out from her lower lip, and her faun-brown eyes flashed with annoyance. The look faded when she realized just who was approaching.

"Brownie!" The troll broke out into a welcoming smile, and she hurried off the bridge before we got there. Donna pulled off to the side of the road and settled in to watch. She was very like her mistress that way.

Bronwynn left her instrument in the wagon and jumped down to greet the troll with a warm hug. When they pulled apart, Bronwynn gave Gerda a pointed look. "It's wonderful to see you here, if unexpected."

"And you . . ." Gerda rubbed her neck, clearly embarrassed at being caught green-handed at a bridge outside of the Dark Enchanted Forest.

I couldn't hold it in any longer. "Do you have a permit to create this troll bridge?"

"It's not a troll bridge." Gerda sent me a defiant look, and Bronwynn raised an eyebrow at the clear tension my words solicited from the troll.

I waved my hands at the unassuming bridge. "Then why are you here instead of patrolling your own bridges back home?"

"Reasons." Gerda crossed her arms and stared at me with a calculating look.

"You'll need to do better than that." I had to admit, my curiosity was getting the better of me. Plus, we really didn't know much about how troll magic worked, and King Keith had been increasingly concerned by its implications, given what we'd learned about Gerda this year.

Bronwynn made an unexpected noise, and I glanced her way. She'd pulled out a pack of nuts and was watching us while she ate them.

At least *she* was having a good time.

Gerda stood quietly in thought for a moment, then nodded. "I'm not making a troll bridge here because it'd be too expensive for me to keep it up."

She sidestepped more than she gave away in that sentence. Common wisdom was that magical enchantment abilities like Keith's automatons or troll bridges cost the user an experience penalty if they were defeated.

"I can understand that; it must be costing you a fortune in experience points to be away from your bridges this long. But that still doesn't explain what you're doing here."

"Bridge troll stuff." Gerda took a step back, her foot almost touching the bridge but not quite.

"You just said—"

"Don't worry about it."

Bronwynn choked on her snacks.

I offered the bard a waterskin from my storage ring. She tentatively reached out and took it; her drink was still on the wagon.

"So you aren't here to capture this bridge, and you haven't officially abandoned your post, *and* you definitely have nothing hidden up your sleeve. We simply ran into you by chance on this empty road over an hour from the border, and we have *absolutely* nothing to worry about. Is that what I'm to believe?"

Gerda's cheek twitched, and I could see the smile pulling at her lips. "That's right, Commander General. Nothing to see here."

Bronwynn piped in. "So do you need a ride back to the Dark Enchanted Forest?"

She reached out and offered her snacks to the bridge troll, who accepted a small handful of nuts. I listened on in interest, politely rejecting the bag when Bronwynn offered me the same.

"That's a kind offer." She hesitated for only a second, casting a side-eye at myself, before letting out a long-suffering sigh. "Actually . . . how about I give *you* a ride? My new [World Bridge] perk lets me connect and fast travel between any bridge I've ever crossed. Even if I don't claim them."

"Hence why you're wandering around in different countries crossing unsuspecting bridges?" I commented. I had to work hard to keep the horror out of my voice. Keith was going to have conniptions.

"Yes." Her innocent smile was almost as worrying as what she'd just said. She checked the air slightly up and to the right of her face, obviously reading a notification of some kind.

I whistled.

Gerda nodded, pleased with whatever she'd found, and pointed her finger at the bridge. "[World Bridge]!"

The entire structure glowed a stunning aquamarine light. Motes of silver lights danced within the blue.

Bronwynn asked, "Where does it go?"

"Wherever I want." The troll shot us a knowing smile. "In this case, a half hour south of the Black Fortress. Figured I'd save you a day's travel."

CHAPTER 50

Lady's Secret

Brownie

Brownie knew that Donna wasn't too keen on portal travel, but the idea of more enchanted carrots harvested from the Dark Enchanted Forest and grown by the Pixie Prim tempted her horse forward. Who would choose regular old Servalt carrots grown in the nonmagical hills when enchanted carrots awaited on the other side of the bridge?

She was *always* willing to do things for enchanted carrots.

Brownie and Rufus were on the wagon, and Gerda stood off to the side with one foot on the bridge and one on the path. The magic of the bridge enveloped them, and it felt like a gentle warm wind that lifted everything ever so slightly. Brownie's skirts slowly billowed, and her hair rose up just a bit. Like gravity was lighter within the magical aura.

Rufus shivered beside her, and she noted that his entire furry self bristled at the sensation. Again, she resisted the urge to reach out and pet him. For calming purposes, of course.

Once the wagon finally passed all the way onto the bridge, Gerda moved her foot off the road and said, "Let's go!"

Brownie had actually had more than her fair share of portal encounters, from that time Marquess Dorset had kidnapped her at the Spring Ball, to the time her maternal cousin Leo had pushed her into a Vort Port and she'd teleported with a crate of cargo onto her Aunt Persia's ship. That had been an unexpected trip to visit her grandparents in Drendil. By the time she'd crawled her way out of the hold and managed to alert the crew of her presence, they'd been long out to sea and couldn't turn back. She'd been seven.

Leo had gotten in *so* much trouble, but she hadn't been mad at him; it beat knife fighting practice!

This portal didn't feel like the jolting, stomach-twisting violent travel that the low-grade but high-cost portal scrolls had. It also didn't feel like the sudden popping sensation of the Vort Port. It felt closer to the slight temporal distortion of walking through Gerda's front door and into her pocket space.

Not *bad*, but strange. Donna was not amused.

One minute, the horse was walking on a bridge surrounded by rolling hills, and the next, she was walking on a slightly more dilapidated bridge surrounded by craggy oaks. She snorted and kept walking until she'd pulled the wagon clear onto the road ahead. The stream bed trickled west.

They would have plenty of time to get to the castle and find an inn if Gerda was correct.

Brownie still had that bag full of gold coins Their Royal Highness had given her, so she could stay wherever she wanted. Before this trip, she'd only known Henrietta out of everyone living in the Black Fortress, and her newly married friend had been . . . distracted.

That had prompted her to sometimes stay at an inn.

Now, Brownie had a borderline flirtatious friendship with Rufus, and she wouldn't be alone at a breakfast table full of random powerful political leaders who didn't know her. Technically, Rufus had been at the table when she'd broken her fast in the past, but at that point, he'd just been another one of said random powerful political leaders.

A nice one, but still.

"What are your plans for the rest of the day?" Brownie left Donna to eat some grass off to the side of the road. She and Rufus both joined the troll, who was busy inspecting the bridge, presumably reviewing her character sheet logs.

"I have upkeep to do." Gerda crouched down and poked at the short wall on the side of the bridge. A small aquamarine spark shot between the stone and the green finger. The troll smiled. "But it shouldn't take long. I'll meet you at the castle?"

Brownie looked down the path. "If you could teleport us to any bridge you've crossed, couldn't you have taken us straight to the castle?"

Gerda laughed. "I don't exactly want to advertise this skill, Brownie. And it's too busy. Unless you want to portal directly into someone already standing there, I don't recommend it."

"That reminds me," Rufus cut in. "Since you're being so forthcoming, how *do* you have a proper troll bridge at the Black Fortress *without* having to toll it?"

"I *do* have to toll the bridge." Gerda continued to feed magic into one particular stone on this bridge but looked at Rufus over her shoulder. When he patiently waited for her to continue, Gerda turned back to her work and sighed. "I didn't want to draw attention to the fact that I'm controlling the bridge. I've just been paying the experience penalty."

"What?!" Rufus exclaimed, incredulous. The beastman actually held up a hand, counting and mumbling to himself, "But that would mean . . . if you added the army rations team . . . though technically, Gimtak *flies*. You have at *least* fifty people a day traveling over that drawbridge! How are you not level one!"

"Lady's secret." Gerda winked at Rufus.

Brownie decided that was enough information from the otherwise private bridge troll. "Then we'll leave you to your magic and meet you back at the Black Fortress."

"Where"—Rufus pointed out—"you'll be required to file an interkingdom business registry for opening portals into other kingdoms . . . How many kingdoms can you cross bridges in?"

Gerda gave him a self-satisfied half smile. "Why, all of them, of course."

CHAPTER 51

Today Was a Good Day for Vengeance

Rufus

I stared at the troll for a long moment.

"Actually," Gerda corrected, "I've never crossed a bridge in the Empire of Sands, or the Untamed Ice Fields to the north. Or anywhere that doesn't *have* a bridge, like Tevl or Plittsmouth."

She named the underwater kingdom off the coast and the underwater city in the Dark Enchanted Forest. Plittsmouth was under Lake Loria, and was probably a short distance south of where we currently stood . . . or a great distance. I couldn't be sure *where* the forest had put the lake today.

Granted, the Empire and the Ice Fields would take weeks to travel by foot; they probably weren't worth it. But then the troll emphasized, "*Yet.*"

The idea of having to file and register all of those bridges was daunting.

Then I had a thought. "I see. Well, we'll meet you at the Black Fortress shortly, and I'll have to arrange another audit."

Gerda's face fell as we trundled off. Today was a good day for vengeance.

"Why are you smiling like that?" my travel companion asked, curious. She picked up Donna's reins, but it was merely for show.

I leaned back into the seat, satisfied, as I said, "I can't stay long, so our dear king is going to have to process Gerda's paperwork by himself."

"What about Henrietta?" Bronwynn asked. "I thought she was helping out these days?"

"True." The reminder dimmed my joy a bit, but I held out hope. I'd barely teased my king about his love life and the Dark Lord had sent me on a bunch of boring kingdom-level quests. With exquisite company I might add, but still . . . "I'll take small pleasure in the extra work anyway. I'm being sent across the continent while my king stays home and enjoys a relaxing honeymoon. I'm allowed a bit of petty revenge."

"Well, I enjoyed having you along for the ride, so maybe I'll thank King Keith while you're busy wishing him mild discomfort," Bronwynn told me. Her relaxed shoulders and playful smile made my heart beat faster, and my tail started thumping violently, so much so that I reached back with my hand opposite Bronwynn so I could hopefully grab the offending limb with stealth.

"If there's one good thing that came out of this," I told the half giantess with a fierceness that burned in my chest, "it's the time I've gotten to spend in your company."

There was a pause while we both stared at each other. Her cheeks were touched with a slight blush . . . and I felt the heat rising in my ears.

Donna snorted at us, breaking the tension. We had just passed where the Gread Roads came to a crossroads. And then, on top of my notification tab that had been blinking incessantly for some time, a familiar feeling of overwhelming pressure climbed up my spine that was harder to ignore. We were home.

It was a beautiful late spring day, birds were buzzing, and flowers were in full bloom as Minstrel Bronwynn and I rode up the road to the Black Fortress, returning to the capital of the Dark Enchanted Forest.

The peaks of the castle came into view above the skyline. There weren't any obvious signs of distress, just the usual army and merchants and civilians bustling about. I decided to continue ignoring the growing tension from my notifications.

They could wait until I was inside, bathed, and lying in my own bed.

There was a brief moment as we reached the drawbridge when I wondered if I should save Gerda the experience by making my way into the castle by some other route . . . but I decided otherwise. If the bridge troll wanted to control the most highly defended drawbridge in the entire Dark Enchanted Forest, then she could afford to pay the price. I was mildly curious how her penalty worked since I didn't receive any experience points, but there was no way to know without asking her—and she didn't seem open to sharing.

We wandered through the market and passed the inn.

Donna was immensely pleased to arrive in the royal stables. Even I could tell, and I didn't have a magical bond connecting us like Bronwynn had. I took some time to help settle the mare and her mistress by unpacking the wagon and administering pets.

To Donna, not her mistress.

The mare seemed to like it when I rubbed the arch of her nose and scratched under her chin. She was a beautiful horse, and a very happy one after I ordered her the best oats and *two* bushels of enchanted carrots to be delivered to her stall.

"Commander General!" a voice squeaked from the stable entry, and I peeked over my shoulder. The ratkin Tuktuk stood there, his impressive frame a surprising contrast to such a high-pitched voice. "I've come to let you know that the king and queen wish to see you at dinner on the hour."

"Tell me I have time to shower." I grimaced.

Brownie stuck her head up from behind the wagon. "Did someone say shower? Who do I have to pay to get a bath as well?"

I grabbed my tail so fast that my claws grazed my skin. The ratkin bowed. "We started preparing the second you crossed the drawbridge. Hot water is awaiting you both upstairs."

"Thank the gods!" Bronwynn exclaimed, dropping back down behind the wagon. She finished whatever she'd been doing back there and hurried out to join us. "Is it my usual room?"

"Yes, Minstrel." Tuktuk bobbed again.

"Then what are we waiting for!" Bronwynn marched toward the stable exit. I smiled and followed the woman—only to stop short of running into her when she paused in the entrance. She glanced back at Donna and pointed threateningly at the mare. "Don't do it."

Donna made a sound not unlike a sigh. If horses could give exasperated sighs, it would sound like that. Since that is what I imagined it was.

"I'm sure Donna will be so well taken care of that she won't think of anything except enjoying her stay," I assured, exchanging meaningful looks with Tuktuk. Despite his size rivaling Bronwynn or myself, the ratkin was timid, and I could see him sweating from my fierce look. But he dabbed at his temple and nodded to show that he'd caught my order.

"We'll make sure your horse is given nothing but the best, Minstrel Bronwynn! I promise!" Tuktuk squeaked. I almost felt bad . . . but I also knew that distracting Donna was the best way to give Bronwynn a relaxing evening. She deserved a relaxing evening after getting chased by murderous bandits. Between them and Gerda, that was two encounters in one day . . . which meant we were still in for one more between now and our arrival in Peldeep.

. . . Unless the fact that Gerda didn't actually give us a riddle for her portal bridge meant it didn't count as an encounter?

I should clarify with Bronwynn later.

Personally, I wanted to count dinner with the Dark Lord and the Dark Lady of the Dark Enchanted Forest as an encounter . . . but that was for me to face, not Bronwynn.

Of course, it was the *after*-dinner conversation I wasn't looking forward to.

Our Dark Lady's Homemade Delights

Brownie

"You met Gerda in Servalt?" Henrietta was on the edge of her seat listening to Brownie while the bard recounted their travels for the last few days.

Brownie smiled. "I did; she said she was going to swing by after she finishes playing with her new magic."

"Bridge troll magic doesn't count as *real* magic," the Dark Lord stated vehemently, drawing everyone's attention.

King Keith had spent the majority of her tale silent up until this point. He'd raised an eyebrow at her missing encounter, chuckled when Donna had been accused of stealing oats, frowned when she'd told him about the duke's assassination attempt, and shot Rufus a *look* when she'd talked about retrieving the beastman from the Assassin's Guild with the story of a dinner date.

Brownie was adept at reading her audience. Henrietta happily "Ooh'd" and "Aah'd" at the right moments and asked an endless line of questions, while King Keith just listened politely. The bard, with her decent Perception, knew the Dark Lord had spent a fair amount of her tale holding Henrietta's hand under the table and presumably toying with it, if the occasional blush on Henrietta's cheeks was an accurate tell.

Rufus also chose that point to add to the conversation. "Just because it's not the [Magic] skill doesn't mean it's not magic. And her new skill is definitely pretty magical."

"What is —? No. Don't tell me." The Dark Lord used his free hand to lift up his glasses and squeeze the bridge of his nose. "I don't want to know."

"If she's free, does that mean we can have a girls' night?" Henrietta was a bubble of joy and adorable energy. Brownie wanted to pet the human woman's head affectionately, but she was sitting across from her and out of reach. With just the four of them, King Keith had chosen not to sit at the head of the table but beside his wife. Rufus sat across from him, and Brownie sat across from Queen Henrietta. Hence the stealth hand-holding.

"I was thinking we could wander out to the drawbridge after this and knock," Brownie offered.

"Are you sure, love?" King Keith faced his wife.

Henrietta looked between Rufus and her husband and finally shrugged. "You can tell me how everything goes later?"

The king's shoulders slumped ever so slightly, but he nodded. "Of course."

"Then it's settled!" Henrietta clapped. "We can visit after dessert! Which I personally prepared, so I hope you enjoy it."

Brownie took her time savoring the lemon custard tarts and dark markle berry torte cake. Henrietta set aside a portion for Gerda, and when all was said and done, they left for the drawbridge.

"I'm so happy Gerda's free." Henrietta was almost skipping beside Brownie down the black cobble street. "I haven't been available since the wedding much . . ."

A blush had come back to the young woman's cheeks, and Brownie resisted the urge to tease the newlywed. The bard outright ignored the small twinge of jealousy at her friend's newfound love and happiness. Henrietta deserved her happily ever after.

The streets were busy around them. Lanterns were lit, and the entire village was alight with an open market. This was the Dark Enchanted Forest, and a significant number of the citizens kept up a nocturnal lifestyle. Brownie spotted arachne, preela, elves, trolls, beastfolk, lizardkin, and more all going about their night to night.

When the pair reached the drawbridge, they recognized a familiar figure waiting for them.

"Gerda!" Henrietta ran forward and grabbed the bridge troll's arm excitedly. "I brought you a present."

Brownie lifted the basket she'd been carrying. "Our Dark Lady's homemade delights."

"I'll never say no to *your* baking, my queen." Gerda smiled, her eyes alight. "I've got a new batch of nettle tisane leaves from an elven crop in Servalt waiting for us below."

The troll walked Henrietta onto the bridge. Two giant golems with long spears stood on either side of it, creations of the Dark Lord's own making. He had golems of all shapes and sizes guarding the Dark Enchanted Forest.

When they got to the other side, the troll led them down the sloped, packed earth of the moat to the underside of the drawbridge. Brownie couldn't help but ask, "Did you just have to pay for Henrietta and I crossing the bridge?"

Gerda's magic flared, and the door to her home appeared on the bridge. Henrietta let go of Gerda's arm so the troll could open her magical door, the frame decorated with beautiful mushrooms and flowers and leaves; it was even more intricately carved than the last time Brownie had seen it.

"Yes," answered the troll as she stood in the entry to her home, looking down on them sideways. Henrietta joined Gerda, and then it was Brownie's turn. It was interesting to feel the spatial magic warp around Brownie as she reached a hand through the space directly overhead and stepped forward into Gerda's home. It wasn't a *bad* feeling, just an *odd* one.

"Wait," Henrietta frowned up at Gerda. "What does she mean you have to pay?"

Gerda shrugged, closing the door. She waved at them to go get seated while she moved to a cauldron of water bubbling over the fire in her hearth.

As she spooned the water into a large teapot and dropped her sachet of the promised nettle tea inside, the troll explained to Henrietta that she had to pay to control the drawbridge without fulfilling her part of the troll magic.

Henrietta listened intently. When Gerda finished, the queen asked, "But . . . *why?*"

That was actually what Brownie wanted to ask. She leaned forward in her chair, putting the basket of treats down on the table.

"Why what?" Gerda tilted her head.

"You're spending hundreds of experience points just to control the drawbridge, and risking angering a Dark Lord . . . Why?"

The troll brought the teapot over and placed it on the table. "I actually have another way to pay for it . . . I found a loophole."

They both stared at the troll expectantly. She hesitated but finally admitted, "I can pay it in taxes."

"But that must be a hundred gold, at least!" Brownie exclaimed, incredulous.

"Well, yes. It costs about two hundred gold a year to manage all of my bridges and take some days off," Gerda admitted. "But it's worth it."

"I can't imagine." The bard shook her head. Henrietta didn't seem as worried, but she was the queen and probably didn't worry about that many gold coins.

Gerda grabbed everyone a cup and added, "Do you have any idea how many experience points I get for holding *every single bridge* in an *entire kingdom?*"

Henrietta and Brownie shared a look before shaking their heads.

"Let's just say"—Gerda put her hands on her hips and looked like a self-satisfied grimalcat when she smiled—"that it far outpaces the loss. I could challenge Commander General Rufus himself for the highest-level minion of the Dark Horde. Not that I'd want his job. No. I'll leave that to General Knolith when the time comes."

"The lizardkin would have to win at the upcoming Winter Solstice Tourney, and I'm not too sure he will," Brownie said. "Rufus won their last duel."

Gerda turned away to grab the honey and cream and three teaspoons, saying over her shoulder, "I'm sure the Commander General title will go to whomever needs it most, when the time is right; no need to worry."

"You're probably right." Brownie felt her own cheeks heat up thinking of the beastman. She *was* worried. It meant a lot to him to keep his rooms and his place in the Black Fortress.

In fact, she hoped he was enjoying the comforts of home right now.

CHAPTER 53

That One Time Her Eminence Feliwyn Sat on Me

Rufus

"Let me get this straight," King Keith said with a wry smile. "You have successfully convinced the Servalt assassins to stop attacking our civilians, you've discovered who was behind the Spring Ball debacle . . . and you've learned that Gerda the Bridge Troll, bane of my life, has possibly hundreds of illegal portals into other kingdoms?"

"Yes."

The two of us had retired to the lounge room in Keith's royal suite with a bottle of fine wine and a cheese platter to discuss my trip. The place had previously boasted a scholarly atmosphere with bare shelves, writing materials, and notebooks lying about. Now, it had flowery cup holders and a small portrait of the king and queen smiling together on the mantle of the dark stone fireplace.

I swirled the wine in my glass, trying to resist a frown as I prepared myself for the worst.

Keith asked. "But you still don't know *how* the assassins crossed the border?"

"I was told to ask Master Derek of Peldeep." I shrugged.

"And you spent *how* many days and nights with Minstrel Bronwynn? Because I'm surprised you haven't mentioned her in your description of the birthday celebration or the Assassin's Guild meeting." Keith was trying to hide a smile, but I could see the pinch in his chin and the slight shake in his shoulders. "For someone who claims to be her biggest fan, you talked more about the grimalcat than the bard."

"Minstrel Bronwynn is . . . There wasn't any—Gods, you can just get on with it," I ground out, dragging a paw down my face in frustration.

Keith obliged and burst into laughter. "The way you almost had a heart attack when you found out that she was Ria's friend . . . I can't believe you joined

Minstrel Bronwynn on the woman's own wagon. That was not at all what I imagined when I told you to follow her."

"I'll have you know I never outright laughed at *you* when you were struggling with your feelings about our queen," I lied. I'd teased him incessantly, and we both knew I deserved what I had coming to me.

I wanted to sigh. Instead, I pulled out the small reading glasses I used for fine print and plopped them on my nose, glancing over the papers I was to submit one last time before handing over the pile.

Keith composed himself down to a light chuckle and accepted the copy of the contract with Guild Master Lina and a brief summary of my findings so far. "Rufus, come on. You can't tell me you discovered nothing about the bard. You were literally with her from the time you left here until that assassin tried to unalive Duke Wyldon. She didn't do *anything* suspicious? *At all?*"

"She literally just traveled around happily playing music . . . Though she was officially investigated when her purse was *wrongfully* placed in the assassin's bedroom." I knew that it sounded bad, so I rushed to say, "But that was Jack's doing, since he'd noticed the same thing we did and wanted cause to interrogate her."

Keith raised an eyebrow. "And?"

"Minstrel Bronwynn is just a friendly bard with a love for adventure and a bonded murder horse," I stated confidently.

A look passed over my king's face, and Keith asked, "So . . . you think it's the horse?"

"What? No! Donna is . . ." I stopped, seriously considering the bard's mare. She was an intelligent beast who could run as fast as the wind, pick locks, and wandered off into the forest sometimes. Still. She was a *horse*.

"Donna is a more likely assassin than Minstrel Bronwynn," I allowed.

"I was joking." Keith shot me a look that questioned my sanity. "You're seriously blaming the horse over your bard?"

"She's not my—Listen, a *rock* is more likely to be an illegal international undercover spy than Minstrel Bronwynn. The woman is as tall as I am, recognized by half the continent, and constantly facing off against her family's cursed *encounters*. She doesn't have time to—"

"Minstrel Bronwynn is under a family curse?" Keith interrupted, leaning forward and showing newfound interest.

"Not like that," I groaned and took a gulp of my drink.

Keith pressed. "Not like *what* exactly?"

"Her mother is the seventh daughter of a seventh daughter. And her father is the seventh son of a seventh son," I explained. For a second, I felt strange not knowing if Bronwynn herself was a seventh daughter since I already knew her birthday, her favorite foods, her mannerisms, how she took her tea, and her shoe size . . . I dragged myself back to the conversation at hand. "And she has three encounters on every trip from inheriting their [Child of Seven] skill."

"I've heard of it, but I've never met someone so tied up in the rules of magical engagement." Keith sipped his drink. "Have you told her you love her yet?"

"What? *No!*" The question came out of nowhere, startling me.

"And she hasn't figured it out?" my king pressed, obviously enjoying my suffering.

I put down my glass and glared at my friend. "What is there to figure out? I love her *music*. You know that."

"Weren't you the one who told me honesty is the best foundation for a relationship?" Keith pointed out, repeating something I'd told him over and over again. "If I recall, you told me that beastfolk just get married when they know."

My magnanimous ruler had a bad habit of not sharing his thoughts until he was sure of them . . . which meant he often just went quiet and didn't tell his wife what he was thinking until prodded. But he was trying to build better habits, and it was just the way things went with relationships: you worked at them every day, or you stopped having a relationship.

"Need I remind you that *I'm undercover*, and following her around the continent on your orders?" I countered, the weight of my situation heavy on my mind. I felt like that one time Her Eminence Feliwyn sat on me, "I don't think now is a great time to tell her how I feel, if I felt that way. Which I don't. I like her, sure, but I *love* her *music*."

"Technically, you're following her around on my wife's orders," Keith countered.

"We're heading out again tomorrow, so I've plenty of time to figure it out while we travel." I ignored his last comment. "Who knows, maybe Gerda will portal us to Peldeep so I can get this over and done with faster."

"Speaking of Gerda." Keith glanced down at the last page in the pile of pages I'd handed the man.

"Ah yes," I stood up, taking off my tiny glasses, rubbing them clean, then slipping them back into their case. I moved them into my spatial ring instead of my pocket, where I'd broken many a pair of spectacles before. I said, " She'll need another audit. I'll leave you to it."

"What—"

"We're leaving early tomorrow and I've got to pack." I ran for the door, hiding a grin. I had no idea what time we were actually leaving.

The king cursed aloud behind me. It was the little things, such as crushing your boss with menial tasks and paperwork, that made life worth living.

That and music, of course.

Speaking of which, I should send a cast to the fan club notifying them that Minstrel Bronwynn's next public performance in Peldeep was on schedule. It had been a while since I'd seen Ross or Frida, and it would be nice to catch a few drinks before the show.

I took my task as leader of Bronwynn's fan club very seriously, and everyone on the list was going to get a message on their crystal shard.

There was going to be a lot to tell the news group, though I wouldn't reveal my identity under the pain of death . . .

I didn't want to get eaten alive by my fellow fans.

Figuratively or literally.

CHAPTER 54

Does He Know?

Brownie

The gentle aroma of simmering strawberry syrup filled the troll's cottage.

Henrietta was telling us about her duel with General Knolith as she used her crushing Strength sixty to whip the unigoat cheese into a creamy, fluffy texture that looked like pillowing clouds. The lizardkin had gone straight to the castle after checking in on Kith Bog . . . and one thing had led to another until they'd had an official duel. She'd defeated him, of course.

Gerda was listening intently while she mixed spices in a mortar. They would go into a bowl of crumbled—also by Henrietta—crackers that were going to act as the base of the cake.

Brownie was using her [Knife Play] to cut all of the remaining strawberries into the shape of rosebuds. They'd saved the tiniest berries to use as decorations, and Brownie was proud that her small flowers were turning out so cute.

"Knolith," Brownie smiled wryly, "is an . . . interesting lizardkin."

Gerda burst into laughter. "You mean he's a pompous, self-assured, young-master type who's reaching for the heavens?"

"Yes." Brownie chuckled. "That."

Gerda shook her head. "At least he's easy to work with; he simply pays me to cross my bridge. It makes everything a lot easier."

Brownie raised her eyebrows. "You mean he wasn't personally offended by you barring his path?"

"He's a good guy; it just took him a while to figure things out. Or in his case, figure out he shouldn't bother wasting both of our time." Gerda finished adding her last spice, an anise seed, and grabbed her pestle. "It took him a few hours the first time."

The pounding of the mortar and pestle filled the room for long enough to create a pause in their conversation. Brownie wondered if she was being too harsh on the General of the East.

"I've whipped the two pounds of cheese, a cup of sugar, a cup of soured cream, a squeeze of lemon juice, and one floofpoof egg." Henrietta put down her bowl beside Gerda. "Am I missing anything?"

The troll scooped a dollop of fluffy cheese onto her finger and tasted it. Her face relaxed in appreciation, and she moved to wash her hand at the sink. "It's perfect, though I'm tempted to add another half an egg . . . It'll be fine."

"Wonderful! Then I'll fix us another cup of nettle tea." Henrietta wandered to the counter designated entirely for the various jars of tea, honey, and tisanes Gerda had collected. Tiny, adorable teaspoons with mushroom motifs hung on a wall frame above the counter.

"What does the recipe say to do next?" Gerda asked. She was mixing her spices into the crackers.

Henrietta read aloud. "Gently pat the crust into the bottom of the dish, and then bake it for ten minutes."

"Alright." Gerda gave the crumble one final stir before pouring it into the baking dish and working to flatten it with her green hands. It didn't take long, and we all watched as she slipped the dish into an oven hole above the fireplace. She used pink oven mitts to close and latch the metal door that sealed the oven.

Henrietta was wearing a familiar hedgehog print apron, Gerda was wearing one with little ducks, and Brownie was wearing one covered in unicorns. They were very nice aprons, with multiple pockets.

"So where are you headed next, Bronwynn?" Gerda accepted the tea Brownie offered before taking a seat at the table. The bard pushed the plate of strawberries forward to have space for her own cup.

"Peldeep. I'm making good enough time that I'm thinking I can stay a few days with my family there." Brownie nursed her tea and enjoyed the warm aroma of the honeyed hot beverage. She'd opted out of milk, though Gerda and Henrietta both added some to their own. Henrietta left the bowl of creamed cheese on the counter and came to join us.

The Dark Lady cast her a sly smile. "So, you're taking Rufus with you to Peldeep?"

"Yes?" Brownie hesitated when her friend used *that* tone of voice.

"Then, are you two dating yet?"

Brownie almost spit her drink. "No!"

Gerda just smiled and sipped her tea.

"Well, I just thought," Henrietta pointed out, her own smile teasing, "that if you're bringing the commander general to meet your family, then you must be at least *interested* in dating."

"I'll have you know that I'm taking him to the Peldeep Assassin Assembly . . . but that's only because that's where he is going next on his quest. There isn't anything else to it."

"Does he know?"

Brownie shook her head.

"Know what?" Gerda asked, intrigued.

Brownie hesitated. She'd only grown close to the troll recently, but eventually decided to share, "My family works for the Peldeep Assassin Assembly."

"So there really isn't *anything* going on between you two?" Henrietta pressed.

"Well, I don't know how *he* feels." Brownie could feel the blush on her cheeks. "But I'll admit I'm . . . *interested.*"

"Great!" The Dark Lady, queen of the Dark Enchanted Forest, giggled.

Brownie suddenly frowned at her best friend. "*You* didn't tell him? Did you? About my family?"

"No! You made me promise when you told me last month." Henrietta placed her cup gently on the table and waved her hands in front. "I haven't even let Keith know. Though I would like to. I think Rufus will find out and report back to him on your trip, so if it's alright with you, can I let him know after you both head out?"

Brownie sighed. "All right. It doesn't really matter because *I'm* not an Assassin, so the worst that can happen is—" She stopped.

"What?" Gerda asked. The troll seeming amused by the entire conversation.

"I don't wanna fae it," Brownie said. "I've been held hostage enough times, and I'm not hoping for another one of *those* encounters anytime soon."

Gerda nodded. "At least the commander general will be there if you need rescuing."

"You know, it's one of the reasons I was so excited he was coming with me." Brownie relaxed, her face lighting up when she thought about her adventures with the golden beastman. "He's wonderful company and scares away most of the inconvenient encounters."

The ten minutes were up, and they paused so Gerda could bring out the pan and add layers of cream cheese to the dessert. The troll placed the filled cake pan in a deep dish with added water, then popped it into the oven for another hour to finish.

Henrietta sipped her tea and made an appreciative happy noise, then said, "I just hope that doesn't mean your encounters are going to change to face obstacles that can deal with him."

Brownie frowned. Hadn't that just happened?

CHAPTER 55

She Was a Good Horse . . . Probably

Rufus

As promised, Donna had had her fair share of enchanted carrots and prized oats, and the mare was in fine form when we packed to head out. Bronwynn loaded her things into the wagon while I administered pets and scratched behind the horse's ears.

She was a good horse . . . probably.

"Gerda let me know last night that we're on our own today," Bronwynn said, jumping up to her seat. "No portal shortcuts."

I gave Donna one last pat before walking over to join the bard. "Is she out walking to a new bridge, then?"

"No, much worse." Bronwynn smiled. "She's registering all of her new bridges with Henrietta and King Keith. We'll still see her at the western bridge though; it's on this side of the Hollow and shouldn't take us long to reach."

"And how was last night?" I asked as I settled in. Personally, my evening had gone about as well as it could have. And His Viciousness, my king, hadn't been as vicious as he could have been. The teasing aside, I thought I'd handled my own quite well.

And Keith's glare from across the breakfast table that morning had left a smile on my face.

"Lovely. Henrietta is living her happily ever after, and Gerda is an enigma. She can't be much older than I am, but every time I talk to her, I feel like I'm getting advice from an older sister. A green one. Luckily, she only had to pop out a few times to troll a bridge." Bronwynn chuckled. "We ate strawberry-glazed cheesecake and stayed up *way* too late."

I hadn't noticed the slight darkness under her eyes until I looked for it. "If we make good timing, maybe we can stop for a nap this afternoon?"

"A man after my own heart!" The half giantess beamed, then coughed. "I mean, that sounds wonderful. And the weather is perfect for it."

The sun had risen only an hour prior, but the day was warm and there wasn't much wind.

"Off we go!" Bronwynn flicked the reins as gently as she could, pretending to lead. Donna rolled her eyes but started walking.

I noted that Bronwynn was wearing her red bag. "Did you ever find out what happened to your money?"

"The duke added the difference in my payment. Or actually, I think Jack added it. Plus a tip." She grinned and patted her bag. "Honestly, the money did its job. People get so focused on the bag and ignore the plain black ring that has my important luggage. That's also why I have a red pack with some spare old clothes in the wagon."

"Smart." I caught myself staring at the bard.

Her red-touched hair was alight in the morning sun, and her smile was infectious. The usual twinkle of mischief danced in her eyes, and I tried not to drown in their dark depths. She was so beautiful, and I felt myself relax even before we pulled out of the Black Fortress. We cleared the drawbridge and traveled west at the crossroads. It took a bit to clear out my notifications, but it wasn't as much of a hassle as it normally felt. As promised, we reached Gerda's bridge almost an hour later.

"Which Pine has the Longest Needle?"

The troll stood on her bridge, hands on her hips, and a half smile on her face. She was wearing a light summer dress with a vest and apron covered in unicorns.

"Oh! Oh! I know!" Bronwynn lifted a hand and waved. She turned to me and asked, "Or would you like a go at it first?"

"Uh . . ." I froze, but drew a deep breath and nodded. I repeated the riddle in my mind a few times and clasped my hands, leaning my elbows on my knees as I contemplated pine trees. "A hilder pine? In Drendil? They grow pretty tall."

Brownie reached over to pat my shoulder in commiseration even as Gerda shook her head and stated, "Incorrect!"

"The answer?" I asked my travel companion, knowing she knew.

"A spearpoint porcupine!"

"Correct. You may pass." The bridge troll moved to the side to let us roll on by. "I'm getting a summons from another bridge, gotta go!" Then the troll disappeared.

We continued down the road for another hour or so, when suddenly, Donna chuffed at us, and Bronwynn nodded. "How far out?"

The mare snorted and shook her head, speeding up a bit. We came upon the exit to the Hollow, the elven city, and passed it by without incident.

"What did she say?"

"There's a herd of unicorns to the north of us making a ruckus. They might cross our path in the next hour, or not. She's just wanting me to know because we'll have to book it if we see them."

"Why?"

Donna chuffed again, her sarcasm almost palpable.

"She turned down Goldenhoof's son, and he's not taking no for an answer," Bronwynn explained. "The colt insists she should give him a chance, and she's put her hoof down—no more unicorns. I miss getting to pet them, though, so I'm hoping the rule doesn't last much longer . . . Maybe Brightstar will find someone else?"

The mare whinnied, and Bronwynn quickly reassured her horse. "Of course I'll respect your boundaries. We'll make a run for it at the first hint of hoofprints."

I looked out onto the thinning tree line, a stunning meadow of wildflowers and green clover peeking through the fir trees. It was too early for an afternoon nap, unfortunately, but I could keep my eyes open.

For a nice, sunny field or a unicorn.

Her Promised Afternoon Nap

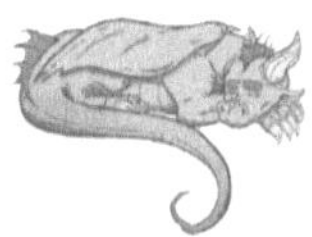

Brownie

They didn't meet any unicorns.

They did, however, pass by a unit of the Dark Horde transporting a wagonload of hats, sun lotion, and waterskins to each of the army bases—preparation for the summer. There were also three mice riding on an owl running down the road. The owl screeched but kept going.

In a dirt clearing off to the side of the road, they saw a regal wagon getting its wheel fixed. Everything looked to be well in hand, so they progressed.

A few minutes later, Donna stopped because a circle of ravens were standing in the road cawing at each other. A few of the birds flew off in each of the cardinal directions, while the rest took to the trees. All of their eyes followed them while they rode past, but Brownie ignored them. It wasn't her story to interrupt. They did manage to find the perfect picnic spot around lunchtime. Brownie pulled out her red-and-white picnic blanket, and a basket full of goodies from Gerda and Henrietta.

The sun shone down on a golden meadow of broomlanding, yarrow, daylily, and scattered snapdragons. Rufus blended in well with his surroundings, his gold coat with ruddy undertones glinting in the sunlight and matching the yellow flowers. He pulled out a bottle of wine and two wine glasses to pair with bimbleberry scones, flying pork sandwiches, fresh strawberries, a round of unigoat soft cheese, and some imported olives from Sumbria for lunch. Brownie played a few songs on her instrument, including "Sally Oh Sally" from Peldeep, "Walk in Shadows" from Sumbria, and one of her own pieces, "The Blade My Father Bore." The last was one she had been trying to perfect for quite a while, and still wasn't right.

"I don't remember you playing that song before," Rufus commented. He was leaning on one elbow splayed out half on the blanket and half off. His free hand held his glass.

The wine was a ruby red that resembled her hair.

Brownie had enjoyed her glass immensely. The delicate aroma of violets and sour cherry blended with warm spice was light and refreshing, and it was probably one of the most expensive wines she'd ever tasted. One she'd finished while sampling the cheese and olives earlier.

She set her instrument aside, but deliberately on the picnic blanket between herself and the beastman—no need for it to go walking because she glanced away for an instant. This *was* the Dark Enchanted Forest, after all. "It's not ready, but I hope it'll be polished by the Masquerade."

"I look forward to it." He nodded.

"One question." Brownie lay back on the blanket herself, both arms crossed behind her head as a makeshift pillow. "How many of my songs have you heard?"

"All of them," Rufus stated before tensing and quickly continuing with, "At least, I've seen enough of your shows that I *thought* I'd heard all of them. You make new ones all the time, so I'm *sure* I only know the popular ones . . . Why? How many songs have you written?"

The innocent question didn't seem so innocent when she noted the intensity of his gaze and the breath he held in wait for her answer. She smiled slowly at the beastman. "Fifty-seven."

Rufus choked on the air he was holding. "F-Fifty-seven?!"

"Fifty-seven," she repeated calmly. Her repertoire was much larger, but of the songs she'd personally written herself? That was about right. Some were juvenile and never saw an audience outside of her family dinners, and some weren't appropriate for polite company. Others were purely campfire songs, like creepy lullabies designed to scare and delight children . . . And then some were too long or too short for a proper show. "I only perform about thirty-two."

"I've heard all thirty-two." Rufus didn't seem happy about his surprising accomplishment. He must have been at any number of her events, since many of her songs were seasonal or scenario based—from wedding to tavern brawl. He'd have needed to slip into her concerts quite a few times . . . and in quite a few countries. She frowned; the only time she'd played "Wings of Ash" was on its debut night in Sumbria.

When the place burned down, she'd decided not to sing it at a concert again, just in case.

And just in case she was overthinking things, she asked, "Oh, have you heard this one?"

We sisters wake up with the day,
And rise in fire to the sun.
The eldest burns in red and gold,
The second shines orange in the dawn.

> I am the youngest fire-touched,
> A whirl with white and smoky-blue,
> And though my sisters love me dear
> They mourn my sky-bright hue.

She played the opening verse. Rufus grinned, "I have. It was sad, but sweet."

". . . I see."

That evening had been a gathering of her fans organized by her fans. Rufus was obviously a great lover of music, and must have procured an invite, but Brownie didn't know how she'd missed someone as large and in charge as the golden retriever beastman.

Unless he hadn't attended in his beastman form.

Her mind drifted to the show as she felt the draw of her promised afternoon nap.

Ever since her big break in Drendil, thanks to Henrietta, Brownie had gotten performance time at taverns and parties all over the kingdom and beyond. Her family in Peldeep had offered to set her up with a musical career early . . . but she'd wanted to find her own voice and her own path. Granted, Henrietta had pretty much done exactly what her family had offered to, but it was still *different*. Her friend might have set up the stage, but she'd had no one standing around with daggers pointed at their backs to clap. Being invited to one garden party on recommendation and being set up by a family of assassins were just not the same thing at all.

And so, when she had instantly become popular, she was suddenly collecting a team of music lovers who loved *her*. Brownie's songs were catchy, and they were new, and her voice was praised in the inner circles. So, for the last five or six years, she'd been followed around by a group of fans, and once a year, they hosted a gathering. Brownie loved it. She could pull out old songs or mix in new ones, and everyone knew the lyrics and knew *her*. She'd met many of them, but respected any boundaries for her anonymous or shy listeners.

For which she assumed Rufus must be in those numbers.

The last fan show she'd performed had been earlier this year in Sumbria, at a large and welcoming tavern near the canyon that *thankfully* was in a village on the edge of the elven forest. The building was made out of wood, but not from a magical tree.

She'd arrived in good spirits, ready for an exciting evening, and accidentally provided the catalyst to burn down the venue.

As one does.

Her mind wandering, she closed her eyes and drifted off into a warm and comfortable sleep.

CHAPTER 57

The Tragedy of Magicians

Rufus

I stared at Minstrel Bronwynn happily napping in the sun and tried to calm my rising blood pressure.

Her words had shaken me. There were songs of hers that *I hadn't heard yet.* For whatever reason.

It was unacceptable.

The thought was almost insulting.

I bet Her Viciousness Henrietta had heard them. She was Bronwynn's sounding board, as I understood, and usually got first ear on the minstrel's new completed work. I wasn't jealous. Not at all.

I was envious.

Bronwynn usually performed only one new song in any given evening performance . . . and the only time I'd heard her perform two new pieces was at . . . the incident.

I shuddered. That night had been one I'd never forget. Actually, the memory haunted me, and I realized with a start one specific song that she'd revealed that evening . . .

Oh no. I dragged a paw down my face, remembering exactly where I'd heard her play "Wings of Ash."

"Excuse me."

The voice I loved spoke right behind me, startling me. Some assumed that changing between full beast form or full folk form changed a beastfolk's senses—they did not. My stats remained the same whether I was a large canine loping over the hills or a furless person walking around and using opposable thumbs. The only thing I noticed right away between any transformation was my size.

As a beast, I was at my largest, but obviously closer to the ground. At about halfway I stood at my tallest, as tall as Bronwynn the half giantess. At full folk form, I lost the extended toes and dropped to my heel, standing as tall as the bard's eyebrows.

The person I was most excited to see stood at the back door entrance, an hour before the front doors opened. "Bard Bronwynn?!"

"I'm here to get ready for the show? Are you in charge?"

The half giantess beamed down at me. She was friendly and open and obviously ready for a good time. Her curls were cut just below her shoulders. She was wearing a purple thigh-length tunic over a pair of black leather tights with her usual belt and pouch and knives.

And a familiar strap slung over her shoulder, carrying her lyre harp Suzette, out of its case. In one hand she carried her instrument case, and in the other hand a bridge red handbag.

I drew a breath and released it slowly, counting to seven. A trick I'd taught my own clients to use to manage their emotions in times of stress.

"Yes, I'm Fergus." That was close enough to my name that it caught my attention. And I was using it for any non-commander-general-related activities. Like meeting my idol. "Let me carry your things."

She handed over the handbag easily and smiled at me again, her dark eyes with flecks of red fire warm and beautiful. At least I didn't need to worry about controlling my tail in this form . . .

"Lead on, friend Fergus," Bard Bronwynn said, following me to the wooden stage. I'd had it oiled so that it shone but wasn't too slippery, and I'd hired a local mage to clean up the place magically that morning, so the entire hall was ready to go. "I'm happy you knew I was the entertainment this afternoon; sometimes, it takes me forever just to figure out what and where I am, and when I actually start."

"Technically, you're not just *the entertainment*. You're the guest of honor," I found myself correcting her. "And I've a rough schedule for the day ready based on your previous shows that we can go over. Which you can of course change to your liking. It's *your* show."

She laughed, deep and wonderful. "Perfect. Oh, can I ask for something?"

"Anything you need," I told her enthusiastically. "Anything, and it's yours."

"Oho?! A man after my own heart. I like you, Fergus," the bard said, and my entire world fell apart at her feet while I stood fixed to the spot. She continued, "If it's not too much of a bother, I would love some water in my mug to start the show."

"No trouble at all; I'll grab you a pitcher," I assured her.

I reminded myself that I was the commander general of the Dark Lord's army . . . and used that to convince myself to move in the manner expected of me: poised, calm, in control.

I left Bard Bronwynn at the back of the stage to get ready. While I finished checking everything one last time before the show started, she looked over the room and thoroughly familiarized herself with the entire space and its staff.

It was short work to place a pitcher of water on a stool on the stage.

When the doors opened, I met up with Frida and Ross, who'd traveled from afar. I, of course, had saved us front-table seats.

A young magician elf and his date shared our table, though they gave us a wide berth. The pair weren't too pleased to be seated with non-elves, but they were willing if only because it was a Bard Bronwynn concert . . .

Then, just before the first break, Bronwynn put it out to the audience for a song request. I yelled out, "The Tragedy of Magicians."

Bronwynn picked out my voice in the crowd and shot me a wink. My attention was all on her, even as my tablemates were distracted by the magician elf asking questions.

"Alright. Here's a little tragic history from my own kingdom to share with you all, for what better way to avoid a curse than to learn about how it came about?"

> King Simon of Drendil was joyous today,
> For the queen would give birth in the spring.
> And they all feasted under the full harvest moon,
> But fate is a terrible thing.

> Oh the moon shone that night
> On the streets and the sight
> Of the people who had read the signs.
> But the prophecy swore
> Of a future that bore
> A curse on King Simon's line.

> The royal astronomer stepped to the front
> Of the festival well underway,
> But his eyes shone with fear of the future he saw
> And all turned to hear with dismay:
> The babe might be born but they would be the last
> To walk with the blood of the throne,
> A magician's curse would be the end of his reign
> And a new king rise when the child's grown.

> Oh the moon shone that night
> On the streets and the sight
> Of the people who had read the signs.

> But the prophecy swore
> Of a future that bore
> A curse on King Simon's line.
>
> The King called to arms, and he sent out his best
> To gather those magically trained.
> And on the next eve, under the bright moon
> He called for them all to be slain—

"What?!" the magician beside me cried out. He was young and had been getting more and more angry as the song went on, but even so, I was not expecting him to be an untrained mage. With his outburst, he lost control of *something* and shot a fireball at the stage.

The stool with Bard Bronwynn's mug caught on fire . . . and the oil from that morning's polish ignited faster than the stage would have otherwise. And the oils burned toxic.

The entire place had to be evacuated, and it was only thanks to Bronwynn being incredibly dexterous that she made it out in one piece.

After it was all said and done, I reassured the bard that the club had a generous donor who would cover everything. I didn't tell her it was me. I just handed over the ring of flowers I'd prepared for her and went off to deal with the aftermath.

I thought for sure I'd be kicked out of the group after that, but everyone turned their ire on the magician. I myself trekked to the Mages Tower to enact my own revenge by asking that the boy be sent to magically clean our castle's privies for a year. We supplied a *lot* of magical ingredients to the tower, and it would be *a shame* if we couldn't deliver as often.

He deserved it for making us miss the end of the song!

I knew it by heart now, of course.

> One by one they were dropped with a rope at the throat
> But the last mage, he slipped through the binds,
> And with his last breath he drew mana and cast
> A curse, on King Simon's line.
>
> Oh the moon shone that night
> On the streets and the sight
> Of the people who had read the signs.
> But the prophecy swore
> Of a future that bore
> A curse on King Simon's line
> A curse on King Simon's line.

CHAPTER 58

Donna's Relationship Drama

Brownie

A gentle breeze played a stray curl across her cheek that tickled her nose. Brownie stretched, arms above her head, and sat up from her nap.

Rufus was deep in thought, his tail curled, his eyes scanning the distance.

Donna had wandered off into the trees, as she was wont to do.

"Thank you for keeping watch," Brownie told the beastman.

"Anytime." He turned to her with a strained smile, but then his ear twitched. Rufus's eyes looked over her shoulder. "But don't thank me just yet."

A flash of white and a rustle in the bushes, and then a majestic unicorn stood with them in the field. If he, for Brownie immediately recognized this particular specimen of equine beauty, had traveled with the herd seen earlier, they were nowhere to be seen now.

"Brightstar."

The white unicorn was recognizable by the golden star on his forehead below his shimmering golden horn and his singular golden sock on the front right leg. He dipped his head. She sensed in the same way she knew what Donna meant that he was greeting her. There was no way that she alone could outrun Brightstar, so she sent a silent apology to her bond before waving him forward.

"It is good to see you again." Brownie extended her hand, and Brightstar butted against it with his head.

Rufus remained sitting. "Well met, Brightstar, heir to Goldenhoof."

The unicorn rubbed his head against Brownie's hand for a second longer before pulling away slightly to acknowledge the commander general. Then Brightstar stamped the ground once and eyed her questioningly.

"Donna isn't here right now," she let him know, at the same time sending a message about what was happening down her link to the mare.

Brightstar's ears drooped. The unicorn swept his eyes across the meadow and peered into the tree line, but there was neither hide nor hair of Donna. He sighed, lowering himself to his knees and resting his head in the minstrel's lap.

Brownie began administering pets.

Rufus raised an eyebrow at her, but she ignored him. Unicorn pets were almost as lovely as squishing his paw beanies—and she rarely got to hold Rufus's hand long enough to satisfy her urges. With Brightstar, she could pet his coat as much as she wanted and bask in the rejuvenating aura of his magic. Brownie could feel the weariness of travel ebb away. Her right shoe stopped pinching, and her lower back twinge abated, and her dry lips softened.

She sighed with contentment, lavishing the unicorn with head scritches until her legs started to lose feeling.

Rufus just stared at Brightstar with a frown. Maybe he wasn't a unicorn person.

Eventually, Brownie had to be the bearer of bad news, and save her legs. "Listen, Brightstar . . . I don't think Donna is coming back, especially if she finds out you're here. She wanted space, and she just isn't ready to see you right now."

Brightstar lifted his head from her lap and eyed her, his displeasure telling.

"I know you like—" The unicorn snorted contentiously. "Fine, but if you truly *love* her, then you should respect her boundaries," Brownie stated as clearly as she could.

"She's right," Rufus cut in. "And I would have thought that a *unicorn* above all others would appreciate a young maiden's no."

It was harsh, but Brownie agreed.

Brightstar was not amused. He stood and looked between the two of them, letting out a sharp whinny.

"We aren't teaming up on you," Brownie assured. "We just both agree that chasing an unwilling mare around isn't the right way to go . . ."

Rufus nodded. "Do you know what *will* help?"

Brightstar focused on the beastman.

"Right now, you're a young prince. But soon, you will rise to take your father's place as the new guardian of these fields. You will have trials, and you will learn a great deal about yourself," Rufus said, pitching his voice to inspire the colt. "If you want to repair any kind of relationship with Donna, you need to become a stallion who respects himself and others."

The unicorn stomped a foot.

"Perhaps, in time, she will see that you have become Brightstar, Guardian of the Herd, a unicorn of great wisdom and strength, and she might choose to accept your attentions," Rufus advised.

Brightstar perked up at that, only for Rufus to swiftly cut him back down. "And perhaps not. Maybe she will never love you back, and if you care for her as you say you do, then if will end there."

The unicorn chuffed, and Rufus suddenly spoke with a firm voice. "It *will* end there, because you are an honorable stallion who will respect Donna's *choice*." Rufus slipped for a second, and he spoke in that same tone Brownie had heard in Thistlecrick. The voice that left a shiver down her spine. A firm voice that threatened getting locked up in his dungeon. "You are an honorable stallion, aren't you?"

Brightstar hesitated, eyeing the beastman, but eventually butted his head forward. The unicorn, when he wasn't a lovestruck colt, was an otherwise noble prince who understood the strength behind the commander general of the Dark Horde, and what it meant when Rufus became serious.

The beastman smiled. "Do you love Donna?"

The unicorn made a loud whiny and stamped the ground.

"Then let me ask you this. Explain to me why she is *afraid* of you?" Rufus said bluntly. "If you truly love her, then you need to allow her to choose when you are safe to be around. Only then can you hope to earn her trust."

Brightstar was considering that last part very seriously.

"At the very least, you should aim to be someone she can respect . . . which goes both ways, honestly." A gentle breeze rustled through his long golden mane and swishing tail, and delicate sparkling magic fell at the unicorn's feet. All around, daffodils blossomed.

"Love starts with respecting someone's boundaries, listening to their desires, and treating them like a person who is worthy of consideration," Rufus urged. "If you stop and think about what she's saying, you'll know what to do."

Brightstar reared back on his legs, kicking the air.

"I think you can." Rufus added.

Brightstar swept the area one last time for Donna before carefully nodding to Brownie and Rufus each, then heading off across the fields and into the woods on the fast western side of the meadow.

"You really think he'll do it?" Brownie asked.

Rufus shook his head. "He might. This is the hardest time, and he needs good role models and some experience. If he can learn to accept no for no, he'll have no end of prospective partners."

"Unicorns mate for life," Brownie pointed out.

Rufus raised an eyebrow. "To other unicorns." She raised an eyebrow because that was obviously not the case if the prince of unicorns had fallen head over hooves for her horse.

Rufus acquiesced, "or not." Brownie lay back and considered her mare's relationship drama.

A few minutes later, Donna popped out of the bushes. She seemed nervous, and did a Perception check before walking over to Brownie. Donna was eyeing every rock and tree as if they were hiding her nemesis.

"He's gone back home," Brownie tried to soothe the mare's unease, quickly packing everything with Rufus's help. He stuck the leftovers from the picnic into his spatial ring, and then they prepared the wagon for travel in record time.

They were making such good time, in fact, that within another day or so, they would clear the forest. Brownie and Rufus discussed plans for their night's lodgings, but decided to simply sleep in the wagon. The option of a detour into the dwarven post or the beastfolk village came up, but it would mean hours off route.

So instead, they laid out bedding next to each other in the back of the wagon and looked up at the stars. It was a warmer night. The summer solstice mere weeks away.

Rufus asked, "So . . . was Brightstar an encounter?"

"I don't know."

"You don't know?"

"I don't know." Brownie shuffled uncomfortably and readjusted her pillow. "It's not like a system quest. More like how your Commander General title gives you recognition among the Dark Enchanted Forest and perks. Except my perk is more bandits."

"I see."

Brownie explained, "So everything is a potential encounter, and even if it isn't, I've been trained to approach it like one. My parents said I should always be ready. It's in the bloodline."

Rufus suddenly sat up and flung open his sleeping roll, asking "What's that?!"

Brownie looked up in time to see the shadow of a creature in the night sky blotting out the stars. It circled overhead. "It kind of looks like a tiny griffin?" she offered, eyeing the creature. There'd been a few baby griffins born last month, and one of them could have flown astray.

The creature swooped down. Rufus raised his hands, presumably to enact a barrier, when a familiar voice called out above them.

"Meow."

CHAPTER 59

Steal an Ogre's Dinner

Rufus

I caught the grimalcat as he landed square in my arms.

"Commander General," the cat greeted, sliding down onto my lap and circling once as if he hadn't just landed on me from the night sky.

"Slake," I replied, reaching out a hand and gently rubbing his head down to his tail—being careful of his wings, of course.

"Brownie," said Bronwynn, not wanting to be left out. We each gave her a wry look, and she grinned.

The grimalcat kneaded his nails in the blankets and made a pleased purr as I continued to give him gentle rubs. After four, the grimalcat freed himself and tromped to the space between Bronwynn and my headrest.

"You traveled much farther than I'd anticipated." He circled three times then lay down comfortably, showing off his soft stomach. "I'm impressed."

Bronwynn lay back down first and then reached out a hand toward Slake. "May I?"

Slake rolled to give her better access to his fluffy chest and inviting tummy.

I saw the trap for what it was, but it was too late to give warning; Bronwynn had placed her hand down on the temptation and was promptly mauled.

Still, she didn't seem all that perturbed. I relaxed when she swept her fingers up to the grimalcat's just below the chin and started scratching the tuft of hair on his fluffy chest. Slake immediately released his hold on her flesh and flopped back to let her continue her adoring administrations.

Rufus wondered if she would be tempted to pet him with such fervor in his beast form . . .

* * *

The next day dawned damp with dew and a little cold. The dry, hot spring had been threatening drought, so the weather was a welcome sign. They were packed and on the road before the rain started.

Slake was not amused and hid in my cloak.

The sun peeked its head out of the clouds by noon, and the rest of the day flew by. It helped that we had the famous Slake Drakeford to regale us with his stories between Bronwynn singing songs. Donna didn't seem that impressed, but Donna was a horse.

The border to Peldeep drew closer and closer . . .

I noticed that, as the day went on, my bard started getting restless. She repeated songs and went longer and longer between playing. The traffic so close to the border was heavier, and we passed merchants, carriages, and travelers all filling the roads. The turn off to Gren's Keep passed on the left, and the path to the dwarven outpost Frolin passed on our right. The only thing of interest was a noble entourage in shambles, but they didn't prevent the flow of traffic.

Eventually, when the border actually came into sight in the distance, Bronwynn asked Donna to stop.

"Is this about your three encounters?" I asked, considering Gerda's bridge and Brightstar and maybe Slake as potential encounters. Though meeting up with a grimalcat who was already invited to travel with us might not have counted.

Everyone waited for Bronwynn to tell us what was on her mind.

"Rufus," my bard finally broached. "I—"

"Fair travelers, please listen to my plight!" And of course, that was when a small red squirrel hopped onto a tree branch on the side of the road and called out to us.

It was almost so quiet as to be imperceptible, but I heard Bronwynn sigh. She must have been anxious. She turned a beaming smile at the squirrel and said, "What troubles you, Daisy?"

The squirrel, Daisy, scampered around the branch she was perched on once and then stood back up. She placed the back of her tiny paw against her tiny forehead dramatically and proclaimed, "The dread Morga has imprisoned Earl Oakley of Sumbria in her lair and is going to eat him this very evening should no one rescue him!"

Bronwynn frowned. "The dread Morga isn't known for eating elves . . . What did he do?"

The squirrel took a deep breath, and then visibly slumped forward, all theatrics laid aside. "Alright, I'll tell you straight, Brownie! He had it coming! He was so mean to Morga and called her . . . Well, he was *very rude*. If he weren't of elven royal blood, every one of us forest folk would've been happy to see him get eaten. But . . ."

"He *is* of royal blood." Bronwynn nodded knowingly. "So you're just doing your job. Thank you, Daisy."

"It's days like these I think about finding new work, but I have an enchanted treehouse overlooking the Pixie Prim's sunflower field to pay off, and I'm not moving." Daisy the squirrel's nose twitched. She pointed a claw off the beaten path and said, "You'll find Morga's lair about ten minutes that way."

I scratched my head. "So, you're . . . a professional quest giver?"

The squirrel stuck up her chin. "The best."

"We'll head out now. See you next time, Daisy!" Bronwynn told the squirrel, who waved then scampered away out of sight.

I crossed my arms. "You aren't really going to go and steal an ogre's dinner, are you?"

"Of course I am," Bronwynn replied, hopping down from the wagon even as Donna pulled them to the side of the road. She had her instrument slung over her shoulder. "It's all in a day's work as a traveling bard."

"It's the proper thing to do in these cases," Slake said from my lap. The grimalcat lazily stretched before jumping onto the bench. He spread his wings and flapped once, a gust of wind carrying him to Bronwynn. Slake landed gently on her back, fumbling for just a second before finding the right leverage to sit on the half giantess's shoulder without getting in the way of her instrument. "Lead on, friend Brownie."

I hurried after them as we abandoned Donna and the wagon to follow a deer trail into the dark woods. The entire place grew quiet at our approach.

"Wouldn't it be easier to just ignore these types of encounters entirely?" I asked, catching up.

Bronwynn physically shivered. "Oh no. Definitely not. If I don't go, I get bad luck."

"The debuff?"

"No." She explained, "It's just that my encounters are all normal and usually fall within a certain danger limit. If I ignore encounters, the next one gets less ignorable."

"But you *can* ignore them?"

"The last time I did that, I got kidnapped and lost my musical instrument," she told me.

I stopped on the path. "What?!"

Bronwynn looked like she was going to shrug, but she had a grimalcat on her shoulder. Slake, for his part, looked interested. He said, "That sounds like quite the tale."

"It was almost worth it," she grumbled. "I was supposed to save the crown prince of Sumbria when I ran into him on the road the day before the Spring Ball. I stopped for thirty seconds before abandoning that cause. That elf was *awful.* Luckily, the maiden traveling with him had a bow and fended off the bandits by herself. If the earl is anything like Crown Prince Darcy, or whatever his name was, then we're in for an unpleasant afternoon. So let's get this over with quickly."

Bronwynn stopped as we crested a hill, looking down into a thicket with a large wooden cottage. There was a desperate and fearful groaning coming from inside, the only other sound from a trickling brook that wound its way through the clearing.

"I wonder if Morga knows people are calling her home a *lair?*" Brownie mused before starting the slow descent.

"And I wonder," I said, following after the bard, "if she's home."

CHAPTER 60

Release the Elf

Brownie

"And then the ingrate had the audacity to call me an old biddy with saggy . . . knees!" Morga thumped her large gray hand onto her thick wooden table. "Which is why I was going to eat him for dinner, of course."

"Of course," Brownie and Rufus said in unison. They smiled at each other and sipped their cups of fresh-pressed pear juice. Slake was too busy lapping cream in a bowl laid out for him on the table to respond.

Earl Oakley, an older elf with long, white-streaked hair pulled back in a ponytail and a sharp hawk nose, lay trussed up on the floor. His brown eyes were bulging, his mouth gagged. He didn't look comfortable, and his clothing was dirty from being dragged.

The three had made it halfway down the trail when the door had opened and an enormous ogre had stepped out to greet them. She was a head taller than Brownie, and quite elderly. Her ashen gray skin was similar to Duke Wyldon's family of elves, but on the ogre, it was more like rock and stone. She was a power to be reckoned with, and the second she'd seen them approaching, everyone had paused in their tracks.

And then she'd invited them in for drinks.

"I suppose you're here on a quest to stop me?" Morga eyed us.

Brownie nodded. "We've been sent to free the earl. Sorry about that."

Morga picked up her own juice and downed the contents of the wooden mug in one fell swoop. She placed it onto her table surprisingly gently, careful of the vessel, and crossed her arms. "So, what are you offering to trade for the earl?"

Brownie tapped a finger on her chin in contemplation. Usually, they would have picked up something useful on the way for this part of the exchange.

Rufus coughed before waving his hand on the table. An untouched flying pork sandwich, a bimbleberry scone quartered for easy consumption, a third of the wheel of unigoat brie, and four remaining olives from their late lunch the previous day appeared there. When they'd been in a hurry to clean up, he'd just quickly gotten rid of everything by storing it in his ring.

"How about a replacement feast?" he said. "As I understand it, you don't like eating elf—"

"They're too wiry," the ogre explained. She happily perused the offering in front of her with a sharp gleam in her eyes. "This will do very nicely as a trade."

"Perfect!" Brownie clapped. It turned out Brownie *had* picked up the perfect thing for this test: a Rufus.

"Then, if you're satisfied"—Rufus stood, downing the last sip of his juice—"we really must be going."

"Hold on just one moment." Morga also stood up, looming over the beastman. Brownie felt her heart race as she debated summoning her dagger. "Let me grab you another glass." Morga's eyes landed on Brownie. "I won't let you leave until you've played a song for me, Minstrel Bronwynn. It has been too long!"

Brownie smiled and swung Danielle into her lap. She crossed her legs comfortably and leaned back in her chair, plucking a series of notes. "How about 'Three Witches'?"

"Wonderful. That and 'One More Song to Go'?" the ogre asked.

Suddenly, Rufus said, "Wait! Are you *that* Morga?"

Everyone turned to face the beastman, and he became outwardly self-conscious. "I mean, I've just heard about you before and finally placed it. Don't mind me. Go on, Minstrel Bronwynn . . ."

Her fingers plucked a heart-wrenching soft, dark melody, singing an old song that her grandmother had sung to her when she was a little half giantess. It was about three witches that balanced their home . . . and the one left to shoulder all of their tasks when her sisters perished.

Three witches lived in Holgrovely
Betwixt the town and fore the sea.
One lived on lime,
One lived on thyme
And the last on a hazel tree.
The lime witch roamed the wave struck bath,
The thyme witch seeped in earthen wrath,
The last was she
Who kept the tree
That birthed the forest path.

One washed the town in sea breeze neat,
One bore the town of summer heat,
One looked and bade
To grow the shade
Which stretched between their feet.
When Winter came the sea witch froze,
Thyme burned in summer sun repose,
But the hazel leaves
Which weeps and grieves
Stood still in her shadows.

They hunt for her but never find
The witch that last is left behind
Who never asked
To shoulder tasks
Her sisters used to mind.
There is one witch of Holgrovely
Betwixt the town and fore the sea,
She minds the waves,
The wood and staves,
But ne'er forgets there once were three.

Throughout the entire conversation and performance, Earl Oakley had remained trussed up on the floor. The grimalcat was receiving pets from Morga, and Rufus had finally relaxed. Brownie finished up her second song and then activated [Liar's Palace] with ease. She wanted to be ready for the hard part that came next.

"Thank you for the juice, Morga," Brownie said after they were all finished. "Rufus, if you can pick up the earl, we'll get going."

"Farewell, everyone, and see you next time, Minstrel Bronwynn." The ogre followed them to her doorway and waved them off. The hill was a dangerous climb, with soft dirt that could slip out from underfoot, but they made the trek.

They weren't anywhere near the main road when Brownie sent word ahead to her horse.

The minstrel stopped on the path. "Alright, I think we're a safe enough distance from Morga to release you now, Earl Oakley. Please forgive our being overly cautious."

Rufus put the earl down on his feet and ripped apart the ropes tying his ankles and knees together like they were fine thread. He plucked the gag out before moving to release him from his upper bindings.

"OVERLY CAUTIOUS!" the elf immediately screeched. "You *dare*—"

Rufus shoved the gag back into the elf's mouth, having stopped just shy of freeing the earl.

"No, no, it's fine!" Brownie urged her travel companion. "Release the elf."

CHAPTER 61

Are You Going to Tell Him?

Rufus

Every bone in my body was telling me to toss the earl down the slope behind us. His level looked to be mid-twenties . . . He would survive.

And he might think twice about yelling at *my* bard . . . But that way lay violence and bad choices, and I wasn't an impulsive youth. I'd never really been an impulsive youth. No, those emotions had only come about after I'd grown a love for music. And an unhealthy adoration of the beautiful Minstrel Bronwynn that I was now letting get out of hand.

"Alright," I agreed, choosing to extend my claw to slice the last rope that held the elf captive.

Earl Oakley reached up with his newly freed hand and grabbed the gag, tossing it to the floor. He turned on me with his full height, which was to say as tall as my collarbone, and yelled, "NOW, SEE HERE—"

"Lord Oakley," Bronwynn cut in. "Do you have any plans now that we've saved you from certain permadeath?"

The earl puffed up his chest and looked down at the half giantess. "You will all return me to my entourage this instant."

Bronwynn, with a patience that left me impressed, asked, "And where is your entourage?"

The earl wasn't paying attention to her.

"My gold-threaded trim! My buttons!" After his declaration that we would escort him, he'd begun fussing over the state of his dress; the fine leather boots were scuffed, his emerald-green hose torn, and his gold-embroidered black doublet was missing a few emerald buttons.

Earl Oakley was growing more and more pale from his personal inspection. I could tell he wasn't having a good day, so I granted him leniency when the elf waved a hand at her and snapped, "What? Oh. We were attacked near the border of Peldeep by that disgusting hag—"

I flexed my claws right in front of his nose, startling the elf into silence. "I would speak more politely about such a lovely old woman." She was also a member of the fan club, though she must have a disguise, since I'd never seen her at a show. I only knew that one *Morga* was on the list of crystal holders getting routine Minstrel Bronwynn updates.

"So you *were* in league with the ogre!" Earl Oakley spat, touting nonsense. "I'm not a fool! You won't receive a copper from me. Now, return me to my carriage at once, cretins!"

I stared down at the delusional elf and then over at Bronwynn, who was focusing on her character sheet.

Slake spoke before I could. "[Silence]."

The elf tried to shout words at the grimalcat—not the best idea, since grimalcats enjoyed a great love for vengeance. No sound left Earl Oakley's mouth, and the elf got red in the face with his growing anger. After shaking a fist at the grimalcat, he stormed up the path.

"You didn't need to do that," Bronwynn said.

I interjected on behalf of the grimalcat. "Actually, it was probably for the best."

We resumed walking as I continued. "It's not my job to rehabilitate him to become a functioning member of society, so instead, I'm going to see him out of our hair as fast as possible. Where's Donna?"

We had reached the road. A road that was missing one wagon and horse.

"I've sent her back to follow behind us," the minstrel explained.

I stared at her. "Why?"

"Because *that*"—she waved at the still fuming elf. He looked like he wanted to have them all drawn and quartered—"wouldn't last five minutes with my horse."

"I see, yes." She was absolutely correct. "So I guess we should start walking."

The earl stamped his foot, but without words, we all ignored him. He was not happy, but after we left him raging on the road all alone, he ran to catch up.

We weren't walking for longer than thirty minutes when we came upon an ornate carriage and five elves calling out for Earl Oakley on the road.

"I'm here, you fools!" the earl shouted, then seemed surprised that his voice had returned at all. "Now, come beg me for forgiveness so I don't cast you out! Do you know that I was ogre-napped while you were dillydallying and twiddling your thumbs over a water break? Useless!"

"Should I [Silence] him again?" Slake stretched, his back arching while his claws dug into Bronwynn's shoulders. The bard didn't seem to mind.

I almost told him *yes* before I remembered that I was an official diplomat of Nilheim and the commander general of the Dark Horde, and maybe I shouldn't be endorsing magic upon a fellow diplomat. At the same time, Madame Potts herself had warned the Sumbrian royals about their behavior while traveling internationally, and this one had let her words fall on deaf ears.

"Now, as thank you for rescuing me," Earl Oakley was done being a menace to his servants and turned back to us. "I won't summon the Dark Horde and have them take you away for disrespecting a royal. Now, begone."

"Are you going to tell him?" Slake asked curiously.

I shook my head, smiling. "He'll find out the hard way. I'm looking forward to bringing it up in Peldeep. In polite company."

Slake smiled a vicious grin. "Excellent."

Bronwynn was distracted again; I'd guess she was trying to relay messages to Donna. She got a specific look when she was trying to communicate with her horse, as dazed as when someone was reading over a character sheet but without the slight back and forth eye movement that came with reading.

Sure enough, shortly after Earl Oakley's group set off, Donna came trotting up the Great Road.

We all climbed aboard the wagon but didn't take off right away, letting the earl get a good head start. Donna took the time to eat the heads off a bunch of flowers on the roadside, and Bronwynn rummaged in the back of the wagon to refill her waterskin from a barrel. I sat there contemplating life while Slake curled up, closing his eyes for a nice nap.

Bronwynn eventually lifted the reins in a mock flick and declared, "Alright, everyone. Next stop, Peldeep!"

Who Would Even Do That?

Brownie

The edge of the Dark Enchanted Forest was an obvious thing. The trees thinned out, and brambles scattered in trailing thickets over fallen boughs and old leaves of seasons past. The forest floor was more brown, the sprigs and twigs and vines weaker . . . and all over, the lack of dense magic left everything slightly less colored.

Rufus let out a breath of pure relief, like a load had fallen off his shoulders and he could finally relax. His smile got brighter, and his entire demeanor relaxed.

"Oh, look." Brownie pointed into the forest off to the south where a giant bunny golem stood with its nose pointed to the sky and its ears taller than the tree line. "The border guard."

Rufus waved at the golem, who didn't pay them any mind. "That's Fiddles. He was one of the Dark Lord's first large automata. Keith quickly realized it cost much less mana if he made his creations closer to their natural form's size. They also didn't blow up as often."

Brownie admired the rabbit, who had one ear flopped forward and the other pointed up. "Bye, Fiddles!"

That got the golem's attention, and its nose twitched. One beady glass eye swept over them, but never stopped searching for intruders.

They weren't its target.

"Fiddles probably wouldn't want pets," she murmured absentmindedly.

Slake's tail flicked onto her lap from where he lay on the bench between her and the beastman she was traveling with. "Pet me instead."

She obliged, and Donna successfully pulled their wagon out of Nilheim and onto a winding road that led through craggy cut paths and steep hills with groves of errant plum trees. The plum blossoms had fallen recently, and the cliffs were covered in the flowers while the trees showed the first signs of setting fruit.

It was now or never, really. And she wasn't going to *not* tell him in some weird, vain hope that he just wouldn't find out her secret while meeting her family.

Who would even do that?

That sounded like a full-blown panic attack that ate away at her soul. Brownie wasn't the quiet type, and she wasn't going to start now.

"Rufus, there is something I need to tell you," she started. Straight and to the point. There were butterflies in her stomach as she considered her words.

He turned on the bench to face her, careful his knee didn't bump the grimalcat she was still petting.

"Alright, what's troubling you?" Rufus leaned heavily on one elbow resting on the back of the bench. "I know *something's* been weighing on your mind."

"I just wanted you to hear this from me. You've been such a wonderful travel companion, and I would hazard to say, friend." Maybe, one day, she would break down and ask if they could be more than friends.

She wanted to reach out and place her hand on his hand beside her on the backrest, but she resisted.

He stiffened almost imperceptibly. "That's . . . It has been an excellent journey, and I would be proud to call you a friend."

"So you will see how important it is that I let you know that . . . my uncle Derek is the leader of the Assassin Assembly of Peldeep." Brownie stopped there, holding her breath.

Rufus's eyes opened wide as she watched him start filling in the blanks. She released her breath and tried to get everything straight to talk to him without making a mess of it.

Not that she was deliberately lying. The second Jack had turned his intense, questioning gaze at her, she'd activated [Liar's Palace] so fast . . . But when Rufus turned a similar curious stare her way, she wanted to bare her heart and soul to him.

Maybe he'd activated a perk? Even as the idea took hold, she ignored it. If Rufus used a perk on her, he'd ask first.

"The same Master Derek Stannard I'm scheduled to meet in three days' time?" Rufus finally spoke.

"Yes."

"And the same Assassin Assembly that's tried to kill my king on multiple occasions?" he continued.

"Yes."

"Those same assassins," he added, "that you informed us were coming on boats and traveling through Servalt. The ones hired by Drendil to attack in a massive group that was close to a hundred people?"

"Technically," she countered, "many of those were regular mercenary rogues on contract to act as a diversion for the army unit marching on the Black Fortress from the south, so there weren't really that many true Assassins . . . And who *counts* Assassins anyway?"

Slake snorted at her use of the saying but didn't so much as twitch his tail.

She was trying to play it off with a light heart, but honestly, she *liked* Rufus. Brownie didn't want him to suddenly turn strange because she was too close to the ones he was investigating.

Before he could say more, she added, "It's just . . . I know my family tried to kill King Keith. But I did have my uncle check, and it was just a normal business transaction. No molten ash vane conspiracy. No deeper ploy. Whoever the great mastermind is out there trying to permadeath all of the rulers on the continent . . . I honestly don't think it's anyone from *my* family."

Rufus stared at her for a long time before saying, "Thank you for letting me know, Bronwynn. If it isn't too much trouble, I do have some more . . . questions."

"I'm ready."

CHAPTER 63

Everyone and Their Human

Rufus

I stared at Bronwynn, whose apologetic rosy blush complemented her flame-tipped curls.

She was from a family of *Assassins*. Not just *related* to an assassin, no, but to a household which accounted for the registration and care for anyone and everyone in that class on this side of the continent. Servalt was a new kingdom with new leadership that had made a name for itself by creating a hub for merchants to gain power and status, which included a new Assassin's Guild. But Peldeep was one of the oldest kingdoms on the map, and the families there had been in power for hundreds, if not thousands, of years.

So if Bronwynn was the direct niece of Master Derek Stannard . . . she might as well have been the young noble miss of an esteemed Peldeep household.

I realized I'd told her I had questions then sat there staring at her while I gathered my thoughts.

"How do *you* feel?" The words came naturally, but I kicked myself when I said them. That wasn't what I needed to ask. I *needed* to ask about her family members, if she knew how they'd slipped assassins past Keith's golems, how to better deal with her uncle, and what exactly *she* knew about molten ash vane.

I had a *job*. But I just couldn't bring myself to care about it at that moment.

"It's just . . . an inconvenience." She shifted in her seat uncomfortably. "Not my family, of course! I love my family, and they could never be an inconvenience. Especially when they've been so supportive and understanding about my own chosen path. No. It's this blasted increase in molten ash vane that's thrown everything for a loop."

I found myself nodding. "It's not helping." Especially when no one, except maybe Duke Lector from Servalt, knew who the poisoner was. Even then, it wasn't certain. The poisoner could have just been adding molten ash vane to all of their orders.

"Everyone and their human is pointing fingers at my family for letting assassins use the stuff, but Assassin is a perfectly respectable trade with a very specific goal. And molten ash vane is an overpowered, if illegal, tool for the task." Brownie sighed. "There's more than one way to permadeath someone, and if those hits get approval, then who cares how it's done?"

"In the meantime"—I clenched my fist—"we're just going to have to get used to more of the stuff popping up, and changing our international contracts to account for it."

Slake drowsily swished his tail. The grimalcat was as invested in molten ash vane as anyone, so I was impressed the creature had remained quiet so long.

Unless Slake was actually napping. I wasn't going to disturb the grimalcat to find out.

The walls of a city appeared in the distance. Usually, I would've turned into my furless folk form while traveling in Peldeep, but my secret needed to be kept for just a little while longer. My mood darkened when I thought about the fact that Bronwynn had just shared *her* secret with me . . . but I wasn't going to share my own.

Yet.

Maybe . . .

Hearthcrest was a city of traditionally older buildings with slanted roofs and rounded doors. The taller buildings were an interesting design with tiny patios at upper floors. Each house had a small, fenced deck, and the cobblestone road turned to brightly colored mosaics as they entered the city gates.

Two guards stood at attention to either side of the entrance.

"Name and purpose?" the city guard on the right asked Bronwynn. She was holding the reins and therefore responsible for answering the questions.

The guard on the left interrupted before she could speak. "You dundering oaf, *that's Minstrel Bronwynn.*"

"What? Really?!" The first guard stuttered, "O-Oh, I'm sorry, Minstrel, please, w-welcome to Hearthcrest!"

"This is Commander General Rufus Triever and—" Bronwynn waved at me and was about to introduce Slake when the cat's nails clawed into her through her skirt; she took the hint—"a grimalcat. We will be staying for the night then leaving from the western gate tomorrow morning."

"Of course! Thank you." The guard's face paled when she introduced me, but he nodded politely and waved us in.

Behind us, I could hear the guard laughing. "I got to talk to Minstrel Bronwynn! Me! Wait until the others hear about this."

The more experienced guard reminded him to fill out his report properly.

And I was reminded again that I'd been traveling with *the Minstrel Bronwynn* this whole time, and we were almost done. I would meet her family, watch her play at the festival . . . then go back home.

There was a weird gripping sensation in my stomach. It hurt.

This wasn't the Dark Enchanted Forest. I wasn't getting drowned in notifications. I wasn't even that overwhelmed by my [Keen Senses] in this clean, calm, and otherwise normal town. There shouldn't be any cause for a tummy ache.

I didn't want to recognize it . . . but I knew. I was jealous. Of myself and what precious time I had with Bronwynn on this trip. I had a problem.

In the stories, love hit like a [Quick Strike]. It was powerful, gripping and changed people's lives.

Here I was, sitting in a wagon on an early summer day, happier than I'd been in a decade. Just . . . happy. The comfort and playfulness. The laughter and music. Happy and very much in love.

There was no earthshaking realization—I'd *always* liked Bronwynn. From the first time I'd heard her sing and every conversation until this moment. It had grown slowly to be what she called friends . . . but maybe I wanted more?

That was it. Where I was beginning to feel a visceral rejection and *need*.

I shouldn't have let myself worry about the *ending*, when I would go back to my life in the Black Fortress and only see Bronwynn when she stopped in on her way between gigs.

I didn't want to let her go.

That was when I felt her hand on my arm.

A rising frustration left me trying to tear my mind away from the sinking feeling in my gut and go back to what precious time I had left in Bronwynn's company.

She and Donna had been figuring out a place to stay that was far from Earl Oakley's chosen inn . . . while I tried to think of a solution. I wasn't ready to let go . . . but I also wasn't ready to propose marriage on the spot as my king had advised.

"Rufus? Are you alright?"

Her voice drew me out of my frustrated circular thoughts. What was next? The Apple Blossom Festival. Then the Hollow. And then . . .

"Bronwynn," I said. Her name felt wonderful on my lips, and I wanted to say it again. So I did. "Bronwynn, would you like to go to the Summer Masquerade with me?"

CHAPTER 64

Her Darkest Desires

Brownie

Bronwynn knew Rufus was struggling with something.

He clenched his hands in his lap and stared down intently as Donna maneuvered them through the small town. Brownie had asked directions to an inn she'd only been to once before. It was a nice inn; it was just out of the way.

"No, I don't want to sleep anywhere *near* a Sumbrian royal," she told Donna after they were guided in the opposite direction of the elf's fancy carriage. "They can find some other half giantess in shining makeup. That reminds me, I need to ask my cousin for more crushed pearls. I ran out on the road, and I need my cheek and eyebrow glitter. What were we talking about?"

Donna sighed.

Brownie nodded. "Well, someone else can keep Earl Oakley out of trouble. Didn't Madame Potts make a warning about that?"

Her horse chuffed and shook her head, plodding on. The Lonely Hearth Inn was just ahead, but they had to stop for a family of trolls with two small children to cross the road. A human in a hurry used the opportunity to dart across the street at the last minute, and Brownie tugged the reins a bit to deter Donna from nipping at the distracted man.

He didn't even wave a thank you.

When the road was clear, they continued, without anyone sustaining injury.

"Almost there. Are you ready, Commander General?" She turned to her handsome and fluffy travel companion. "Rufus?"

Maybe she should have spoken louder to get his attention, but he was looking rather downtrodden. Even his tail hung low, unmoving. Brownie gently placed a hand on his arm, and he startled, looking at her with intense golden eyes. The same eyes that sometimes made her self-conscious when she caught him staring at her. She pushed those feelings aside.

"Rufus? Are you alright?"

"Bronwynn." Her name was like a whisper on his lips. He made her doubly self-conscious. "Bronwynn, would you like to go to the Summer Masquerade with me?"

"What?!" She couldn't help the loud outburst, her cheeks flushed as she squeezed his arm in surprise.

His paw, claws sheathed, covered her hand.

That was too much for her.

The commander general of the Dark Lord's army had just asked her out. Probably. That was an important question.

"Wait!" Brownie cleared her throat and tried to speak calmly. "Do you mean you want to take me on a, on a date? A real one? To the Masquerade?"

"Yes," Rufus replied.

Brownie pointed at her chest, checking one final time. "Me?"

A slight smile tugged at the corner of his mouth. "Isn't this normally where you would say, 'Of course you want to take me on a date. I'm *the* Minstrel Bronwynn'?"

"I'm not normally asked out by Commander General Rufus Triever, the most powerful beastman of the Dark Lord's army!" she countered, but she was grinning from ear to ear.

Donna cut in with a snort. Brownie ignored her horse.

"One more question," she added, pulling her hand free but then running it down his arm and gently taking his hand so she could squish his paw pads. Before she said yes to a date, she needed to see if he would be alright with her darkest desires. The beastman shivered, but it wasn't from rejection, and she grew bolder when he let her play with his fingers.

"Is this an 'I'm interested in a relationship with you' ask to the ball, or an 'I like you and want to go dancing with you' kind of date?" Her heart pounded in her chest, and she dragged her attention from his soft palm to his emotionally tumultuous expression. He was figuring it out and struggling with finding the words, she could tell, but Brownie didn't regret asking.

These were important questions!

"Both?" he finally said.

"Both is good," she replied, squeezing his hand. "Now, let's hop down and get sorted for dinner."

She dropped his hand and collected the reins again. Just in time. Donna didn't wait for anything, not even an awkward but intense confession by the Dark Lord's right-hand man. The mare had brought them right to the Lonely Hearth Inn and was ready to check *herself* in for some hay and a good brush.

"We're just staying the night." Brownie jumped down and tossed Donna's reins to a nearby stable hand. Then she faced her horse. "Donna, please, for the love of all the gods, let me have this night?"

Her mare gave her a half-hearted neigh that Brownie took well. She hugged her horse before dragging Rufus inside to secure room and board.

"Greetings," a naga woman welcomed them inside the inn.

"Rooms for me and my companion," Bronwynn said, then hesitated. "Separate rooms. And board for my horse and wagon."

"Right this way, miss."

Brownie followed the innkeeper and Rufus followed her. Brownie felt the weight of his gaze on her back. She enjoyed his company and his personality and his sense of humor. He was patient and kind, and sometimes fierce.

And she'd managed to shove it aside with a laugh until now. But now, it was an uncomfortable sense of pressure that she didn't know how to handle. In the span of an hour, she'd finally told him her secret, and he'd asked her out. She knew it wasn't because of his investigation into her family business . . . probably. But she'd thought of it, and would continue to think of it.

The pressure built enough that she turned to look at him while putting on a dazzling smile to hide her uncertainty. "Can we finish our conversation over dinner? There's a curry shop around the corner that will make your mouth water."

She met his eyes again, and almost tripped.

"Alright." Rufus could, when he was serious, speak in a deep, rich voice that sent shivers down her spine. She quickly faced forward again.

They were shown to their respective rooms, dropped off their respective things, and then met back in the hallway.

There was a moment where they stood facing each other, and then Brownie took the initiative and offered her hand.

For a powerful general, he was *very* soft.

CHAPTER 65

I Want to Be Honest with You

Rufus

In a moment of weakness, I'd thrown my entire plan out the window. And less gracefully than Bronwynn herself could defenestrate, I imagined. My original plan had been simple.

Step one, investigate Bronwynn.

Step two, find her innocent.

Step three, confess.

Specifically, confess that I was investigating her. Then, depending on how things progressed . . .

Step four, confess.

But what had I done? Betrayed her trust even as she held my hand and dragged me off to go eat dinner together. Bronwynn was grinning from ear to ear, a bounce in her step, as she led me to a shop that smelled *divine*. Actually Divine. I only caught the sense because I spent so much time with King Keith's Demi, quarter-demon self.

"Here we are." Bronwynn held open the door to a bright blue shop. The spices hit me; mostly garam masala, with hints of cardamom and cumin and cinnamon.

I thanked her and went inside. The restaurant was busy, with three bushy-tailed foxkin waiters that were servicing the front of the house. An elderly foxkin sat at the front and greeted us.

"A table for two, please," Bronwynn requested, and I noted for the first time that Slake hadn't followed us. I didn't remember seeing him leave the wagon.

We were alone, for once.

What was it Queen Henrietta had told me during one of her sessions? No sense in having perks if you don't use them? Or, in my case, what was the point of having high Perception when I was so lost in my thoughts that I didn't pay attention.

"Right this way."

I ignored my internal screaming as I smiled and pulled the chair out for my bard before taking a seat across from her. She immediately started regaling me with the menu and the flavors of her favorite dishes. Usually, at this point, I'd be taking mental notes to share with the group via Cast Crystal later . . . but not today.

If I was going to ask Minstrel Bronwynn to a ball, I didn't want to invite *Minstrel Bronwynn* to a ball. I wanted to invite just Bronwynn. The person. The woman I'd gotten to know over our trip, not the idol of my dreams.

She hadn't said *yes*, per se, but she'd implied it . . . Maybe I should ask again?

I took her advice and ordered the simmering floofpoof bird medium-spice mixed fruit and nut curry with dried cherries and flat bread. She ordered a cheese paneer curry with rice.

After our orders were taken, I spoke. "Bronwynn, thank you for accepting my request to take you to the Summer Masquerade." In all things, I could fall back on common courtesy. I would need *something* to fall back on while having dinner with the bard of my dreams as we discussed the prospects of . . . well . . . whatever she wanted.

"You're welcome," she answered. Then she waited.

In the beastman culture, there was a very straightforward style of courting: you didn't. When you knew, you knew, and you were honest about it. You spent time in someone's company, and if feelings developed, you just told them. Usually this was ruled by desire, but comfort and security were also a type of relationship.

The General of the West was in a lifelong relationship with his wife. But the wolverine beastwoman who owned Logan's Noodle House had three husbands and an open relationship with any one other person at any given time. I would know, for she had propositioned me in front of her husbands enough times.

I remembered that time I'd told Keith that he should just go ask Henrietta to marry him, and felt my own advice come back to bite me.

"Bronwynn," I started. "I want to be honest with you."

The bard flashed a frown at my words so fast I almost missed it before it softened into a receptive nod of her head. "Go on."

"You've shared your secret with me, and so I want to share one of mine as well . . ." I paused, wondering exactly what I *could* say? That I was hiding my identity as the leader of her fan group? That I was spying on her? That I thought she was an amazing woman who deserved to be treated with respect, and I was failing on all accounts already?

The beginning. I would start at the beginning. "I have liked you from the moment I first heard you sing. I love your music, and I enjoy your company, and this entire trip has been one of the most wonderful times in my life."

"Really?" Her amazed smile lit up her face, and my stomach twisted in a knot.

"But . . . you should know that I only joined you on this trip as an order from Henrietta."

"What?!" Her amazed smile fell to a frown, but I continued.

"She was worried . . . and asked me to keep an eye on you since we were practically going in the same direction anyway. There's more, but I can't speak of it until the end of my quest," I explained. It wasn't a perfect truth, but it was a start.

Bronwynn frowned. "I can't believe she . . . Alright, I *can* believe Henrietta would do that. And she made you join me this whole time?"

"I did *not*," I stressed, sensing the misconceptions already forming in her mind, "*have* to join you. I could have checked in on you or followed you without your notice. I *chose* to venture with you because I enjoy your company."

That must have alleviated some of her worries, because she started laughing, the sound full of her usual good humor. "So instead of stalking me in the bushes, you hitched a ride and rode comfortably?"

"Yes. Do you forgive me?" I asked.

She paused a second, and it was the longest moment of my life. Finally, slowly, she said, "Alright. I forgive you. Honestly, it's been wonderful having you along, and *you're* wonderful and—WAIT!"

I was about to pick up my glass of water when her sudden outburst startled me into fumbling. My high-level Dexterity was the only thing that saved our table from an awkward spill. "What?"

The minstrel pointed her finger at me from across the table and yelled, "IT WAS YOU!"

CHAPTER 66

It All Made Sense Now

Brownie

It all made sense now.

Something that had been weighing on Brownie's mind for most of their journey, the unease and frustration, and a few restless nights. She ignored the various people sitting around them who'd turned to stare at her outburst. This was more important.

"You were my first encounter!" she accused Rufus. Seeing the shame and embarrassment that played across the beastman's face revealed something even worse. "*And you knew?*"

"I did . . ." he confessed. "I realized that night at the inn, and I didn't tell you because, well, for obvious reasons, I suppose."

Brownie dropped her head into her hands and groaned. "All this time. I've been wondering all this time, and it was *you.*"

"I'm sorry," Rufus offered. He'd been apologizing a lot recently. They both had. Rufus was a polite, common sense, and logically based beastman—who'd been stalking her. *Her.* The leader of the Dark Lord's army was following her around because . . .

She took in the sight of him. Rufus always had an air about him that was calm and relaxed without giving much away . . . and it was complete rubbish. She could tell. She could always tell. Sure, he *looked* fine, but his tail was curled up under his chair, his claws were in, and his eyes—*his eyes were guilty.*

"You're not just protecting me—you're spying on me!" She stood up from the realization, then sat back down again, glancing around to see if anyone had paid attention to her outburst.

Everyone had.

Rufus sighed, but it wasn't from impatience. He was taking a deep breath to steady himself. "Yes. I was stalking and spying on you, but on orders. I would never—"

He trailed off, and an unease crawled up on Brownie. She felt more nervous from that one cutoff sentence than the first time they'd met when she'd walked into the Dark Lord's keep to get captured just to see if Henrietta was alright.

"I'm assuming it had something to do with your quest . . . Did you think I was the molten ash vane assassin? Did . . . Did Henrietta?"

Rufus nodded, and Brownie reached for her glass. She finished the water in one gulp, and then forgot herself in the moment, bringing it down too hard on the table with a loud thunk. Controlling her body had been a constant awareness her entire life. She'd been born with +5 Strength from her Half Giantess title, and was naturally bigger and stronger than her peers; a lifetime had taught her to be careful around handling objects.

It was actually the reason she'd become enamored with music so early. If she properly controlled her grip and her hands, then she could produce beautiful sounds. Her mother loved to sing, and some of Brownie's fondest memories were of singing and playing with her family as a child.

Still, she wasn't told every day that the beastman she'd been slowly falling for was actually stalking her to uncover if she was an assassin. An *illegal* assassin at that! She was lucky the cup didn't outright shatter into a million pieces when she put it down . . . it just splintered a little.

Rufus waited for her. He was always waiting for her. She wondered for just a second if the patience she knew and loved was actually an order . . . but no. When she saw the worry lines on his brow and the concern in his eyes, she knew he was being considerate.

He wasn't supposed to tell her any of this.

"And now?"

"*Technically*," Rufus said, "*I* didn't think you were the assassin, and neither did Her Viciousness. I was sent to prove that. And to keep you safe in Servalt."

"Excuse me," a foxkin waitress appeared at Brownie's shoulder, her lips smiling but her eyes not. "May I take your cup?"

Brownie blushed and nodded. "My apologies. I'll pay for a replacement."

The waitress relaxed. "May I get you a fresh drink?"

Brownie looked at Rufus, then back to the waitress. "A bottle of Yorik's Bimbleberry Mead. To share."

The waitress hesitated, probably uncomfortable with bringing them such a drink when Brownie had already shown she was upset. Yorik was a renowned brewer in Peldeep famous for one thing: his liquor could knock out a Master class warrior with Strength sixty. It tasted divine, like dewdrop sun-kissed bimbleberries on a midmorning in late spring, and Brownie wanted a bottle to share between them. The bard flashed a silver coin from her storage, twiddling it between her fingers.

"Of course, miss." The foxkin pocketed the bribe and hurried away.

"That's a rare vintage," Rufus idly remarked.

Brownie shot him a look. "After the night I've been having? It's just the thing."

This trip was burning through her pocket money faster than usual, but she had plenty to spare. Recently, she'd had a number of wealthy patrons who made contributions to her travels, but she was usually more frugal and restrained.

Today was not that day.

The dishes were cleared from their table, and a bottle of shimmering purple bimbleberry mead glistened in the magical lamplight. The server had brought two glasses for the wine, two glasses of water, and a dessert menu.

A few minutes later, the bottle had aired nicely, and they had two small lavender scones for dessert—compliments of Rufus.

"Rufus," Brownie started by pouring a glass for her crush and then one for herself.

". . . Yes?" The beastman hesitated but picked up his glass and returned her mock toast.

The bard looked Rufus in the eyes before downing the entire glass of mead. Then she gently placed her glass down, moved her elbows onto the table, and rested her chin on her now interlaced fingers.

"Let's play a game."

My Constitution Was Kicking Me in the Assets

Rufus

The bimbleberry mead was fruity and nutty but smooth. The unique undercurrent of honey brew meant it had a natural light sweetness that went down easy. It was like drinking freshly pressed berry juice without the bitter or tart flavors so commonly mixed in. It was also strong enough to give my Constitution twenty-four a challenge.

Still, my greatest vice was a fine glass of wine. Or mead, as the case may be. I enjoyed a long sip before setting the glass down on the table. My fingers played with the rim of my glass.

"A game?" I asked. Brownie eyed my hand, distracted. The mead had already hit her, I could tell, causing a rising blush to creep up her neck and flush her face. Her prominent cheeks, often dusted with glitter, were bare save for the heat.

Settle down, tail. I was lucky she was even still talking to me.

"Yes." Bronwynn wagged a finger at me.

I liked her fingers. *No, concentrate.* "What kind of game?"

"Fifty questions!" she stated. "Actually, twenty questions. I don't want to be here all night."

The hair raised on my arms and my tail curled, but I remained poised. The show of a confident general was a skill that came in handy in all areas of life, but more so now than ever. "I don't think we have the time—"

"You can ask me *anything*. And I'll answer the truth," Bronwynn whispered seductively. Or maybe she was just speaking normally, and I was overthinking everything.

I took another sip. Somehow, my glass was already almost empty.

The facts remained, I'd lied to her, stalked her, and taken advantage of her hospitality. I didn't know if she would be able to trust me again, even if she understood where I was coming from. Which it sounded like she did. And there were so many things I wanted to know . . .

Still, better to play it safe. "Ten questions each."

"What . . . is your favorite song?" Bronwynn asked so quickly that she almost cut me off.

The answer was obvious. "Any song you sing."

She slapped the table. "That's not a real answer!"

"Fine." I thought about it. "'Balthorn Rose.'"

"Really? Why?" Bronwynn raised an eyebrow, then quickly waved her hands in front of her. "Wait, that wasn't my second question! Hm . . . When did you first hear me sing?"

"The first time I heard you sing was in Peldeep last year. You were playing at Herman's Club," I recalled, remembering the night my entire world had changed. "And I'll tell you this for free: I love 'Balthorn Rose' because, even though I can barely understand half the lyrics, I love the harmonies and the melody. It gets stuck in my head all the time, and it drives me crazy that I won't get to hear you sing it until hopefully the next concert."

"You could always ask," Brownie pointed out.

I was spoiled. And I was an idiot. Because I'd been asking for specific songs all the time, I'd missed out on hearing the songs that I *didn't* know about.

She offered and after I nodded, Brownie refilled both of our glasses.

The second glass hit harder than the first, but I had impressive stamina. I'd accepted the second glass, but I wouldn't accept a third. My king was always talking about my monstrous Constitution; little did he know I didn't min-max my stats. I had a healthy amount of points distributed among my attributes.

Name:	Rufus Triever
Occupation:	Commander General
Level:	54
Experience Points:	13397/13500
Hit Points:	616/616
Mana Points:	900/900
Class:	Commander

Titles:			
[Beastfolk], [Protector], [Mediator], [General], [Commander], [Connoisseur]			
Attributes:			
Strength:	26	Intelligence:	30
Dexterity:	19	Perception:	30
Constitution:	24	Charisma:	19

Hey, I was about to level up. Anyway, my "impressive" Constitution was heavily reliant on the fact that my predictive attack meant I could mitigate damage while pretending to take hits. And while I enjoyed the *taste* of wine, I never drank to excess. Most wines were made for the common-level folk; those who had an average Constitution of fifteen.

I looked away from my character sheet and back at Bronwynn, who had just finished refilling her third glass. If my Constitution was kicking me in the assets, I couldn't imagine what she was suffering.

"Are you even drinking that wine?" The words were out before my mind caught up to me, and the minstrel looked up at me with shock.

"Not very much, no," she grumbled. "I'm good at pretending to drink. And I'm not using a skill or perk, just basic Dexterity and my storage ring. Most don't notice."

"Why?"

"Because this is my revenge for stalking me," she said, taking what I *assumed* to be a real sip of the mead. "And *that* was *two* of your questions!"

If I was paying attention, I could focus on watching the liquid fall past her rosy lips . . . and her tongue licking her lips afterward.

"We're going to have a rousing night, and you are going to be a mess tomorrow when dealing with my uncle, and I will feel better about you taking advantage of me. Also . . ." She paused. I had to wrench my lascivious eyes away from her lips and drag my eyes up to her own. "Are you just being nice to me because you've been ordered to?"

"No!" My fist hit the table as hard as hers did earlier . . . Alright, maybe a little harder. Our waitress appeared at my elbow.

"How are your desserts? Can I get you the bill?" The foxkin stared at my fist, and I self-consciously withdrew my hands into my lap.

"Everything is delicious," I said, before realizing I hadn't even taken my first bite of my lavender scone. I hurriedly did so now.

Bronwynn came to the rescue. "We're almost done, promise. You can bring the bill anytime. I've got it."

The foxkin nodded. "Two gold, four silver."

Brownie handed over three gold, and the waitress left them smiling. The amount was exorbitant, and I stared at the half-empty bottle of bimbleberry mead that'd cost my bard two gold.

Speaking of my bard, she was beaming at me despite my outburst. Brownie took a bite of her scone, then appeared distracted for a second as she closed her eyes in obvious enjoyment.

"I was going to buy dinner," I told her. "At least let me pay for half?"

"No, and that's another question."

"Wait, no it wasn't—"

"My turn." She finished off her scone. Then she leaned forward across the table. "Rufus . . ."

She so rarely called me by name that it startled me. I drew back and asked tentatively, "Yes?"

"Can I pet you?"

CHAPTER 68

This is More Important Than Scones!

Brownie

As much as she'd *said* the bimbleberry mead was for Rufus . . . Brownie had wanted liquid courage to help her ask the *important questions*. Especially since the absolute shock that dawned on Rufus' face was *not* inspiring. She tripped over her tongue as she added, "Or not! You don't have to—"

"Yes."

"What?"

Golden eyes locked onto hers, serious and intense. "Yes, you can pet me. I consent. Let's do it right now."

"Wait—"

Rufus stood up and almost knocked over his chair. "We need to leave."

"What about the mead, and your scone?" Brownie laughed but stood up as well.

"Leave them. This is more important than scones!" Rufus offered his hand, and she took it. Instead of linking it into his arms politely like he normally did, Rufus slid his fingers between hers and gripped her hand gently. The soft fur and rough beanies were an interesting feeling that she immediately loved.

Rufus all but dragged her from the restaurant. He couldn't actually drag her, she had a skill for that, but she let him pull her along.

He didn't get very far, stopping in the middle of the quiet evening street and turning back to her. "Where are we going?"

"Is that your fourth question?" she teased. "We can just go back to my room at the inn."

"Is that your fifth?" he countered. It was actually her sixth, but she might have lost count. He waved in the general direction of where they were staying for the night. "You want to pet me in your room?"

Brownie imagined herself lying in bed cuddling a giant golden wolf dog. It was very appealing. Then the image of waking up in Rufus's arms took its place, and she noted that it was equally appealing. Heat burned her cheeks, but there was a gleam in her eye as she asked, "Why, have you never been in a woman's room before?"

Rufus choked on air. "I have . . . but I've never been to *your* room before. And I'd *never* go to a woman's room if either of us had been drinking. Where's the consent in that?"

She laughed. "We aren't . . . you know. This is just petting!"

"Petting should still involve consent!" he declared.

"So I'm not allowed to pet you because you had bimbleberry mead?" Brownie frowned.

"No. Forget I said anything," Rufus hurriedly rejected the idea. "I've been wanting this for too long to give up now."

"But—"

"No buts." Rufus lifted her hand to his heart. "Unless you don't want to pet me anymore?"

"I do. I'm just worried about consent now."

Rufus had had two full glasses.

"I've got it!" Rufus pulled out a high-grade antidote. One he'd packed at their stop over at that Black Fortress. He popped the cork with a thumb and downed the bottle. He rubbed his lips.

"Now I'm stone-cold sober," Rufus declared, storing the now empty bottle. "Or I will be by the time we get to your room."

"You just wasted so much gold!"

"It wasn't a waste, and I'd do it again." The beastman smiled.

"Just so you know," Brownie said, having completely lost count but still wanting to continue, "I get two more questions, and you have four."

"Why are we playing this game?" Rufus asked as they started walking again.

"I've been wondering so many things," Brownie admitted. "Do you like me as much as I like you? Is it wrong to pick up a commander general while he's on a quest? What do you look like in all of your forms?"

"I thought I'd already answered that; I like you *much* more. More than I care to admit, actually. Yet. Also, that was more than two questions," he pointed out. The inn was in sight.

Brownie squeezed his hand. "Does that mean you won't answer them?"

"It means"—Rufus squeezed her hand back—"that it's my turn."

She waited. They were almost at the front door. She waited still. They were inside the inn. She was almost done waiting when Rufus stopped them in the empty hallway outside their rooms.

He let go of her hand and took a step back, opening his mouth to ask, "Meow?"

They both looked down as Slake wound his way through Rufus's legs.

"You are *really* good at that," Brownie told the grimalcat.

Slake's tail flicked once, but he ignored her statement. "I'm going out tonight to meet a friend. Don't wait up."

The grimalcat sauntered down the hallway and out of sight. The pair shared a look.

"You were saying?" Brownie crossed her arms.

"Will you go to the Summer Masquerade with me?" Rufus asked, his voice strangely quiet.

"And *I* already answered." Brownie raised an eyebrow, wondering if Rufus was more drunk than he seemed. "Of course I'll go with you to the Summer Masquerade."

Rufus sighed. "Thank the gods. You *didn't* actually say yes! You *implied!* And . . . I was worried you might have changed your mind."

"Well, I haven't. I'm looking forward to it."

"Then what about after?"

"What about after?"

"Never mind, that's all of our questions, I think."

"It is not, you still have . . . one?" Brownie sighed. "Alright, I admit I've lost count."

Rufus opened her bedroom door and asked, "Are you ready?"

There was a moment where she hesitated, but then her face broke out into a huge smile. "I was born ready."

She marched into the room, Rufus following behind her. There was a shock of awareness that ran through her as he closed the door and she heard the faint click of the lock, but it was from excitement.

Rufus nodded at her once before he fell forward, landing as a giant golden beast that resembled a golden wolf-dog. He was huge, coming up to Brownie's elbow. He walked up to her and rubbed his head against her hand as she crouched down to give his ears a scratch. That sent his tail thumping violently.

"Rufus," she spoke, her voice only slightly sweeter than normal. Brownie was resisting the urge to go full adorable on the commander general, and she was proud of her restraint. "You're the best."

He happily splayed out on the floor as she rubbed his tummy and chest and back and head. She played with his left ear that was slightly floppier than the right, and she squished his beanie paws and toes at length. By the end of it, her willpower had started to wane, and she was giggling and lavishing the golden beast with unrestrained love and affection.

Eventually, Rufus fell asleep on the carpet in front of the hearth. His breath was deep and steady. Brownie thought about climbing into bed, but rejected the idea. Instead, she pulled down the blanket and got comfortable leaning against the giant wolf. As a half giantess herself, she wasn't used to *leaning* on people.

But Rufus didn't seem to mind it while he was awake, so she didn't let it worry her now. If she recalled correctly, he was nearing level sixty, and could probably lift her one-handed.

As she was drifting off to sleep, she thought about their conversation over the evening. He was so fluffy, so considerate, but so hesitant.

"I hope your other secret isn't going to ruin this, Rufus," Brownie whispered into the quiet night. "Because I think I'm falling in love with you."

CHAPTER 69

I'm a Very Nice Grimalcat

Rufus

The door opened in the middle of the night.

I raised one eyelid to peer out into the darkness as a small figure walked closer. It stopped just within reach.

Glowing green eyes met mine, and I lifted my head slowly, careful not to wake the half giantess leaning against my stomach. There was a moment of stillness, and then the grimalcat sniffed. "The room stinks of dog."

He turned and walked back to the door. In the doorway, he paused to look over his shoulder as if expecting me to follow.

I really, really didn't want to go . . . but I wasn't a fool.

It was short work changing back into my usual beastman self, and I caught Bronwynn in a princess carry midtransition. She grumbled and cuddled into my embrace as I walked over and placed her gently on the bed, but she didn't fully awaken. I tucked her in with the blanket she'd been holding and had to stop myself from kissing her on the forehead at the last minute. My fingers lightly brushed a stray curl from her cheek instead.

Bronwynn was displeased with the cold bed substitute, curling in on herself. I sighed and dragged myself away to follow the grimalcat. Once we were in the hallway, I gently closed the door and asked Slake, "Can you relock the door from out here?"

"Of course," Slake scoffed. "It is done."

"Thank you."

I followed him down the hallway and into my room. The inn was silent, as even the nightlife of the city had settled down in the dark hours before dawn.

Slake jumped onto my bed. "Commander General. I had my party members search for the Blackfog spies that attacked you in Servalt, and I believe we've found something."

"Go on." I sat beside the grimalcat, frowning. It wasn't that I was ambivalent about being attacked by a band of Blackfog spies, but I wasn't in such a rush to hear about this in the dead of night when I could be cuddling my bard.

I didn't mention this to the grimalcat, of course.

"The spies had an order to permanently kill most of the Dark Horde, as well as fifty other people from around Valaria; Their Royal Highness Rowen, Regent Havork, Grand Duchess Calisto, Countess Julia, and the entire Oakley family, to name just a few." Slake frowned. "None of the spies were carrying molten ash vane on their person, but that means nothing."

The grimalcat touched a paw down on the bed and a piece of paper appeared. It was a copy of the list of names. "For your records."

"I see." The evidence was incriminating, though it left many questions unanswered. The rash of assassination attempts across the continent could be the work of the Blackfog spies . . . but if so, why had they been caught without any molten ash vane when the Assassin's Guild master had a bag full of it? "You are *sure*—"

"Lina is a good girl." Slake's tail whipped back and forth menacingly. "She might unalive people for a living, but being an assassin is a perfectly respectable career option. Her recent misadventures are a direct result of that *fiend*, Duke Lector. When I get my claws on that elf . . ."

"He should already be behind bars, no?" I raised an eyebrow. "Duke Wyldon would surely have already arrested him by now?"

Slake bared his sharp teeth and flexed his claws in the blanket. "While we were uncovering Duke Lector's schemes with the guild, the elf made an appearance at the castle and announced his intentions to visit the Silver Star Festival in the Hollow next week. He left the birthday celebration before Duke Wyldon received Jack's report, and no one has seen him since."

That wasn't ideal—for *Duke Lector*. Anyone sane would choose the full weight of the law over an irate grimalcat. There was an old nursery rhyme my mother used to sing when I was a very young pup that I still remembered clearly.

> If you ever bring back, a winged horned cat,
> Then you lived to escape your ill fate.
> The grimalcat favors the young and the bold
> But chooses the death it will sate.
>
> Its eyes are as bright as the stars in the sky,
> Its heart is as dark as the night.

> Beware what you promise and keep to your word
> For a grimalcat's strength is by spite.
>
> So never betray you a grimalcat's trust
> And never a lie pass your tongue.
> The creature will hunt you until the blue moon,
> And the damage returned or undone.

There were so few grimalcats, but everyone knew they were not to be trifled with. Guild Master Lina would've been a fool not to listen to Slake.

And so would I.

"Then I'll let you know if I see the duke. In the meantime, we still don't have all the pieces." I yawned and lay back on the bed. "Is there a reason we couldn't discuss this in the morning?"

"Minstrel Brownie is a suspect in the case, and not a member of the investigation team." Slake stretched and let out a tiny yawn.

"And you are?"

"Of course." Slake straightened and sauntered over to the vacant spot beside my head. I considered getting up and properly pulling the quilt over me, but the cool night air was refreshing. The nights were getting warmer with summer right around the corner. The grimalcat circled once, twice, thrice, and then lay in a ball. He said, "I offered to go when Their Royal Highness brought up sending an envoy to the investigation."

"Really?" That would explain why we'd never run into the Peldeep representative . . . We had and just hadn't realized it.

Slake continued. "It isn't something I would normally be interested in, but when I learned that Lina was throwing away the life I gave her, I was very disappointed."

"So you do save children." I smiled into the darkness, knowing Slake could hear my amusement.

"Sometimes. I'm a very nice grimalcat," Slake answered, deadpan. "I've got three lives roaming around right now."

I wasn't sure how to take that. I hummed a bit of the grimalcat song, and Slake snorted in amusement. Sleep was reclaiming me, and I regretted for a second that I wasn't still in front of the banked fire in Bronwynn's room. I would apologize for slipping away in the morning.

"I'm happy you've joined us, Slake." My words had grown soft. I pet the grimalcat once, and he kindly didn't maul me when I brushed my hand over his fluffy tummy.

The last I heard before sleep claimed me was a confident purr and, "Of course you are."

CHAPTER 70

It's Another Potts's Cast!

Brownie

Brownie snuggled deeper into her blankets, sad when Rufus left. She was sadder still to wake up without the warmth of the beastman beside her.

Maybe she could convince him to sleep with her again . . . and maybe she would phrase it differently when she asked. Or not. They were adults, after all.

It was time to go down.

The inn was bright, and travelers were signing in and out with a lizardkin woman behind the counter. Brownie dropped her key in the return box and was ready to go. Her companions were standing a few feet from the door, Slake on her beastman's shoulder. They waved her over, and Rufus greeted her with a winning smile that had her elated all the way to her toes.

"Good morning, I'm sorry I had to slip out."

Brownie shook her head. "No worries. Are you ready to grab something and—"

The door to the inn burst open, and a preela shoved their head inside. "Ruby! It's another Potts's Cast!"

The lizardwoman gave a shout, and everyone rushed out to hear the news, Brownie and Rufus and Slake near the front of the throng.

. . . and anyone going to Julia's Grotto this week for the Peldeep Apple Blossom Festival shouldn't fear the fireworks. The knight commander's wedding will have some unexpected magical guests who weren't invited, and Their Royal Highness Rowen of Peldeep is going to get to show off that they still got it.

Anyone in the Dungeon Valley Crest will notice an increase in tulip belles on the third floor for the next few days. And the monsters

on the second floor will have a +10% drop rate for ravenwing grass circlets. Please remember your Sleep and Paralysis antidotes.

Tinker Tate has made an appearance in the Dark Enchanted Forest and has some of the rarest and most sought-after materials. If you have the chance to see the tinker, be sure to offer up a song. If he likes it, you might get a discount.

There's a pink portal user who's causing everyone grief these days. You know who you are. I'm here to say that you probably shouldn't be going up against an enchanted forest that can eat you.

The Summer Solstice Celebration is only a few weeks away. For anyone who doesn't know, the festival will end with the wedding between Countess Julia von Slyke from North Sumbria and Necromancer Chloe Watercress from the Dark Enchanted Forest. This enchanter has it on the best authority that the newest popular trend in North Sumbria is a fine herringbone weave, tassels, and a boot dagger. If you have a favorite dagger, might I suggest not hiding it in your boot, because that is the first place anyone will look?

This was Madame Potts with the latest news. I hope everyone is enjoying the fine weather!

As a note, starting tonight, it's going to rain for five solid days, so be prepared. I'm not.

The lizardkin inn staff, who was standing beside Brownie, patted the preela on the shoulder. "My thanks again. How did it start?"

"The usual, 'This is Madame Potts with the latest opening, and then she said something about a Baldorin thief running around Drendil."

"Really?" The lizardkin chuckled. "Serves the kingdom right."

Brownie shared a look with Rufus. That was not very kind to Drendil, and yet . . . up until recently, the kingdom had been ruled by an abusive, vicious tyrant who would rather conquer the neighbors than pay trade taxes. Poor Henrietta. Brownie couldn't even imagine having to live under the same roof as the deposed king and queen. Having to hide the thing she loved for fear that her parents would discover the truth and punish her . . . Luckily, Regent Havork was ruling the place now. The man was doing his best and trying to raise Henrietta's cousin as the new Crown Prince Nathaniel. A crown prince who had been revealed on his hundred-day celebration to have dark-red hair and black eyes that looked nothing like his father, Duke Francis . . . or his mother, Dowager Princess Beatrice, for that matter. The woman had been conferred a new title upon her divorce from Duke Francis, and Beatrice was thriving with the newfound political freedom.

She was a menace, in the best kind of way.

"She also said"—the preela leaned in to her friend—"that we'll be in for a smaller fruit harvest this year. Come to think of it, Madame Potts forgot to mention *where* the rain was going to hit. "

"We'll find out tonight."

All about, the people returned to their day-to-day, but Rufus, Brownie, and Slake remained on the sidewalk.

"Still think Madame Potts is Their Royal Highness?" Rufus asked, a bit teasing. "They *would* compliment themselves live on Crystal Cast."

"Do you still think it's me?" Brownie countered, resettling her instrument by tugging a bit on her strap.

"I think it's Feliwyn," Slake commented offhand.

"Her Eminence?" Rufus shook his head slowly so as not to disturb the grimalcat on his shoulder. "That dragon's been asleep for almost a decade, and she's more the kind to just eat anything that irks her, not warn people about their own problems."

Brownie felt the urge to hold the beastman's hand, and so gave in. She reached out until her fingers brushed his with the barest touch. Rufus noticed her intention and gave her a tight smile, taking her hand. Her Eminence Feliwyn was the regent who had chosen him to be Keith's playmate, effectively dooming him to live far from his family and take up his life in the Black Fortress. It wasn't advanced magical theory to guess that he might have some mixed feelings about the dragon.

Slake licked his paw, "That doesn't mean she isn't doing it."

"Did you know," Rufus admitted, "that the King's Crystal, the specific crystal that we use to activate our own kingdom-wide Cast system in the Dark Enchanted Forest . . . was misplaced in Her Eminence Feliwyn's horde?"

Slake smiled. "Furthering my point."

"The Dragon Feliwyn was *right there*, asleep, for the entire wedding. But Madame Potts's Cast made it sound like she was sitting around sharing tea and cake with the rest of us." Brownie tugged Rufus's hand, walking them over to the stall next to the inn where her horse had *miraculously* behaved herself all evening.

"She could've lied," Slake proposed. "And what happened to your horse?"

Or maybe miracles only happened over bimbleberry mead.

"Donna," Brownie sighed. "*Whyyy?*"

CHAPTER 71

Dazzled the Eyes

Rufus

I'd admit I wasn't ready to go meet Bronwynn's family.

Having dinner with a household of assassins wasn't the problem, no. It was that I was going to a household of assassins, and I had a nebulous relationship with their daughter. Because whatever we were had changed since yesterday . . . I hoped. If she was going to bring me back to her room and pet me all night, I could *reason* we were something more than we'd been the day before.

She'd accepted my invitation to the Summer Masquerade. I'd like to think it was obvious we were dating, but as someone who dealt in marriage counseling, a position without a label wasn't kind or respectful to either party.

It would be nice to take our time traveling to her family home and talk. Of course, I wasn't expecting this type of delay.

Donna the murder horse was covered head to foot in glitter, rainbows, and bow ties.

She looked like she'd walked out of a princess tea party hosted by four-year-olds at a Pixie Prim childcare center. The only pixie I'd gotten to know that well, Ross, was just as pink and sparkly.

Donna shook herself and then stood straighter, her majestic tail whipping from the bum wiggle. Her hair dropped sparkles like the drunk fairy godmother I'd met at Princess Tamara's sixth birthday party; she was Their Royal Highness Rowen's youngest, and eighteen now.

The mare stamped one hoof in the dirt and glitter of her stall.

Bronwynn placed her hands on her hips, standing her ground.

"What do you mean you want to keep it?!" she exclaimed. "You want to travel across the continent inconspicuously dressed like a rainbow? How did this even happen?"

Donna looked at her neighbor in the stall next door. Inside, a black horse with shimmering purple wings stuck her head up over the ledge and blew out her nose. Donna leaned toward her friend, and the movement brought her flank into a beam of morning light that dazzled the eyes.

"Cassandra! I should have known!" Bronwynn slapped her forehead.

Again, I wasn't in a hurry to visit Bronwynn's family home before my actual meeting, especially since we hadn't had a sober talk between the two of us . . . but I knew my bard had wished for an early start. I couldn't imagine washing all of *that* off was going to take a short period of time.

"What's happening?" I asked Bronwynn for clarity. Usually hearing only one side of the conversation wasn't this confusing.

"My horse," Bronwynn scoffed, "gambled away the last of your gift oats and got herself enchanted with a rainbow mane by Cassandra Moon here." The bard jutted a thumb at the black horse, who looked all together very pleased with herself.

"And she doesn't want to change back?" I confirmed. After a quick glance, I spotted our wagon at the end of the hallway, in a small alley behind the stable. At this point, a stable hand noticed us and slithered up the hallway to come and help.

Bronwynn slumped. "She's lost a bet. Of course she'll have to keep the coat until the spell wears off. Still . . . it's so *shiny.*"

I reached out and placed a palm on the bard's shoulder just in time for the help to arrive.

"Hello, Minstrel Bronwynn!" The naga woman was wringing her hands in front of her chest. "I'm sorry about the mess. We caught the horses playing cards this morning, and we have *no idea* when the changes happened."

My hand slipped from Bronwynn's shoulder.

"*Cards?*" the words slipped out of my mouth, incredulous.

"I haven't seen Cassandra's partner yet today"—the naga bowed low—"but as this happened at our inn, we are willing to try and undo the spell—"

"We'll be fine." Bronwynn waved off the stable hand. "I understand there wasn't any ill intention, and Donna doesn't seem to mind. Do you know how long it will last, exactly?"

"Ten hours, give or take." the naga said with enough confidence I realized this probably wasn't the first time something like this had happened. It wasn't my place to interrupt, so I simply stood in support beside my bard. "The spell lasts half a day, and I caught them two hours ago . . . though I'm not sure how long they'd been playing."

Donna leaned down and sniffed the latch on the stall door she'd been staying in. Suddenly, the latch was loose, and the door swung open, releasing the mare. She sent a fond farewell, or what I imagined was a fond farewell, to the black horse who'd caused all the mischief, and then walked over to us.

"I'll bring up the wagon." The naga nodded, as if horses magically opening their stalls were the norm around here, and slithered off to the back of the stable.

Bronwynn reached out and gripped her horse's head, rubbing her hand on the mare's long nose and marveling at the copious amounts of glitter that fell as she did so. Or at least, I marveled.

"I can't bring you *anywhere*," Bronwynn mumbled, and then set about grabbing Donna's equipment and dressing the mare. A saddle, even though Donna barely needed it while she was pulling a wagon, and some things to help hitch her to said wagon. Bronwynn would know better than I about preparing a horse and wagon, so I grabbed our bags and brought them to load into the back.

We were set and ready to head to Vitol, the capital city overlooked by the Emerald Palace.

Within a few hours, we would be standing at Bronwynn's family home and . . . I decided it was probably time to have that important conversation with my bard.

CHAPTER 72

Born for Greatness and Biting People

Brownie

Brownie's beautiful, sparkling, gloriously foolish mare had on more than a few occasions gotten into trouble after meeting other intelligent horses like herself. If Brownie had known Cassandra was going to be lodging there, she might have planned better and moved the mare.

Or not.

Donna was a very sociable horse, with a need for adventure. She was also very popular, and Cassandra was all too happy to get up to mischief with Donna. No one was ever really hurt in their antics, though one time, Donna had somehow shaved a picture of a stoneskin wombat's butt on Cassandra's flank. Brownie didn't even want to *know* how the mare had handled a pair of trimming scissors.

"Bronwynn." Rufus' smooth voice immediately had the bard focusing on her travel companion. He'd thrown an arm up on the backrest and casually turned to face her. Slake was having a catnap in the back of the wagon, and they'd just exited the city gates with little to no fuss.

"Yes?" She smiled across at the beastman general. For a bare instant, she wondered if she might just cancel visiting her family and go find a place in the city where she could spend some time petting Rufus instead. Or talking to him. Or going to a festival . . .

Rufus leaned closer, his golden eyes searching hers. "May I court you? Officially?"

Brownie burst into a huge smile. She felt the rise of excitement, uncertainty, hope, and more build as she positively yelled out, "Yes! Of course!"

Brownie let go of a small fear that had been secretly worrying her since that morning; that Rufus had left last night because he wasn't interested after all and he wasn't going to let her pet him again anytime soon.

Rufus didn't even flinch at her shout. Brownie, self-conscious of her outburst, tried to calm down. "What type of courting?"

"Well . . . how much do you know of beastfolk customs?"

"I know that the second Olen the bearman and Princess Penelope looked at each other, Olen practically carried the princess off to be wed," she stated. "But other than that? Not much."

"We *are* very . . . quick." Rufus nodded. "When you know, you know."

"And do you know?" Brownie asked, intrigued.

"I know."

"Is this why you keep saying you love me more than I love you?" Brownie coughed, mortified at the slip. "*Like* me more, I mean. That you *like* me more than I *like* you?"

The beastman stared at her long and hard. He stared at her until she was wondering if he wasn't going to answer at all, then finally, he said, "Yes."

Simply that.

"Does this also mean you want to get married, have kids, and settle down in the Dark Enchanted Forest together?" Brownie dropped the reins and folded her arms. She didn't know how this was going to work beyond petting friends. Or maybe *heavy*-petting friends . . .

But he answered, "No."

Again, no further discussion. That was, until he drew a breath.

"Your music is your soul, and you are not going to be happy settling down in one place for very long," he stated matter-of-factly. "So, if this is going to work, we'll have to get used to not seeing each other for a bit every month. If we marry, I can be the stay-at-home husband, and you can continue working across the continent."

"You'd have to buy a house," Brownie said, also calmly, like she wasn't discussing her entire future and subsequent change in marital status. Pretending to be calm was helping, though she was actually a torrent of emotional damage on the inside as she continued the pretense.

"That I would . . ." Rufus stared out over the beautiful craggy path that led them down toward the western sea. A very gentle incline for hours.

She waited, knowing he was thinking about it. After everything she'd learned, she wondered if he was ready to move out of the Black Fortress?

It was his home. She just didn't want it to be *her* home. There were few things Brownie had a strong opinion on, but *home* and family were up there with music and storytelling. If Rufus was offering to be her new *home* . . . then a temporary set of rooms in the Dark Lord's castle wouldn't do.

And he knew that she knew that he knew that. He also knew that she knew that he was still hiding something—or somethings. Maybe they were just about his current quest, but she was unsure.

At some point, she was going to need to demand an explanation. If nothing else . . . she was going to visit Henrietta in the Hollow after this, and she could interrogate her friend for answers then.

It would be nice if Rufus could tell her himself, though.

"Would you play me a song while I think about this?" Rufus asked.

She obliged. Donna knew the way just fine.

Vitol, the capital, sprawled out on both sides of the Gordan River before it reached the sea. The Emerald Palace was at the northern tip of the city, followed by the ministry and noble districts. The guild district was attached to the central market and the main heart of the city, closer to the water's edge. The shores of the Gordan were lined with floating houses tied to docks on both sides, and the river was full of boats ferrying passengers. Two major bridges stretched across the river to the south side. The inland bridge led to the military district, where the mages college and the knights academy was surrounded by a fort and military housing. The bridge closest to the sea led to the merchant's district, where her family lived. From her family home, it was fifteen minutes to cross the bridge north, and then another quarter hour to walk to the Assassin Assembly building in the guild district.

At some point, Slake rejoined them up front, and conversation turned to plans for performances and the meeting with the Continental Council. After a while, Slake went for another nap in the back of the wagon, and that was how they all rolled into her family's estate a few hours later, leaving a shining rainbow of glitter and bedazzle in their wake.

The guard griffins at the front gate made a fuss as they approached, the pair of them looming over the wagon.

She waved to the griffins. "Hey, Ricco; hey, Oscar. How are things?"

Ricco fluttered his wings excitedly and flew down to land, gripping the back of her seat. He was large enough to cover the entire wagon width with his wingspan, but he was well-balanced, and leaned down to run his beak through her hair. A clear sign of welcome.

Oscar was busy eyeing Rufus.

"It's alright, Oscar," Brownie assured the griffin. Oscar was an amazing griffin guard, strong and powerful and instinctively observant. He was born for greatness . . . and biting people. He could always tell when someone had ulterior motives, and her family knew to listen to Oscar's intuition.

"This is Rufus . . . my, um, *suitor*."

CHAPTER 73

The Big Bad Wolf

Rufus

[You have taken 46 points of Damage from Oscar the Griffin. Health 570/616. You suffer **Bleed**. Continuing Damage may apply.]

Oscar bit my hand, drawing blood. I didn't stop the griffin. He had landed beside the carriage and stood on his hind legs to reach up and sniff me before biting my offered hand.

He was guarding Bronwynn's family, and I was her first encounter. I had nefarious intent. I'd lied my way into her life and left out the fact I was a fan who's been stalking her for months and investigating her entire family for international war crimes.

Of course the guard griffin would bite me.

"Oscar! Let go of Rufus this instant!" Bronwynn ordered. The griffin refused, sinking his teeth into my hand further and shaking it violently.

[You have taken 20 points of Damage from **Bleed**. Health 550/616. Continuing Damage may apply.]

"Hello, Oscar," I said, debating whether I should activate my [Calming Effect] perk. "If it helps, Minstrel Bronwynn already knows that I'm not a good person."

The griffin turned to face my bard, and she nodded. "He's coming today as my guest, but he'll also be visiting Uncle Derek on *business.*"

"I promise to cause no harm to your people while visiting, save in self-defense," I vowed, still being mauled by the griffin. He was indeed very good at biting.

Ricco let out a screech from beside Bronwynn, and Oscar let go, dropping back down to sit on his haunches on the ground beside the wagon. He eyed me with suspicion and licked the blood off his beak.

[You have taken 20 points of Damage from **Bleed**. Health 530/616. Continuing Damage may apply.]

"And don't—Actually, never mind," Bronwynn started to say to the griffin, but changed her mind. "If that's everything, we'll head in—"

"BROWNIEEEEEEEEEE."

Beyond the gate, the wall encircled an entire collection of huge houses divided by patio walkways covered in sloped awnings with one tall three-story building in the middle. . . and there was a gaggle of children racing down the main path toward us.

They descended upon us with a wave of chaotic energy and excitement that convinced both griffins to wisely fly back up to their posts before getting tackled.

We were not so lucky.

"You're back!" said a young foxgirl running around to Bronwynn's side of the wagon. At the same time, a younger puma beastgirl clambered up and over my lap to get to Bronwynn from this side of the wagon, saying, "Auntie Brownie, can I show you this bruise? Dennis tripped and fell on me."

"Did not," a boy said, approaching Donna. He was one of two giant youths the size of a teenager, but still obviously under ten.

"Did too!"

Upon closer inspection, the two youths petting Donna were *not* the same age. Dennis was around five, and a giant. The girl beside him was around ten, and a half giantess, and I'd mistaken their ages due to their similar height. The pair laughed as they pet the horse, coating their arms in glitter. Donna put up with the attention, but I could tell she was being magnanimous only due to their family relation with the bard.

Movement behind me revealed a human boy with glasses sitting at the back of the wagon, petting and whispering to Slake.

"Up, up!" a soft voice said down by my feet. I would have missed it without my [Keen Senses]. A tiny troll girl, no more than a toddler, holding a tiny griffin stuffie lifted one hand up at me and repeatedly opened and closed her fist, telling me she wanted *up-up*.

It was the hand sign for *milk*, but context mattered.

I reached down and lifted her with both hands, placing her on my lap. She seemed content and just sat there, watching the older children crawl all over Bronwynn.

"Mimi!" a troll boy standing on Bronwynn's side called over the clamor. "Come here."

While accosting family was perfectly acceptable, the idea of bothering a guest seemed to embarrass the boy, and he motioned for the little troll girl to join them.

Mimi stuck up her nose and refused, perfectly content to sit on my lap.

Oscar grumbled but didn't make a move. I was no danger to the children.

"I'm Mimi." The chaos of conversation beside us was forgotten as the girl reached out a little hand to steady herself by grabbing my shirt.

She asked, "Who are you?"

"I'm Rufus. It's nice to meet you."

She stared at my bloody hand, her black eyes with hints of red, so similar to Bronwynn's, and then back up at me. "Are you a bad man, Brufus?"

It was the hand that Oscar had mauled earlier. The bleed effect had stopped, at least, though I still needed to wash up. For some reason, staring into her big dark eyes, I couldn't muster up the willpower to lie. I pushed a stray pink curl out of the little girl's face with my clean hand. "Yes, but I like your Auntie Bronwynn a lot, and so I'm trying to be good."

She leaned in, and I bent my ear for her. "Are you the Big Bad Wolf trying to eat my Auntie Brownie?"

I choked on a combination of laughter and shock. "I mean—"

Suddenly, a pair of green arms whisked the toddler away. The older troll boy, probably around ten, had come around to my side of the wagon and was staring daggers at me while holding his sister. "Mimi, we don't climb on the guests. You could get hurt, and mama will be angry."

"But Julep—"

"No buts."

"Children."

A voice as gentle as a soft summer breeze carried its way through the chaos, and the mini horde stilled. As one, everyone present turned to see a giantess walking toward them. Her long gray hair was tied back in three braids, and she wore a stylish mix of silk tunic, fine leather pants tucked into plated boots, an embroidered vest, and protective leather arm bracers.

The size of the buildings was explained next to the giantess. I was tall, elevated onto my haunches in half-beast form, but even I only came up to her elbow. Brownie was tall among the crowd, but a full giantess towered above *everyone*.

Except maybe a dwarf.

"Come here," the woman said, her voice still whisper-soft yet clear.

"Yes, Aunt Glindy," Most of the tiny horde replied, but the two trolls and the giant and half giantess, who said, "Yes, Grandmama."

They lined up tallest to smallest, with the exception of Julep still holding Mimi, and waited.

"Good." Glindy nodded. "Now that you've greeted your cousin, it is time to go back inside. She will need to unpack and get ready—"

"Aww," a sorrowful mix of whining and displeasure met the announcement, but Glindy held firm, and no one was willing to actively disobey the giantess.

"You will all have a chance to see her when she's settled," Glindy told them. "Inside. Now."

After the children had finished marching out of sight, Glindy turned back to us. Her eyes lingered on my injured hand, which was already mostly healed due to my Constitution, but she made no move to kick me out.

Instead, she announced, "Welcome, Commander General Rufus. Linden and Marigold are waiting to see you in the Rosewood Terrace."

"Wait!" Bronwynn exclaimed. "My parents are *here*?"

CHAPTER 74

Welcome Home, Dear

Brownie

Brownie stared at her Aunt Glindy in confusion and unease.

Her parents were *supposed* to be staying with her maternal family in Drendil, investigating the changes being implemented in the kingdom. The new regent was promoting acceptance of nonhumans, but that didn't mean it would change overnight. Her parents had been chosen to inspect.

Most of her mother's family had moved to Peldeep, since her aunts had, one and all, married nonhumans, but her maternal grandparents still lived in Drendil. Brownie had been raised there for half of her life. Drendil hadn't been the best place to grow up as a half giantess, but she hadn't spent very much time there until her teens—and then, she'd had music and Henrietta to keep her busy. The previous king and queen had promoted intolerance and violence against nonhumans; how they begat a sweet princess like Henrietta was anyone's guess.

"Your parents traveled here with Persia on her last delivery. They wanted to meet your *partner*." Aunt Glindy waved a hand at Rufus, who'd jumped down to join them.

"But how did they *know*? We've only just started courting today!" Brownie accepted Rufus's offered hand. He tucked hers into the crook of his elbow and smiled down at her.

"Just because it took us a while to figure it out doesn't mean it wasn't obvious to everyone else that I was chasing you," he teased.

"You weren't chasing me," Brownie grumped. "You were sitting in the wagon right next to me."

"That's because you let me ride with you," Rufus pointed out. "Otherwise, I *would* have been chasing you, all the way to Servalt and back."

"Nevertheless"—Aunt Glindy took a step to the side and waved them forward—"your parents *are* waiting."

Brownie drew a deep breath. "Then I'll leave Donna to you, Aunt Glindy. Her enchantment should run out in the next hour or so."

"I'm going to head out as well." Slake hopped up from the back of the wagon and shook himself. "I've a report to make at the palace. But I'll be back to visit before your meeting with the guild leader."

The grimalcat flew away before anyone could do more than bid a polite farewell.

Aunt Glindy raised an eyebrow at them having traveled with the mythical beast, but joined in the goodbyes, adding a slight bow to be polite. "That wasn't *your* grimalcat, was it?"

"No." Brownie shook her head.

Aunt Glindy sighed before waving the pair of them on as she led Donna away.

Brownie's family home was almost a fortress in its own right, with a two-story wall that guarded the compound, a stable to the left, and a training field to the right.

Rufus followed Brownie as she tried to explain her family and the grounds as simply as possible. In the center rose a giant elegant tower with a few balconies and windows placed in strategic positions in case of attack. Eldest Uncle Derek lived there with his foxbride Sue, their foxson Luke with his human wife, Jasmine, and the fox granddaughter Lily. Luke's sister, the storm giant Candace, had moved out to be an adventurer.

Strategically placed in four corners around the tower were four houses also build for giants, each with sliding doors and covered wooden patios that bridged the large and smaller units. In the front right, herforever single-and-happy Uncle Tobias; the back right was Brownie's parents'; the back left was Uncle Ulric and his wife, Aunt Glindy; the front left was Uncle Ulric's son and his troll wife Lucy and their four children.

There were smaller-size buildings in between which housed all of her nongiant uncles and their wives and children and grandchildren. It was a busy place.

They passed by her human uncle Bruce on his way to the palace. He lived in one of the smaller units, but he was rarely home, as his ratkin husband Benji lived in the palace, and they mostly stayed there.

Brownie explained all of this as they walked . . . and assumed that Rufus retained *none of it*. Her family was *huge*, and just explaining this much was pretty overwhelming.

And she didn't include her mother's side.

Rufus, for his part, listened intently.

"And this is my house." Brownie motioned toward a large building with open windows and delicate wind chimes hanging from the eaves. A collection of marigolds hung in planter boxes off the patio railings. The entire place was warm and welcoming.

Her father, wearing all black and sharpening a collection of throwing knives while sitting on a seat on the patio, was less so, though her mother, wearing a flowing green summer gown with floral trim along the seams, was watering the plants happily. They could not be more different; her father a rogue assassin and her mother a priestess of earth who specialized in blessing crops.

But they loved each other, and they loved her.

"Mother, Father!" Brownie beamed up at them, still linked arm and arm with Rufus. "Welcome back. I wasn't expecting you."

"Greetings." Rufus nodded.

"It's a good thing we arrived when we did." Her father eyed them, focusing mostly on Rufus as he slowly *ka-shinked* a knife across the sharpening stone before resting the blade flat side down on his knees. "As I'm sure there is *much* to speak about before dinner."

The slight to Rufus by not returning his greeting wasn't a good sign, and was actually kind of rude, but Brownie didn't worry.

Her father was one for dramatics, while her mother . . .

"Welcome home, dear." Her mother put aside the watering can and smiled down at them. "Why don't we all go inside for a nice cup of elder-raspberry tea? I just picked up a fresh tin of leaves from the Pixie Prim booth at the market this morning."

"Alright." Brownie squeezed Rufus's arm, and they walked up the stairs together.

Her father placed the sharpening stone aside and stood, holding the shining knife in his hand. He flipped the blade a few times in the air, deftly displaying the [Knife Play] skill that all of her family prided themselves on. He finally sheathed the blade and clipped it to his belt, resting his hand on the clip. With a sweep, he gestured them forward with his free hand, all the while leaving the other in place and staring daggers at Rufus.

The entry of her childhood home remained the same, opening into a mud-room used for taking off their shoes and donning indoor footwear. Rufus accepted a pair, sliding his wolf feet into ill-fitting slippers. In the common room, her mother was pouring hot water into a teapot to steep. She'd also placed out a few snacks: lotus blossom cakes, fried vegetable dumplings, mixed nuts, and a small platter of dried meats.

The sentiment warmed Brownie's heart. Her mother was a vegetarian and never served meat unless they were hosting a purely carnivorous guest of honor.

Marigold didn't know what Rufus could eat, so she'd added meat just for him.

Brownie resisted the sudden urge to cry; she loved her parents, which was why convincing them to accept Rufus was all the more important.

Her father sat down cross-legged on a pillow at the low table. At least, low by half-giant standards. While standing, it came up to Brownie's shin and her mother's knee.

"So, Rufus," Linden Stannard said. "Tell us about yourself."

CHAPTER 75

You've Been Stalking My Daughter?

Rufus

Somehow, I'd gone from admiring Minstrel Bronwynn from afar to sitting across from her parents the night after she'd pet me to sleep, trying to convince them I was a worthy husband for their daughter.

I still couldn't quite wrap my head around it.

"My full title is Commander General Rufus Triever, leader of the King's Dogs of the Black Fortress, and I'm also mediator to the Dark Horde. I live full-time in the Dark Enchanted Forest but enjoy a fair bit of travel—mostly to go see Bronwynn's concerts." I thought that telling that much of the truth wouldn't hurt. What *did* hurt was my tail, which I'd deliberately sat on to prevent difficulties.

My tail was not meant to be sat on.

"I'm also a sitting representative on the Continental Council," I added, trying to impress.

Marigold Stannard nodded. Bronwynn had mentioned that she'd used her mother's maiden name, Lyriel, in her bardic career. Something to separate her from her assassin family. "That's nice, dear, but what my husband wants to hear isn't your job but something about *you*."

As someone who'd lounged comfortably on the asking side of this style of interrogation most of my life, it was somehow nerve-racking to find myself sitting and being scrutinized on the answering side.

Of course, [Natural Poise] let me relax into my seat with an appearance of put-togetherness . . .

"I'm a simple beastman. Every morning, I enjoy breakfast and a swim to get me going. I like reading, and recently picked up all of Her Eminence Feliwyn's romance novels, though I read educational books on the habits of people in equal measure. My favorite music is anything your daughter is singing. I have a sister in Gren's Keep I still keep in touch with. My favorite food is flying pork–breaded cutlets on rice. And I am a connoisseur of wine, but rarely overimbibe. I simply enjoy the taste."

"And can you explain"—Linden slapped his knee—"why Oscar bit you?"

"The griffin probably sensed my own guilty conscience."

Even under the intense eye of my potential future in-laws, I admired their honest straightforwardness. It was something I promoted in my own people. Why beat around the bush when you could ask direct questions? It helped that I had [Sense Lies] and [Detect Fake] and [Sense Threat], and could very easily ask all of the same questions and know for fair certain if the answers given were true. Between her parents, I wasn't certain they didn't have a similar skill.

"I hope you were planning to elaborate on that," Marigold said sweetly, pouring each of us a cup of tea. It was then that my sense of self-preservation made me viscerally aware of the human woman. There was a matter-of-fact hint of murderous intent in her dark eyes. Something primal told me that while Linden Stannard would happily shank me in an alleyway if he saw fit to do so, Marigold would feed my body to her plants, where even the bones would be used for fertilizer.

The Black Fortress had a man-eating carnivorous castle garden planted by Her Eminence Feliwyn, and I'd had my fair share of walks among the corpse roses.

"I have a few kingdom quests that involve following Bronwynn around," I stated, "which she has kindly—"

Linden cut me off. "You're *spying* on my daughter?"

"Yes." I nodded.

"How long have you been 'following her around'?"

The question caught me off guard, and my eyes flicked to Bronwynn for the first time since we'd sat down side by side at the table. She was happily eating a mooncake, her cheeks full and her smile radiant. When our eyes met, her smile somehow grew bigger. I thanked all the gods that for this meeting, I'd sat on my tail.

I dragged my eyes back to her father and stated, "A year."

"*What?*" Bronwynn choked on her mooncake. The word was a garble of pastry, but I could recognize it by the tone. I held back a wince. In for a copper, in for a gold coin, I supposed. *Sigh.*

"Ever since I heard her play last year," I explained. "I've joined her fan club, traveled to her concerts, and attended her shows . . . I've been following her far longer than my orders . . ."

"So you've been *stalking* my daughter." Linden's voice grew a shade darker.

"Well, that's fine," Bronwynn shrugged. "A lot of people have told me they're my fans. I even have a fan club with events! I don't think that warrants being called a *stalker*, dad."

She had no idea, though I *did* try to respect her privacy as much as possible. All of the information I collected and coveted was public knowledge. In all this time, I'd remained true to that limitation . . . despite the temptation to abuse my power and authority otherwise.

I was still holding on.

Bronwynn followed up with, "I thought you were going to tell them that everyone thinks I'm the molten ash vane assassin."

"What?!" Both of her parents asked at the same time. Her mother coughed and turned an intense stare on me, following up with, "Does that mean?"

"It means I am guarding Minstrel Bronwynn as instructed by my Dark King and Queen . . . and she's already found out I was investigating her at the same time. We aren't the only ones who've noticed that Bronwynn has been spotted at every molten ash vane assassination attempt in the country."

Bronwynn's parents shared a look. It wasn't a "Who has our daughter brought home this time?" expression. Instead, it was very much an "Are you thinking what I'm thinking?" type of look.

"Could it be?" Linden asked his wife, proving my point.

Marigold shook her head. "Derek wouldn't ship molten ash vane. Do we even *have* a poisoner that can make it?"

Bronwynn spoke up then. "We have three poisoners contracted; surely one of them could make it if they had the ingredients? But that *still* doesn't mean anything—I'm not in the family business, remember?"

There was a pause, and my [Sense Lies] immediately activated when Marigold nodded and faked a smile. "Of course, dear."

The pit dropped out of my stomach. Linden and Marigold were hiding something from my bard.

Something important.

"Let's get back to the matter at hand." Linden turned his stormy gray eyes my way. "You've not given us a very good first impression, Rufus."

I took a sip of my tea. It wasn't poisoned, which was nice, and it actually tasted very smooth. "I'd rather tell you everything I can up front. I *could* try winning you over before you find out the truth, but that's never been my preference. Statistically speaking, one in four beastfolk from the Dark Enchanted Forest find that our open approach to relationships and family structure causes problems when finding mates elsewhere, but the recommendation remains to be honest. It's a cultural difference that has been extensively studied by my peers."

Linden's lips twitched. "Go on."

If the opportunity arose to discuss principal theory on interpersonal relations between cultures, nobody needed to ask me twice. "The basic family structure in Gren's Keep, for instance, is built on a community approach. There are spaces and places for people who are interested in such things to frequent, a big one being tourney days, where prospective lovers challenge each other. It used to be a free-for-all bloodbath, but the introduction of duels in recent years has really mellowed things out."

Marigold laughed quietly but covered it behind her hand.

"Love is love, and beastfolk are not prudish by any means. We are just honest," I explained. "Some people marry many; others are seasonal mates . . . I've always taken longer to develop feelings, but I do want to fall in love, marry, have children, and grow old with the person of my choosing."

There was a quiet pause for a few seconds until Linden broke the silence.

"And do you love my daughter?"

CHAPTER 76

Mind the Furniture

Brownie

Brownie slapped the table then, drawing everyone's attention. "Rufus! *Don't answer that question!*"

From the moment they'd sat down, Brownie had been on the edge of her seat enjoying the snacks and the drinks and the interrogation of her potential partner. She'd let her parent's get away with verbally cornering Rufus and asking him all kinds of poignant questions because she'd also wanted to know more about him. If she wanted to do more than just pet the man, then she was going to have to figure it out sooner or later.

But!

"I want Rufus to say it to me first," Brownie explained. "If and when we fall in love will be relayed to you *after the fact*."

Linden raised a single eyebrow. "You brought a man to visit us before you were sure he loved you?"

"I didn't bring him to visit you! You weren't even supposed to *be* here," Brownie countered. "I just came by to visit my cousins and have a nice home-cooked meal before going to the festival."

Rufus cut in. "And I already happened to have a meeting with Guild Master Derek planned. So either way, I was going to be in the area."

"A meeting to discuss if our Bronwynn is the culprit of an international poisoning spree," Her mother said dryly.

"We both know that she isn't guilty." Rufus shrugged. Brownie smiled at her prospective suitor. He really was darling.

Then Rufus continued. "Though I'm not so sure about the Assassin Assembly at large."

Her father's hand curled into a fist on the table. "Say that again."

"I'm not certain if the Peldeep Assassin Assembly isn't involved in some way with the molten ash vane case," he repeated. "Which is only fair; I haven't spoken with Guild Master Derek yet. I'm not fool enough to judge an entire family of rogues based on their bardic cousin."

Brownie nodded. "Does this mean we can wrap things up and go visit *my* cousins before dinner? I was going to sing Mimi a bedtime song before she goes up."

Her mother stood and summoned an oak staff from the next room. It flew into the priestess's open hand, and she used it as a proper cane. After a bad fall last winter, her mother had been relying more and more on it. One too many times cleaning up poisonous foliage, her healer had told her, had left her bones a little too brittle and prone to break.

"I'll walk you over to Andreas and Lucy's house," her mother said. "Your father will have a word with your suitor, alone." That last wasn't a suggestion, and a vine carrying two glasses and a bottle of red liquid bobbed over to the table. "We'll see you both at dinner."

And then her mother all but dragged Brownie out of the room by the elbow.

"I don't know if it's wise to leave them behind like that?" Brownie said.

Her mother stomped her cane down with vigor. "No need to worry, love. Worst that could happen is they come to blows."

"I think the worst that could happen is father picking a fight with a level fifty-something general who blows up the building," she shot back, but continued to let her mother pull her along.

"I'm sure Linden will mind the furniture," her mother replied, with more hope than Brownie felt was realistic.

The entire compound was a series of houses that circled the main building, and each house had a full patio and walkway between. Brownie and her mother made their way through the back of their house, along the patio, through a family vegetable garden, around the main building's patio, and then back across a small yard to Cousin Andreas's house.

He and Lucy, the troll, were married with four children. Mimi was two, and the youngest of anyone in the entire family. That little troll had everyone wrapped around her tiny green hand, including Brownie.

"Aunty Marigold! Cousin Brownie!" Dennis the giant five-year-old rushed forward, laughing. He hit Brownie in a hug that would have crushed weaker mortals. Luckily, she had [Sturdy] ready.

"Hello, Dennis. How're your knife classes going?" Brownie set her cousin down and started walking with him to the house. Lessons on weapons handling, reading and writing, [Silent Step], and improved dexterity started at five years old. Goodness knew Brownie had done them all herself.

And usually the kids were most excited about the sharp pokey part of their new schedule.

"I hit the target today *three times*." Dennis puffed up with pride, and Brownie reached out to ruffle his hair.

"That's brilliant." Brownie nodded.

Marigold brought up the rear as they all entered the house. The entire place looked too delicate to house four kids, with ornate wooden doors and some paper walls, all on bamboo floors. But Brownie knew how much reinforcement magic went into every square inch of the house.

They didn't want one kid's tantrum to destroy half the building.

Everyone slipped into indoor shoes as Dennis yelled, "Mom! Dad! Aunty Marigold and Cousin Brownie are here!"

"COUSIN BROWNIE!" A tiny troll toddled about the corner, curly pink hair bouncing up and down. She was in her sleepwear and had her stuffie ready for bed. The child also tackled Brownie, but with much less force than her older brother.

Brownie laughed and picked up the little girl. "I'm here, I'm here. I promised you a bedtime song, didn't I?"

Mimi nodded.

"Have you brushed your teeth?"

Mimi nodded.

"Said goodnight?"

Mimi nodded.

"And have you picked a song?"

"Can I pick a song too?" Dennis shoved his face in front of them.

Mimi stuck her tongue out at her brother and hugged Brownie around the neck. "Mimi first!"

"Yes, yes," Brownie soothed. "Dennis, I'm going to go put your sister to bed; I'll be there shortly."

"Awesome! I'll go tell Mom!" The boy shot off down the hall in a hurry, bumping a table at the end of the hall.

It, of course, didn't even rattle.

"I want 'Wings of Ash,'" Mimi requested, cuddling into her arms. "Peas?"

"Of course, sweet."

She waved goodbye to her mother, who followed after Dennis. Uncle Graham was supposed to be playing a game of chess with Julep before bed. He was the lead administrative authority in the family. Between her mother, who was Uncle Derek's personal assistant, and Uncle Graham, the lead paper shuffler, they'd get everything ready for Rufus in short order. Even if Brownie couldn't do anything to help the beastman in his quest personally, she could at least make it easier!

Brownie hoped the dinner tonight went well.

CHAPTER 77

Take Off Your Clothes

Rufus

"Alright," Linden slapped his knee the second his wife and daughter were clear of the house. "Let's get you ready for the dinner party. Is that all you have to wear?"

That . . . wasn't what I was expecting. The fierce stare and gruff demeanor made me ready to catch a fist at any second, not suddenly prepare for a change of wardrobe.

"I have formal attire in my storage?"

"Bring it out," Linden ordered. He took a swig of his wine and placed it to the side, then reached forward and moved my own drink to make space. "Let's see what you have."

While strange, I accepted this sudden turn of events with my usual outwardly laid-back self. Inside, I was confused and concerned . . .

"These are the clothes I was going to wear to meet Guild Master Derek tomorrow," I said, laying out a dark-blue silk tunic with golden thread running in swirls along the cuffs, neckline, and buttonholes. I brought out matching britches with a tie at the calf so the pants fit snug, also with golden embroidering at the ankle and the sides. I had a golden brooch in the shape of a shield with a green tree and four drops of green blood, one in each corner, that I would wear as a symbol of the Dark Enchanted Forest army, and I'd planned to sweep my hair back into a low ponytail.

"This is perfect for your meeting, but not good enough for dinner," Linden stated, matter-of-factly. He eyed me intently, his gaze trailing from the crown of my head to my toes. Finally, the half giant stood up and marched toward the back of the house. "Come with me."

I obliged.

The house was a combination of wood and paper walls, with long hallways and sliding doors. After a few turns, Bronwynn's father led me into a storage room. There were some boxes, a wardrobe, a few chests, and a ceiling-high shelf covered with enchanted knickknacks.

Linden threw open the wardrobe and rummaged inside. He and I weren't of a height, since the half giant was even taller than his daughter, but presumably he had been my height at one point in time in his life. He pulled out a black silk robe with block-printed red blossoms. The flowers weren't too pronounced, and they reminded me of the color of Brownie's hair.

"Let me show you how to wear this, and then you can help me into my own," the half giant said, seeing that I was appreciating the high-quality clothing.

"What do I do?" I knew that King Keith had servants to help him dress when he saw fit, but I'd rarely made use of the privilege.

"Simple," he said. "Take off your clothes."

The banquet hall was in the main building, and Linden led me there while we talked. We'd spent a surprisingly long time getting to this point.

The process to put on the outfit he'd picked out for me was somewhat arduous, but it certainly looked regal—and more importantly, it felt comfortable to wear. And his decision to finish the bottle of wine before changing into his own clothes might have prolonged the task.

". . . and any Sumbrian who thinks that we would let that happen is a fool." Linden was telling me about the ambassador of the elven nation who put forth a proposal to the house of servants, what Peldeep called their governing body, ordering a ten percent reduction in port taxes for five years as a part of the marriage agreement between Knight Commander Bastian and Countess Peregrine Fern. The couple were set to be wed this week at the end of the Apple Blossom Festival, and Sumbria was in full form with their usual diplomatic arrogance.

This was why the Dark Enchanted Forest did not host resident ambassadors like most of the other kingdoms . . . Her Eminence Feliwyn would have just eaten them if they proved too much of a bother, and Keith was too distracted with *golemancy* to bother.

My friend was a lot like the dragon who raised him, even if he denied it.

"I'm still surprised they place so little weight into the prophecies," I said, walking up a half flight of stairs.

Linden shook his head. "Fools, the lot of them. Though Benji, that's my brother's husband, was telling us Peregrine isn't so bad. Her father has always been a reasonable elf to bargain with. He's also an exceptional talent; nobody's managed to assassinate anyone in his family yet, and not for lack of trying!" The half giant laughed heartily. "Count Valin just sends our assassins back with a polite note every time. He's a good sort."

I recalled the number of times we'd had to send assassins back to Peldeep or Servalt, and the troubles figuring out which one belonged to which organization. I said as much. "How can he tell if they're yours? The assassins, I mean. They're usually tight-lipped about where they come from."

"Is that why King Keith is always sending us Servalt's operatives?" Linden shook his head. "Did Derek not let him know that you can tell by their blades? Peldeep uses pettle steel pommels. It's subtle, but it lets everyone know who's whom without anyone having to break their professional confidentiality oath."

"I'll be honest with you, no. I don't think anyone knew that. Now that we are on the topic, I have to ask; of the twenty-odd assassins we sent back from the Drendil Bridge Battle," I asked, "how many were yours?"

"Eight."

Linden stopped outside a set of sliding doors and squared his shoulders. I followed suit, settling comfortably into a confident and poised position.

My stomach flipped twice when he opened the thin paper door and let us into the dining hall.

First, because I was not ready to see an entire room of Bronwynn's roguish relatives who might not rival me in level but were mostly giants and in all honesty intimidating by the sheer fact that they were *Bronwynn's relatives.*

And second, because *she* sat in a red dress with black accents that complimented my own so perfectly. Bronwynn was smiling at something her mother said, the light catching the fire in her hair and the joy in her eyes.

There was that moment at the table, when her father had asked me if I loved her . . . the answer had come so readily.

Suddenly, standing in a room full of assassins didn't seem that bad.

I was ready.

Until my prospective father-in-law reached out and slapped my back with enough force to topple a tree. My Constitution barely let me keep still, and I took twenty points of physical damage from the attack.

"Alright, all," the half giant's voice pitched over the room. "Let me introduce you to Commander General Rufus Triever of Nilheim."

There was a dramatic pause as all eyes bore into me with a mix of curiosity, reservation, or indifference. Until Linden added, "He's come to court my daughter, Bronwynn."

That was when the room exploded into a ruckus.

CHAPTER 78

That's The One Oscar Bit

Brownie

Brownie was born and raised with a large family, so she was used to the loud, boisterous cacophony of giants, trolls, foxfolk, and humans all talking over each other during dinner. Rufus, she knew, was *not*, and she felt that he handled the onslaught of questions admirably.

"What? No!" Cousin Terra, a human Courtier, gasped, hiding her smile behind a colorful fan.

Uncle Tobias, a storm giant and her sixth uncle, asked, "How long has *this* been going on?"

"That's the one Oscar bit," Jasmine, a human Arcane Assassin, explained to her fox husband, Cousin Luke. She wasn't trying to be quiet about it, either.

"I'm surprised she landed someone so—" Cousin Terra's husband, the puma beastman Mark, began to mutter. He didn't finish his sentence before his human mother-in-law, Aunty Martha, jabbed him in the side.

Brownie's father headed off most of the inquiries while escorting her beastman to the seat beside her. "He's only just arrived, so don't overcrowd the man," Linden ordered. Instead of taking his usual seat beside her mother, he sat beside Rufus so the two of them were defended on both sides by her parents.

It was strangely comforting, and Brownie was reminded for the hundredth time why she loved her family. Even if they made her want to tear her hair out sometimes.

A deep voice quietly carried over the din of noise around the table. "*If* you have good intentions for our niece, then I'm happy to welcome you to our table, Commander Rufus." Everyone stilled as Uncle Derek spoke from the head of the table. He was the eldest, in his fifties, and sat with Aunty Sue, a foxfolk. Aunty Sue was the quiet type, but her thin eyes were lifted in amusement even as her husband masked threats in a greeting.

"I assure you that I only have the *best* of intentions for Bronwynn." Rufus bowed at the waist as low as he might to someone a rank above him, showing her uncle a great deal of respect.

"We shall see." Uncle Derek nodded in acknowledgement. He faced the gathering then, and announced, "Now that everyone is here, let's eat."

Brownie reached out with her sticks and plopped a small glazed duck breast onto her plate, then added some long broccoli and wild rice. Rufus hesitated but selected from a tray of steamed buns and some sauteed mushrooms. She passed the ladle to him, and he scooped some of the rice onto his plate as well.

The table was long and rectangular, and repeat dishes were prepared to serve every four people down the line. Since her father was the seventh son, he was seated at the end. That meant they weren't surrounded by curious family members, just sandwiched.

"How long have you known our Brownie?" Her Uncle Tobias asked over his own plate of steamed buns. He was the forever-single-and-happy-about-it uncle who spoiled his nieces and nephews, including Brownie.

Rufus answered, "I've been to her concerts long before we officially met."

"And then my best friend got married to his best friend," Brownie explained, "so we saw a lot of each other in and around the Dark Enchanted Forest, even before he joined me on my trip to Servalt."

"Servalt is not the safest place right now, so I'm happy you had someone traveling with you," Lucy the troll pipped up, and Cousin Andreas nodded in agreement with his wife. He was the son of Brownie's fifth uncle, Ulric, who was on shift that evening guarding their home.

Cousin Andreas asked, "And how were your encounters? Nothing too arduous?"

Brownie shrugged. "Same old, same old; though we did need to save a Sumbrian elf that I was tempted to let get eaten."

"You wouldn't be the first," her mother muttered darkly beside Brownie. She stabbed one of her sticks into her bun to let out some of the steam. "Uncle Bruce and Benji have told me horror stories. I'm surprised at how few hits have been taken out on the Sumbrian court royals currently visiting."

"It explains the Sumbrian rebels' requests, though." Her mother sighed. "They've ordered twice their normal amount of poisons recently. And put out a hit on at least five royals. I don't know how they could suddenly afford it; they must have a new sponsor."

Her father shook his head. "I think our locals are just waiting until negotiations are settled, the wedding is done, and the lot are on their way back home. Who's to say that we won't have a sudden increase in contracts next week?"

"I'm planning on it, actually," Cousin Terra said from slightly further up the table. She was the daughter of Brownie's human third uncle, Graham, who wasn't present. They were in charge of managing the family's business and administration side, and it was nice to know they were preparing.

"Terra, any chance you have some crushed pearls I could steal?" Brownie pleaded to her favorite cousin, hands linked in front of her heart.

Terra fanned her face in mock haughtiness. "I guess this kind and generous miss can spare a bottle or two . . . For a song!"

"I'll swing by after dinner!" Brownie beamed, then she turned back to Cousin Andreas. "Aside from that, it's been the usual bandits and troll riddles. Though we did come across some Blackfog spies in Servalt."

She didn't mention they were, in fact, attacking Rufus, or that she was just there for the ride.

"You know, I've seen a lot more of them around recently." Uncle Tobias crossed his arms. "We've even had some delivered to the guild with a batch of assassins from Nilheim. Speaking of." The giant turned his attention to Rufus. "*Must* you send us so many Servalt operatives? I'm in charge of handling trade with the Assassin's Guild, and it's time-consuming."

"I'll be meeting with Guild Master Derek soon to discuss that very topic," Rufus said. "I'm sure we can come to some solution."

"Commander General Rufus." There was another pause in the conversation as Uncle Derek spoke. Between her uncles and aunts and their children and their children's children, there were fourteen people at the table, even with some of her family absent. It was noticeable when everyone stopped to listen to the head of the family.

"Yes?" Rufus replied.

"As you are staying in my home, why don't we move up the meeting to tomorrow after we break our fast?" her uncle offered.

Rufus nodded. "Alright, if it's not too much trouble to organize the paperwork here instead of the Assembly?"

"No trouble at all."

Brownie placed her hand on Rufus's paw. "That's perfect. Once you're done with Uncle, we can go to the festival together. And you can come to my show!"

Rufus stiffened noticeably under her touch, but his demeanor never faltered, and she wondered if he was just distracted by her hand on his, or if there was something she was missing.

"Ah, yes." He smiled, though it didn't reach his eyes. "I did hope to catch at least one of your concerts."

Brownie didn't know why . . . but that feeling of unease slowly settled in her gut again. The same one she'd had before she learned that Rufus was following her around on orders.

No one else seemed to catch it, but she knew. She knew, and all night, she wondered.

CHAPTER 79

The Dark Enchanted Forest is a Dark Enchanted Forest

Rufus

"As per the records from the Assembly relocation project, the operatives responsible for torching Kith Bog were hired mercenaries from Drendil, and not our responsibility," Guild Master Derek explained while I read over a tidy report logging the statements of each Rogue class we'd shipped off to the Assembly after the mass attack during the day of the Bridge Battle. "You will find the contracts individually signed by our guild members that specify *royal targets only*. As such, there was no breach of treaties, and we will not be offering reparations."

"Thank you, this will be enough to reassure my king." I carefully reviewed each page in a stack placed before me, my reading glasses perched on my nose. Everything was meticulously organized. "I shouldn't be long."

Very unfortunate.

I'd been hoping to leverage the Peldeep assassin's breach of treaty for information on how the giant had even gotten assassins across the border, but it didn't look like that was going to be the case.

And . . . now I was courting Bronwynn. It would've been so much easier to threaten to bring down the entire weight of the Dark Enchanted Forest when I didn't need to calculate how that would affect future family dinner parties.

Guild Master Derek's office had a giant desk in the corner appropriately sized for the storm giant, but I was currently sitting on a comfortable-size couch across from him with papers stacked on a short table between us. There was tea and snacks, and two copies of each report so that I could bring back a set for our records.

Dealing with the long-standing Peldeep guild was night and day to meeting with Servalt. While Guild Master Lina's entire business was cloaked in shadows, secretive, and bordered on the illicit, Peldeep was an established guild with centuries of history and reputation.

"Any chance," I broached, knowing it was a lost cause; still, it weighed heavy on Keith's mind—and by that, I meant it was driving my king up the wall with irritation, "you would reveal how you suddenly bypassed my kingdom's defenses?"

"Trade secret, I'm afraid," the guild master refused with a smile. He was missing one of his teeth; his lower left canine. I hadn't gotten a good look at the giant last evening, but from across a table, he was a very confident older man with salt-and-pepper hair, sideburns, and stormy gray eyes.

As for size, I came up to just below his elbow.

"Just thought I'd ask."

"I'm sure the Dark Lord will figure out the loophole any day now." Derek chuckled. "And I'll have a new magical defense to puzzle through. It's been a pleasure working against his border guard all these years."

"I'll let him know you said so." I nodded, tapping the files. There were only ten or so left. "As long as Peldeep continues to respect the safety and security of Nilheim citizens during contracts, then we may lay this to rest."

The guild master nodded. "Of course . . . and we appreciate that you've diligently adhered to the same restrictions."

We didn't send many assassins to other kingdoms, anyway. There were only six who had registered their Assassin class in the forest, and they enjoyed using their skills for other occupations, like maid or nanny. Keith's old wet nurse, retired now and living her best life in Gren's Keep, had been an Assassin class. There were a few other rogue classes, but they were highly prized and guaranteed a well-paying job with a pension in the Dark Horde. Since the Dark Enchanted Forest offered high-paying jobs with salaried four-day workweeks at four-hour shifts, not many thought about leaving.

I checked the clock and saw we were making good time for what was an arduous task.

After I'd survived the dinner with Bronwynn's giant relatives the previous evening, I'd been shown to a room one building over in Guardian Ulric and Tracker Glindy's home. As their titles suggested, they were very skilled at protecting visitors . . . and protecting the family *from* visitors.

I hadn't minded.

The black with gold trim outfit I'd prepared for meeting Guild Master Derek wasn't as *impressive* as the clothing gifted to me by Linden, but it was still perfect for this meeting. Comfortable but fashionable. Marigold had been waiting for me at breakfast with Ulric and Glindy. The priestess would act as my official escort while conducting business with the guild master, and after we'd finished a meal of fruit and flying pork bacon with small hotcakes had showed me to Derek's office. When asked, she'd let me know that Bronwynn would be busy with the children all morning.

She'd stepped out for our main discussion, but was waiting on hand outside.

Now that I was finishing up my meeting with Guild Master Derek, who was proving very helpful even without the grimalcat, there was another worry distracting me.

How was I going to meet up with the rest of the fan club *without* changing into my folk form? No one had ever seen me in beast or beastfolk form, as I'd managed to keep my work and my hobby completely separate thanks to the introduction of my hidden identity, Fergus.

There was a need to appear as myself in the royal court while visiting Their Royal Highness and when I was representing Nilheim on the Continental Council, but otherwise, I spent my days in Peldeep in a furless form, using the anonymity to relax.

Now I was courting the very woman I longed to hear, and I was expected to meet up with Frida and Ross as soon as they contacted me to let me know they were in the city. The rest of the group would be there too, though I knew few personally outside of the Crystal Cast correspondence . . . My opportunity to mingle at the yearly fan event had been stopped short when the entire place burned down. Maybe I should host another fan event this year. A fall affair, or a winter solstice concert . . . By that point, I should have revealed all to Bronwynn.

"Alright, that's the last one." I waved a hand over my copy of the documents, and the pile disappeared into my storage ring. "I'll report these back to the Dark Lord."

"And what will you be reporting back to the council?" Derek asked. He retained a friendly businesslike demeanor, though his low voice couldn't hide his suspicious curiosity.

I paused in the process of standing up. Honestly, I was going to wait until Slake came back and then speak with the guild master again. The original meeting was supposed to be tomorrow . . . But, as he'd brought it up himself: "That depends. Are you the one secretly delivering molten ash vane?"

The guild master didn't reply right away. Instead, his eyes searched mine, and whatever he was thinking about was hidden behind a calm outward mask. I waited.

Finally, he asked, "Rufus, who does the Dark Enchanted Forest order its poisons from?"

"Anyone and everyone," I replied. "Every market has a pop-up apothecary and any number of stalls with homemade antidote or poison bottles for sale. Or just locally harvested ingredients that have similar effects. Even if the castle was looking for something specific, we could have the army find it or ask the Pixie Prim to grow it. The Dark Enchanted Forest is, well, *a Dark Enchanted Forest*. Stumble around long enough, and the forest will figure it out."

Guild Master Derek nodded.

"The rest of the continent isn't like that. Instead, you have a few famous poisoners who will brew up batches of poisons and hire someone to distribute the goods to potential buyers."

Back in Servalt, Guild Master Lina had said something similar.

"And you have three such poisoners?" I recalled Bronwynn mentioning it.

"Yes." Derek waved his own hand—and four bottles of molten ash vane appeared on the table. The giant didn't have any visible rings or jewelry, so either it was a skill or he was just very good at sleight of hand. Both were equally likely. "We have three poisoners, and recently, these have been popping up in the inventory lists."

"And you are telling me *because?*"

"You're one of the lead investigators, are you not?" Derek waved the molten ash vane back to where it came from.

"I am."

"Then you would come back here with a signed writ from Their Royal Highness to audit my supplies sooner or later. I have the registry of each bottle, and the records show that each bottle we've received is untouched. The problem is that our poisoners are located across the continent, and I can't be absolutely sure *who's* been adding MAV to the batch."

It was an amusing thought, that both Guild Master Lina and Guild Master Derek shared the same scheme. If it was a good plan, it was a good plan. "Could you figure out which one is the poisoner?"

"With enough time, yes. Though there's someone here who might already know." He trailed off, obviously hesitating.

"Who?" I prodded. There was no sense in stalling when he'd come so far and told me so much already.

"It is against the guild's confidentiality contract to tell you her name, but you already know her," he sighed, "since she isn't a normal guild member and spends a lot more time traveling than most."

I felt my heart sink as I offered a name and he didn't say no.

"One last thing," he said as we stood. He was towering over me, as giants were wont to do. "Linden and Marigold have approved of your match, and I'll honor my brother's choice. But I'm sure you know what would happen to you if you *ever* hurt my niece?"

"Of course." I was a perfectly legal target, as per the treaties with the Peldeep Assassin Assembly. I offered my paw, and we shook hands before summoning Marigold to escort me.

But not back to Bronwynn. No.

I had a date with a horse.

CHAPTER 80

One Night by Candlelight

Brownie

Brownie met up with Rufus at noon after a long morning with her cousins. She hoped that Rufus had had an alright time of it without her.

For all she could see right through him, the beastman was a well-respected, confident commander general of the Dark Lord's army—and from what she'd gathered, most of her family already liked him.

Her father had even given Rufus a set of family robes. He was practically married in already.

Not that they were getting married anytime soon, or even engaged. They hadn't even admitted to love yet. She wondered if she should just tell him. It might not be the overwhelming storybook love of legends . . . but she *adored* the beastman and loved spending time with him, and wanted to live happily ever after with him.

Once he'd finished his task and all of their secrets were out of the way.

Brownie had always thought that *she* was full of secrets. A hidden family of assassins wasn't something you just sprang on somebody on a one night by candlelight. Rufus, for all his stalwart golden retriever energy, had a boatload of secrets and a hidden agenda you could park a wagon in.

She sighed over a lunch of roasted spicy hummus and flatbread, with a side of stuffed olives and a bowl of salted nuts.

Rufus and her mother arrived late to lunch. And both of them seemed strangely tense.

"How was your morning?" Brownie wondered if her uncle hadn't been polite. Any *number* of things could've gone wrong in the negotiation.

Rufus shared a look with her mother, and his left ear drooped a bit. But he hid his unhappiness pretty well behind a reassuring smile. "It was fine."

It was most certainly *not* fine. Brownie picked up her half-forgotten cold cup of tea and took a sip while she further inspected her beastman general as he settled in and helped himself to a plate.

"Did you at least sign a new treaty?" Brownie inquired. She wouldn't be sad to stay another day while they hashed things out, but she liked leaving early when she had things to do.

If she didn't leave extra, extra early . . . she usually ended up late.

"The guild master and I sorted everything easily." Rufus ate an olive, and surprised pleasure shone on his face; they were very good. He ate another before adding, "He's a very well-organized giant, even if he wouldn't tell me how Servalt and Peldeep operatives keep getting past the border spells. They're enchanted to let no foreigner in with ill intent to the kingdom or its people. The only other person to get through the enchantment was Henrietta . . . and I'm pretty sure there's only *one* Henrietta."

Brownie replayed the words of the enchantment over in her mind . . . and maybe it was all that time spent answering riddles over the years, but it seemed obvious to her. She even opened her mouth to say the answer, but closed it under her father's scrutiny. It wasn't good to reveal that kind of trade secret at lunch . . . Maybe when they were alone, she could give him some *helpful hints*.

Marigold was sitting across from her, Linden to the left, and Rufus to the right. Her mother reached out and placed a hand on her father's arm, drawing his attention. Brownie ate her own olive, wondering what they were discussing. Her father had a perk that let him communicate through the system chat logs.

Chat logs were a party system unique to dungeon delving, where party members could chat or message each other through a pop-up in their notification log. Some perks afforded the same, and her father's was called [Stealth Com] and required touch.

Rufus was also staring at her parents with fierce eyes . . . and a bit of disapproval. She didn't know if she liked the idea of Rufus *disapproving* of her parents. Or that they might have done something to him worth disapproving.

All in all, disapproval was *not* a good look on him.

And so, she sought to distract him. "Does that mean we can leave this afternoon? Where are you staying?"

Rufus sighed. "Actually, I'm going to be staying in the Emerald Palace. I have other work for the Dark Enchanted Forest that I need to get done, and a meeting with the Continental Council, and then I'm hoping to slip out and watch, ah, one of your shows."

Brownie's shoulders slumped. She'd thought they would be spending more time at the festival. *Together.*

Rufus' eyebrows pinched into a pained expression as he hurriedly added, "But I have some added time since my meeting with your uncle is done early.

And we can visit every morning? Grab breakfast, go see the apple blossoms, and maybe catch one of the competitions? I'll rent a room at your inn just in case."

"There's going to be a knife fight I was hoping to catch . . ." Brownie tried to cheer up. It wasn't *his* fault they'd fallen for each other on his workcation. Well, it was, but he wasn't *responsible*.

"Really?" Rufus reached out and placed his paw on my hand on the floor beside the low table.

It definitely helped.

"The knife fight is actually between my cousin Luke and the leader of the Adventurer's Guild, Warren Jones." Brownie stopped for a second to remind Rufus, "Luke is Uncle Derek's son, and on the path to inherit. He was the fox our age at dinner. Now, the relationship between the Assassin Assembly and the Adventurer's Guild took a turn after Guild Master Warren got trapped in a newly discovered dungeon—"

"The one that Madame Potts foretold?" Rufus cut in, amused.

"The very one!" Brownie had a gleam in her eye. "Assistant Guild Master Gemma all but begged my aunt Glindy to use her tracking skills to find Warren before his prophesied demise. She had nine days to save him, and she found the Thia Dungeon *and* the guild master in *six*."

"So where's the problem?" Rufus used his free hand to plop another olive into his mouth, closing his eyes with happiness. Brownie would have to remember to get the recipe from her mother before they left.

"Since Warren was happily battling his way through the dungeon without difficulty, he didn't know why there was a rescue party trying to drag him back home. He's not a *bad* person, but he was incredibly rude to my aunt and she . . . Well, her contract was to bring him home dead or alive."

"Did she seriously?!"

"He was alive *when he arrived back at the guild*." Brownie shook her head. "After that, Luke ran into him, and he still wasn't very happy about the whole thing. One thing led to another, and Their Royal Highness Rowen found out. He's ordered them to work it out like civilized folk."

"With a knife fight. Goodness, they'd fit right into the Dark Horde."

Brownie nodded. "Of course. The pair were last year's finalists, and that puts them in the final rounds already—"

"Ahem." Her father coughed, drawing their attention. Her parents were also holding hands, and they were a surprisingly adorable bunch, all holding hands around the table.

"Bronwynn," her mother spoke, using her full name in a show of seriousness. Brownie sat straighter and dropped Rufus's hand as her mother continued. "Your father and I have something to confess."

CHAPTER 81

Enchanted Carrots

Rufus

Thirty Minutes Ago

"Donna is staying over here." Marigold brought me to a sparkling clean stable that stretched along the western side of the compound. It had eight empty stalls and two open doors with a free-range cultivated meadow for horses.

The mare I was looking for was happily cooling herself in the shade of a tree. Summer was here, and it was bright. There was another horse, a black stallion, who was eyeing Donna nervously from the other side of the green.

"You knew, didn't you?"

Bronwynn's mother sighed. "It started out pretty harmless, actually. And then she kept accepting more and more jobs. She expressly made it clear that she would tell Brownie in her own time . . . That time just hasn't come yet."

"But . . . how? She's a *horse*." Even after spending all this time with the mare, I found it hard to suspect a *bonded companion* would go behind their partner like this. Granted, Donna was an exceptional horse.

"As I said, it started out small." Marigold waved a hand at the black horse. "Pascal had injured his tail and was on recovery when we got a request to send a letter of reference to Drendil's royals. They were interested in hiring a few assassins, and Persia had already set sail. Without Pascal, it was going to take weeks . . . Donna overheard us posting the quest on the board and walked over to accept it herself. She was going with Brownie to my parent's house in Drendil, and it just lined up."

"When was this?" As far as my Bronwynn intelligence network—as in, *the fan club*—had been able to tell, Donna had become Brownie's bonded companion four years ago.

Marigold thought for a second. "About two years ago."

"Who usually rides Pascal?" I asked.

"No one; he's a hippocamp and travels by sea," Marigold explained. "We have people in the ports who receive his deliveries. He's pretty smart, though not as intelligent as our mysterious mare over here."

We'd stopped outside the paddock, and Pascal wandered closer to say hello. He didn't actually *say* hello, but he greeted Marigold with a sniff. After carefully observing me, he turned away and went to browse for grass.

Donna had seen us arrive, but she was content to relax in the shade.

"Why are you telling me all this and not Bronwynn?" The memory of Bronwynn happily boasting about how her family was so supportive of her life as a bard separate from the assassination business sat heavy on my mind.

And now, I had *another* secret between me and the minstrel. My stomach lurched, and my gut tightened.

Marigold stepped into the meadow, and her foot was immediately covered in happy plants that moved to hug her soft shoes. The woman smiled down at the grass but kept walking. To me, she said, "We will discuss with Donna about her latest deliveries and tell her it's time to come clean."

I trudged along behind her, trying to be careful of the nicer wildflowers in the meadow. "Alright."

"Donna!" Marigold reached the mare first, standing in front of her with both hands on her hips. She was human and barely came up to the mare's shoulders, but the ferocity in her stance had the mare double-take and pay heed.

They stood staring at each other for a second, and I wondered if Marigold could speak to animals like her daughter.

"Have you," Marigold suddenly asked, "noticed anything interesting about your shipments?"

Donna blew through her nostrils and stuck up her nose, imperious.

"I'm not saying that. You're one of our best," Marigold stated. "We've just noticed that *someone's* been making molten ash vane, and it might be one of ours, so we're here to ask what you know."

The long look that Donna gave me, from my feet to my eyes, spoke volumes.

"Guild Master Derek has approved his involvement. So?" Marigold waited for the mare to answer her question.

Donna eyed me one last time before whinnying loudly and nodding her head like a person might. The mare walked up and extended her face, lipping Marigold in the ear. The woman let her, frowning.

"You think they're coming from the Hollow?"

Donna turned away and walked back to her shady spot.

"One more thing," Marigold said.

Donna gave her a side-eye before settling back in to enjoy her noonday sun.

"It's time you tell Brownie you've been working for us as an undercover contract delivery mare," Marigold announced. Donna blew air out of her nose and started eating some grass. The human continued. "You've had long enough, and now it's affecting poor Rufus too. We'll give you some time, but this is your last chance. If you don't say anything, we will."

"I'll agree to wait"—the words were dragged out of me by the expectant look of my future mother-in-law—"until the end of the Apple Blossom Festival. But no longer than that."

Donna stared at us for a long time, but we held firm against the displeased horse. Finally, Marigold stated, "We are going to lunch, so we'll leave you to think about things."

Before I left, I said, "And Donna?"

The mare snorted. I didn't know what that meant, but I continued. "Thank you for the poisoning lead. If you think that the poisoner is from the Hollow, then I'll use every resource at my disposal to uncover the truth."

Donna flicked her tail once then turned away and set to grazing. But I felt, somehow, that she was pleased I'd thanked her.

I followed Marigold back. Before we reached her house, I asked another question that had been playing on my mind. "What was the quest reward that convinced Donna to work for you? And have her come back for more quests?"

"Enchanted carrots, of course," Marigold replied over her shoulder as she opened the door to her home and welcomed me in. "And a bag of golden-grade oats."

I recoiled. "She's been going behind her bonded companion's back, *for some carrots?*"

Marigold didn't seem to find anything wrong with this, stressing, "*Enchanted carrots.*"

I was risking another secret ruining my relationship with the most amazing woman on the continent . . . for carrots.

CHAPTER 82

Attacking the Beastman

Brownie

Bronwynn waited, pretending patience.

"We have discovered that one of our poisoners might be the one brewing up molten ash vane," her father said slowly. "The timing of the assassinations matches with one of our deliveries."

His eyes glanced at Rufus for a second, and she realized he must've already known and was waiting for her parents to tell her.

"Alright." She shrugged.

It seemed bad . . . but a small part of her thought that if *someone* was going to flounce around the continent dealing out the most powerful poison known to kind, she would've been a bit *offended* to learn her family had *no* part in the party.

They were a centuries-old assassin guild, and she was proud of them.

She should've been more concerned since Rufus, *one of the head investigators,* now knew about their involvement . . . but again, why worry when *he* was calmly sitting beside her eating olives? He might have his perks active, but that was not the face of a beastman coming to tell her that he would be dragging her entire family before the Continental Council.

"There's more." Her mother pulled out their family crest and placed it on the table in front of them.

Brownie didn't pick it up; she wasn't an assassin.

"We would like you to take Rufus with you to the Hollow and introduce him to our people there," Mama said, her voice unwavering.

The bard still didn't pick it up. Brownie knew what holding the family crest meant—and that was why she'd never accepted the proof of her Stannard lineage before.

"I could simply hunt for the poisoner myself?" Rufus offered, frowning at the crest. "No need for Minstrel Bronwynn to do anything she doesn't want."

"You won't find them without the crest, dear, and you're *obviously* not from the Assassin Assembly. You're *the Commander General*," her mother pointed out. "Everyone will recognize you."

They were correct, but that didn't mean Brownie was going to pick up the crest.

Her mother continued. "We have two poisoners in the Dark Enchanted Forest, and if it were Sanders, then I would say go for it. He lives in Plittsmouth and is a well-known apothecary. He even has a shop on the main boulevard selling all manner of concoctions. But the other poisoner we have a contract with isn't so easily found."

"Mia doesn't like *people*," Her father stated.

"She lives deep inside the Dark Enchanted Forest," her mother explained. "And drops off her delivery in a cave behind the Hollow that's warded. Even the person picking up the poisons hasn't met her."

She further explained. "The poisoners don't work for *us*. We work for them. They make what they can, and then our operatives deliver their poisons to respective paying customers. We act as a protective shield and middleman. It's one of many, many contracts we have as a long-standing family in the business."

"I still don't see why *I* need to do it?" Brownie cut in, crossing her arms. "Why don't you send a message to someone in the Hollow to meet us, and they can sort everything out."

Rufus coughed. "Does the . . . *person* picking up the poisons have a family crest?"

"No," her father stressed. "They're a contractor. They just do pick up, no contact."

Her mother tapped the table. "If you want to speak to someone and receive an *honest* answer, then you'll need to bring this and show it to them. *Even then,* Mia might not see you. She's very private."

"My point still stands," Brownie repeated, "I am happy to bring Rufus with me to the Hollow, but I won't be helping him with that part of his quest. I am not, and will never be, involved in that part of the family. I promised, and *you* promised."

The crest remained on the table, untouched, as her parents shared a look. Even in the silence, Brownie remained unmoving.

"Alright." Her father sighed and reached out to retrieve the badge, but he didn't put it away and instead tossed it at Rufus.

The beastman caught it midair.

"Why are you giving me this?" he asked, inspecting the palm-size silver plaque. It was a calligraphed, jagged black spiral that ended with a small drop of red blood in the center. The spiral was a whip, and there was a small mark near the start of the outside that represented the handle.

"Even if Brownie cannot help you," her father said, "maybe the *person who delivers the poison can.*"

Rufus ran his fingers over the surface of her family crest and turned to Brownie. He must have seen something in her because a second later, the crest was placed politely on the table and pushed back toward her parents.

"Thank you, but I'll find my own way to complete the quest," he stated. He flashed Brownie a reassuring smile. "Though I'll still take a ride, if that's alright with you."

"Absolutely." Brownie nodded eagerly.

"Rufus, the guild master has ordered us to help facilitate your quest in any way we can. First, because we know you will consider this in your report to the Continental Council; we have not accepted any illegal contracts to use molten ash vane, nor have we any plans to do so in the future." Her mother reached out, but took up her cup and sipped the drink, leaving the crest where it was. "And secondly . . . if you really are going to be seeing our daughter more formally, then you might become part of the family."

Brownie opened her mouth, but her mother didn't let her interrupt, instead adding, "And not the assassin guild part; the Stannard part."

The sentiment was very sweet, and Brownie was distracted from her earlier defensiveness by the feeling of love and welcome her parents were offering Rufus. In all her life, she'd never brought home a lover or prospective mate, so it was a new experience. And they'd welcomed him with open arms.

She hadn't thought his stalking talk would've won them over so easily.

"I would be honored to formally court your daughter," Rufus said, reaching out and taking Bronwynn's hand. In a show of affection that made her positively *swoon*, the beastman lifted it to his lips and kissed the back. It was romantic and sweet, and she didn't know how she stopped herself from attacking the beastman then and there.

Brownie said the first thing that came to mind to distract her. "I'm sorry I'm not able to help you more than this . . ."

There was a smile teasing at the corner of his lips.

"You don't have to worry," the beastman stated. "No matter how much someone tries to hide in the woods, I'll find them. I think you all keep forgetting *I am the Commander General of the Dark Enchanted Forest.*"

CHAPTER 83

A Curse Word but Luckily not a Cursed Word

Rufus

I pulled out a small golem thrumming with the barest hint of power. We were a *long* distance from Keith, and it was going to cost the Dark Magician King an arm and a tail's worth of mana to activate—not that he had a tail. I did not care. "[Activate Call]."

The orb flashed, and the sound of the golem connecting echoed statically throughout the room. The sound was fuzzy, and I attributed that to the distance even though I knew absolutely nothing about golems.

Keith's voice came through clear. "Report."

There were a few ways Keith typically responded to calls. "Report" was the usual. If he was casting spells or spending private time with Henrietta, he just wouldn't answer. There was also "What do you want?" for off-hours contact, and "But why?" that one time I'd called first thing in the morning to check in before going to a council meeting. My attempt to make morning small talk with the ruler of the Dark Enchanted Forest had been met with a curse word—but luckily, not a *cursed* word—and a dropped call.

"I've found a lead in the Hollow," I explained.

"The duke?" Keith asked, referring to Duke Lector.

"Actually, both our poisoner and the duke will be in the Hollow. We will arrive at the elven city in five days' time. I'll need a tracking team."

The rest of the table waited quietly. No one wanted to cut off the Dark Lord on a voice call.

"Alright . . . Does that mean you'll be searching during Ria's stay?" There was an edge to the Dark Lord's voice that I ignored. He was probably just envious that I got to go when he was stuck at home working.

"Yes. Minstrel Bronwynn is here with me now, and she's offered to drive me," I stated, letting my king know there were others present.

"Brownie's there?" Queen Henrietta's voice sounded distant, like an echo in a cave. "Hi, Brownie!"

Bronwynn smiled and leaned in closer. "Hello, Your Majesty. My parents are here too."

"If we may, love?" Keith said softly. She must have agreed because he followed up with, "Rufus, who are you moving?"

"As soon as I'm done here, I'll order Puma's guard unit to mobilize and move Chikli's unit north of the Hollow, between the mountains. It'll be a delayed post so they leave closer to the date, of course."

"Of course," Keith agreed. There was never a guarantee that the forest wouldn't move everything between now and then.

"And I'll be there if we need some muscle!" the Dark Queen said excitedly. Henrietta might by tiny, but her Strength was high enough to pick up a napping dragon.

Not that she would be so foolish.

I could hear the frown in Keith's voice when he said, "Report again *when you're closer to the border.*"

"Yes, Your Viciousness." I smirked. The words let me know I had indeed inconvenienced him with the range of the call. Hah!

I could hear the aggrieved sigh from the other side of the golem, but it was faint enough that I didn't know if anyone else on this side would have caught it. The golem went dark, and the Dark Lord was gone. I was already opening my character sheet.

To everyone in the room, I explained, "I'll select a few of the high levels to encircle and sweep the region around the Hollow, including the best Tracker in the Dark Enchanted Forest, Mistress Puma."

Name:	Rufus Triever
Occupation:	Commander General
Level:	54
Experience Points:	13397/13500
Hit Points:	616/616
Mana Points:	900/900

Class:	Commander		
Titles:			
[Beastfolk], [Protector], [Mediator], [General], [Commander], [Connoisseur]			
Attributes:			
Strength:	26	**Intelligence:**	30
Dexterity:	19	**Perception:**	30
Constitution:	24	**Charisma:**	19
Skills:			
Keen Senses:	2	**Leadership:**	4
Secure:	6	**Bureaucracy:**	4
Patient:	6	**Examine:**	6
Perks:			
Sense Threat, Redirect Blow, Claw Strike, Force Palm, Empathy, Calming Effect, Inspire Honesty, Commanding Voice, Natural Poise, Sense Lies, Personnel, Detect Poison, Detect Fake, Identify Craft.			

There were a few notifications I could preview in my logs at any one time before opening the notification or scrolling through the list.

[Passive Skill: **Mediator** has been activated by your **Patient** Nicole Fernand. Primary emotion: Fear, Anxious. Subject may run away.
Threat Level: 1]
[**Sense Lie:** Linden Stannard attempted to use **Subterfuge**.]
[You have activated **Golem: Daniel**.]

Nicole was a selkie from Plittsmouth who was probably in the city to watch Bronwynn's concert, as she was a crystal holder. She was also cripplingly shy and struggled with leaving her house. Or talking. Or being near people. It would be a good idea to check in on her because she was wont to yell at people when she was too overstimulated . . . and her class-based sound attack was Area of Effect [Paralysis] . . .

It was fine for now.

I turned to my abilities.

Commander General

The kingdom is safe with you ready to guard against injustices. All denizens of the Dark Enchanted Forest recognize your leadership and wisdom. Bonus +4 Charisma when dealing with members of the Dark Horde.

Military Update:
Morale: 98%
Resources: 81%
Readiness: 90%
Reserves: 14958
Troops: 8279
Elites: 8/10
Total Defense: 89%

I paused for a second, realizing there was one more elite than I remembered there being.

Myself, General Knolith of the East, General Quinton of the West, General Derilla of the North, Chloe the Necromancer (who was supposed to be the General of the South but outright refused to let anyone call her that. Ever.), Lieutenant Patina of Plittsmouth, Puma of Gren's Keep . . . The king and queen didn't count, so who could've joined the army in the last month over level forty? Did I not notice a level up—Ah.

The bridge troll.

I had the titles Commander and General, both of which afforded me access to Dark Horde intel, including a map of the troop placements and any active battles. I could use my Commander points to issue orders to any member of the army, which I did now, reallocating experience points for job quest completion and paying out an advance travel fund to the teams.

When I finished, I found my three breakfast companions watching politely.

"If I can't have the poisoner come to me," I said confidently. "Then I can bring the army of the Dark Enchanted Forest to *them*."

I took a deep sip of my tea and almost spit it out when Marigold said, "Are you sure you haven't fallen in love yet? 'Cause you'd better jump on this one quickly, sweetheart."

CHAPTER 84

How They'd Met

Brownie

"Mother!"

Brownie was a grown woman, but even that was going a bit far. She stood up and pulled Rufus to his feet with barely enough time for him to put down his cup safely.

"We're going to head out now. See you next time I'm in town!" The half giantess all but dragged Rufus from the room while her parents shared a knowing look and bid their quick goodbyes. There was usually a round of hugs, but not this time. This time, she was making a well-considered, hasty retreat.

Rufus let her pull him along, which gave her courage. It wasn't far to their rooms, and she stopped outside his door.

"Are you ready to go?" he asked, an amused smile on his face. She nodded, thrusting a thumb over her shoulder at her own room a few doors down. "I just left my instrument on my bed. Everything else is packed . . . As long as *you're* sure you're finished with my uncle?"

"Unless Slake wants to come back tomorrow. But the guild master was more . . . transparent than I thought. Are *you* sure you don't want to spend tonight with the family?"

"Absolutely." Brownie squeezed his hand. "I thought we could . . . you know. Stay at an inn tonight? Closer to the palace. Together?"

Rufus dropped her hand, and it crushed her confidence. She fumbled to save her request by adding, "You know, since the palace is on the other side of the river. . ."

She realized then that Rufus had taken his hand and covered his mouth. His eyes were closed.

His tail gave it away before his reply.

"Do you want to . . . pet me?" His breathing was ragged, and when his golden eyes found hers, she was lost for a second. They were usually bright and smiling when he looked at her, but as his eyebrows lowered and his eyes narrowed, his gaze turned dark and passionate.

She felt it all the way to her toes.

Instead of answering aloud, she nodded, strangely too embarrassed to speak.

He reached out and gripped her hand again, and for a second time, he lifted it to his lips. He smiled as he kissed her hand, and it brought back a bit of his natural playfulness. "Then you'll be happy to know I'm already ready to go now."

Brownie nodded, again, and wondered if she was going to be able to resist *herself* when petting Rufus that evening. Then again, he was a higher level and could probably fend her off with a stick when she crossed the line.

If! *If* she crossed the line. And being outright rejected like that wasn't a good thought.

Maybe they should have a safeword? "Look out!" or "No, thank you" or just "Safeword." It was hard to forget the safeword when the safeword *was* "safeword."

"Then we can grab Danielle, go pick up Donna, and be on our way," Brownie found her voice.

"Alright."

She collected her instrument, and they went to the stables. They'd no need for a wagon in the city, so Bronwynn stored it in her storage ring. It took up the entire space, so it wasn't ideal, but she wanted the freedom to head out whenever.

A normal horse might have preferred the grassy paddock to a city inn stable, but Donna was no normal horse. She was a social butterfly who enjoyed gossiping with her stable neighbors. The mare would take a walk if she was getting stuffy, and do her own thing.

Donna was always one to get into trouble. That was how they'd met.

One autumn four years ago, she'd met the mare while en route to visit Peldeep for her Uncle Faren and her Aunt Larraina's wedding. Brownie didn't have a wagon back then, and would either walk or hitch a ride or rent a horse, depending. She'd caught a lift, and they were making good time. On the second day in the Dark Enchanted Forest, while they were passing Lake Loria, Brownie's ride was beset by griffins.

The monsters were drawn to the fish that the lizardkin merchant had picked up back at the lake. He was headed to the Dark Lord's castle first, and then Gren's Keep second, at which point Brownie would go on alone.

The griffins swooped down and plucked at a guard's spear.

Brownie, never one to miss an opportunity, ran away.

As much as her family had trained her well, Brownie was *not* and *never would be* a combat class. She could assist with her bardic skills and perks to buff the party, but the entire group was in utter disarray, and when the attack started, the merchant tried to hide behind Brownie. Which was fine in and of itself, but then he'd tried to push her out of the wagon. One of the griffins had landed beside them, and she'd only survived by the skin of her [Sturdy] skill.

No sense defending someone like that. She was only a few hours down the road when she heard *another* battle.

Off the road a bit, there was a white unicorn attacking a dappled roan mare.

Donna held a stone in her teeth, and every time the unicorn tried to stab her, she would hit away the deadly horn with the rock. Donna had been the only one injured as far as Brownie could see, and she was barely standing her ground.

As she drew closer, she discovered it was a young stallion who was pacing around Donna and stamping the earth in frustration. He lashed out, but this time when Donna's rock parried his horn, the stallion slipped and fell hard. When he got to his feet, Brownie could see his pride was hurt, as well as his leg. As with most creatures of intelligence, their body language was pretty recognizable. To Brownie, at least. Donna flicked her mane in a show of defiance and snorted at the unicorn. She was refusing to yield.

A dark expression crossed over the stallion's face; one full of rage. He reared, letting out a bloodthirsty neigh that rent the field.

When he landed, he charged.

It was obvious he had gone from playing with her to trying to hurt the mare. And Donna was not going to survive the encounter . . .

Brownie couldn't bear it, so she made a very foolish choice.

She struck a chord on Suzette.

[You have activated the Perk: **Strength of Sound**. You may target listeners up to or equal to your level: 26. Target(s) gain +2 Strength for 10 minutes.]

[You have activated the Perk: **Inspire**. You may target listeners up to or equal to your Charisma 17. Target(s) abilities cost 10% less for 10 minutes.]

It was a small boost, but it was enough. Donna managed to face off against the unicorn in a horn-to-rock collision that only ended when the stallion's injured knee gave out. With a violent whip of her head, Donna hit the side of the unicorn's head with her rock, rendering him unconscious. But alive.

Donna came over to nod a curt thanks to Brownie for her assistance . . . and the rest was history.

Not to say Donna had trusted Brownie right away. They'd traveled for a few hours in silence before Donna had let Brownie patch her up.

It took a long time to figure things out between them, and Donna rejected the bond a few times.

Whether it was by fate or her own bloodline, the Dark Enchanted Forest kept pushing them together . . . and eventually, they formed a bonded companion pact.

They had been together ever since.

Brownie had never asked Donna about her past in the Dark Enchanted Forest because the mention of it obviously upset her friend.

Similar to the way Donna was upset now.

CHAPTER 85

I Appreciated the Headbutt

Rufus

Donna had not come clean on the way to the inn . . . and neither had I.

How was there so much to do in so little time?! Between reporting to the Continental Council, meeting up with the fan club, and getting up the final ounce of courage to actually tell Brownie that I was, in fact, the leader of her fan club, well, there wasn't enough time. I could feel the pressure build even as we made our way across the bridge, up the hill, and through the market to Bea's Bed & Breakfast. Our stop was just in sight, and we'd traveled in relative silence. Relative because the streets were anything but *quiet*.

What made Bea's the obvious destination was that it sat across the street from Herman's Club, and only one street off from the central marketplace where the largest part of the festival was taking place.

The city being scattered across the river into districts meant that each area of Vitol celebrated in their own way. The military quarter put on contests all week at the training grounds, and the civilian martial contests were set up in the guild district Juniper Square a few streets down. Mercenaries and adventurers and everyday people would compete in the city games, and the finalists would face off against the military in a friendly rivalry that came to a close tomorrow.

The streets were loud, as the civilian side finalist matches were *today*.

"Niomi of the Grim Reaper's Adventuring team won against Kyle Killer of the Red Panda team in a tiebreaker round!"

"Torren Tully is battling Stormbringer Candace next! Can the up-and-coming youth defeat the giantess? Or will her wind blades prove his undoing?"

"Wait!" Bronwynn stopped us, reaching out and grabbing my arm excitedly. "We have to go to Candace's fight!"

"We do?" I asked, letting Bronwynn drag us away from the inn toward the crowds of excited onlookers. My senses weren't too keen on a small space full of emotional onlookers, but I let Bronwynn pull me along anyway.

"Candace is one of my cousins! I wanna go and support her," Bronwynn explained. Our respective heights let us see pretty easily over the crush, and even with Donna, it wasn't too much trouble to get to a viewing spot.

The idea of leaving Donna behind flashed through my mind, until I realized the murder horse was just as excited as her mistress to attend the fight . . . if not *more*.

"How many cousins do you *have*?" I saw Candace the giantess stretching on her side of the elevated battle platform in the middle of the cleared-out city square. She was the tallest of any of Bronwynn's relatives, curvy and fit with long silver hair that fell to her knees. The giantess stopped stretching and swept one straight lock over her shoulder, planting her feet in a fighting stance.

"Perfect timing; they are starting now!" Bronwynn yelled at me over the din. "I have twenty-four cousins. My parents are one of seven children each, remember?"

I nodded, beginning to feel the pressure than the usual overstimulation of sights, sounds, and sensations from the press around me. The match started, and the unease was still there, still nagging at me and distracting me, so I clung to the other thought as an easy distraction.

The half giantess I was courting had enough family to make up for my lack. Maybe there would be time to swing by Gren's Keep and introduce Bronwynn to my sister. Jessica was always saying I should come by . . . Maybe it was time?

"She's so good!" Bronwynn laughed, dragging my attention to the stage. Candace had her blades spinning around the dwarf holding an ornate hammer. Torren had sustained a few superficial cuts but otherwise seemed to be holding his own.

I realized, with my discerning eye, that the dwarf was enjoying himself. After he blocked the next volley of shadow daggers, he used the momentum of his swing to finally get close enough to the giantess to be right under her. With a triumphant yell, Torren activated, "[Control: Size]!"

The otherwise shorter dwarf used the famous racial skill that allowed him to shrink or grow in size. Suddenly, he was bigger than Bronwynn's cousin, with enchantments on his clothing and weapon to grow with him. The hammer hit Candace in full force, knocking her back.

With a single step too far, her heel landed just outside the line.

"Victory to the fresh blood! Torren wins again!" The audience went *wild*, and I found my arms unconsciously wrapping around the minstrel cheering beside me. I couldn't even register if she was actually cheering or booing at that point. "Rufus?"

It was just as bad as I remembered it being, and I tried to will my hands to let go of Bronwynn, even when she was the only thing keeping the ever-growing sensory overload from cloying its way into overwhelming me as hundreds of people pressed against me. They weren't pressing on me *physically* but with each wave of shouting building on top of the constant notification tabs sending me notice that there were more and more messages waiting *and* the feeling of being trapped, hoping to be there with Bronwynn while she enjoyed a show.

"Guild Master Warren's Penalty Bout is up next!" a young voice cried.

The date. Their date. I used my own recommended breathing technique to calm down and tried to separate myself further from the crushing weight of everything.

Bronwynn had, at some point, turned and shoved my nose into her collar. The smell of her, a bit of resin and cinnamon and citrus from her hair product filled my nose. Donna snorted nearby and headbutted my shoulder. I didn't know if she was telling me to get over it or concerned, but I appreciated the headbutt either way.

[You have taken 60 points of Blunt Force Damage from Belladonna Windrunner. Health 556/616.]

Bronwynn's voice, my lifeline, whispered in my ear, "This way," as she all but dragged me from the town square.

CHAPTER 86

Something Wrong with Her Beastman

Brownie

There was something wrong with her beastman.

It started as a simple thing that she should have noticed sooner. The way he'd tensed as they made their way inside the square. The way his eyes couldn't focus on the fight. The way he'd leaned into her grip on his arm and only relaxed a bit when they found a spot to stand. She'd just figured he was distracted trying to find a place that could fit a horse like Donna.

Then, when Candace lost, Brownie had let go of his arm for the first time since the battle started.

Candace had gotten to her feet in an instant and was shaking the dwarf's hand, looking impressed. Brownie pumped a fist in the air, joining the crowds. Then she felt Rufus step toward her and wrap his arms around her. When she looked up, his eyes where focused on her and only her, but it wasn't the usual bright smile playing on his lips. Instead, he looked pained. And every time the crowd cheered anew, he visibly flinched.

"Rufus?" she spoke softly, her words otherwise lost to the noise around them. Still, she thought he heard her because his grip started to loosen. But it didn't give way.

"Guild Master Warren's Penalty Bout is up next!" Norton Novic, a young adventurer from the guild, called out, announcing the halftime show.

She turned into Rufus's arms and reached up to pull him closer. He collapsed into her embrace, letting her run her hands over his back a few times as she tried to figure out what was wrong.

Did someone have wolfsbane nearby? Or was there something else? Her eyes searched for an easy way out, and Donna caught on to Brownie's plan fast. The mare headbutted the back of the beastman. Not the best way to get his attention, but it worked. She thanked the gods for her extra strength as she managed to drag Rufus out of the square and up the road. Donna did her part clearing a path.

Her mare wasn't exactly nice about it, but she only had to inconvenience the first few onlookers to have the masses squish aside and give her space to leave. She was a good horse.

In an attempt to distract her Rufus, Brownie started talking about anything and everything that came to mind.

"The next match isn't a part of the city battles," she explained, "but a penalty bout issued by Their Royal Highness Rowen on Guild Master Warren when he got lost in that new dungeon. You know the one. Thia Dungeon, as it was called, was only discovered a few months back. The guild master himself was dealing with a high-level monster sighting at Thia Falls when he accidentally activated a portal pad into the unknown dungeon. The dungeon was building into a dungeon break. It wasn't going to explode monsters into the countryside that day, but it was close enough that it wouldn't have lasted another month."

Brownie took a breath. She was amused that Guild Master Warren, a level fifty-two Paladin, had taken it upon himself to thin the numbers instead of reporting first, going against the legal protocol from hubris.

Which might have worked for him . . . if a certain Madame Potts hadn't dropped a Cast.

Hello, everyone, this is Madame Potts.
It's a little late, but I hope you'll excuse me.
The Peldeep adventuring guild master of Vitol stumbled upon a new
dungeon around Thia Falls and is trapped on the sixth floor. He will
die in nine days if rescue fails.
Thank you, this is Madame Potts signing out.

The guild master had been saved thanks to the Cast and Aunty Glindy's tracking skills . . . but Guild Master Warren wasn't in the clear.

"Did you know that Assistant Guild Master Gemma was beside herself with worry when they found him?" Brownie told the whole story to Rufus, keeping her voice light. "Gemma's had a crush on the guild master forever. We all know it. And after she dragged him back to Vitol, I heard that she made him sit on his knees in their office for *six hours*."

She chuckled. "One for each level he'd gone down. And he didn't get off there, of course, because as soon as she was done, Their Royal Highness summoned Guild Master Warren for a *talk*."

Their Royal Highness of Peldeep was a fox. One who was renowned for their cunning and trickery and playfulness. "As final punishment for going against protocol, they ordered Guild Master Warren to fight a warm-up bout with *every single civilian contestant* in the Apple Blossom Festival."

It had doubled the number of contestants, because who wouldn't want to have a bout with one of the most powerful fighters in Peldeep? It was practically a free personal lesson from the guild master himself.

Donna successfully led them to one of the side streets, but even as she pulled Rufus clear, his eyes were still pinched shut. "We are out of the crowd; how are you doing?"

He breathed a little easier, and he ground out a short, "I'm fine. I just . . . I need a minute to process the notifications."

She stopped, letting him take a few more shallow breaths. Donna prevented passersby from disturbing them, but they were still awkwardly shoved up against the side of a building to not deter traffic.

"Would this be easier inside? Can you make it to the inn?" Brownie squeezed his hand.

Her beastman didn't reply right away, but after a long moment, nodded.

She pulled him along.

"It's just . . ." His voice hitched as he tried to talk and walk even while he was obviously dealing with the notifications in his tab still. "I don't like crowds."

There was a little more to this than not liking crowds, Brownie guessed, but she simply nodded. "Now I know. We don't have to go to big events like this again."

His voice dipped low and aggrieved when he whispered, "Sorry for ruining everything."

Brownie's heart broke at the self-hatred she could hear in his voice. They were so close to Bea's, but she stopped him short right then and there. "Don't say that."

"But—" His golden eyes opened and found hers, but they were empty of the usual warmth and joy she loved.

"Do you know," she cut him off, "when I started falling for you?"

"What?"

The change in subject brought him out of himself and closer to her; she could feel it. She continued. "When we were in Thistlecrick, you thought General Knolith had hurt me, and you were so . . . so *intense*."

Rufus didn't reply, but he was blushing. They continued walking up to Bea's Bed & Breakfast, and Donna blew out her nose at having to listen to them being all lovey-dovey.

"You said, '*If he hurt her,*' in the sexiest voice I've ever heard," Brownie confessed. "When did you first start, you know, *liking* me?"

"I—"

The front door of Bea's Bed & Breakfast opened, and a tall elk fae stepped out, speaking to a group of people behind her. "We will meet back here at a quarter to, since Minstrel Bronwynn's performance starts tonight at—Minstrel Bronwynn?!"

Everyone stopped and stared. Brownie recognized a few of her regular listeners and stamped down the urge to brush them off so she could find a quiet place to cuddle Rufus and hear his answer.

The group stared at her holding onto Rufus's hand.

"Commander General—" A pink pixie fluttered off the fae's shoulder to greet Rufus, but stopped and squinted up at her beastman. "Wait, *Fergus?*"

CHAPTER 87

Scape-Cat

Rufus

I admit it; I considered running . . . but that was futile. So I said the first thing that came to mind. "Hello, everyone."

"Really?" Frida turned a quizzical eye on the pixie. "How could you *tell?*"

Ross pointed. "Those are Fergus's clothes, and who else has such pretty golden eyes and hair? How could you *not* tell?"

The heavy weight of anxiety I'd been battling moments before felt like nothing compared to the gaping hole I was sinking into as Ross nodded knowingly after revealing my deepest darkest secret.

"Fergus?" Bronwynn herself turned to me and stared. She squinted, searching for something—and finding it. "You're *that* Fergus?"

Sometimes, there are moments that live down as the most horrible, no good, absolutely dreadful moments in a lifetime. This was that moment. I should have told Bronwynn this morning. I should have told her yesterday. I should have cut Ross off and confessed right then and there . . .

But no. A pink pixie had beaten me to it.

At least Donna looked impressed. She was eyeing me with newfound respect.

With a sigh that let go of a year's worth of secrecy, I *poofed* into my folk form, one hand waving. "Surprise?"

I was slightly shorter than Bronwynn in this form, since I was standing on my heel instead of my canine toe pads. I had a military frame, muscular like a troll, but with light-brown skin like a human. I wouldn't be mistaken for one of the lithe elves, but my ears were pointy. My eyes were still the same. I could barely pass for a human if someone wasn't looking closely.

"Wait!" A catkin from Gren's Keep named Nelly pointed her finger at me.

"If Fergus is also Commander General Rufus . . . does that mean *the leader was dating Minstrel Brownie? And didn't tell us!*"

I'd told them that Commander General Rufus was traveling with their minstrel . . . and I'd left out that Commander General Rufus was *me*. If a sharp gaze could cut, I would have been sliced to ribbons as everyone except Frida and Ross glared daggers at me. The latter just looked a bit disappointed and shell-shocked. Even Nicole, the shy selkie from Plittsmouth, had popped her razor-sharp claws while hiding in the back. I was surprised she wasn't hiding in her room until the show; she was usually *that* anxious about crowds.

"If it helps," I confessed, "I didn't tell Minstrel Bronwynn either?"

It didn't help. Brownynn dropped my hand, and the feeling of loss left me wondering if I was ever going to be able to breathe freely again. The grip on my chest made it hard to draw anything more than a shallow breath . . .

And all the while, my cursed [Natural Poise] was keeping me from falling apart at the seams.

One of the fans at the back of the group, a naga named Lance, whispered to the preela girl beside him, "I hope we get a cool song out of this."

I searched Bronwynn's eyes, and there was something in them that gave me hope. She wasn't angry or sad or frustrated . . . She was *considering*.

Finally, she opened her mouth. "Meow."

And there was Slake, arriving at the *least opportune moment*. His black body wound its way through the group, and then the grimalcat leaped onto my shoulder, settling himself in. "Rufus, I've just come from the palace. Their Royal Highness has summoned you."

"What?" I didn't ask how the grimalcat could also recognize me. He was a grimalcat; it could be as easy as recognizing my vest or recognizing the taste of my soul. Grimalcat lore was still questioning if the beasts ate souls.

Slake lay down comfortably on my shoulder and licked one paw delicately. "Since Their Royal Highness is worried about the excitement around Bastian's wedding and everyone is already here, the meeting has been called early."

Bronwynn was still looking at me, considering, when she said words that crushed my heart and ate away at my own soul. "You should go."

The fan group was quiet, staring between their idol, myself, and a *grimalcat*. It was probably the grimalcat that truly prevented them from hauling me off in an angry mob for questioning.

"Bronwynn—" Her name was on my lips even as she shook her head, rejecting anything I might have to say.

"You need to go and do your quest," she decided. "We can talk later." A strange look passed over her face. She glanced between me and the fan club and back. "You'll know where to find me."

I stood there as she waved politely to everyone and pulled Donna to the stable around back, leaving me standing rooted to the spot like a dejected treant. The entire situation had gotten out of hand.

"Frida, Ross . . ." I started, trying to salvage what little calm I'd left. "I wanted to tell you in person. I'm sorry you had to find out like this."

The fae woman tilted her head, and the vines draping from her antlers swayed delicately through the air. The faint sound of wind chimes accompanied her head tilt. "You speak the truth, so I will think on this matter."

"Thank you." I reached up and pet Slake. The grimalcat allowed it. "Well, everyone . . . maybe I'll see you at Minstrel Bronwynn's performance tonight— assuming she doesn't have me barred."

"She didn't outright dump you!" Nelly the catkin tried to cheer me up.

Lance added, "And she's still talking to you, even if it's to dump you later."

"Lance." The preela shook her head.

"I'll hand over my crystal tonight if everyone wants to pick a new leader." I sighed, slouching forward as much as my [Natural Poise] allowed.

There was a quiet as the group processed what I'd said. For a mob on the verge of ripping me to shreds mere minutes ago, they were surprisingly calm about the entire affair, though Ross fluttered about with his arms crossed and a frown on his face.

The little pixie said, "Why?"

"Why what?"

"Why are you stepping down as the leader?" he asked. He touched down on Frida's shoulder again and promptly sat down. There were murmurs among the group that reflected the same confusion.

"Because . . ." I paused. There were so many reasons, and yet none of them came readily to voice. The hidden identity, courting Bronwynn, or simply that the group had lost faith in me should have been enough.

"*Are* you dating Minstrel Bronwynn?" Nelly asked, her sleek brown ears twitching. She was in a purple dress with a serviceable apron with both hands on her hips demanding an answer.

"I am, was? I *am* courting the half giantess." What our relationship was going to look like by tomorrow might change . . . but as of right now, that still remained to be seen.

"So," the catkin reasoned, "you will have firsthand knowledge of what she likes, all of her shows, what her favorite foods are, and what she's doing? All the time?"

"I mean . . . yes? Again, assuming she doesn't leave me."

There was a satisfactory agreement among those present that came about incredibly fast. Frida was the one who nodded deeply and said, "Then it is good that you keep the crystal."

"But . . . it's *Minstrel Bronwynn.* Why aren't we all dragging me into a dark alley for a special talk?" I finished petting Slake, who was still my assumed scape-cat.

"Because you're our leader!" Ross shook his head. "You're one of us. *Of course* you fell in love with Minstrel Brownie. I'm just envious that she likes you back."

"If the leader's courting her, then he can give us updates more often!" Nelly smiled viciously and caged her hands in delight.

"Our minstrel deserves *at least* a level fifty member of the Continental Council." The preela nodded. I wondered if she was Gisele of North Sumbria? She was another fan I'd spoken to only over Crystal Cast.

"But—"

"No buts." Ross pointed a finger at Slake. There was a hint of fear and respect in the pixie's voice when he said, "Now go do what the grimalcat wants, or we might *all* find ourselves in a dark alley."

I twisted my head to get a good look at Slake, who was smiling fiercely at the fan club.

"That would be wise." Slake's tail whipped once. "I do not wish to be late."

The walk to the palace wasn't far, but it felt like an eternity as I walked away from the Bea's Bed & Breakfast.

CHAPTER 88

How Could You?

Brownie

Brownie walked straight into the busy stable, past the already occupied stalls, and into a free spot at the back. Donna followed her. The stable hand had recognized them and given Donna a wide birth, so Brownie had some privacy when she turned and threw her arm's around her horse's neck and hugged her tightly.

"Donna."

The mare snorted, having been privy to the emotions running through her bonded half giantess the entire conversation.

"He's even more handsome in folk form," Brownie complained, frowning at the image of Rufus with his shoulder-length hair swept back, and the same piercing golden eyes. She wanted to run her fingers through his hair and draw a finger along the line of his strong chin and see how soft he was compared to his beast form.

Did he have chest hair?

Questions ran through her mind even as she tried to calm down. Donna had limited patience but allowed Brownie a few minutes more to hold on for dear life before the mare sniffed loudly and lipped at the bard's hair.

"I know, I know," Brownie said, pulling away and taking a deep breath. "But was that *really* his big secret? It's not so—"

Donna whinnied and stamped a foot, looking imperious and unyielding.

"What? No! I don't need to make him grovel. He's literally just the leader of my fan group? What's the problem with that? I already *knew* he was a fan?" Brownie took a step back and leaned against the frame of the stall. She was trying to rack her brain for anything and everything she knew about her beastman and his love of her music.

It would explain why he'd been so nice to her in the castle from day one. And stood up for her during that first dinner when she had come forward to warn Henrietta about the assassins.

Donna turned her head to stare intently at the bard with one eye, incredulous.

"Maybe you're right . . . As much as I don't see the big deal, Rufus certainly felt that it was his dark secret. The look on his face when I told him to go with Slake could have melted a dragon's heart." Brownie crossed her arms and tapped a finger to her chin. "But, I mean, *I practically already knew*? He loves my music, knows the lyrics to every one of my songs, and I figured he was at the fan-run concert this year because he knew the lyrics to 'Wings of Ash,' and that was the only place I sang it. So was that really the secret? Are there more secrets? What am I missing?"

Donna almost rolled her eyes.

The horse was very good at conveying feelings and expressing herself, and for that, Brownie was thankful. A bonded companion who could outright talk was rare, but one as intelligent and fun as Donna was even more so.

"I mean, yes, he *did* keep it a secret. And there shouldn't be important secrets between us . . ."

The mare suddenly looked away and to the left, and Brownie grew suspicious. "You already knew about Rufus, didn't you?"

Donna shook her head like a horse would, but that feeling of unease still remained in the bond. Brownie waited patiently, sending her own gentle nudge to the mare to ask her what was on her mind.

Eventually, Donna sighed and did something she'd never done before.

She was . . . apologizing? It wasn't straight remorse, but a begrudging, rueful sorry.

"I don't understand; is this still about Rufus?" Brownie asked.

Donna hesitated, so Brownie questioned further. "It's not about Rufus, but Rufus knows about it?"

Donna nodded, dropping her head to the ground. Brownie wasn't sure what the mare was doing until the gem on her collar shone rainbow bright, and a bottle of Belladonna poison appeared in front of her.

It was followed by twenty other bottles of poisonous potions and antidotes.

After a second, the horse put everything back into her storage and out of sight again. She waited for Brownie to process what she'd just revealed.

A frown tugged at Brownie's lips. "You're saying you have a collar full of poisons? Why—*Oh no.*"

The sheer audacity her horse had to look innocently up at her like what she'd just revealed *wasn't* the most horrible, no good, absolutely dreadful moment of Brownie's adult life was unbelievable. A torrent of emotions washed over Brownie as she stared, betrayed by her own bonded companion.

"You *know*." Brownie bit her lip and tried to push down the rising pressure in her throat. Her eyes stung as she accused, "*You know why I don't do this.*"

Donna made to argue, probably something along the lines of it being the mare's own life and her own choice separate from Brownie. She had always established boundaries around her horse business, never letting their bond get *too* strong.

"It's not about that, and you know that!" Brownie waved a hand at the spot where she'd revealed the bottles, even without the evidence laid out in plain view. "Donna . . . how could you? I'm not . . . I *can't*."

The mare had the grace to look sheepish, grumbling a contrite huff.

"How long has *this* been going on?" Brownie thought back to all of her performances after bonding with the horse all those years ago, and her stomach clenched with anger. "You took a quest at my uncle's house the *first time I brought you?*"

There hadn't been a molten ash vane poison yet, but someone *had* used Belladonna on the marquess of Cavenish in Drendil during her trip to Terpenlily on the southeast coast. The entire performance had had to be rescheduled for the *new* marquess of Cavenish that stepped up three days later.

"And Rufus *knew?*" Brownie started, then slapped a hand to her face, drawing it down. "Uncle Derek. No wonder he was so upset this morning."

The mare chuffed a bit and stamped her foot.

Brownie argued, "At least Rufus isn't secretly taking assassin jobs. Now *I'm* a suspected illegal assassin!"

The bard slid down the wall until she sat in the stall with her knees against her chest, her face in her hands. It was too much. What was she going to say to her grimalcat, Momo? She'd have to explain it somehow . . . But what if Momo decided she'd broken her oath? What if he took back his favor?

Brownie sat there like that for a while until Donna came up and sniffed her hair. The mare was trying to reassure her that she was overthinking things and everything would be fine . . . but Brownie wasn't ready to forgive her horse.

She pushed Donna away.

"I need space." Brownie took a deep breath, wiping any stray tears from her eyes with her shirtsleeve. "And I have to get ready for my show."

Her horse tried to say something, but Brownie needed to calm down first. She'd need to sign in and wash up, switch to her comfortable shoes, apply glitter on her cheeks, and find her cloak. And a lyre harp tuner. And a comb. Her curls would fray with a brush, but she had some oil and a wide-toothed comb tucked away in her red decoy bag.

Brownie climbed to her feet and steadied herself. Or *sturdied* herself, as the case was. She left Donna without looking back.

The pair of them had more to discuss . . . but Brownie needed to go sing her heart out. And maybe get drunk.

Alright, she wouldn't get drunk. But she'd think about it.

*   *   *

Herman's was one of her favorite places to perform because the stage was in a corner that better carried her voice without having to use too much magic to amplify her sound. The bar was directly across the room from the stage, and Ol' Malley the tigerkin had been a very good host for all of her shows.

He'd managed to sell out every performance and keep the crowd's spirit lively without destroying the place. The man being a retired level forty-one Assassin made it easy for him to go around, unseen, dealing with everything neat and tidy.

"Minstrel Brownie!" Ol' Malley greeted her with a smile when she arrived, early as per her usual. If he saw any signs of her frustration or tears, he hid it well. "Come on in. I'll grab you a honey licorice root tea for your voice, and a full jug of water for your set."

The tigerkin let her do some practice sound checks onstage while his staff prepared for the dinner and show. She always kept water onstage, even if she had a full waterskin. People were more patient between sets if they saw her physically pouring herself a glass of water and taking a drink. It gave her more time than if she just chugged back her waterskin; little tips and tricks that helped a bard make the most of a show.

The other tip was to keep a wooden tankard that her patrons could fill for her at the bar but would actually contain a very low alcohol content or simply more water. That let the bar split the difference of the drinks with her, and Brownie never risked drinking until she sang off-key . . .

She didn't ever want to repeat the one time she'd been so drunk that her Bard title amplification magic had gone full blast, dealing sound-based damage to the audience and letting her off-key rendition of "Sally Oh Sally" be heard across the entire city of Danbrook in Drendil.

She'd never gone back to that city, and she never would.

But tonight, Brownie immersed herself in the magelight. She pulled out every song and sang twice as long and didn't finish until Ol' Malley almost had to carry her from the stage. The fan group she'd met with Rufus today were all there, cheering for her.

She missed her beastman. Even as she fell into bed that night, she missed him, and she hoped that things were going to turn out alright.

For both of them.

CHAPTER 89

Taxes

Rufus

"You would have us believe that a *horse* is to blame, Commander General?" Agatha demanded. She was the Witch of Winter's End, otherwise known as the Sorceress of Ice.

Which was actually incredibly impressive, since witchcraft and sorcery were completely different schools of magic, and both required a lot of study. To have titles of each implied the human was exceptionally talented . . . if mocked for having a heart of ice.

And a tongue to match.

"Belladonna Windrunner was simply a courier, Witch Agatha," I stated. "The molten ash vane, as I believe, is being added into circulation by a poisoner in the Dark Enchanted Forest and made deliverable through a contract with the Peldeep Assassin Assembly."

"So Peldeep is to blame? Or the Dark Enchanted Forest?" the Wizard Lorthar asked, stamping the cane that he held onto even while sitting in a half circle with the rest of the present council members. The wizard was a representative of the Mages Tower.

The Continental Council was made up of high-level individuals representing each of the major nations on the continent. Chloe or myself usually sat in for Nilheim. Today, Witch Agatha stood in for North Sumbria, Prince Lucial Neftor for the Empire of Sands, Earl Oakley from Sumbria, Master Thomas Martin for Servalt, and Knight Commander Bastian for Peldeep. No one came from Drendil, but the new regent had sent an apology and assurance that he would attend the Summer Masquerade event.

As the host, Their Royal Highness Rowen presided over the council meeting. The monarch was guised as a young lady in blue silk robes with ornaments in their long black hair. They wore heavy coal eyeliner and glossy lipstick, and a touch of glitter on their cheeks. The glitter reminded me that I was missing Bronwynn's performance at Herman's to be here.

I'd had some time to calm down on my way here. I was used to using my job as a focus, and today was no different. I wasn't saying that was healthy, just that I was doing it.

Slake casually lounged on my shoulder, and were it not for the grimalcat, I might have thrown caution to the wind and told Their Royal Highness I was *not* available until the appointed time.

Even *if* the appointed time was during an explosion of fireworks and magic.

"Well, Sumbria is innocent," Earl Oakley huffed, his nose stuck in the air. Knight Commander Bastian was staring at the man with such an empty expression—purposely devoid of emotion to the point it was uncanny. The earl, for his part, kept sneering at the drakin noble every chance he got.

"The situation is not as clear as it was when I saved you from an ogre," I said, rubbing in the fact the elf had required saving. He'd gone pale and angry when he saw me, and then outright panicked when he realized I was the Dark Lord's right hand. It had done wonders for my nerves.

I placed my palm on the podium in front of me and leaned forward to look each member of the council in the eye. "No ruling nation has condoned, registered quest, or acted against the international treaties. In fact, the *targets* of each case *were the nation's own government.* As such, it is with little doubt that I direct our attention to the *individuals* who are violating their respective sovereign law."

"Are you not saying that because the poisoner is from Nilheim and you don't wish to face repercussions?" Master Thomas asked. The half elf had pale gray skin and mixed blue-green hair, closer to aquamarine than teal. His parents were friends with the king and queen of Servalt, a selkie and an elf, and one of the leading forces in the revolution. Despite only making his debut at the Spring Ball, Master Thomas was already a force to be reckoned with.

His tribal tattoos glowed faintly if I looked closely. He was activating an ability.

"No," I said simply. "As I'm sure Jack Laverick reported in Servalt, the Assassin's Guild took a contract from Duke Lector Yarrow for the hits on King Keith, deposed King Simon and Queen Thalia, and Servalt's own Queen Delia and King Astor. I am of the belief he was attempting an insurrection to make himself king of Servalt, and using his connection with Marquess Dorset to assassinate the Drendil rulers so the marquess and the kidnapped Princess Henrietta would take the throne, effectively gaining control over two kingdoms at the same time."

"We are not fools; we were there for King Keith and Queen Henrietta's report." Witch Agatha shot me a look that said, "get on with it."

I'd adopted a casual stance behind the hip-high podium they'd provided for my evidence; the bottle of molten ash vane acquired by Slake in Servalt, copies of the registered poisons from each assassin's guild, and the assassination quest receipts from Duke Lector in Servalt over the last year—many of which coincided with molten ash vane sightings—were all laid out in front of me.

"If the poisons are being made in Nilheim, then as per Section 42 of Trade Violations in the treaties signed by the Continental Council, all goods traveling through the Dark Enchanted Forest of Nilheim will receive a tax cut of one point seven percent for twelve months from the time set out by the Continental Council. The earliest account of the poison I have on file is summer of last year, when a civilian tried to assassinate Duke Francis of Drendil at his own birthday party.

"Too, Servalt's Assassin's Guild was blackmailed into using molten ash vane three times by Duke Lector, and as an authority of Servalt, they are in violation of Section 43b. Servalt would be issued a fine of one thousand gold pieces for each infraction, to be levied and paid to the Continental Council.

"As individual civilians of each nation, excepting the Empire of Sands, have been caught in the handling and use of a restricted potion, Servalt, Peldeep, Nilheim, North Sumbria and Drendil would all be subject to a vote of confidence to continue standing on the council for the duration of the investigation."

Unease swept through the council at that last part, though Their Royal Highness only smiled an amused fox grin. Their Royal Highness was very aware of my intention for calling to motion the vote of confidence, which would force each nation to step back until I had time to further my investigation back home.

"I am in favor of beginning the tax reduction for twelve months starting on the first of *next* month," Their Royal Highness voiced their opinion. "Allowing each trade guild the opportunity to prepare and report moving forward."

Earl Oakley, moved by his emotions and not his business sense, argued, "But if they're at fault, they should be punished from the time of the breach of trust!"

"As long as the molten ash vane case is completed before we pass the first sighting date from last summer, there is no difference. They'll still be penalized for twelve months either way." Witch Agatha pointed out. "And if it is *not* resolved within the year, we will extend it to a two-year penalty."

There was something to be said for dealing with my peers. If the tax change started *now*, going into summer, then each nation would be able to push forward more than their usual commercial sales and take advantage of the new rates with careful planning and consideration for profit. If they set the twelve months' starting date to last year, then it would cost everyone in time and resources to backtrack receipts and distribution of refunds.

Their Royal Highness stood then, putting to motion each order of business. As expected, no one decided to vote themselves off the council, Nilheim would reduce taxes, and fees would be paid.

Now, I just needed to find the poisoner in time to save my kingdom . . . from taxes.

CHAPTER 90

Day Drinking, Rufus?

Brownie

Brownie rolled over and threw one arm across her eyes, trying to block out the midmorning sun.

The birds were chirping, the wind was rustling, the city was in full festival mode . . . and Brownie wanted to go back to sleep instead. She wasn't feeling the desire to go anywhere, and she didn't want to speak to anyone—even her fluffy boyfriend.

Sometimes, when things were hard, she wanted a little bit of alone time. That wasn't too much to ask for, was it?

The longer she stayed in bed, thinking, the longer she realized she was hungry, dehydrated, and in need of the washroom.

Sigh. It was past time to get up.

When she came downstairs, her beastman was in his nonfluffy folk form, leaning back casually in the big armchair beside the banked fireplace. He was drinking a glass of wine, and as much as he *looked* relaxed, she could tell from the pinched crease around his eyes as he read his novel that he was *anything* but. He sadly didn't have a tail to give away his emotions, but she knew him well enough by now to get a good feeling.

"Day drinking, Rufus?" she asked, having walked up to the commander general of the Dark Lord's army without him noticing.

Rufus, to give him credit, didn't spill his wine on the book. Just everywhere else. "B-Bronwynn?"

The glass shook, sloshing liquid onto the hand holding the wine and splattering droplets onto his white shirt and tan vest. He stood hurriedly and placed his book and glass out of harm's way on a small table beside the chair.

"Don't stand up for me." She laughed, pulling out her kerchief. "Here, let me get that for you . . ."

Brownie stopped because Rufus had lifted his hand and licked the red wine off the inside of his wrist. Her mouth went dry. Drier? She was already thirsty . . . but this was next level. He had no right to be that attractive. Beastman form or folk form.

"Thank you," Rufus said, taking her kerchief and running it over his hands. He dabbed at the splotches on his shirt but finally decided, "I'm going to change into something new. Wait for me?"

His golden eyes were still dark with anxiety and a nervousness she wasn't used to seeing. Brownie nodded. Rufus didn't wait, rushing to the bathroom to go and quickly change.

It was too bad he didn't just strip his shirt right there in the lobby. She was still curious about his chest hair.

When the thought crossed her mind, Brownie shoved it away and turned to stare at the book Rufus had been reading so intently. *The Wizard Needs a Lady*, book fourteen in the Berkshire Belles series.

He really was reading all of Her Eminence Feliwyn's lurid romance novels! Brownie picked up the book and flipped through it. He had a glowing bookmark with a grimalcat on it tucked into the middle of the novel. To her surprise, there were markings in the book. Paragraphs were circled; dialogue highlighted.

> *"Don't leave. Please, Rebecca. I know you thought that I proposed because of the love potion . . . but the potion was a lie! I was afraid of showing my true feelings too soon, when dwarven culture is so meticulous. I can't live without you. Food is like dust, water like acid slime on my throat. I can't cast an air spell strong enough to fill my lungs—because I cannot breathe without you. Please, I will do anything, just . . . don't go."*

She flipped through a few more pages until another highlighted section caught her eye.

> *"From the moment you fell out of that tree and landed on me . . . I knew."*
> *"That's ridiculous, Zach. You couldn't have known—"*
> *"I knew. I might be a cat, but I am still a beastman. If you don't want to live in this Wizard Tower, then we can move to Peldeep or Gren's Keep or anywhere you want. As long as we are together, that will be my tower."*
> *"But—"*
> *"Shh, love, no buts.*

The following paragraph wasn't highlighted, but it was . . . spicy. Brownie found herself enthralled reading through an intimate scene on a garden bench.

"Bronwynn?"

The bard flinched, snapping the book closed and slamming it on the table a little too excitedly.

Thank goodness she'd turned the page, reading to a spot with no highlights. Even if he'd caught a glimpse of her page, it wouldn't be obvious she had been reading his notes . . .

Just the racy scenes.

"Rufus! Wow, this is such an interesting book. I—" Brownie stopped when Rufus, wearing a new black silk tunic open at the throat, stood close enough that she could just kiss him. Since his folk form was slightly shorter, she finally got to see his chest dusted with golden hair.

He reached forward, his hand resting on top of hers and the book. Why was he so close?

"Bronwynn." The book disappeared into his spatial ring as he wrapped his hand around hers and drew it toward himself.

He frowned, searching her face and probably spotting the telltale sign of last night's tears.

"It's not what you think," she said, trying to explain to Rufus that he actually had little to do with her current state, and in fact was one of the shining moments of her day so far.

He didn't let her finish, but she forgave him the interruption, if for no other reason than he was baring his heart sincere. "I'm sorry. I'm sorry I didn't tell you sooner, and I'm sorry you had to find out from Ross and I wasn't strong enough to tell you myself. I've been hiding the fact that we've known each other already this whole time. When I said I've been stalking you for a year, I *meant* it. I've been obsessed with your music, I've followed you across the continent, and I even ran that catastrophic event in Sumbria—"

"It wasn't *that* bad." Brownie found herself smiling genuinely for the first time since yesterday, amusement pulling her out of her anxiety and woe.

"I was trying to keep my personal life separate from my work life. But that wasn't fair to you." He lifted her hand and kissed it, sending shivers down her spine. Brownie wondered if she should let him continue or just jump him.

She was feeling more vulnerable than usual.

Rufus finished with, "Do you forgive me?"

CHAPTER 91

Her Eminence Feliwyn's Lurid Romance Novel

Rufus

My heart was racing as I laced my fingers with Bronwynn's and kissed the back of her palm.

She had walked into the lobby looking utterly devastated, and the bottom had dropped out of my stomach. Her eyes were red, her cheeks were puffy, and she looked like she'd gotten next to no sleep. Even with a show last night, it shouldn't have been this bad.

Yesterday, she'd fallen quiet and contemplative after learning everything, but now, her grief was *palpable*.

She had been reading my book when I came back, and I spared a thought to which page she might have been so distracted by.

At the same time, fear of losing her, of hearing goodbye, wrenched my stomach. Nothing felt worse than the short moment before she opened her mouth and said, "I forgive you, Rufus."

The tension gripping my body didn't suddenly relax, but I drew a deep breath that felt lifesaving.

"Thank the gods," I sighed, then I tucked her arm into mine and started walking her toward the door. "Now, I have a surprise to make it up to you."

I stopped when she hesitated near the entrance. She looked between me and the second-floor rooms, and I wondered if she'd been up so late that she wanted to just grab breakfast and go back to sleep. As we stood there, her eyes finally focused back on mine, and I decided to throw the surprise to the wind. "I've rented a spot on the patio of Vivian Vermillian's Eatery so we can watch your cousin fight the guild master in the final round of civilian combat today."

"You didn't?!" That perked her up, and she leaned back into my hold.

"I most certainly *did*."

*   *   *

The midmorning heat pushed down on the city with a vengeance. The marketplace and streets were busy, but the real crowds were up by the fighting. The closer we drew, the noisier and more oppressive it got.

I wiped a bit of sweat off my brow but kept moving forward.

We weren't going to be standing in that mob. No. I'd booked us seats for the entire morning at Vivian's, with plenty of time to come back to the inn for her to nap and eat. I could finish my reread of *The Wizard Needs a Lady* . . . Speaking of which, I was a little on edge thinking that Bronwynn had read my highlighted notes inside Her Eminence Feliwyn's lurid romance novel.

The image of her, blushing and panicked, made me smile.

It was a bit unpleasant shouldering through the crowd in the street to get to Vivian's, but once inside, we were sitting with our own table overlooking a bout between a catkin ninja and a human archer. Not a good match, and the stage had to erect a shimmering shield that would prevent stray arrows from volleying into the crowd. The glittering wasn't too distracting, thank goodness.

The catkin used elemental earth magic to erect random barricades around the ring to hide behind. The human was meticulously walking around and firing flaming arrows off at any minor noise.

The human eventually won with a lucky shot. The catkin had tried to jump the archer from behind, but the human had turned and fired on them at the last second, hitting the catkin in the shoulder.

The audience had gone wild. Bronwynn and I'd been mostly distracted ordering some snacks and iced lemon with elderberry water.

Multiple times I made to say something but thought better of it. Bronwynn was sipping her drink and watching the arena with mild interest.

Anything to distract her.

Even on the way here, her face would lose some of its shimmer when she wasn't talking or she thought I wasn't watching. She should have realized by now that I was always watching. That was the *problem*. Even here, when a preela with twin swords was battling against a B-class adventurer lizardkin with a battle axe, I was having a hard time focusing on the battles.

"When do you think Cousin Luke is going to fight the guild master?" Bronwynn suddenly turned and caught my eyes.

I casually took a sip of my own drink and replied, "Your cousin is in the last round of five today. Then the penalty bout."

The information about each bout and contestants, the general schedule, the best view of the fights, and where the betting booths were all sat in carefully written scrawl on a sheet of paper in his storage. The morning had proven his investigation skills were still on fire. Just like the preela was when her opponent used a special Lizardkin title fire breath that caught the lanky swordwoman's tunic.

I continued.

"This morning, there was a presentation by the palace dancers and a pie-eating contest. Then the first fight. A selkie maiden sang her giant opponent to sleep, then took a while rolling him off stage."

"I'm sad I missed it." Bronwynn chuckled at the image, placing her chin on her palm. Below, the preela had managed to put out the fire, but in doing so, she'd lost one of her blades.

"The second fight was between a sloth beastman and a healer. Apparently, the healer had sworn a vow of pacifism, and she only entered the contest on a dare."

"Really?"

I was happy my knowledge was successfully lightening the mood. "Yes. The sloth had gravity abilities that made everything slow . . . but the healer had a debuff that made everything cost more mana. The beastman ran out of mana long before he could reach the healer to attack her. The difficulty with being a sloth beastman."

Bronwynn nodded, taking a sip of her water and eating a mochi cake made with Lady Green tea.

"The five winners today face off against the five winners from the military tomorrow. The royal knights' academy and the army are having their finals on the other side of the river as we speak," I said, though I assumed she already knew, having grown up in Peldeep. I brought it up only because I had an important announcement. "I don't know what your plan is tomorrow, but if you're free, we could go?"

Originally, I was going to be fully booked with meetings during my stay in Peldeep. I needed to find the Peldeep investigation team—which turned out to be Slake—then meet with the Assassin Assembly guild master—which turned out to be Bronwynn's uncle—and then meet with the ruler of Peldeep and the council—which was moved ahead due to Madame Potts's warning.

Suddenly, we had an extra day to just *relax*.

"Aside from performing, I'm free." Bronwynn said; she didn't sound as calm as her usual self and she continued "Actually, I was wondering if . . . Well—"

The sound of hundreds of voices cheered when the preela dealt a finishing blow on the lizardkin, distracting her.

Then her cousin flew in on a flying sword and landed in the middle of the ring. His robes were elegant black-and-red silks, complementing his fox fur. Luke was a direct heir to the Stannard family and held himself with grace and dignity.

Guild Master Warren sauntered onto the stage. He looked almost human, wearing standard adventuring attire. The only thing that would have had him stand out from the rest of the crowd was a brooch haphazardly pinned on with the symbol of the guild: a silver circle with a blue shield, and then a silver crescent moon on the shield.

He smiled casually at the audience, saying something to Luke that made the fox shifter sigh.

"It looks like the guild master is ready to go!" the announcer said. The roar that followed was intense, and I shivered. Both contestants nodded at each other before taking position.

Luke placed his palms together in front of his chest and squared his stance. His whip appeared in his hands, and he slowly lifted the hilt, bringing the tail down with a snap, moving into the first stance.

Guild Master Warren rotated his shoulders and cracked his neck, then he balled his fists and crouched.

The announcer's voice carried over the square, "Let the final battle . . . BEGIN!"

CHAPTER 92

One of the Grimalcat's Lives

Brownie

Brownie dropped her question and turned her full attention to her cousin. Part of being in a big family was showing up and supporting each other. It was one of the few things that could have dragged her outside today, when she would otherwise have just climbed back into bed with a cup of tea and a pastry.

"Go, Luke, gooooo!" she hollered with the rest.

She still felt bad that she'd rejected her family name, but promises were promises, and she'd traded her life of knife for music.

If anything, having Rufus as the secret leader of her fan club *eased* some of her worries. Having the commander general of the Dark Lord's army coming out to every show was a real morale booster . . . especially today, when she needed it.

While she was pretending to be fine, Donna's betrayal had hurt her deeply . . . even if she understood the ridiculous need her mare had for unfettered freedom. Her unhinged and chaotic stance had left Brownie in trouble on too many occasions to recount.

And this time worst of all.

Brownie knew Donna wouldn't think twice about doing whatever she wanted . . . but this was different. It was different because Donna shouldn't have done it, and she knew she shouldn't have done it. The mare could argue the importance of confidentiality until she was blue in the face; it wasn't going to change the fact that Brownie could not do anything to even remotely connect her to her family business.

She also knew about Momo and Brownie, and her promise to the grimalcat. It was just not the right thing to do, especially when you were running around with one of the grimalcat's lives.

Donna might think that acting on her own wasn't breaking that promise . . . but Brownie didn't feel that way.

The battle began, and the fighters were almost evenly matched.

Sure, Cousin Luke was pretending indifference as he whipped out into the space where the guild master had been, while Warren dodged the whip and attempted to go in for closer quarters.

"I thought you said this was going to be a knife fight?" Rufus asked.

Brownie flicked her eyes to her date then back to the arena. "Warren usually uses knives. Maybe he's saving his mana for the penalty bouts? I could also just be wrong."

"You?"

"It's alright to be wrong sometimes!" She turned her attention back to the fight. "It happens!"

The guild master finally managed to wrap a hand around a part of the whip long enough to yank it. Luke was thrown, but a bolt of silver electric power he'd inherited from their grandmother's side blazed up the whip and paralyzed Warren's right arm.

Warren took a step back, rubbing his arm and grimacing. It wasn't for long, though, as his face burst with an intrigued smile.

There was plenty of time for him to pop a potion while Luke landed and retook his stance, but no such potion was produced. Her cousin quirked an eyebrow at the choice then flicked his whip gently, sending out sparks.

"I have a spare antidote," Luke told the guild master, "if you need one."

It was meant to be an insult, but Warren visibly perked up. "Really? Thanks. I'll take it after the battle, though. For now . . ."

Brownie flinched as the guild master suddenly crouched and flexed. His eyes started leaking a bright purple aura, and gravity started to warp as his hair rose into the air and his clothing billowed. One arm hung limp, but the other was tense and bulging with ever-growing muscles. He was suddenly *huge*. Not like a giant huge but like a bodybuilding-musclehead-that-spent-all-his-time-in-the-training-yard huge. The crowd went wild.

"[Spirit Blast]," Warren said, activating a spell.

Finally, her cousin's face broke its serene facade. With a panicked look, Luke dropped to the ground. In the split second before the blast of energy hit him, Luke touched the floor of the ring and activated, "[Static Force]." He was hit by a wave of purple energy that sent him flying as the entire floor erupted in silver arching sparks.

Warren, standing on that floor, had a spark explode at his feet which discharged him into the force field that encircled the arena. Both Luke and Warren hit the boundary of the ring hard enough to send waves rippling through the dome.

Luke hit the ground first.

"And the battle goes to Guild Master Warren Jones!"

The announcer was yelling, and everyone was yelling, and Brownie suddenly remembered yesterday's excitement with Rufus, so she turned to the beastman and reached out a hand to his.

He held her hand like a lifeline, but otherwise seemed to be taking the ruckus in stride.

"I didn't know Guild Master Warren was a demon." He nodded back at the fight.

She explained. "Ah, yes. He's been the guild master for a hundred years at this point. Their Royal Highness Rowen's grandfather won a bet with the demon, and so he's been forced to lead the Adventurer's Guild for a full hundred years. I think he's stepping down later this summer, actually."

"Really?" Rufus eyed the demon who had walked over to shake hands with Brownie's cousin. He happily accepted the antidote from the amused but also annoyed fox. When he regained control of his arm, he reached up and scratched the back of his head before turning to wave at the audience.

It was a good thing that Luke had given the demon the antidote, since he was about to fight all the contestants who had lost going into the preliminary rounds.

"Rufus?" Brownie squeezed his hand. "Can we go somewhere else?"

Her beastman stood up, nodding. "Of course. Where would you like to go?"

He didn't hesitate, simply tossing a few gold coins onto the table. Brownie reached for her instrument and realized she'd been so out of sorts that morning she'd actually left Danielle back in her room.

For some reason, that was enough to send her over the edge. All of a sudden, tears sprang to her eyes, and Rufus visibly panicked. She let him pull her to her feet and then she leaned down and hugged him.

Rufus stiffened.

Brownie rubbed her eyes. "Let's go back to my room. I wanna talk."

CHAPTER 93

Say It for Me

Rufus

My heart was racing as we walked back to the inn, hand in hand. Bronwynn waved away my concern as she sniffed. She was holding back as much as she could.

The second the door to her room closed behind us, she fell into my arms and started crying.

I held her, gently patting her back as she let it all out. After a moment's hesitation, I scooped her up into my arms and carried her to the bed. I sat, Bronwynn in my lap. The half giantess leaned down into my shoulder, sniffling again, and got out, "I talked to Donna."

Ah. I hugged her tighter. "I'm sorry . . ."

"You didn't do anything." She pulled a kerchief from her storage ring and blew into it loudly. Then she stilled and cast a look full of suspicion. "Did you?"

"I found out. And told her if she didn't tell you . . . I would," I explained. There wasn't anything I could regret. It needed to be done.

I was reminded of the fact that Bronwynn's emotions were hidden from my senses and my notification sheet, if not my sight. Her family heritage and upbringing were a testament to that, and I appreciated it even as I worried. If I was going to love this woman, I wanted her to have her own private thoughts and emotions. Even if it left me on the edge of my seat for a day worrying.

Bronwynn blew her nose a second time and nodded. "Donna already told me you knew."

"I imagine she had a lot to say." My hand swept her hair out of her face and tucked a curly lock behind her ear. She was so beautiful, splotchy crying face and all.

"Our relationship is full of secrets," she stated. "My life is full of secrets."

"True." I nodded.

"And even my bonded companion had secrets!"

I continued nodding.

"And I have secrets."

I tensed, suddenly worried. Although, when was I *not* worried? "You do?"

Bronwynn sighed, looking sheepish. "It's one of the reasons I've completely separated myself from my family business."

There wasn't much I could do except wait for her to tell me. It took some time to gather her courage, but she finally whispered, "Rufus . . . when I was seven, I had a bit of an adventure with a grimalcat."

Everything stopped as I stared at my bard with a mix of horror and understanding. Still, I didn't interrupt her.

"I've never told my family all of the details because it happened when my cousin accidentally shipped me off to Drendil," she started, slipping into storyteller mode as easily as she did breathing. Her emotions slipped away, and only the art of recounting the events remained, giving her voice strength.

"My aunt Persia on my mother's side found me in the hold, but it was too late to go back." She smiled. "My grandparents were only too happy to have me stay with them for a summer while Persia finished her trip east up the coast to North Sumbria.

"But Drendil isn't exactly safe for nonhumans, and I got cornered by a gang of children trying to 'show the giant that she ain't welcome.' There was an accident, and as I was running away, I reached a dead end. That's when I met Momo. I'd been terrified, but the second he showed up, I thought that everything might be alright. He asked me what my dream was, and I told him. I told him I wanted to be a bard and travel the world, and how much music meant to me."

She glanced at her lyre harp and then down at her hand, clenching it. I had to remind myself that the king and queen of Drendil—the ones responsible for creating a culture of hate—were already undead.

Bronwynn continued. "He asked what was stopping me. I told him I was supposed to grow up and help my family business. I was so much in shock from my wound that I added, 'If I survive,' and the grimalcat snorted.

"Then he sniffed my hand and said that if I was willing to follow my dream and abandon my family business, he would help me . . . and I agreed. Momo pulled out the knife in my side, and the wound healed with magic, and I was fine. But I'd made a promise."

The song jumped right into my mind, and I spoke the ending to my bard.

> Never betray you a grimalcat's trust,
> And never a lie pass your tongue.
> The creature will hunt you until the blue moon,
> And the damage returned or undone.

"Exactly!" Brownynn put her head in her hands. "What if Momo thinks that my bonded companion completing my family's quests is the same as me breaking my word?"

"You could ask Slake?" I offered; my free hand rose to play with the ends of her hair. "He would know."

Her body shifted delicately on my lap, making me exceedingly aware of her. At least I didn't have my tail to give me away as well.

She stopped, blushing at me, but not immediately running away.

"I *could* ask Slake," she agreed, her voice soft. She leaned closer, her breath tickling my neck. The sensation was heightened without my fur, and I shivered. Bronwynn pulled back, searching my face. "*Later.*"

The red tint in her dark eyes was like a fire. Her arms came up, one wrapping gently around my neck while the other was toying with the ends of my hair by my shoulder. I turned my face and kissed the hand. My arms were still holding her on my lap.

Looking up at her, I nodded. "Later."

She leaned down to kiss me, but I spoke just before our lips touched. "Bronwynn?"

"Yes?" she asked, pausing.

"I love you."

She smiled, pressing her lips to mine in a gentle exploring exchange. When she pulled back for air, she whispered, "Good. I would hate to be the only one."

Chuckling at her teasing, I rolled her underneath me on the bed and kissed her nose. "Say it for me."

"I love you too." Then she laughed and added, "And this time, neither one of us has been drinking, so there are no problems with consent, right?"

I lifted her hand to my face and kissed the inside of her palm. "That's right. But I'll be checking things as we go, just to make sure."

CHAPTER 94

He Went Mostly Unmauled

Brownie

"Momo?" Slake Drakeford, Adventurer Extraordinaire, sat on the bar at Herman's. "Of course I know him."

After spending the entire afternoon at the inn, she and Rufus had ordered a bath, washed up, and gotten ready for her show. She would perform one more night at Herman's, and then tomorrow she was contracted by Their Royal Highness to play in Juniper Square. She was scheduled for the lunch break, just before the last champion match between the military and the civilian finalists. When Rufus had ordered the bath, he'd also sent a messenger to the palace to ask Slake to join them for dinner. They'd not received word back, but when they'd walked across to the tavern, the grimalcat had been waiting for them.

The establishment let Slake lay on the bar as if he owned the place, and once or twice, the troll barkeep would walk by and pet the grimalcat.

He went mostly unmauled.

"Then we would like your opinion on something." Rufus held Brownie's hand and urged her to explain.

And she did.

Slake listened quietly, his tail flicking once or twice but otherwise intent on her story. When she was done, Brownie sat back and waited for the grimalcat's verdict.

"I see . . ." Slake stretched then stood up, walking across the bar toward her. When he was directly facing Brownie, the grimalcat reached out a paw and poked her forehead. His eyes began to glow.

She held still, letting Slake do whatever a grimalcat did. He frowned, then shook his head sadly. "I don't know what Momo will say, but your feelings of guilt will summon him soon, I'm guessing. It's hard to hide something like this from us."

Brownie slumped. "What should I do?"

"I will speak for you," Slake offered, "but I cannot promise he won't be angry."

The grimalcat from her memories was her savior, and she didn't want to disappoint him. "Alright. Thank you, Slake."

"You're welcome." The cat jumped down onto the seat beside hers and proceeded to lick his paw.

"What is Momo like?" Rufus asked them, arms crossed.

Brownie recalled, "He is fluffy, with feathered wings, and bright yellow eyes."

"He *is* very fluffy." Slake agreed.

"You ready for tonight, Minstrel Bronwynn?" The tigerkin Ol' Malley came up to the group and stopped to politely acknowledge the grimalcat.

Brownie pushed her near empty plate away and finished her light pear cider in one gulp before gently slamming the cup on the bar. "You bet I am!"

Ol' Malley nodded. "Got any new songs for us tonight? I'll have Samson run around to let everyone know you're playing. After yesterday, I don't think we'll have a problem filling tables."

The previous evening had gone harder and longer than any she'd previously performed. "I'm afraid I sang everything I've ever written last night. I don't think I'll be able to top that."

"You what?!" Rufus interrupted. "You sang *everything*?"

"Nothing you haven't heard before!" she assured him.

The only reason she'd been able to remember the lyrics to some of those songs with such alacrity was because she'd been singing them for him on their trip from Hearthcrest to Vitol.

Rufus deflated. "I can't believe I missed that."

"Serves you right!" Ross exclaimed, flying over and plopping himself down on the counter. "This is what they call *karmic justice*."

Brownie waved at Frida as she slowly walked toward them, hands clasped in front of her. The fae woman moved with an unnatural grace. Her Dexterity must have been even above thirty, or maybe she had a title trait that made her presence so subtly pronounced.

"Ross." Frida smiled. "My friend, do not tease our leader overmuch. Would you not have jumped at the opportunity to travel with Minstrel Bronwynn?" Frida returned Brownie's greeting with a small bow. The vines dangling from her antlers swayed gently, and her robes barely moved out of place. "How do you two fare?"

Before Brownie could speak her pleasantries to the fae, Ross pointed a tiny finger at Rufus. "He's positively glowing. I think they're doing fine."

Her beastman smiled a very pleased-with-himself smile, his furless ears only a little pink with embarrassment. He offered Ross his hand, and the pixie hopped onto his palm. "You're right, Ross; we're doing wonderfully."

"It's true," Brownie agreed.

Rufus moved the pixie to his right shoulder, and Ross stepped off, taking a seat near Rufus's ear.

Frida took the free seat beside Rufus, and the bartender appeared like magic. He might have appeared *with* magic, going by the stupefied look on his face and his hands in the position to dry a plate with no plate to be seen.

"One glass of elven myst dewdrop for my friend here"—she waved at Ross—"and I'll have the Carol's mead."

The bartender blinked a few times then cowered before the elder fae, running to do her bidding.

Brownie resisted the urge to chastise the woman for manipulating the troll without his permission. On one hand, she was a fan who would be more likely to listen to Brownie's advice . . . On the other, she was an all-powerful fae elder who could probably separate Peldeep from the continent and set it adrift on the ocean.

There was something to be said for the small number of creatures over level eighty on the continent who walked around like they were ordinary citizens.

There were more who filed into the tavern, and Ol' Malley called Brownie away to her evening's performance.

"Fine friends and good gentles." The tall tigerkin stepped onto the stage as the room filled with more and more people. He smiled, his sharp white teeth flashing. "I would like you all to welcome the one, the only, Minstrel Bronwynn Lyriel!"

Brownie walked onstage to cheers, the lights dimming a bit, though the magical light above the stage remained bright. Three waitresses waited off to the side of the bar: Flow, Faun, and Flora. They would descend about halfway through Brownie's first song, delivering drinks to tables and then coming around again to take food orders. They had a nice stew, fried potato sticks, a pasta salad, or rice bowls with flying pork cutlets.

Bard

The joy of a bard is in the audience. **Bard** allows you to target an audience equal to your Level 31 x Charisma 21 = 651. Targets will be able to hear you at your control and will feel the full effects of any Charisma-based abilities unimpeded by distance. When performing for an audience of max capacity, gain additional experience. Unless defended against, automatic success when buffing a member of your party with a level of equal to or lower value.

Her titles let her absolutely slay on the stage. The ability to target her audience and control her own sound were the two she concentrated on now.

Minstrel

What sets a **Minstrel** apart is their ability to control their sound.
Unlocked: **Reverb**, **Drone**, **Repeat**. Unlocked abilities stack.

Reverb

Creates an echoing wave of sound that trails off.

Drone

Creates a lingering, steady sound that remains constant.

Repeat

Creates a mimic of a select length of sound that can be replayed.

She chose [Reverb] and raised her hand to the sky. It came down strumming a wave of echoing chords off her lyre harp. The room hushed in an instant as everyone drew in a breath.

Then her hands played, and she let her repeat build each section so that her chords were playing behind her as she then plucked the melody to her chosen opening song. She chose this one because it was Rufus's favorite: "Balthorn Rose."

How like the rose to wither,
How like the petals to fall,
The blood-red flower is cut down—
And she fell in Eleran's Hall.

CHAPTER 95

Better Battle with a Grimalcat

Rufus

After an amazing night and an even more amazing sleep cuddled up together in my room, we had breakfast and then I escorted Bronwynn to her big show. The contests for the morning had finished with time to spare. She played five songs, a mix of her own and some popular pieces in Peldeep like Sir Eglamore and Tammy's Tavern. She was fantastic, as expected, and I watched the performance from the comforts of Vivian's Vermillian Eatery.

Afterwards, we decided to head out right away for the Dark Enchanted Forest. But before that . . .

Bronwynn had deliberately taken time away from her bonded companion, paying the inn to take care of Donna for the entirety of the time she'd needed space. The mare, for her part, had stayed in her stall without much trouble. As I understood it, that was a first for the murder horse.

I wouldn't call her a murder horse to her face, of course, but I would admit to thinking it.

"Donna?" Bronwynn called out to the mare.

I took a step back while the two of them talked it out. There wasn't much I could add when I only heard half of the conversation.

"I know."

"I'm still angry. And unless you can explain—I thought so."

"It did mean a lot to me. I'm still upset, but I'm trying."

"No, I've definitely made Rufus apologize . . . Oh, stop it! Just wait until you find a mate."

"Alright, we can try. What did you even get—"

I shook my head, knowing the answer to that one already.

"*Enchanted carrots? Really?*" Bronwynn frowned, and a hint of anger hitched in her voice. "You chose enchanted carrots over *me*? No, I *do* think that's unreasonable! I thought this had something to do with your obsession with independence . . ."

By this point, she'd started walking Donna out front of the inn. The mare sniffed at my . . . her . . . *our* bard.

"It *is* an obsession. It took me *forever* to convince you to bond, and I was happy to let you wander off and have your own life. I didn't realize you were delivering packages for poisoners! What if you got caught—Never mind, don't answer that." Bronwynn petted her horse on the side of her head. "But still. *You're* going to have to talk to Momo about this."

The horse turned and butted her head against Bronwynn's hand, rubbing the bridge of her nose.

"Slake said he'd help, and Rufus is the lead investigator, so I'm sure . . . I'm sure it'll be *fine*." She didn't sound fine, but I wasn't going to interrupt Bronwynn in the middle of her own pep talk.

Donna had no such compunction. She whinnied.

"*I don't know, alright?*" Bronwynn snapped, and I decided it was a good time to come in as tactical support. I sidled up beside the bard and softly placed a hand on her shoulder.

She turned to me and faked a smile. "It's fine. I'm just not sure how our trips are going to be going forward. I don't want to restrict Donna or stop her from having the freedom she needs . . . but I don't know if I can trust that she won't be out there taking jobs and not telling?"

The mare huffed and stuck up her nose, eyeing us.

I had no idea what she was replying, but that didn't stop me from saying, "Your family let her join the guild on contract because they felt the same way you do; Donna is her own horse and has the right to her own life outside of being your bonded companion. You have never put a stop to her before, and never asked what she was doing."

The horse stomped her foot in what I imagined was agreement.

"But," I continued, "she hurt you, and your family realized that the two of you have to work this out. So Marigold took Donna off the contract list, and she won't be able to take any new jobs until you come to an agreement."

Donna blew out a breath of air.

Bronwynn reached up and covered my hand with her own. "Thank you, that helps. And *no*, we *haven't* come to an agreement!"

Bronwynn squeezed my hand once before pushing it off her shoulder. I didn't mind; she needed to summon the wagon.

She waited until there was enough space to bring it out of her storage ring, and then started strapping Donna into the breastplate and girth.

"If it helps," I told the horse, "you'll probably have your answers after we meet Momo."

"That reminds me. Do you know what Slake's plan is?" Bronwynn checked everything once over just in case.

"Slake is going to meet us later." I waved at the stable hand and tossed him a copper coin for a tip. The lizardkin lad had just been standing there the whole time while we spoke, politely waiting to see if we needed assistance. He bowed, and I hopped into my seat on the wagon. "I think he's spending the day with Their Royal Highness. I heard the fox ask Slake if he was free today."

"What would they do with a grimalcat?" Bronwynn joined me on the driver's seat.

"The same thing we did when Slake traveled with us, I imagine: give pets and get mauled?"

It was nice not having to worry about maneuvering my tail between the seat and backrest. And it was nice not having a full coat of fur under the afternoon heat.

Sadly, I hadn't packed a hat.

"Good point." Bronwynn picked up the reins, but Donna started moving before the bard could guide her.

"You know," I said as we traveled over the bridge heading toward the northeast city exit by the military district, "it's unfortunate that we had to leave so soon."

"Why?" Bronwynn asked. She set her reins down and pulled her lyre harp out of its case. Instead of playing a song, she summoned a cleaning kit from her storage ring and prepared to give her instrument a fine tuning and maintenance.

I smiled, staring over my shoulder at the great Emerald Palace on the other side of the city. Its beautiful ornate towers shone under the bright sun. "I'm sad we're going to miss the fireworks display, and Their Royal Highness showing off why they're still the ruler of Peldeep."

Bronwynn gently wiped her instrument clean, and then pulled out a bottle of oil. "The last time I saw Their Royal Highness use their skills, I was four. They pushed back a level forty-eight kraken that had decided the inner harbor was a great place to make a lair."

I whistled slowly. Kraken were giant sea monsters that looked like squid the size of a building, with ten extra tentacles. They were very territorial and prone to eating things. Like people.

We left the city and started the gentle incline toward Hearthcrest. I thought about Madame Potts' Cast again, and wondered if that wasn't the reason why Their Royal Highness had invited Slake to join them . . .

Any battle would be a better battle with a grimalcat.

CHAPTER 96

Tinker Tate's Traveling Tokens and Tales

Brownie

Brownie was still angry at Donna after a good night's sleep. And on the road to Hearthcrest. And she was still angry at Donna when they rode up to the inn—the same Lonely Hearth Inn that was her new favorite inn because it was where she and Rufus first got to petting. She was angry that night, despite only renting out one room this time and getting ample amounts of petting, cuddling, and canoodling.

She was having a hard time letting go.

It was almost a good thing that Slake wasn't there yet. He'd be the first to tell her that spite was an excellent motivator, and vengeance the only option.

To a grimalcat, revenge was the best form of flattery.

But she didn't want revenge on her horse; she wanted . . . well, to not disappoint Momo. The grimalcat had saved her life and befriended her, and trusted her to keep her promise.

One did not simply break a promise to a grimalcat.

Brownie was *still* angry when they all loaded up and set on their merry way to the Dark Enchanted Forest the next day. It was a very distracting thing, being angry.

She was so busy being upset, in fact, that she almost missed her first encounter.

"Look over there." Rufus poked her shoulder and stuck a finger toward a vardo, a covered caravan wagon, that had pulled off to the side of the road. Despite the sunny weather, the preela was busy hanging up a soaking wet waterproof canvas cover on a rope secured between the vardo roof and a tree. He was standing on a single-person landing at the front door of the vardo.

Brownie sent a message to Donna to slow down. The horse didn't mind a stop and pulled up next to the disgruntled, mumbling preela. He'd noticed their arrival but was busy straightening out the heavy damp cloth.

"Fine weather!" Rufus called out politely. Brownie waved.

"And fair luck," the preela replied. He tugged three more times and nodded, stepping back to make sure everything was wrinkle free. Then he fully turned to face them and lifted an eyebrow.

This preela had three gold earrings in one ear. He was very tanned, darker than the usual brown-skin and fur, thin-winged, floppy-eared preela who lived on this side of the mountain range. The humans, fae, and dwarves that came from the empire were all darker skinned. That was where the grand duchess of North Sumbria's family came from. The Empire of Sands had two main routes, south to Peldeep and East through the mountains to North Sumbria and the Ice Fields, making North Sumbria a duchy teaming with the most diversity. Peldeep had a mix of beastkin and beastfolk; Nilheim had different cities for each beast-folk and elf and lizardkin and naga and selkie; Drendil had mostly humans; Sumbria had elves; Servalt had elves and half elves; and Baldorin had dwarves. Sure there were exceptions, but there was an obvious majority.

North Sumbria was a near equal mix of *everyone*.

The duchy also imported the latest research out of the Empire of Sands, making it more magically advanced and modern then its neighbors. Peldeep might share a border with the empire, but they didn't have the passion and drive for education and knowledge that North Sumbria was famous for.

The preela were originally from the Empire of Sands, but a few had moved south to the rest of the continent and set up shops in the bigger cities like Vitol or Thistlecrick or Gren's Keep. When they did, they usually had an entire clan helping with a family business or trade.

This preela was very much alone.

"Welcome to Tinker Tate's Traveling Tokens and Tales!" Tinker Tate patted his hands dry and then waved one hand at his vardo. "As you can see, I'm not set up, but I'm happy to listen to requests for buy or sell or trade."

Rufus smiled and leaned forward. "I heard you enjoy music?"

The preela's eyes glinted with interest, and he crossed his arms. "I do."

Brownie saw where this was going and pulled out Danielle. Rufus did not disappoint; his smile got bigger, and he announced, "Then may I introduce Minstrel Bronwynn Lyriel."

A slow smile broke out on his face. "I've heard tell of Minstrel Bronwynn. This *is* fair luck!"

"And I've heard about you, Tinker Tate." Brownie laughed.

"You and everybody else," the tinker sighed with exasperation.

Madame Potts's portents were announced across all of Valaria. The poor preela must have suffered a bit under the international attention.

Brownie had Danielle on a shoulder strap while she and Rufus clambered down from their own wagon. Donna pulled the wagon to off the road.

Tinker Tate reached out and pulled a tasseled rope hanging beside the door. Suddenly, the entire wall of the vardo swung down on hinges until it had completely flipped around and sloped to show a velvet pad covered in the preela's wares. He leaned on the railing of his tiny front doorstep and smiled down at us. "Anything catch your fancy?"

There were all sorts of knickknacks, poisons, antidotes, herbs, and even a few weapons. Brownie grabbed Rufus's hand as they inspected the traveling merchant's wares. A pair of hand shakers drew her eye. Brownie was always looking for easy instruments to add to her [Reverb] title ability . . . and she also just collected instruments like a dragon collecting shiny things. She had a problem.

"I'll take the two shakers, this bracelet with a +1 Charisma modifier, and the jar of killer bee honey," Brownie said, pointing at each.

Tinker Tate snapped his fingers, and each of the above listed items rose in the air, packaging themselves neatly into a small cloth bag that floated toward the bard. "Excellent. That'll be five silver pieces, or three silver pieces and a song."

Brownie took the bag in one hand and flashed her three silver. The money vanished with the transaction, and Brownie stored her purchase in her storage ring. Instead of pulling around her lyre harp right away, she checked on Rufus. The beastman was still in folk form and was tapping his chin with his fingers. They were very nice fingers.

"I'll take the wolfsbane and its antidote," he said. He caught my eye and smiled. "You can use the antidote on me if we run into any more Blackfog spies."

With a wave of Tinker Tate's hand, the items also packaged themselves neatly in front of the beastman. "That'll be four gold, thank you."

"And the wolfsbane?" she asked, eyeing the package dubiously. Tinker Tate hadn't offered a discount to Rufus, so she would only be singing one song. Perhaps "The Traveler's Tale" would be a good pick?

Rufus looked at the bags and eventually handed them over to her. "I was just going to buy it out of circulation, but why don't you take both?"

Brownie didn't like the idea that she had Rufus's greatest weakness just hanging out in a bottle in her storage ring, but she accepted the potions anyway. It meant there was one less poison out there that could be used against him.

Without further comment, she plucked a delicate tune on Danielle and set about entertaining the tinker.

As far as encounters went, these were her favorite kind.

CHAPTER 97

Storm-Giant Storm

Rufus

It wasn't that I thought Bronwynn would ever need to defend herself against me or have cause to attack me, but it wasn't really fair that I was twenty levels above her. Maybe we could swing by a dungeon after everything was said and done and level her up a bit. Only if she was interested in that, of course.

We said farewell to Tinker Tate and made our way to the Dark Enchanted Forest. As we approached the border into the magical wood, we prepared for the storm ahead.

The literal storm. The great trees and dense forest were covered in rolling black and gray clouds billowing in a magically charged rainstorm sweeping from the north to the south. Sheets of water fell from the sky, making it hard to see directly in front of the wagon.

Donna was not amused, stopping and backing up a bit when we got close to the enchanted tree line.

"Well, I guess we've found Madame Potts' rainstorm." The bard reached behind her and put the hay, water barrel, decoy bags, and boxes from the wagon into her storage ring. The wagon was left empty.

"Good idea." I donned a hooded cloak with magical water-repellent spells cast on the fabric. When she was done with loading everything, Bronwynn put on her own red cloak. She tucked her stray curls under her hood and looked up at the sky.

Donna whinnied. I didn't speak horse, but even *I* could guess it was probably something along the lines of "Do we have to?" or "Why don't you have a horse cloak?" and I felt bad for the mare.

Bronwynn, however, had it covered. Donna covered, that was. She pulled out a giant coat designed just for the horse and hopped down to properly put it on the mare. "I'm sorry, but I'll make sure you get a special treat when we get there."

The horse sighed.

"I've only seen this kind of summer storm a few times." I marveled at a bolt of lightning that shot into the sky instead of to the ground.

"It's a storm-giant storm," Bronwynn mused, returning to her spot on the seat beside me. "I've seen them a couple times while visiting my grandparents' family in the mountains."

"Oh?" I'd only been to Baldorin, under the mountains, a handful of times, and never had the pleasure of traveling over the peaks.

"The storm giants collect ambient mana until they have a good storm going, and then release it toward the sea. They do it to help prevent dungeon breaks from too much mana build up. It also serves to strengthen the land where the water falls, giving mana back to the earth." Bronwynn double-checked everything one last time and then called out, "Alright, Donna, let's go!"

The pressure from the rain hitting us was accompanied by the sudden onslaught of my notification tab. On top of my usual commander general notifications tracking the Dark Horde and the King's Dogs, my own unit of mediators, I had tabs from my passive skills.

> [Passive Skill: **Mediator** has been activated by your **Patient** Cressy Verily. Primary emotion: Anger, Hostile. Subject may act irrationally. Threat Level: 2]
>
> [Passive Skill: **Patient** has been activated. A **Patient** within the area of your Skill is in need of counsel.]
>
> [Passive Skill: **Mediator** has been activated by your **Patient** Nelson Hedgemore. Primary emotion: Sad, Guilty. Subject in danger. Threat Level: 2]
>
> [Passive Skill: **Patient** has been activated. A **Patient** within the area of your Skill is in need of counsel.]
>
> [Passive Skill: **Mediator** has been activated by your **Patient** Jenny Verily. Primary emotion: Sad, Guilty. Subject in danger. Threat Level: 2]

And on and on the list came. I mentally scrolled through the first thirty or so updates in case of imminent danger, but Bronwynn and I were safe.

I sighed.

It would be better to just get everything out of the way on the outskirts of the Dark Enchanted Forest. Even though I couldn't see Fiddles lurking in the rain, I knew he was there and guarding. My Commander title would have informed me if a position of border defense had been left unattended, and when I checked to confirm, just in case, there he was.

I could spend half an hour indisposed, so I closed my eyes and directly assumed the information from my notification tabs. It wasn't so bad when I was managing the information on a daily basis, but I'd been away for a few days, and things had piled up. Luckily, we weren't close to any of the major cities, or I'd be fielding the information from those places on top of my usual slog.

When Keith read a wall of information in a split second, he seemed otherwise unconcerned. He didn't have a measly Intelligence thirty trying to process all of that information.

Alright, thirty was double the average Intelligence stat . . . but it wasn't Intelligence eighty-five. And it wasn't enough to let me get away with doing my job without a headache at the end.

I rubbed my temple with a hand and realized I still *had* hands. We were incredibly lucky that we hadn't immediately had that encounter on this side of the border. People recognized me right away, and changing my form wouldn't have affected that . . . though the rain might have.

I changed back.

We rolled down the road for an hour or two, the roaring of the storm making it impossible to properly converse. Donna was unimpressed, Brownie was unhappy, and I . . . Well, I was reminded I couldn't just galivant about the countryside and enjoy life. I had a job to do.

A hand reached out and touched the paw I had balled into a fist in front of my face.

Brownie leaned in close and yelled over the rain, "When did we hear Madame Potts's Cast? Was it the day before last?"

My Intelligence thirty wasn't good enough to handle an entire kingdom's worth of military information without giving me a headache, but it could recall these kinds of things easily. "It's been four days."

There was a mumble beside me, and when I leaned closer, she yelled again. "Madame Potts said five days of rain. We can't wait it out if we're going to make it to the Hollow in time for the festival."

"At least it'll be gone by the time the festival starts," I yelled back.

We pressed forward for another hour, until all of us were at our wits' end. It was one thing to be wet, and another to be doused with heavy rain so loud it made it hard to think straight.

And as Brownie said, there was *mana* in the rain. I wasn't sure if that made it better or worse, and I didn't care—I needed out of this rain.

As luck would have it, the turn off to Gren's Keep appeared.

We could stay at the Damp Gizzard and have some of their famous stew.

I couldn't wait.

CHAPTER 98

Literally on a Quest

Brownie

"Come in, come in!" a singsong voice welcomed the pair into the inn.

Since everyone could recognize Rufus as their commander general, they'd barely had to stop for ten seconds before getting welcomed through the gate.

Donna was happily munching on high-grade hay in the stables attached to the inn, and Brownie and Rufus were trying to take off their cloaks in the doorway without shedding too much water on the floors. A mat had been rolled out in the entry that let them stamp their boots a few times.

Both chose to hang their cloaks on the wall beside the door instead of shoving the sopping wet fabric in their storage rings. If they had to go out into the rain again, then it would be nice if they *didn't* have to wear already damp apparel.

"A table for two, princess," Rufus called out, shaking himself as an animal might to get any water droplets off his fur. "And a room if you have one."

The infamous Princess Penelope—daughter of Their Royal Highness Rowen of Peldeep, and wife to the tavern owner Olen Orrin—glided toward them so elegantly she might as well have been dancing.

She probably *was* dancing.

"Commander General! Minstrel Bronwynn, what a pleasure it is that you've chosen our inn!" Princess Penelope curtsied gracefully, straightening with a gleam in her eye. "One room, you say? Right this way!"

Brownie beamed at the musical princess who was leading them to a table. She had her long black hair in a ponytail that fell to just below her waist, and she was wearing a beautiful light pink gown under a crisp white half apron. The place wasn't too busy, as it an hour before dinner, and who knew how many locals would be making their way through the deluge.

Two birds flew up to Penelope and circled her once. "I know, my loves, I know. Could you bring me the room key and then you may go?"

The bluebirds fluttered away and came back with a key and an ordering slate. They dropped the key into Rufus's awaiting paw, and the slate with Penelope.

"That will be your room, 203." Penelope smiled, then she pulled a pencil from her apron and tapped the slate. "And what can I get for you both to eat?"

"I'll have the stew!" Brownie said, excited. The specialty curried stew was full of spuds and carrots and meat so soft it fell apart in the mouth.

Rufus nodded. "I'll have the same, and whatever Lavender is making tonight."

"Me too." Brownie looked towards the kitchen. A familiar purple Lizard Wizard was happily at the bar mixing coctails and setting off plumes of sparkles as she made enchanted drinks. They were a novelty all on their own, and paired with the rest of the cozy inn made for an enchantingly magical experience.

"Two stews and each a foaming floral coven." Penelope nodded as she wrote.

"Sounds fun." Brownie dragged her eyes from the lizard at the bar and back to their hostess. "What's in the drink?"

Penelope opened her mouth to reply but was cut off.

"Wife, your timer just rang." A bear beastman stuck his head out of the window leading into the kitchen.

"Can you take the buns out of the oven?" she asked, her voice loving and lovely. Brownie longed to sing a duet with the fox . . . and she would. If Penelope managed to go the whole evening without bursting into song, it would be a first. The princess told the bard, "She's made a concoction of rosehip and nettle, topped with a whipped foam on warm milk from the kettle."

After the day they'd had, a hot drink sounded wonderful to Brownie. "Thank you, that's perfect."

Penelope dipped into a curtsy then danced back to the kitchen. She stopped just outside as the two bluebirds alighted on her extended index finger. They chirped a fond farewell to their princess, and she bid them both goodbye with a kiss.

A squirrel arrived to start it's own shift. It put on a tiny apron Penelope handed over and then got to it, removing dirty plates and cutlery to a trolley that followed it around.

"I love a four-hour workday," Rufus remarked, also staring at the birds. "It's the perfect amount of time to get things done and still have energy to enjoy the day."

Brownie laughed at her beastman. "*You* work only four-hour days? Really?"

"What does that mean?" He raised an eyebrow at her from across the table.

Brownie teased, "How is this quest a four-hour work day? "

"I used to work more." Rufus shrugged. "Now I take off weeks at a time to visit your shows, so it all balances out in the end."

"I don't think it does." Brownie shook her head. "I'm not saying that a four-hour work day isn't *nice.* I'm saying that I haven't seen you stop working since I met you."

"I'm literally sitting in a restaurant with the most charming companion a beast could ask for," he stated. "*Not* working."

"Rufus, you're *literally* on a quest! Right now!" Brownie countered. She smiled at her beastman.

He frowned. "This doesn't count. I'm normally happily tucked away in my dungeon around this time with a good book and a fine beverage. And I will be again, once I've locked up Duke Lector and straightened out our resident poisoner."

The image of Rufus in a dungeon was tempting, but the fact that she was going to *only* see him in a dungeon was not. At that moment, their future didn't seem as solid as she wanted it to be.

What was she going to do, just stop in from time to time on her travels?

She didn't want to let her reservations dampen their already rain-logged evening.

"Rufus?"

A voice cut into her thoughts, and the pair of them looked up. A golden-haired beastwoman with sharper canine features than her travel companion and an obvious resemblance had shed her own coat and walked up to their table.

"Hello, sis."

Rufus stood up and added a chair from an empty table to their own.

"I came as soon as I found out you were here!" the beastwoman said, taking the offered seat.

Rufus made a long-suffering sigh at her words but smiled at his sister. "Jessica, this is Bronwynn. We are courting. Bronwynn, this is my sister, Jessica."

The beastwoman flashed the bard a smile that showed a lot of teeth. "It's nice to meet you!"

CHAPTER 99

He Beat Everyone

Rufus

It had been a long time since I'd directly visited Gren's Keep. Or my family here.

Being the most powerful beastman in the Dark Enchanted Forest meant that a lot of people were *interested* in me. Needless to say, if I wasn't traveling with Bronwynn and could use her as a shield against unwanted attention, then I would have rather slept in the wet bushes than chance coming here.

Even if I *did* miss my sister and wanted to spend more time with my niece and nephew.

"You can call me Brownie if you like."

"And you can call me Jess."

My bard shook hands with my sister, and Bronwynn immediately started asking the important questions.

"How did you know we're here?"

Jessica put her fists on her hips. "This is Gren's Keep! And by that, I mean the city guards are veritable gossips. I think half the town's heard by now."

I shivered, remembering the mob of challengers I'd had to fend off the last time. "Good to know."

"Your drinks." Olen, the owner of the Damp Gizzard, appeared beside our table and placed two drinks before us. Then he eyed Jessica expectantly.

"I'll have a regular nettle tea, please, Olen. I need something soothing," she said. "But just a small one; I can't stay long."

"How are the little ones?" I asked, picking up the foamy concoction that smelled like a warm hug in a cup. The nettle was a soft, deep, yet smooth flavor complemented by the faint sweetness of the honey. The whipped cream was sweet and foamy with magic. Bronwynn took a sip of hers and then licked the foam off her mouth with her tongue.

"Busy, like always." Jessica chuckled. She was looking between me and the bard. "Are you wanting children?"

The question caught us off guard. I, conveniently, had already swallowed. My bard, however, was in the process of a second sip.

She coughed directly into her mug, sending the enchanted foam gently pluming up onto her face.

Jessica covered her mouth with her hand. She was just as much of a tease as . . . well, as I was. So I couldn't fault her.

Without much thought, I reached out and rubbed my finger on Bronwynn's cheek, scooping up a bit of the foam. It didn't help much, so I pulled out a kerchief and let her run it down her face aggressively.

"Your family is just as straightforward as mine, it would seem," she grumbled at me. To my sister, she said, "I've not really thought about it. Maybe one? I would need a stay-at-the-castle father to even consider it."

She threw the words I'd said back at me, and for some reason, the idea made me blush now. I imagined for a second a tiny curly-haired toddler like Mimi running around the dungeon . . . She would destroy the place.

Maybe it really *was* time to get my own house? Somewhere close to the Great Road so Bronwynn could find her way home easier. Or, when the kids were old enough, we could just live with her in a vardo like Tinker Tate. . .

I resisted the urge to hide behind my own hands—I was *not* planning my entire future in my mind over dinner with my *sister*.

"We just started seeing each other, Jessica." The words were accompanied by a stern look that I hoped said we should change the subject. Worrying that might actually inspire the opposite, I added, "When are you bringing the family to visit me in the Black Fortress?"

"Food's up, and your drink, Jess." Olen plopped everything down on the table.

My sister picked up her plain tea and sipped it happily. "It'll have to be soon, now, won't it? Or maybe we'll wait and see what happens with General Knolith."

"What do you mean?" I paused in the process of lifting my spoon full of highly anticipated and delicious soup.

"He came here a few days back, just before the rains. Lieutenant Patina was with him, and I'll tell you *that* was a ladies' night I won't forget." Jessica laughed and pushed back from the table, leaning against her backrest and folding her arms.

I put down my spoon and frowned. "What was the General of the East doing in the territory of the General of the West? Who's guarding Kith Bog and Plittsmouth?"

That very morning I'd processed *all* of my notifications. I knew. There weren't any flagged locations over the last week that were lacking in defense.

I'd even checked the border myself this morning.

"You're asking if the general who went into closed-door cultivation for *months* is properly guarding his territory?" Jessica outright laughed. "The lizardkin only *has* that job because he's trying for *your* job."

Bronwynn lifted her licked-clean spoon in the air, drawing attention. "So why was Knolith *here?*"

"He'd gone and spent a day in the dungeon leveling up and practicing with his newfound powers." Jessica ran a claw around the rim of her mug. "And . . ."

"And?"

"He challenged anyone and everyone in the Keep to a duel."

I gave in and rubbed the bridge of my nose like my dark liege tended to do. It helped, but only a little.

"How did he do?" Bronwynn piped up from the side. She had happily consumed half of her bowl of stew in the time it took me to try and wrap my head around the lizardkin general.

"Well . . ." Jessica's smile faltered, but she regained herself.

I raised my eyebrows. "Well?"

My sister breathed a frustrated sigh. "He did *well.* He beat everyone, even General Quinton—"

"That's not hard." Olen leaned over from where he'd just dropped off food at a nearby table. "That tiger's been talking about retiring all year . . . It's time we get some fresh blood running things."

The customers at his table shared a chuckle. They were two rabbitkin, one white and one black, both with adventuring attire and cutlasses at their hips. The white rabbitkin said, "He's right; everyone knows Puma is practically the general already!"

"She's been doing the bulk of the work for a year now," the black rabbitkin added.

Olen resettled his platter, which still had two bowls of soup for a waiting table against the far wall. A mixed adventuring party of dwarf, catkin, and beastfolk were distracted talking amongst themselves and wouldn't know that Olen was delaying delivering their dinner. "So I think it's a good thing General Knolith defeated him so easily—it finally convinced Quinton that it was time."

The entire conversation settled in my gut, wrenching my stomach. I had to push aside the momentary, overwhelming feelings of . . . jealousy? *Envy.* That Quinton could just finish up the year and retire with grace if he so chose.

But I had a dungeon waiting for me. A comfortable dungeon. With wine. And lurid romance novels . . . and patients.

But was I even needed these days? Truly? I mostly holed up down there because Keith had installed some enchantments that let me have a reprieve from the otherwise endless notifications that I had to deal with all day.

Feeling sorry for myself was helping no one, least of all *me*. I'd missed a bit of the conversation even, coming back to things when Bronwynn asked, "We all know Mistress Puma is the best, but how does everyone feel about General Knolith becoming the new commander general?"

CHAPTER 100

General Knolith Is Incredible

Brownie

Brownie noticed when Rufus flinched from her question, but she didn't regret asking it.

If he was battling the lizardkin for his job every year, she would like to know if he needed to worry about what would happen in the worst-case scenario.

Olen answered first. "General Knolith is *incredible*."

"That's right!" the black rabbitkin agreed. "He's one of the more terrifying fighters I've ever battled, and his ability to read the flow of battle is outright brilliant."

"When I fought him, he was already calculating the exact amount of knock-out damage it would take to propel me from the ring without losing momentum to carry through to Baker Annie."

"I saw that!" Jessica cut in. "Baker Annie didn't even get a chance to swing her axe before he blew her out of the square."

"And he was able to manage his own abilities so well that he could defeat *all of us* with enough left over to help fix the city wall." Olen decided it was time to move on before the soup got warm. As he walked away, he added, "It was really well done of him to do so."

"Well then." Brownie never took her eyes from Rufus during the exchange. Her beastman wasn't responding to the information at all. His tail hung as usual, and his carefree face didn't crack once while they listened to the tavern extol the virtues of his competitor. "That's good to know."

"Jessica." Rufus suddenly turned to his sister, who was fiddling with her empty cup of tea.

"Yes?"

"It's probably time you head back." He stood, having never even touched his soup.

The two shared a look, and then Jess sighed. She looked out at the dark rainy storm unloading buckets of water onto the town just beyond the doors of the Damp Gizzard, and then she took a deep breath to convince herself it was time. "You're right. I have to get back soon, or my husband's cooking will go to waste. I'll tell everyone you said hi."

Rufus got up to hug his sister goodbye. Brownie stood as well.

"Nice to meet you, Jess." She stuck out her hand at the beastwoman.

Jess moved right past the hand and gave Brownie a big hug. "You take care of my brother, alright?"

"Of course." Brownie squeezed the beastwoman's shoulders a bit and then they released.

Jess gave them both a big smile and a mock salute. "When next we meet!"

Then she and Rufus were standing alone. As alone as you could be in a slowly filling tavern.

"Are you two done?" Princess Penelope came up behind them, a bright smile on her face. "Must you run? I'll clear the plate if so. But please decide, and say you tried, my stew before you go?"

Rufus stared down at the full bowl of soup, then over at Bronwynn's remaining magical drink. He visibly hesitated, his eyes glancing at the stairs and back to Brownie . . . He drew a deep breath. "We'll stay a bit longer to finish."

There were so many things going on with the beastman that Brownie would have gone with him anywhere. Magical drink abandoned or not.

Though honestly, if he'd dragged her off to bed upstairs without eating his dinner, she would have stored it and brought it out for him later.

They sat back down, but Penelope lingered at their table.

"Excellent, a wonderful choice. I'm happy you're staying downstairs." The princess winked at Brownie. "Any chance for a song that we can both voice, or some music to that you'd care you share?"

Princess Penelope was so enthusiastically excited, clasping her hands in front of her clean apron, but it was Brownie's turn to hesitate. Her eyes flickered to Rufus and back.

"I don't know . . ."

Her beastman reached out and squeezed the hand she had clenched on her thigh. "I'm sure everyone would love to hear a song, myself included."

She nodded, summoning Danielle to her lap. Before she checked if her strings were on key—which as a magical lyre harp from a dragon's hoard, Danielle was *always* on key—Brownie double-checked with her partner. "You're sure?"

"Actually"—Rufus picked up his spoon and smiled reassuringly—"it'll be less awkward than if you just sit there staring at me while I eat."

Brownie couldn't resist laughing out loud at that.

"Wonderful. I'll fix your bowl, with a very simple [Reheat]," Penelope used a perk, then she waved her hand at Brownie. "Something lively would do well, with a catchy tune, and a beat?"

"Alright." Brownie plucked a chord, and it *twanged* instead of *twinged*. She and Penelope both flinched.

Brownie couldn't resist glaring at the magical storm raining magical rain through the small window. The Damp Gizzard had an overhanging roof, and the two-story building was covered in vines and ivy that draped down to provide much appreciated shielding from the wind.

"One second." The minstrel pulled out her tuning peg and carefully tightened each string by half a note.

Penelope motioned to her husband, letting him know he would be in charge of the kitchen for the next little while. Olen finished taking the orders of a beastman wolf and a beastman goat, before heading to the back. The squirrel hopped down from the bar with some ale for the pair.

Don't ask how he carried the mugs when each was as big as he was, but that squirrel delivered.

Brownie played the opening chord to her chosen song, "The Dragon's Wife."

You say that you have heard the tales,
And rightly so you may.
But I have one that I would love
To sing for you, today.

CHAPTER 101

Welcome to the Pixie Prim

Rufus

The next morning dawned miserable and raining, today marking the last day of the foretold magical storm. Hair tickled my nose, waking me. I smiled, gently unwrapping myself from the half giantess and sitting up.

Conveniently, I was in folk form and could use the soft pad of my fingers to gently tuck the lock of hair behind Bronwynn's ear. She mumbled a complaint as I placed a kiss on her forehead and got up, letting in the cold air under our blankets.

With a stretch, I transformed into my usual self and set to putting on my outfit for the day: a thick long sleeve undershirt, knit sweater, and heavy cotton pants. No socks or shoes were required in this form, but I slipped on a pair of awkward ankle-high boots that were custom fit to my canine feet. Better to be uncomfortable than covered in mud.

I slipped downstairs to order breakfast, a hot bowl of water, and a pot of black tea with cream to be sent up to our room before ducking outside by way of the stables. The wagon was parked outside in the rain, but Donna and all of her tack were inside. The mare eyed me as I walked up to the edge of the shelter, water cascading off the hanging roof and puddling on the ground. There wasn't much to view.

"Well, wish me luck," I said. Wrapping myself in my cloak, I pulled the hood up and took a step out into the deluge. There was a faint whinny behind me. I guessed it was the mare calling me all sorts of a fool for going out into the rain, but this was important. I had something I needed to do before we left.

The streets were bare, and only a handful of cloaked figures hurried about. Lights from inside the houses and shops shone as a haze of yellow against the gray storm.

"Welcome to the Pixie Prim," a cheerful voice sounded as I pushed open the door to my intended destination. "Please stand still while we assist you."

The efficacy of [Life Magic] practiced by the Prim was renowned. Not to be confused with necromancy and the ability to control life and death, [Life Magic] opened up an entire skill tree with powers useful to everyday *life*. Other practicing mages might acquire a *few* [Cantrips], but the Pixie Prim racial trait gave them hundreds.

"[Cleanse], [Quick Dry]," the pixie who flew up to greet me cast, waving a tiny finger at me.

"Thank you," I said, greatly appreciating the spells. My cloak and boots were granted the same treatment, so I didn't bother storing them, instead leaving them in the entry.

They were safe with the Pixie Prim.

The shop was fit for one giant to squish in awkwardly between the door and the counter, but tall enough to accommodate me just fine. The wares behind the counter covered many different shelves. There was an elaborate collection of bottles, drying herbs, potions, stills, and about twenty or so pixies flying around the shop checking on the wares and carrying bottles, or fetching things for the crafters in the back.

There were more pixies sorting through swathes of trays containing everything from paints, dyes, soaps, and medicine. I was led through a door into the work room beyond, where a veritable warehouse of finished products sat waiting for delivery on the left side, and the Pixie Prim worked on the right.

Any form of compounding imaginable took place in pixie-sized designated workrooms that climbed to the tall ceiling twice my height in a honeycomb pattern. Hundreds of pixies worked in their respective areas, magicking ingredients. Drapes covered what I knew to be a glass skylight; there was no view of the thundering sky above today. Instead, the place was illuminated by floating magic lights, enchanted string lights woven through the branches of ivy that ran along parts of the shop and bioluminescent mushrooms.

"Commander General!" A pink pixie with long green hair fluttered up to my face. "Welcome! How can we be of help to you today?"

"Hello, Mateo. I'm here on two pieces of business." I tilted my head in respect to the high-level creature. Mateo was the grandson of the head of the Pixie Prim, and in charge of their major storefront. He was also just shy of level fifty, but he used it for crafting instead of combat.

Mateo flew over to land on my shoulder, sitting in much the same way that Ross did. Now that I was comparing them, the two had similar coloring as well . . . but I didn't know if it was rude to assume that coloring was a distinguishing feature among the pixie.

Curiosity won the better of me. "Do you know a pixie named Ross?"

Mateo looked very taken aback. "How do you know my da?"

The silence stretched between us as the pixie on my shoulder squinted up at me, suspicious of my hesitation. I finally said, "I met him in Peldeep."

Mateo nodded, as if that explained it. Which technically it did, since I had just had dinner with Ross a few days ago. In Peldeep. He didn't look old enough to be the father of a fully grown pixie. Then again, Mateo also looked surprisingly young for as long as I had known him.

"I'm actually here to ask if you are supplying poison ingredients to someone in the Hollow?" I changed the subject, leading back to the reason I was here at opening hour.

Mateo tapped his chin. "Lucee."

"You called?" A pink pixie with purple wings and purple hair flew up to us, a small notepad in her hand and a quill in the other.

"A list of long-standing buyers in the Hollow, please," Mateo requested.

Lucee nodded, sticking her quill behind her pointy ear and using both hands to open her notepad. She flipped through more pages than I thought could possibly fit inside, and I accepted the magic without question. "Isla Fens; carol white paint, hulid nectar, and treant marrow, every blue moon. Tilly Lilly; three jars ratha root and one floofpoof hen jaw, quarterly. Duke Briarthorn one gold-grade floral bouquet, quarterly. The duke's staff all order through the chatelaine; I will include a list of the last four quarters here. And the Hollow Glade, the household of the saintess, also has a long-standing order which I will include."

The pixie waved her hand over her notebook, and a copy of everything she listed appeared above it, floating between us and growing in size until each page was as big as she was.

"Thank you," I replied, catching the pile and slipping it into my storage ring for review later. "You've been an incredible help."

"Thank *you*." The pixie bowed lower than was required, and when she straightened, there was a fierceness in her gaze. "You helped my cousin a few years back, when he was in a very dark place. He's decided to be a blacksmith now, and is loving life. The Marrowgrove family owes you a great debt."

I accepted her bow with grace. I remembered her cousin. I remembered all of my patients, and it was good to hear that Lex Marrowgrove was doing well.

"It was my pleasure . . . and speaking of pleasure, there's actually one more thing I need."

CHAPTER 102

[Bond] Level 2

Brownie

Rufus hadn't returned by the time Brownie checked in on Donna. The mare was not pleased with the prospect of travel today and said as much.

"You know we have to leave now if we're going to make it to the Hollow . . . unless you want to get us there faster?" Brownie raised her eyebrows at her horse.

The name Belladonna Windrunner wasn't for nothing; when she wanted to, Donna could run the length of Servalt in a few hours. It might take a day or so to cross Nilheim, but that was because the Dark Enchanted Forest stretched wide across the continent.

Brownie had never seen Donna push herself to her limit before, so even those were rough estimates. Needless to say, Donna could have them at the Hollow in no time if she so pleased.

Her horse snorted, looking away.

Brownie understood. "You know that Rufus will be with us? We could stay with you until your mana replenishes—No? Alright then."

The bard didn't pressure her mare. Donna's fast travel was an overpowered skill, but it cost her a great deal in stamina and mana, and her cooldown on the ability was cripplingly slow, so if she needed to use it again right away, she would be out of luck. Sometimes, Donna didn't seem to mind. Other times, especially while traveling through the Dark Enchanted Forest, Donna wouldn't . . . Wait.

"Donna . . ." Brownie eyed her horse suspiciously. Donna, for her part, eyed her back. "Do you use your fast travel while you're 'taking a walk' to go and pick up the poisons?"

Donna looked up and away, feigning innocence. She even tapped her foot once in a nervous twitch.

"It's not that you *wouldn't* fast travel! It's that you *couldn't!*" Brownie slapped her forehead. "Really? *Really?*"

Donna gave a very unhorse horse shrug. More like a flex of each shoulder blade, but Brownie recognized her bonded companion's tells. "You know, I've never questioned your love for enchanted carrots . . . but really?"

It had been a few days and a good cry since Brownie had started to process her steed's evitable betrayal. It still hurt, and she was *trying* to understand. Brownie grabbed her horse by the nose and swung Donna down to face her—sideways, since horses had monocular vision. "Tell me for real: Do you have an enchanted carrots problem?"

Donna made a weak attempt to resist, but her heart wasn't in it. She blew out in an aggrieved sigh and looked Brownie in the eye.

"You *do!*" Brownie dropped her horse's chin and crossed her arms. "All this time, I thought you were still anxious over that unicorn that attacked you in the forest!"

Donna stamped her foot and looked out into the heavy sheets of rain pounding the earth outside their stable shelter. She chuffed, almost too softly for Brownie to hear against the storm.

"Are you still anxious?" Brownie reached up and petted her horse's flanks comfortingly.

Donna continued to stare out into the rain, but she nodded.

After all this time, they'd still never spoken of that day. Brownie kept petting. "Do you wanna tell me what happened? You don't have to if you're not ready . . ."

[You have leveled up **Bond** with Belladonna Windrunner. **Bond** Level 2 unlocked.
What started as an unlikely kindred spirit has turned into a true friendship. Belladonna Windrunner has decided to trust you and take the next step forward in your **Bond**.]

[**Bond** now allows you to communicate more than concepts and understand basic directions. Ability to share senses unlocked. Ability to share memories unlocked. Ability to share character sheets unlocked.]

[**Bond** now allows you or your bound to share 30% of Mana or Hit Points as a temporary buff, duration of Constitution 15 x Intelligence 17 = 4 minutes and 15 seconds.
Ability to sense **Bond** condition unlocked. You will be notified when Belladonna Windrunner is critically low on Hit Points. You will be notified when Belladonna Windrunner is critically low on

Mana Points. You will be notified when Belladonna Windrunner
is under the effects of a physical debuff. You will be notified when
Belladonna Windrunner is under the effects of a mental debuff.]

Brownie was surprised by the notification . . . but she was more surprised by
Donna leaning more heavily into her and the new information coming through
their shared connection. It wasn't with words or language, but the information
was flooding in with a mix of images and emotions and *knowing*.

Donna had grown up in a herd of unicorns that lived in the southeast of the
Dark Enchanted Forest.

But Donna was not a unicorn.

Brownie had always assumed Donna was something more than the usual
knowing animal like the other talking squirrels and badgers and birds of the
Dark Enchanted Forest. Those animals did not have magic, while Donna was
the opposite.

The family structure of the herd was ambiguous to Brownie, since there was
no feeling of *mother* or *sister* or *wife*. Donna's mother, whom she had few memories of, was a *unicorn*.

But Donna was not.

After her mother was gone, there was only *the herd*. Including Donna, though
she had a strange hesitancy and frustration that clouded her perception of the
head stallion and the head mare. At this time, though, Donna wasn't trying to
explain everything; Donna was just letting it all out in a torrent of anger and fear
and *memory*.

Brownie pieced things together while she continued to pet her mare slowly.

The southern unicorn herd were the protectors of the Moondew Meadow
that held a magical pond. Brownie knew the name already and could fill in the
blanks. This pond was enchanted, and any creature who drank from its waters
would become *knowing*. The unicorns used it to enhance their magical powers,
and some unlocked specialized skills when they leveled up that made them even
more powerful.

The herds would roam between the Drendil border and Lake Loria, all the
way east to Kith Bog. But no matter where the forest took them, every unicorn
would always return to their meadow. Donna always knew where the wildflower
fields and enchanted pond waters lay. All throughout the memory, Brownie never
felt a sense of belonging except for when Donna felt the pull of the enchanted
waters guarded by the herd of unicorns.

The herd had a few troubles, like the dire wolves who came down to the
meadow to try their luck. Or that one frog prince who kept trying to get the
young mares to kiss him. Or, Brownie thought, the loneliness. Still, Donna was
able to grow up with others who could understand her.

And the herd was *strong*; the herd was *one*.

Until *he* leveled up.

The unicorn that had attacked Donna.

In her memories, he'd tormented her first. Angry that she was with a part of the herd and using every opportunity to make her feel that unwelcome. After he became stronger, he pushed her further and further from the safety of the herd, refusing her access to the enchanted pond and it's replenishing magic.

Brownie suddenly knew his name as clear as she knew her own: Bodum Brightcharge. A stallion whose level up granted him immense power and agility.

Not enough to catch Donna, who had unlocked her own fast travel skill, but he didn't need to catch her right away.

He just needed to catch her when her ability was on cooldown.

Brownie kept petting her horse through the memory. She even managed not to cry.

And Brownie realized why Donna, her magical and wonderful and funny mare, was addicted to enchanted carrots.

CHAPTER 103

Fast Travel It Is

Rufus

I found Bronwynn in the stables with Donna, and immediately felt the air had cleared between the two.

Whatever level attributes Bronwynn had that let her hide from my skills didn't matter. When I saw the soft smile that graced my bard's face as she talked to her horse, I knew.

"Are we ready to head out?" I asked, standing under the overhang and dripping water everywhere. No sense taking off my cloak if I needed to go out and get the wagon ready.

Bronwynn exchanged looks with Donna and nodded firmly. "Yes. Let's get this over with."

Donna neighed.

"Really?" Bronwynn asked, surprised. Then she chuckled. "I've been saying that a lot today. Thank you."

I raised an eyebrow.

"Donna said she will fast travel us to the Hollow!" My bard smiled. She set about saddling the mare and preparing to get her strapped into the wagon. "It will save us the day's travel. I bet we could get there by noon if nothing, uh, *exciting* happens."

"Don't we still have two encounters to go before we reach the elven city?" I watched her prepare everything in the comfort of the dry stable. If I tried to help, it would instantly be soaked.

Bronwynn rubbed her neck. "I mean, yes, but it might be something simple like crossing Gerda's bridge. Or meeting someone in Gren's Keep before we get back to the road."

Donna chuffed, and it sounded like a laugh.

"Don't you start. I wanna be at the Hollow as fast as we can so—OH!"

"What is it?" I took a step forward, worried at the bard's outburst.

"If we meet Gerda, we can ask her to portal us closer to the Hollow!" Bronwynn put her palms together in front of her face and tapped her chin a few times, thinking. "Rufus, can you tell where she is with your abilities?"

I could send her an order as one of the kingdom's elites, but hesitated. "If it is not a matter of kingdom business, it's impolite to use my occupation abilities."

"Have you ever used it to find *me*?"

The innocently voiced question held no malice, only genuine curiosity, and it wrecked me. I'd used the border guards to let me know when Minstrel Bronwynn left the forest so that I knew when I needed to portal over in time to hear her concerts. More reminders of my shameful past.

". . . Yes."

She nodded. "Just double-checking."

"Bronwynn—"

"So do you have an ability that will show you where the closest bridge is?" she asked. Donna chuffed again, and that time, I was *sure* the horse was outright laughing. At me.

"My kingdom mini map isn't as detailed as Keith's," I explained, crossing my arms under my cloak. "I see the cities and the army movements if they are on a quest for me . . . of which Gerda is not."

"Then fast travel it is!" Bronwynn patted Donna on the back. "Let's go!"

The journey was miserable.

And unfortunately, Bronwynn's hope of an encounter in the city never happened. We made it through the gates no problem and down the road a bit before Donna started to shine with a magical light.

"Hold on tight!" Bronwynn instructed, reaching out and tying the reigns securely to the dashboard ahead of us before bracing herself against the backrest.

My Dexterity nineteen wasn't impressive on a beastman of my level, but it was enough to save me when we were suddenly traveling at breakneck speed through a downpour.

"[Protector]." I immediately activated my shield, curving it so the rain would hit and slide off easier. Those first few seconds cutting through the water had been painful and unpleasant.

"This is perfect!" My travel companion threw back her hood. "Why didn't you use this during our trek in the rain yesterday?"

"I didn't think about it," I said honestly. Using a shield to block the rain wasn't something I'd done before, and I'd activated it almost on reflex. "I am not strong enough to hold off the magical equivalent of a lake falling on top of the wagon, but I can create a big enough shield to keep the pressure off us for about fifteen minutes."

Donna would be on her own, though. She didn't seem to mind, continuing at high-level speed. She reached the Great Road in a minute, then she actually *sped up* once we reached the main stretch.

There were people few and far between on the roads on a day like this, but we did pass a few.

"What's that?" I asked, my [Keen Senses] identifying a group of travelers ahead.

Before I could call a warning, the mare had already managed to magically pass them, winding through a unit of the Dark Horde, wagons pulled by alligator-dogs and the minions of evil marching east. I recognized them. My order to deploy Mistress Puma had gone out, and the tracker was en route. I nodded, pleased, and continued concentrating my abilities to keep us dry.

When my skill ran out of durability, I had to wait an uncomfortable minute with both myself and Bronwynn hiding our faces in our cloaks while the sting of water droplets hit. As soon as the skill was available again, I spent the mana to activate it.

I could go through all of my mana without much worry, since I had three mana potions in my storage in an emergeny. I knew I'd be fighting Duke Lector, and potentially the poisoner, so that left one high-level mana refill to spare.

A note to self: I should pick up some in the Hollow just in case.

We very quickly passed the turnoff to Frolin and a few trails, but no Hollow. I was wondering which we would meet first, the turnoff or a bridge, when the answer brought Donna to a full stop. I didn't know how it exactly worked, but it was by pure magic we all weren't sent flying off into the forest from the force of that stop.

Instead, Donna was standing in front of a very miserable Gerda the Bridge Troll.

"What falls from the sky
And makes me want to go back inside?"

CHAPTER 104

Belladonna Windrunner

Brownie

Brownie burst into laughter. "You can't be serious, Gerda?"

"Just answer the question. I'm cold and wet and I was reading a good book." The bridge troll was in a cloak with a heavy canvas parasol open above her head. Despite the cover, the falling rain hit so hard it bounced up, and a mist of water wet her boots and the bottom of her dress. The troll's braided tresses frizzed, fuzzy green locks framing her face and sticking up all over her head.

Brownie's own curls were suffering as well.

"Rain?" Rufus answered beside her.

Her beastman looked so pleased with himself, and Brownie didn't have the heart to tell him that Gerda was going the easy way out.

"Yay," Gerda said, deadpan. "You guessed it. Now you've finished an encounter and—Oh, for the love of—"

The bridge troll cursed, activated her teleportation skill, and vanished, presumably for another bridge.

"Well," Rufus said, smiling. "That was nice of her. Shall we go on?"

Donna stamped her foot and then carefully walked forward to cross the bridge. Since it was a magical bridge, she wasn't surprised Donna didn't just barrel across.

"Have you hit one of Gerda's bridges before?" she asked. Her horse sent her an aggrieved reply, including the faint memory of her broken nose. Then Donna followed it up with stealing a heal root from the bag she'd been delivering. The operative she'd dropped off the bag to hadn't been pleased, but he hadn't suspected the *horse*. The more fool he.

Brownie was sad they'd crossed the bridge so easily because she was hoping to stop in for a short visit, or even convince the troll to transport them closer to the Hollow.

They made it to the other side, and her horse promptly kicked off again.

"Donna, are you alright if I look at your character sheet?" Brownie asked, knowing the horse could hear her through their bond even if she couldn't hear her with her ears.

That was met with begrudging consent.

Brownie activated the [Bond] level-two ability, wondering what a knowing animal's stats looked like.

Name:	Belladonna Windrunner		
Occupation:	Bonded Companion		
Level:	35		
Experience Points:	4670/8720		
Hit Points:	450/450		
Mana Points:	240/240		
Bonded Companion:	Bronwynn Lyriel		
Condition:	Enchanted Horse		
Class:	Arion Mare		
Titles:			
[Arion Mare], [Windrunner], [Thief], [Destrier]			
Attributes:			
Strength:	25	Intelligence:	5 (+5 Enchanted)
Dexterity:	18	Perception:	15
Constitution:	36	Charisma:	30
Skills:			
Magic:	2	Unbound:	2
Swift:	5	Battlemare:	4

<table>
<tr><td>Perks:</td></tr>
<tr><td>Siphon Mana, Dodge, Surehoof, Lockpick, Parry, Knockout.</td></tr>
</table>

Alright, Brownie thought, so Donna really was a magical murder horse . . . That was fine. At least she was Brownie's magical murder horse. And she saw why Donna horded enchanted carrots; her intelligence as a knowing animal, as a *person*, was directly tied to her enchanted horse condition.

If she stopped eating enchanted carrots, she would lose *herself*. Brownie wished she'd just said something.

Donna's [Swift] skill *did* take a long time before she could reactivate it, but it actually let her go a certain *distance* before she ran out.

"There's the turnoff," Rufus said, bringing Brownie's attention back to the road. Thank goodness the Hollow hadn't moved too far east. She didn't want to be in this weather all the way to the castle.

The Great Road was a large highway that was well suited to wagons. The road leading into the Hollow was smaller, single lane, and surrounded by lush trees that caged the road and provided some shelter from the rain. The closer they got to the elven tree city, the more the surroundings became dense woodland.

"What's that?" Brownie saw a shining white light on the path ahead, and Donna came to a stop with plenty of space between her and the magical creature standing majestically in their way.

Her mare nickered a graphic expletive that made Brownie's jaw drop. "Donna!"

The unicorn in front of them leaned his head forward, double-checked that it was, in fact, us, and took a polite step to the side.

Brownie could *feel* the waves of suspicion rolling off her mare, who did not wish to take even half a step forward toward the prince of Goldenhoof's tribe. Brownie held her breath, and Rufus remained silent beside her. All paused to see what the two were going to do.

Donna neighed loudly, confronting Brightstar.

Brightstar remained where he was, standing to the side to let them pass. He shook his head with a very horselike shake. Donna hesitated still.

With his own heavy breath, Brightstar grumbled but then stood taller.

Donna immediately took another step back, and Brownie was afraid she might bolt back the way they'd come. The rain clouds weren't the black pillows of aggressive thunder and lightning from the day before, but they were still getting soaked just waiting there . . . and there wasn't any other way to the Hollow except maybe begging Gerda to see if she could portal.

Otherwise, worst case, Rufus was going to have to go on this adventure by himself.

As Brownie was worrying, Brightstar bowed his head low. He flicked one of his ears, but otherwise waited.

Donna reached out through their bonded connection to let Brownie know that she was alright. Her mare was going to try and do this. She was going to walk past the unicorn.

He'd apologized to her and told her he would respect her wishes from now on . . . including her desire for space.

Brownie got the feeling like he was on a quest and wasn't able to simply leave and give them the road. Also, the mix of bush and vine and bramble that was the forest floor off the path didn't look appealing to walk through. It looked prickly and branch-stabby.

Donna huffed but stood straighter herself. She didn't make use of her active skill to race past, but calmly walked up to the unicorn . . . and then kept going. After the wagon was clear of Brightstar, Donna visibly relaxed. She swung her head around to look over her shoulder and whinnied at the unicorn.

Brownie caught Rufus flashing Brightstar a thumbs-up.

The unicorn stood straight again and bobbed us all a nod of his head before walking back to the middle of the road and taking his position once more.

Brownie thought that was going to be the last encounter on her trip to the Hollow . . . and it was, for *her*.

Rufus had his own encounter waiting for him at the gates of the city.

CHAPTER 105

A Little Bit Carnivorous

Rufus

Green Oak Hollow, otherwise commonly referred to as the Hollow, was the oldest city on this side of the continent, built by the elves who worshiped the great tree that was the Dark Enchanted Forest.

The Hollow Gorge was a dungeon south of Gren's Keep, not to be mistaken with the Hollow.

Centuries ago, the Hollow elves managed the Hollow Gorge *and* the Green Oak Hollow, but now, they mostly stayed in their city.

Lithnilheim, the forest itself, was a benevolent dungeon spirit that had broken through to this world thousands of years ago. It was a part of the Green Oak Dungeon, a tower dungeon that stretched into the sky and looked like a giant green oak tree. The dungeon break had brought the elves here with it, and they'd created a home in the forests that burst from the high-level dungeon break. The descendants of those elves were the Hollow elves, and they had a culture all of their own.

It had been a millenia, and the generations of elves living on Valaria resembled very little to their dungeon born counterparts. Almost all of the thinking races came from dungeon breaks—except for the beastmen, humans, and selkies. Who, so far as anyone could tell, had never been found in a dungeon and thus native to this world.

The Hollow elves were born with the forest, and so they had been here since the beginning. They'd agreed to abide by Nilheim law, but it was a tentative relationship at best.

Lithnilheim was a wonderful forest to live in. Though it had a will of its own and enjoyed playing with weary travelers, once you became a citizen of the Dark Enchanted Forest, it mostly left you alone. Sometimes, it even helped out. If you asked it, Lithnilheim might move a meadow or bring you a lake or build you a house . . . but having the attention of a sentient forest was not advised. Who knew what else it would do with you once you had its attention?

Also, it was just a little bit carnivorous.

The elves worshiped the forest, and their city was built in a crescent moon shape formed along the roots of the tree branching out to either side. The city wall completed the full circle, and the entrance was directly opposite the great tree. The gate was wide, a part of the two-story city wall. The gate was also wide enough that a wagon could comfortably fit under the peaked roof dripping rainwater onto the path.

And standing under the gate was General Knolith.

The lizardkin held an enchanted parasol to keep off the rain, and at his belt hung his sword. He was in robes fit for dining in a palace, which were magical dry despite the weather. His long blue-gray hair flowed in a magically created breeze, probably a by-product of his high Charisma. Or a perk.

To the sides, the elven city guards were standing at attention and looking bored. I knew there were many more on top of the gate, and there had been some in the trees on the way here.

We weren't stopped because I had my class active.

"Commander General." Knolith nodded imperiously at me. He dipped his parasol in an arc to close it, and as he did, his clothing shifted into combat-appropriate attire: strapped pant legs that ended in steel-tipped leather shoes. A tunic and shirt that looked like a robe cut at the thigh and tied with a white cloth belt. Arm guards, wrapped with silk and bracers.

I had no idea why he chose silk; it was terribly clingy when wet, and not heavy enough to provide support like a durable cotton.

Perhaps it was arachne silk.

"Knolith." I replied, leaning forward in the carriage.

The lizardkin stared up at me with fire in his eyes. "I challenge you to a duel!"

"No," I said. Simple. It was easier if I was straightforward from the get-go.

"I *insist*—"

"I'm busy," I cut him off. I was wet and cold and wanted to find an inn to cuddle in front of a fire. We'd already battled in Thistlecrick, so there was no way I'd accept again so soon.

Knolith crossed his arms. "Fight me."

"How long have you been standing there?" Bronwynn interrupted. Knolight shot her a glare and turned back to me for an answer. I sighed.

"Three hours, miss." One of the elf guards said from his post against the wall, appearing otherwise stoic and uninterest.

"I'm going to the Hollow, and then I'm getting out of the rain," I laid out my plans. Donna neighed. I continued. "Besides, our last duel should have followed the usual rules: you win, I step down; I win, you leave me alone."

"What do you mean you 'step down'? I thought that was an only-at-the Winter Solstice-kind of thing?" Brownie asked. "Henrietta said she was looking forward to the challenge."

"You can't say *no* at the Winter Solstice Tourney. And if you want to have the job for the following year, you have to win the tournament," I amended. "It's highly improper to duel for the position during the year because everyone should have the right to their annual post. If Knolith wins this duel, then I can choose to not fight at the upcoming tourney, or step down now in dishonor."

"But if Knolith wins he'd only get the job for half a year?" Brownie asked. "Why bother fighting now?"

"Rufusss has been commander general long enough." Knolith glared. "If I defeat him there is no one left who can challenge me!"

Donna swung around to look at me. She considered me for a second and then chuffed.

"Donna wants to know," Brownie translated, "why we're still standing here, and can she bite him?"

"Maybe don't," I replied without enthusiasm.

"I will prove to you that I am the superior fighter in a one-on-one duel." Knolith straightened. "The tournament is all well and good, but who knowsss how many people will ssstand between us. By the time the finalistsss compete, we've already been fighting for hoursss."

"You almost beat me last year," I lied.

"I will beat you *now*," Knolith retorted, taking a stance.

"Here?" Bronwynn cut in. "If you're going to fight, shouldn't we move this to a more, I don't know, combat-y area?"

"Combat-y?" I repeated, laughing.

"You know what I mean." She stuck her tongue out at me. It was a nice tongue.

"Very well." Knolith stepped aside. "We will battle in the arena."

"They have an arena?" Bronwynn asked.

"We *aren't* fighting!" I declared. "Now, let's go. I want to settle in and get dry before dinner."

Donna agreed, apparently, because she jutted out her chin in a horse nod and started walking forward. General Knolith cursed and walked beside the horse to try and convince me to fight him.

I thought he was playing a dangerous game.

He was awfully close to a very murdery horse.

I chuckled to myself at the thought, even as the downpour of water hit me going through to the other side.

CHAPTER 106

I'd Rather Face Off Against Assassins

Brownie

The Hollow was a huge circle with the giant green oak hanging over much of it. The road led straight down a slope and far off to the dungeon tree, but otherwise, the center of the city was covered in rolling fields and garden beds. The majority of the buildings stretched around the outskirts in a crescent shape against the tree.

The road ahead branched off into hundreds of paths that wound through the green, like the roots of a tree.

There was a delegation waiting on the other side of the gate.

"Greetings, Commander General Rufus." The leader had long brown hair pulled back into a tight ponytail, and his eyes were green. He held himself with noble bearing, nodding politely at Rufus.

Rufus nodded back. "Sir Vainbark."

"You arrived early," the prim and proper elf stated. "Sorry about this."

"About what—?"

An arrow whizzed through the sky, and Knolith reached out to catch it just before it hit Donna. The horse reared up and kicked the air twice in surprise.

Rufus promptly took a step to shield Brownie with his body and his skill. "[Protector]."

"This belongsss to a Blackfog ssspy," Knolith said, inspecting the arrow.

"So it would seem." Rufus sighed.

"They came in this morning, and they're proving to be a *nuisance*. Every time we're about to catch them, they portal elsewhere." Sir Vainbark frowned. The elf made a symbol with his hands, and a volley of arrows shot from the top of the wall above us, landing somewhere in the gardens below. The elven group formed a shield in front of their wagon, facing toward the assailants. Swords were drawn and bows ready.

"Why didn't you report this to the castle?" Rufus spoke through ground teeth. "What about the festival?"

Sir Vainbark looked at the beastman with disdain. "Any guest of importance who was invited early is safely in the estate. You need not worry about *our* affairs; if we don't find them today, Duke Briarthorn will ask Lithnilheim to deal with it."

There was a scream in the distance.

The elf knight sighed. "Come back tomorrow when we've cleared them all out."

"Honestly," Rufus replied, "I'd rather face off against assassins now than travel back through the storm."

Brownie agreed; she summoned Danielle into her hands under her cloak. The magical rain wasn't the best on her strings, but they played in some semblance of key. She promptly activated her buff skills, affecting Rufus, Knolith, and the city elves in front of her.

Except, she noticed, that Knolith was *gone*. Brownie had no idea when, but as she opened her mouth to say as much, Rufus spoke first.

"I'm assuming that Duke Lector made it here with his entourage?" Rufus asked, blocking an arrow that splintered against his shield.

"Yes . . ." Sir Vainbark turned from giving more hand signal orders to staring at the beastman. "He's at the banquet now . . . Why?"

"I'm here to arrest him for illegal international assassination, use of molten ash vane, and cavorting with Blackfog spies," Rufus replied, waving a hand toward the general direction of the assassins. The lightness in his tone as he blocked a third missile—this time an axe—made the elf leader frown.

"He's currently having dinner with Duke Briarthorn and Lady Amy," Sir Vainbark said, alarmed. "I must get back. Lady Hazelglade, notify the green guard to protect the duke."

"What about the assassins?" An elf woman separated herself from the group, her eyes suddenly glowing green.

"What about the assassinsss?" Knolith repeated, landing in front of everyone on the path. He held two black-clad figures by the scruff of their tunics. He tossed the pair to the ground in front of Sir Vainbark. "Those were the only ones shooting at us."

The elven knight nodded, raising a hand and issuing another silent order.

"Everyone, follow me."

The elves used some form of quick step that let them all disperse at not-Donna-speed down the main road.

"Are we helping them?" Brownie asked, picking up Donna's reins as if she were driving.

Knolith and Rufus shared a look before Rufus said, "Straight ahead to the palace."

Knolith vanished again.

"So much for a relaxing evening reading and drinking tea while we wait out the rain." Rufus reached out and wrapped an arm around the bard. He seemed in good spirits as Donna raced them down the road at a quick-but-not-that-quick gallop.

"At least we're together," Brownie pointed out, smiling at her beastman. She wouldn't have expected to see him in such a good mood from everything that was happening.

"You know," he added, "if we get everything done *today*, maybe we can go for a nice walk around town tomorrow morning? I wanted to show you one of my favorite spots."

"That sounds nice," Brownie agreed. Donna snorted, but the minstrel ignored her sarcastic horse.

"Perfect."

As they made their way past the last of the flower fields and toward the actual city, Brownie couldn't help but admire it all up close. Everything in the Hollow was crescent shaped, not just the city itself. The streets were lined with crescent-shaped cobblestone mosaics, the signs on shops were crescent shaped, the bread sold at the bakery they passed was crescent shaped, and each building had crescent-shaped windows.

The palace started to the left of the Green Oak Tree, and rose in twisted spires like unicorn horns. The main body of the palace wrapped itself in a crescent shape over the dungeon gate platform, ending high in the tree on the right side.

It was very artistically pleasing, and Brownie wondered if she should write a song about it.

She couldn't wait to see it on a clear day, and promised herself that she would spend tomorrow getting a better look in the sunshine. With Rufus.

Upon closer inspection now, the estate was in a state of disarray as countless palace workers streamed into the courtyard outside. They all stood in the rain as the sounds of battle rent the air.

Rufus kissed her on the cheek before jumping down from the wagon. Brownie covered her cheek with a hand.

"I have some work to do," he said. "Promise me you'll stay with everyone else where it's safe?"

Donna whinnied, and suddenly, the mare was shaking free of the wagon.

"I'll stay with Donna," Brownie promised, climbing down to join the horse.

He nodded. "I'll be right back."

And then, her beastman raced toward the screaming.

CHAPTER 107

Did Someone Call for Backup?

Rufus

I entered through the main doors and found Lady Amy at the bottom of a grand staircase that started smaller at the top but swooped down and wide at the bottom. The elf saintess, chosen avatar of the Green Oak Tree, stood with her bow drawn. Her long brown hair was intricately done up in braids, and her dress was torn high at the hip on the left side but longer to her knees on the right.

She was crying silent tears even as she restrung her bow with a strange untipped tree-branch arrow.

A gray elf in comfortable black evening attire with a pair of glasses and a short wand stood at the top of the stairs. "You should have drunk the poison like your father."

"You will never get away with this!" Lady Amy declared, releasing her arrow. The shaft shifted midair, twisting into an elemental missile that would've hit Duke Lector if he didn't portal suddenly three steps to the right.

The duke nodded at a cloaked figure obscured from Lady Amy's viewpoint, but I managed to catch a glimpse of the small woman with shoulder-length blonde hair peeking out from her hood. To the saintess, he said, "Ah, but I already have."

"Did someone call for backup?" I asked, running up beside Lady Amy just as ten Blackfog spies poured out from behind the duke. Weapons drawn, the group split in half, and each jumped down to attack us.

"Commander General Rufus?" the saintess asked, a new bolt already pulled back and flying. "How did you—?"

[You have attempted to use the Skill: **Examine**. You have succeeded. Six targets may be observed. 5 **Blackfog Spy** selected.

Duke Lector selected. Target(s) under observation. Predictive
analysis: 12%. Available predictions: attack trajectory.]

Faint lines appeared, letting me know the oncoming attacks of each Blackfog
spy that jumped me. There were a few extra lines where the skill offered multiple
trajectories, but the longer I fought, the easier this would be. There were two
humans and three elves attacking me.

My claws grabbed an arrow out of the air and turned around to stab a close-
combat human spy that had foolishly come within arm's reach. I dropped the
arrow, ducked a [Sword Art: Slash], then caught the close-combat spy by the
ankle. Righting, I swung my human spy in an arc. He took a blow from an ally,
knocked over an elf, and when I let go, he flew off into a group of three elven
knights that came running into the lobby from a hallway on the left side of the
grand staircase.

[You have defeated a **Blackfog Spy (Level 21)**. + 21 EXP]

"Any chance," I said to the human Swordsman, stepping cleanly out of the
way of another [Sword Art] skill, "that you want to defect to evil? Your form is
excellent."

The elf that had been knocked down jumped to his feet. "Don't listen to him!
[Fireball]."

At the same time, I easily dodged another arrow from the elven archer
who hung back. The other elf, a fighter type by the looks of his brass knuckles,
attacked the knights.

The fireball was avoidable, but I didn't want to dodge it. I was sure the
wooden palace in the wooden tree in the wooden city was spelled against fire . . .
but just in case. "[Protector]."

My shield's durability from the previous fight meant that it could only take
one or two hits before the cooldown, then I wouldn't be able to activate it again
for fifteen minutes.

The shield dissipated the flames but didn't break.

"I'm serious." I turned to the swordsman. For some reason, my senses were
telling me that *this* Blackfog spy wasn't happy with his lot. "You're what? Level
twenty-five? You shouldn't be lost in a group of masked figures. We have an excellent afterlife plan."

He hesitated for the barest instant, and the mage elf threw up his arms in
exasperation. "Seriously, Barry! We've been through this! You are a valued member of this team. Now *stab him*."

The human, Barry, took a half-hearted stab at me, which I easily parried. "We
also have free health care. And a four-day workweek."

Barry lowered his sword. "For real?"

"Argh!" the mage said. "That's it!"

[Update: Predictive analysis: 40%. Available predictions: attack trajectory and perk activation.]

The notification came just as the mage lifted his hand high in the air. I thought he was going to cast an area of effect spell, but there were no predictive lines showing that. Instead, he slammed a small ball to the ground.

Billowing plumes of wolfsbane exploded at my feet, knocking me back from the sheer unpleasant experience.

[You have taken 14 points of Critical Damage. Health 602/616.]
[Warning! You have been poisoned by **Wolfsbane**. You will lose consciousness in 00:00:10]
[Unique Effect **Wolfsbane** triggered: **Beast Form**. Spend mana to maintain current form or revert to **Beast Form**.]
[You have taken 14 points of Critical Damage. Health 588/616.]
[Warning! You will lose consciousness in 00:00:09]

Wolfsbane was the poison best suited to hunting down and trapping any of my kind of canine beastman—werewolf, wolfman, coyotekin, foxkin, foxfolk, fox spirit, or mythic jackal. It also trapped us in beast form so we couldn't hide, and it was an almost automatic critical hit.

I coughed and jumped back toward the exit. It wouldn't matter if I popped my antidote now if I was standing in the poison radius.

Lady Amy had successfully defeated all of her Blackfog assailants and was already running up the stairs. And the knights had successfully detained the human that barreled into them *and* the elf archer. "You were supposed to save that for Their Royal Highness!" Barry's voice criticized. "Now what do we do?"

"The portal mage can make another for all I care! Let's get out of here." the mage elf grabbed the swordsman by the scruff of his neck and dragged him off to the unguarded hallway to the left side of the hall.

The fresh air from outside filled my lungs, and I collapsed to the ground.

With little time to spare, I summoned a wolfsbane antidote from my storage.

CHAPTER 108

Is That a Horse?

Brownie

Brownie saw Rufus burst out of the palace in beast form. He caught himself and then collapsed to the ground.

Her heart almost escaped her chest, and without heed to her earlier promise, she ran up the stairs to him. She was on her knees in front of him when she saw the antidote and swiped it into her hands to pour it down his muzzle for him.

Rufus didn't look too happy to see her this close to the open doors of the palace, but he accepted her help. Slowly, his body shrank to his beastman form. His head was in her lap, and he looked up at her with a mix of love and frustration. "You aren't a combat type, remember?"

"What's the difference between standing over there," Brownie teased, pointing to the bottom of the stairs where the rest of the noncombat classes were waiting under the gray sky and light rain. "And up here?"

"The area of effect damage radius, and you know it." Rufus sat up and rubbed his head, shaking off the effects of whatever had hit him. Wolfsbane, from her experience.

"Well, let me [Buff] you again before you jump back into the battle." Brownie pulled out Danielle, not caring at that moment if the lyre harp got soaking wet. She promptly struck a D chord.

[You have activated the Perk: **Strength of Sound**. You may target listeners up to or equal to your level: 31. Target(s) gain +2 Strength for 10 minutes.]
[You have activated the Perk: **Inspire**. You may target listeners up to or equal to your Charisma 17. Target(s) abilities cost 10% less for 10 minutes.]

Brownie stood up and hit a G chord.

[You have attempted to activate the Perk: **Piercing Wave**. You
have succeeded. The area of effect attack hits targets equal to **Siren
Song**, dealing piercing damage. Targets available: 1]

An elf maiden with long auburn hair and light green skin wearing a maid's
outfit was running out the palace doors. Brownie's attack hit the panicking
woman at full force.

"What?" Rufus asked, concentrating on the now angry-looking maid as both his
eyebrows shot up. Brownie knew he had skills that would let him see exactly what
she already knew. "I was wondering where the fifth spy had run off to. But how—?"

"You think I wouldn't recognize an assassin in disguise? *Please*." Brownie
flicked a wet strand of curl out of her face.

Rufus shot her a smile and a nod before pouncing on the elf.

[You have defeated a **Blackfog Spy (Level 21)** with Commander
General Rufus Triever. Experience Points halved. +12 EXP]
[Your bonded companion gained +12 EXP from her **Shared Expe-
rience** Perk.]

Even in the heat of battle, Brownie was a touch jealous. Rufus should only
be pouncing like that on *her*.

A throwing knife flew out of a window from the second floor, arcing down
and landing very close to Brownie's shoe. She decided then that it was time to
hightail it out of there. Donna met her at the bottom of the stairs.

Her mare was actively pouting.

"You really wanna fight *that* bad?" Brownie sighed, reaching out a hand to
rub her horse's neck. It was hard to keep Donna from all the fun. And experience
points.

The mare chuffed sadly.

"Alright, how about this." Brownie gripped Donna's reins and pulled her to
the side of the courtyard. The giant door to Green Oak Dungeon was just to
their right, and the towers of the estate wrapped around and over, stopping still
high in the air. There was no way out from that side of the palace except to get
lost in the roots of the tree or to fall to the ground below.

And the tree, as she understood it, was carnivorous. She couldn't imagine
anyone foolish enough to go that route, but . . .

Brownie let her horse stand under a window far below the treetop estate, and
sure enough, two spies floated down with magic about five minutes later. The
pair, a mage and a swordsman, were arguing quietly as they descended.

"Every time. You do this every time," the mage accused.

"Not *every* time," the swordsman countered. "Just, you know, most of the time. I don't like the Void Mage; she gives me the *creeps*."

"So? We're *spies*, who else are we going to work for—Is that a horse?"

The mage was hit with [Knockout] before he knew what headbutted him. Donna, not wanting it to end too soon, even let the swordsman draw his weapon.

It was more fun for her that way.

> [Your bonded companion has defeated a **Blackfog Spy (Level 24)**.
> You have gained +24 EXP from Donna's **Shared Experience** Perk.]
> [Your bonded companion has defeated a **Blackfog Spy (Level 23)**.
> You have gained +23 EXP from Donna's **Shared Experience** Perk.]

Brownie tied them up and dragged them back to the waiting area.

CHAPTER 109

Pink Magic

Rufus

I knew I couldn't go back through the main entrance, but luckily, the elven knights were just inside the doorway rounding up the spies.

There were a few of my skills and perks designed for exactly this type of situation. My Protector title had a [Secure] skill tree, which on its own allowed me to secure and detain all manner of targets. I mostly used it to prevent anyone sent to the dungeon from escaping until we had had a good heart-to-heart, but I could use it skillfully to keep prisoners of battle as well.

The elf I'd caught outside had a low enough level that I didn't need to use a skill. I simply knocked her out and tossed her at a knight who'd been walking toward me.

I was tossing a lot of spies tonight.

After that was dealt with and I looked to see that Bronwynn had gone over to Donna and was busy petting her.I leapt to a second-floor balcony and grabbed a ledge, swinging myself up and onto the landing. The balcony led into a ballroom with a long table set for dinner.

On the floor at the head of the table was a *very* messy puddle, and Sir Vainbark helping a very disoriented elf to stand on his still regrowing leg. A healer wearing all green stood nearby, visibly shaken and sweating.

Sir Vainbark looked up when I walked inside.

"I owe you a great thanks," the knight said. And this time, he wasn't speaking to me through a thin veneer of politeness.

"As do I, it would seem," the recently healed elf said, turning around. It was Duke Briarthorn. He had the same rich brown hair as his daughter, though he was a much darker green. "The guard called the warning as I took the first sip. There was barely enough time to cut off a foot so they could [Revive] me."

"Please, Your Grace," the healer said. "The potion is going to take a while to recuperate your health points. We must get you to safety."

Duke Briarthorn looked grim. "No, I must protect the Hollow. Bring me to the Sanctuary."

Sir Vainbark nodded, offering his arm to the duke but getting only a dignified shake of the head.

It took him a second to find his feet, but Duke Briarthorn stood straight and tall before taking that first unsteady step. He caught himself and slowly marched toward a door off to the right.

After a few steps he paused and turned to face me. "Commander General?"

"Yes?"

"My daughter . . ." The duke hesitated, trying to find the words.

"I'll see that she's safe," I replied, walking toward a door I knew led to the grand stairs. "Lady Amy was hunting down Duke Lector the last I saw her."

Duke Briarthorn clenched his fist. "My cousin has *a lot* to answer for. *If* he survives."

That was the last he said before continuing his walk toward the private sanctuary of the palace. It was a good distance through the palace to get there, but that gave me time to inspect the place and catch Duke Lector myself. If Lithnilheim dealt with the duke, there wouldn't be any remains left to [Revive].

Keith and I had been to this estate a few times in our youth, which hadn't very much endeared us to the elves. As much as it was my job to keep Keith safe and out of trouble . . . the man had a knack for exploding things.

Needless to say, it wasn't hard to find my way to the top of the grand stairs and then follow the trail of Lady Amy.

And there was a trail.

It was hard to miss the aftermath of a battle between a mage and a magical bow-and-arrow-wielding saintess who was too grief-stricken over the potential death of her father to aim away from the priceless heirlooms of a thousand generations.

I was particularly drawn to the floating vase suspended midair, surrounded by a Void Dimension bubble a mere inch off the ground. Whoever the blonde mage working for Duke Lector was, she was a fan of historical arts. A few more pieces were encased in the pink with black spotted bubbles as I went deeper and deeper into the palace.

At some point I had to backtrack to a tower entry, but I found a scorch mark on one wall. From one of the crescent-moon windows, I saw a contingent of elves gathering up fifteen or so Blackfog spies and hauling them out into the courtyard in front of the palace doors.

"You won't stop me!" Duke Lector's voice shouted ahead, echoing down the tower stairs.

Lady Amy yelled back, "Lithnilheim will never accept you! Servalt has called you *traitor*; give up now or else—"

"Or else what?"

The voices were louder. I'd reached the top of the spire.

"Or else this," Knolith answered quietly. I would barely have heard it if not for my [Keen Senses].

"Argh!"

I came into the room in time to see Duke Lector standing there, missing a few parts. They would grow back eventually, or quickly with a potion, but I realized that was Knolith's plan all along.

"You cannot use portal scrolls now," Knolith said. There was a brutality to his work. Then again, I wasn't the type to lop off limbs.

I wasn't a very bloodthirsty commander general. I was a *mediator*.

I ignored my notification tab letting me know that my predictive analysis for the duke had risen to forty-three percent. I still only had attack trajectory and perk activation warnings available.

Really, I was most interested in the woman standing on the far end of the room, on a balcony with waist-high railings. Her hood had fallen off, blonde hair blowing in the wind. The rain was still falling, but in a hazy drizzle light enough that it didn't obscure anything.

The woman looked human of middling height, with shoulder-length blonde hair and bright blue eyes. Her Charisma score must have been in the forties at *least*, but she couldn't have been older than eighteen herself. She was glaring at Knolith with what would have been an adorable pout that would have made me want to please her somehow—to turn that frown into a smile—if not for the fact I was already in love with Brownie, and the feeling of her passive perk was shallow and easily ignored.

"Teleport us!" Duke Lector screamed at the woman. She flinched once, raising her arms to do as she was bid.

I, of course, wouldn't allow it. "[Secure]."

[You have attempted to use the Skill: **Secure**. You have succeeded. Target under the observation of **Examine**. Target is restrained and cannot activate or be affected by movement abilities. Time remaining: Strength 28 x Level 54 = 00:25:20]

Knolith and Lady Amy acted in tandem, and it was too late for the duke.

The void mage, sadly, was either the same level as me or higher and not effected. She vanished in a burst of pink magic.

CHAPTER 110

Lithnilheim Is Here

Brownie

Brownie was very wet and tired, and all she wanted to do was cuddle up to a fluffy Rufus in front of a warm fire while they relaxed for the evening.

Instead, she was standing outside with the others in the light misty rain while the Hollow elves found and restrained Blackfog spies.

Everyone was on edge because no one could be sure that all of the invading force had been captured. No one was allowed to leave while Lady Hazelglade and her knights thoroughly investigated the people who had escaped the palace.

At least the Green Oak Dungeon Gate was nearby, glowing with magical green light that made the otherwise miserable gray courtyard ethereally beautiful.

"Until Duke Lector is apprehended, I want everyone on branch to guard the city. Anyone off duty should head to the wall. We want to make sure no one slips away." Lady Hazelglade stood, ordering the knights. She was calm and collected, and everyone jumped to do her bidding. "Take Arcos Andres to lead the archers to the east—" She paused, and Brownie felt it; the world suddenly *shifted*.

The rain itself felt like it paused for a single strange instant. Brownie looked up to see the overhead canopy of the Green Oak Tree *moving*. The minstrel reached out and grabbed her horse just as settled rainwater from a tree bigger than a literal palace fell down on them like a lake.

It soaked everything and everyone with so much water that Brownie barely remained standing with [Sturdy]. Donna neighed in discomfort, and many of the palace staff were forced to the ground under the weight of the water.

"The Forest!" Lady Hazelglade shouted. "Lithnilheim is here!"

Panic and elation filled the city. People disobeyed lockdown orders from around the city to peek out their windows and cheer. The roots of the giant tree that framed the city remained stable, but beyond and behind the great tree, roots as long as the city itself pulled free from the earth, rising into the sky. Roots like tentacle arms rose high into the air and then swept over the elven city. Brownie stood there, mouth agape, heart pounding, as the literal Dark Enchanted Forest turned its attention on them.

"*NO ONE MOVE!*" Lady Hazelglade ordered, her voice taking on an echoing effect that carried over the entire city and beyond. She had activated one of her abilities. Reaching out, she grabbed the arm of an elf knight who'd tried to run back into the palace. Many were just now regaining their feet. "*STAND STILL, AND YOU MAY SURVIVE.*"

The last didn't promote confidence, but Brownie was rooted to the spot watching the tree do its work. As she watched, the green doorway nearby pulsed. The courtyard cobblestone rustled around the palace workers and Brownie and Donna. It separated them from the elven knights and their prisoners. Someone screamed, but it was futile to resist, and Brownie felt more awe inspired than terrified of the sentient dungeon.

She had done nothing to anger the forest.

Strangely, Donna didn't seem that perturbed either, and that lack of concern helped Brownie ground herself.

"What?" she whispered as the rustling cobblestone split and earthen walls rose up to pen them in. A roof formed overhead, blocking out the rain, and benches formed themselves against the walls. Brownie could no longer see what was happening from inside the shelter.

"Thank you, Lithnilheim," a senior maid said, bowing her head. She took a seat and started ringing out her long black hair while another maid joined her. The younger maid held out her hands. "Let me help you, Maybelle. [Quick Dry]."

The palace staff happily took the opportunity to take a seat. A few maids and a noble elven guest came forward to help everyone dry off, and a steward summoned magic lights to illuminate the temporary shelter. Some fifty people, and a horse, were making themselves comfortable.

Brownie stood with Donna at the side of the shelter open toward the palace, just out of the rain, and remained standing with her mare even after being offered a seat. She inspected the wooden roof overhead and peeked outside to see the tendril of the Green Oak Tree rooting around the city for invaders. Every once in a while, it would toss a spy onto the pile at the palace door.

The minstrel nodded her own head, whispering, "Thank you, Lithnilheim."

It never hurt to be polite to sentient forests.

Everyone was so happy to be dry, and secure in the knowledge that Lithnilheim would deal with the threat, that even Brownie found herself relaxing. Donna snorted.

"I mean," Brownie replied, "it's better than that time the wagon got stuck in Kith Bog, and it took me an hour to untangle the weeds from the wheel while waist deep in bog water."

Donna lipped Brownie's shoulder, and the minstrel pulled out an enchanted carrot from her storage.

Another spy shouted in surprise as they were dragged by the ankle into the sky and casually tossed with the rest. Lady Hazelglade had her hands full subduing the panicked spies, and the knights needed extra effort to tie up their latest gift.

Brownie watched and then cast her eyes up at the quiet palace. Rufus was still in there, and she hoped he would finish up faster. The magically sentient shelter had formed benches, and now tables and chairs as people made space. That was a kind gesture, but she wanted out of her travel clothes, bathed, and bedded. In that order.

Another spy landed on the pile.

Brownie just leaned into her horse and waited.

Finally, Rufus walked out of the palace with Lady Amy and General Knolith, an elf thrown over the lizardkin's shoulder. They stopped in the doorway as another spy flew through the air and landed with the rest, a giant root tendril swooping past on its way to search for more.

Rufus looked around, clearly panicking, until their eyes met. Brownie smiled up at him and waved.

He looked at Lithnilheim. And back to her.

She shrugged.

He sighed.

CHAPTER 111

What It Takes to Be the Commander General

Rufus

This wasn't my first time seeing the forest moving around, but it was my first time seeing the actual Green Oak Tree uproot and boss-monster itself on a city. The fact that it was its own city was all the more fascinating.

The tendrils were so delicate with the houses, gently unlatching a window before snatching a spy hiding inside. No carriage overturned, no herb garden disturbed, no shop damaged. If anything, the place was *cleaner* than before. A canopy from a shop down the road that had collapsed under the weight of the torrential magical storm-giant rain was righted and tidied. A new roof magically appeared on someone's house, and an old trellis near the community gardens was refurbished to look like new.

When a Blackfog spy tripped over a flowerpot in their attempt to escape, a nearby tendril was utterly offended at the mess. It scooped up the fallen spy, scolding its captive by wagging its root tip in the spy's face and then pointing at the pot. Another root tendril came forward and quickly righted the pot and fixed the flower.

At this rate, the forest would have everyone sorted shortly. Bronwynn smiled up at me and waved.

I sighed.

"Knolith," I said, staring at my adorable bard but addressing the lizardkin who was standing beside me, mouth agape.

"What?" The general closed his mouth and promptly stood straighter, as if he hadn't been shocked by the colossal forest monster hunting down interlopers. It was a good hunter; I counted almost forty people haphazardly piled up around us.

"Do you think you have what it takes to be the commander general of the Dark Enchanted Forest?" I asked.

Knolith lifted Duke Lector and dumped him unceremoniously onto the ground beside the others. He took a deep breath and said with unwavering conviction, "I do."

"Prove it."

"What?"

My eyes moved between the rampant forest and the bard standing there, waiting for me.

"Prove it," I repeated, lifting my paw toward him. He flinched, but I just grabbed the lizardkin's shoulder in camaraderie, smiling at his confused face. "Deal with *all* of this." I waved my free paw at the mayhem before us. "Meet with the nobles, file the reports, transport the prisoners to the Black Fortress, and *prove* it. You have only ever run your own domain, but the commander general deals with *everyone*. Do this, and I will accept your challenge. You can duel me for my job."

General Knolith picked my paw off his shoulders and daintily dropped it as he had the elven duke earlier. Then he cracked his neck and smiled, showing all of his sharp, pointy teeth. "Deal."

With a swish of his robes and the noble bearing of a leader, the lizardkin swept forward to join in the heated conversation between Lady Amy and Lady Hazelglade.

I waited half a second longer to make sure they didn't just throw him in the pile of prisoners with the rest; the Hollow elves were notorious for their independence. When Lady Amy happily welcomed the general and mentioned teaming up, I turned and walked away.

Quickly.

Out of the combat area and straight into Bronwynn's awaiting arms.

"I'm happy that *that* quest is done," I said, nose buried deep in her surprisingly dry hair. Behind me, a spy cursed as they were being detained by the knights, shouting something about being right all along and "I told you so." Turns out it wasn't just Barry who wasn't too keen on their current assignment.

Bronwynn looked over my shoulder. "Are you sure it's done? It doesn't look done to me?"

"General Knolith is handling it," I stated, pulling back and smiling at her. I took her hand and started walking down the road toward a nice inn with a tavern and a kitchen and a stage that I'd stayed in previously. "Shall we go grab dinner?"

A giant tendril traveled past us as I continued escorting Bronwynn down the main road, Donna following behind us. The wagon was somewhere in the chaos, but I didn't care to go back for it. That was tomorrow's Rufus's problem. Right now, I only cared about dinner and a bath and bed. In that order.

"I would *love* dinner," Bronwynn replied with feeling. It had been hours since we'd stopped for lunch. Donna neighed behind us, and Bronwynn added, "Yes, I'll buy you some of the special elven horse feed."

"What's so special about it?" I asked. The forest seemed to be calming down now, as less roots were combing the city and some even returned to their place in the ground, sinking back into the earth. As each root did so, a light tremor rumbled under our feet.

Brownie squeezed my arm and said, "Donna and I have sorted some things out, and I'm paying her in enchanted food now."

I looked over my shoulder at the horse, who managed to look both proud and sorry at the same time. And I didn't even speak horse. "Oh?"

"We had a good heart-to-heart, and our bond leveled up!" Bronwynn said, trying to reassure me.

I was *not* one to judge a murder horse in the secrets, since I didn't want to be a raging hypocrite. "Congratulations."

"Thanks," Bronwynn replied while Donna huffed, looking away.

"And here we are!" I opened a door just in time to catch a frying-pan-wielding elf innkeeper bent on protecting their inn from whoever was dumb enough to walk around during Lithnilheim's rampage. The tree was almost completely settled at this point, though, so I wasn't worried about more assassins or spies myself.

"Lovely to see you again, Hemlock," I said, lowering the pan as I gently pushed the elf aside so we could go in. "I'm looking for a room, and board for a horse."

Donna neighed again.

"And some of your best magical feed," I added, guessing what Donna was going to say even before Bronwynn translated.

"And a bath," my bard spoke up. "And dinner."

Hemlock lowered his pan and stared between the three of us. The tavern part of the inn was full of elves, a catkin, and a wolfman, all staring out the crescent windows deathly still.

Since he wasn't responding in a timely manner, not that I blamed him, I looked back at Donna and said, "The stable is over there, if you wanna go in out of the rain."

She didn't need to be told twice.

CHAPTER 112

Is It Morning Yet? Because I Refuse

Brownie

Brownie woke up wrapped in Rufus's arms. She curled into his embrace, grumbling, "Is it morning yet? Because I refuse."

A chuckle rumbled in his chest. "It's morning. I thought you were excited for the festival? Our Dark Lady is going to be here and—"

"Refuse," she repeated, pulling the blanket over her head to block out the morning sun.

Rufus leaned over and whispered in her ear, "We could go on a date. I have a few hours before Mistress Puma arrives and we start the search for the poisoner."

Brownie poked her nose above the blanket. "I guess I could be convinced."

Rufus laughed and kissed her nose before sliding out of bed. He was in his beast form, and pulled on his calf-length pants and a clean white tunic. Brownie stretched, wondering if she should wear the same outfit she wore yesterday. An elf maid had cleaned and dried her with skills while she waited for Rufus. Still, she thought, if they were going to go on a real date, she should dress up a bit more than her usual travel skirt.

She summoned a blue day dress from her storage ring and cinched it at the waist. The puffy princess sleeves pleased her, and the skirt fell to the calf. She pulled on an underskirt for a little bit of extra definition, and Rufus helped her tie a bow in her hair after she used a leather string to secure a half updo.

They swung by the washroom and were downstairs in under thirty minutes. Hemlock, the elf who owned this particular establishment, was busy checking in guests. The Hemlock Haven was a good inn, close to the town courtyard where the Green Oak Dungeon Gate was located.

Since the Hollow rarely welcomed visitors, and then only on festival days, the lineup of people who had arrived early this morning when they opened the city gate must've been impressive.

There were at least twenty people trying to secure lodgings.

"Let's grab food on the way." Rufus offered his arm, and they wandered off in search of sustenance. Donna seemed content to stand around eating her enchanted oats after her excitement yesterday, and bid Brownie to go have fun.

The street was *packed*, all manner of people from about the Dark Enchanted Forest wandering around the stalls shopping.

"I want that!" Brownie dragged Rufus over to a crepe stand where an elf was carefully making elaborate crepes with fresh fruit and berries and nuts. It was delicious.

"So, how long do you think it is going to take to find the poisoner?" Brownie asked, leaning her head in and whispering to her beastman.

"As long as it takes." He sighed. "Though the search is already started, since one of the units reached the other side of Green Oak and is sweeping the forests around the city."

"Then let's make the most of it. You said there was somewhere you wanted to take me?" Brownie smiled. The dark clouds of the day before were nowhere to be seen, and blue skies stretched out around the great oak canopy that stretched out over this part of the city.

She was scheduled to perform at the stage they had set up in the square that afternoon, and in the meantime, she wanted to see as much of the city as she could.

Rufus took her through the gardens and toward the main gate they had come through the previous day. Traffic going toward the city down the main road was steady, but they were alone as they walked back up the hill. It was a gentle slope, but it was still a hill, and when they were about three quarters back toward the gate, Rufus pulled her off the road and up a small path.

There were elderberry trees planted in a small crescent shape facing the city below. A bench was placed in the arc of the trees; a perfect place to sit and watch the city. The flowers were few due to the storm, but a few of the remaining happy blooms were open and facing the sun.

They sat on the bench, watching the festival and the gardens, the giant unassuming tree monster that could eat them all staying dormant and providing shade with its large canopy.

"Hey, Bronwynn," Rufus said casually, his arm wrapped around her, and their heads cuddled together watching the Hollow.

"Yes, Rufus?" She wondered if it was time for him to go hunt down a certain poisoner causing trouble for everyone. Brownie didn't have the heart to be angry at them, though; without them, she wouldn't have gotten to go on this adventure with Rufus.

The beastman was silent for a long second. "I love you."

"I love you, too." She looked at him, and he was blushing.

"I was thinking now would be the perfect time to make a grand confession." He squeezed her a bit closer.

"Alright, I'm ready." She nodded, waiting expectantly.

"Ever since you fell out of that tree—"

She was not one for violence, but she thwacked Rufus in the chest, catching him off guard. He was quoting the part of his romance novel that she'd sneaked a peak at back in Peldeep. "What—?"

"I thought you might like it." He was laughing and holding his side. "Since you were reading it so *intently.*"

She blushed, remembering the very racy scenes she'd opened up to. "How did you know?"

"I have an enchanted bookmark that keeps track of my reading history; doesn't everyone?" he asked, fully turning on the bench to face her.

"Do you need *me* to make the grand confession?" she demanded, flipping her hair over her shoulder in a power move that gave her strength. "Because I can do that. I can make the grandest confession ever, with music and lights and a live audience—"

"I love you, Bronwynn Lyriel," he interrupted, leaning forward and kissing her.

"You've said that," she retorted, her breath against his. Then she grabbed him and kissed him back.

When they broke for air, he said, "And I want to spend the rest of my life with you."

Brownie was grinning. "That's a good start."

"I can't imagine going back to a life without you," he confessed, pressing their foreheads together. "I can't imagine *anything* without you."

"Go on." She grabbed his hand and interlocked their fingers together.

"I love everything about you." He squeezed her hand. "I love your smile and your laugh and the way you snore—"

"Hey!"

"And I love the way you look at the world, full of adventure. I can't wait to start a new encounter with you every day." He kissed their hands and then disentangled their fingers so he could hold her palm in his.

He pulled out an ornate wooden ring intricately engraved in gold knotwork and set with rubies. "Please, Bronwynn, would you marry me?"

CHAPTER 113

I'm Going to Have to Eat Her

Rufus

I resisted kissing Bronwynn again long enough to hear her answer as she inspected the ring with a mix of joy and shock.

The ring was one of a pair I'd bought from the Pixie Prim in Gren's Keep. It was enchanted to fit, rounded on the edges, and flatter than some of the more popular styles. I chose it so it wouldn't impede Bronwynn playing her instrument, and because it reminded me of our colors; her red-tipped hair and my golden coat.

She dragged her eyes away and beamed at me, opening her mouth to answer, "Meow."

"Momo. Slake." Bronwynn released her breath, and her lips quirked into a sad half smile as I whipped my head around to look in the elderberry tree above us.

Two grimalcats lounged on a branch, a familiar black one with green eyes and horns and bat wings lying down and relaxing, and a brown one with golden eyes and horns and fluffy owl wings licking its paw.

"Not funny, Slake," I said, my voice slipping into a growl. I probably shouldn't have growled at a grimalcat, but I didn't care. I might've still been just a little bit bitter about him interrupting me back in Peldeep and dragging me off before Bronwynn and I could clear the air.

"You know"—Bronwynn reached out and put a hand on my cheek, guiding me to look at her instead—"I really like it when you do that. You should growl more." Then she kissed me one more time. It was short and sweet. Too short. She smiled. "Of course I'll marry you."

"Really?" I didn't know why I felt the need to question her at that moment. Probably the panic.

"What can I say?" Bronwynn poked me in the chest. "With beastmen, when you know you know."

After saying that, she looked up into the tree. "Momo, thank you for coming. We have a lot to talk about."

"We do," Momo replied, his voice softer and higher pitched than Slake's. He was so much fluffier than Slake, too, with a big poof of fur on his chest and wide eyes that made him look like he was permanently startled or confused. He took a step on the branch and slipped, but righted himself and tapped the branch twice as if saying he'd meant to do that.

I managed to keep a straight and respectable face.

Momo's poofy tail flicked twice and then he jumped down, landing in a patch of grass. Slake yawned and closed his eyes, choosing to remain in the tree.

"I'm sorry to say," I told Slake, "that you missed all the fun last night."

The grimalcat opened one eye. "If you think we were going to take one step into a magical rainstorm crafted by storm giants, then Intelligence must be your dump stat."

"It was truly dreadful. I could never," Momo agreed as he bound around to the front of the bench, sitting and staring at us with his very wide eyes.

"Good to know." I grimaced. "In case I ever need to escape a grimalcat."

Slake snorted. "There is no escape. We can *smell* your intent."

"It would make for a good hunt," Momo added. "Now, let me get a good look at you."

I held Bronwynn's hand while she exchanged a very long stare with the fluffy grimalcat, his eyes glowing a steady gold.

"Hmm . . . yes. I see," Momo said. Whatever magic he was doing had Bronwynn held fast.

What did I know about grimalcats? They saved children, dealt in lives, were incredibly powerful and fickle and rare.

And there were two right in front of me.

Momo sneezed and froze, his gaze going distant. We waited patiently.

Finally, the grimalcat sneezed a second time and was back. "You are living my life very well, but I don't like this part here. No, no at all. What a mess."

Bronwynn's face fell; she looked incredibly guilty. I regretted not going and lifting Donna here bodily. Where was the murder horse when you needed her?

"I'm sorry," my bard said.

"Mm." Momo blinked slowly, the light of his powers dimming. "I guess that is the way of things."

"What does that mean?" I asked.

"Momo," Slake called down from the tree, momentarily startling the brown grimalcat. Momo shivered in puffy consternation and gave Slake the side-eye.

"I know, I know. But I can't. Even for you, old friend," Momo argued. "There's no help for it; I'm going to have to eat her."

I stood up so fast it startled the cat. Momo's claws popped out, his hair rose, and he flinched. Bronwynn's hand on my arm held me back from doing something I might regret.

"You can't eat her," I spoke up, putting my own arm out to block my bard. Slake leapt down from the branch, walking over to the brown grimalcat, who looked like he was still a bit frazzled at my outburst. Momo glared at me with his wide eyes, and for some reason, my [Keen Senses] was warning me that I was in more trouble than when I'd watched Lithnilheim rampage across the city.

Slake circled Momo, and after a full turn around, sat beside him, facing the couple.

"Actually, technically, he can," Slake said.

Momo nodded, settling himself and looking around. His eyes caught on a white butterfly nearby but dragged themselves back to Bronwynn. "You have lived a wonderful life, have you not?"

"I have," Bronwynn assured the grimalcat.

"And followed your dreams?"

"Yes, but—"

"And then you broke your promise." Momo tilted his head to the side. "So I should eat you. You've got nothing left to lose."

"Momo," Slake spoke, fulfilling *his* promise to speak for us. "She did recently get engaged . . ."

"To a *dog*," Momo stressed, looking me over with disdain. "See, nothing left to lose."

"Well, that was rude," I stated.

Bronwynn sighed. "Rufus, I *did* break my promise."

"No," I stressed, "*Donna* broke your promise. Can she even *do* that?"

"Minstrel Bronwynn feels responsible," Slake explained. "Momo can feel it in her soul."

"I could eat the horse?" Momo mused, but then shook his head. "No, that still wouldn't change the way you feel."

"Wait." I realized something, lowering my arm. "Did you say *the way she feels*?"

Slake and Momo exchanged looks. Slake was the one who finally spoke. "Yes. As long as she feels responsible for her bonded companion's actions, her promise will be broken, and Momo's soul construct will demand payment."

"It is a shame; I really did like your music." Momo's tail twitched twice; the white butterfly was back and fluttering closer than ever. The grimalcat jumped up onto his hind legs and tried to grab it with his paw, batting a few times but not catching the butterfly. He landed on all fours and turned back to the bard. "Still, this is the end."

"Actually," I informed everyone, "it's not."

[You have activated **Mediator** title ability. +2 Charisma. Targets equal to or higher will recognize the title.]
[You have attempted to activate the Perk: **Calming Effect** against Minstrel Bronwynn. It was uncontested. **Calming Effect** was successful.]
[You have attempted to activate the Perk: **Inspire Honesty** against Minstrel Bronwynn. It was uncontested. **Inspire Honesty** was successful.]
[Passive Perk: **Empathy** still in effect.]

CHAPTER 114

I'm Not in an Abusive Relationship with My Horse

Brownie

It was an hour later, a bit past noon, and she was technically supposed to be performing right now.

Or already eaten.

She knew it'd been an hour because [Calming Effect] had worn off.

"Repeat after me," Rufus said, gently cupping her chin in his paw as they both sat facing the other on the bench. "*Donna is her own person.*"

"Donna is her own person."

"*I am not responsible for the actions of another.*"

"I am not responsible for the actions of another," she repeated, her eyes wandering off to the white butterfly as it fluttered about.

"This would be so much easier in a dungeon." Rufus sighed.

"This would be—" Brownie cut herself off, smiling. "You can take me to your dungeon another day. *Why* am I not at fault? I rode with her across the continent. I'm her bonded companion. I was *there.*"

"You *are* her bonded companion and you *were* there, sure, and you can be responsible for *your* actions and choices at that time. Namely, you didn't do anything." He tried again. As had happened for the last hour, Rufus would answer her question with a simple statement and then explain further using anecdotes. "When a person is in a healthy relationship, both parties give and take of each other. In a *toxic* relationship, one partner puts their needs above the other without consideration. When it devolves into one person *giving* pain, and the other partner *taking* blame, then it's moved into abuse. You *made* me do it. You *deserved* it. *You should have been better.*"

"I am *not* in an abusive relationship with my *horse*," Bronwynn protested.

"No," Rufus agreed, "But right now you are behaving as if you were. You *feel* that Donna abused your trust. That she purposefully did things behind your back."

"I . . . Sure, but that's not the same! I was the one who connected her with my family; I was the one who drove her places and provided her cover! I should've paid better attention! I was an *accessory* to an *assassination quest!*"

"Bronwynn." Rufus poked her playfully on the nose.

She covered it with both of her hands. "Hey."

"It wasn't your fault that I poked you on the nose, no matter how much your extremely cute and very pokable nose tempted me to do so. It was *my thinking and my choice.*"

"But that's *different!* You know the difference between right and wrong!" Bronwie argued. "Donna's a *horse!* She doesn't understand ethics! I should've been looking out for her, making sure she didn't go down the wrong path!"

"You are *still* assuming responsibility for your companion? Do you think it would have been better to limit her freedom so you could control her?"

"No! I . . ."

"You do not *own* Donna. Donna is her *own* person. You cannot be responsible for the actions of another person."

"Oh, I'm *certainly* not her owner," Brownie acknowledged, then sighed. "Or even a close friend."

After all that time they'd been together, Brownie thought she'd been closer to her horse. A Bond was still a bond. . . but they'd never really had the deep connection she'd hoped for. Brownie was Donna's half giantess, and Donna was Brownie's horse. That was just the way it was. And Donna had kept a healthy distance, with ample alone time granted to go *apparently* be an undercover assassin contract delivery mare.

Bonded companions were supposed to be friends of the heart, with a magic that bound the two in mind and spirit. Brownie hated how she'd had to corner her mare to tell her things, and that that had inspired the mare to finally open up.

Because Brownie had already loved her stupid horse.

Rufus repeated, "The person who was betrayed is not at fault. You are assuming guilt for the actions of another person because you feel responsible for her."

"Yes? But doesn't everyone take responsibility for the actions of their loved ones?" Brownie asked, discomfited.

"*No,*" Slake and Momo joined in, sounding offended, while Rufus gave his rebuke softly.

"Donna is not a child or a pet; she is her own person, and she makes her own choices. And if you think she isn't fully capable of being responsible for her actions, then I think we need to call her over here so you can actually talk to your bonded companion."

"Still . . ."

"If Jill burns down old Tammy's inn, it's nobody's fault but Jill's," Rufus said, using one of her favorite songs to repeat the same point.

"I only eat people who deserve it," Momo told Slake. "And Jill sounds delicious."

Funnily enough, it was what Momo said that finally sparked something in Brownie's subconscious. The grimalcat *did* eat people who were at fault, and it'd been almost a year since Donna had started delivering potions. If it'd truly been her fault . . . wouldn't Momo have come for her sooner?

"Close your eyes and repeat after me," Rufus repeated. "*Donna is her own person. I cannot be responsible for the actions of another.*"

Brownie repeated the words, and as she did, for the barest moment, she wondered if maybe Rufus was right. Brownie had made her stance, had accepted the horse's reasons, and felt guilty for *letting it happen* . . . but was she really at fault?

"She's got it," Momo spoke, and his large golden eyes that burned into her soul blinked slowly. "And nyaow I need to find something else to eat."

He sniffed once and got to his feet. The white butterfly was back, and he turned, his bum wiggling as he prepared to pounce.

In front of her, Rufus practically *deflated*, going from a supportive and relaxed counselor to an exhausted mess clinging to her shoulders in a desperate hug.

"Rufus?" Brownie reached up to put her arms around her beastman.

"Hmm," he grumbled into her collarbone.

"I'm late for my show," she pointed out. The festival was lively, but it lacked that musical touch.

Her beastman took another deep breath and then kissed her silly.

CHAPTER 115

Tracking the Lead

Rufus

"We have found the drop-off location," Chikli reported over Cast Crystal. The army had a few to use between units, and I was standing on top of the wall to the outer city as it trailed off into the dungeon tree roots. Behind Green Oak, there were trails and a lake and a small hill that could be seen peeking out of the regular forest.

"And?" I asked, looking out over the wood. Chikli's unit had spread out to search in a grid pattern North of the Hollow since yesterday. The group consisted primarily of lizardkin, who enjoyed the magical rain. They'd arrived too late to watch the Green Oak assault.

"We can't sssee anything," Chikli said. "It is as warned. The cave is hidden. Mage Lina is trying to find a way through the illusion now."

"Good." I nodded, turning and looking back at the city. It was in full festival mode, and I resisted a sigh. "I am going to check in with Mistress Puma."

I silenced the crystal then opened up the connection it had to the Tracker's unit. The Cast Crystals were designed to be able to connect to any other crystal that had been cast in the spell with it. You could connect to multiple crystals at once, but it was difficult to manage conversation. You could also pick and choose the crystal you wanted to call. Each crystal had its own small symbol that represented it, and you just needed to activate the symbol.

"Mistress Puma, reporting." The feline beastwoman's voice was rough, for all she was in her thirties. Gravelly and fierce. "I am still tracking the lead."

"Excellent." I had given Puma a bunch of poisons that had previously been picked up from the Dark Enchanted Forest when Donna was doing her deliveries. How had I found a bunch of poisons that were never delivered from the poisoner in the Dark Enchanted Forest? Easy, Donna had stolen them.

That horse had a real problem; she wasn't paying taxes on her stolen wares. That was going to be more paperwork for me, and an audit for the murder horse conducted by some poor unsuspecting member of the Dark Horde's accounting unit.

I resisted another sigh.

"Where is it taking you?" I used my [Keen Senses] to focus my sight on movement far off. Puma's unit was mostly hidden behind the giant roots of the forest, as she'd started near the suspected drop-off location on the northeast side of Green Oak and then tracked her way west.

I was going to need to head that way myself.

"West. The trail is sticking very closely to the roots and heading towards the Hollow," Puma said.

"Less likely to suddenly find yourself in some other part of the forest," I agreed. "I'll swing around from the front of the tree, and we can meet up en route."

"Alright, Commander General."

I cut the connection before pocketing the crystal in my dimensional storage. To better travel in comfort, I shifted into my beast form. The fact that the poisoner didn't just run there from across another kingdom to pick up and drop off like Donna did was a stroke of luck. Also that it wasn't a flying creature who wouldn't leave much of a trail.

Puma *could* track a flying foe, but it would have taken a lot more time.

I jumped off the city wall and onto the roof of a nearby house. If I wanted to cross the city quickly, I wasn't going to be running through the city streets. The idea of navigating festival crowds made me want to vomit. Instead, I bounded across rooftops and leapt high over the city square. My landing was gentle as I kicked off again, making my way to the western wall.

Since Puma wasn't just running at full speed to get into position and instead carefully tracking the poisoner through the woods, I arrived at the wall well in advance of the beastwoman. I changed back into my usual beastman form, resisting the urge to sit on the edge of the wall and take a break before they arrived.

I was the commander general of the Dark Enchanted Forest, and that meant I should probably be ready to meet them properly.

Not relaxing with a romance novel.

When Puma arrived a few minutes later, assisted by two other beastfolk, I was still waiting on the wall, feet apart, shoulders back, and hands on my hips.

"I've sent the rest back to do a second sweep," she explained when I stared at her two assistants.

"Alright, what did you find?"

Mistress Puma and the others leapt onto the wall with ease. This would normally be the point where thirty Hollow elf soldiers descended on anyone who even got close to the wall, but they were on official business. The beastwoman pulled out a frayed, muddy piece of string and let me examine it. "I found this half buried in dead leaves and caught on a fallen branch. It has the same faint trace as the poison bottles."

"Then lead on." I took a step aside and waved her forward.

She nodded, jumping down into the outskirts of the Hollow. There was one big street lined with stunning wooden architecture and a mix of living treehouses that stretched in an arc with the roots of the Green Oak, but there were some smaller houses and shops two to four streets deep on the inner circle side.

Puma trekked through the smaller streets, around a local food stall with a vendor who looked like she'd rather be *anywhere* else—probably the festival— and then to a half-moon house built around an oak tree.

The beastwoman walked up to a door and sniffed. "This is it. I'm certain of it."

I reached out and knocked on the door.

Nothing.

I knocked again, louder.

"Mia isn't home," the food vendor called out from three doors down. She stressed the beginning, the name sounding like "My-ah."

We all turned to look at the elf woman, who seemed a little intimidated despite being a healthy distance away. She said, "Mia's dungeon delving right now. She won't be back for at least an hour, maybe more."

"She's an adventurer?" I asked, slowly walking over to the elf. I was much taller than her, and I sighed when she shrank back. She suddenly squinted at me, and I thought that my occupation was probably the only thing keeping her from running away.

"N-no, Commander General." She shook her head a few times. She didn't bow or nod her head in greeting. The elves were a proud race, and they considered themselves equal to the most powerful members of the Dark Horde. Even food shopkeepers. It was one of my favorite cultural nuances about the Hollow. The elf continued. "She's a porter."

I raised my eyebrows at that but smiled. "Thank you."

She blushed, but I only nodded and turned back to the group. The pit in my stomach tightened as I ordered, "Everyone, we will wait at the dungeon gate. And someone go tell Slake that we've got something."

CHAPTER 116

So What Did I Miss?

Brownie

Minstrel Bronwynn, Lady Amy, and Queen Henrietta all sat round a table at Brownie's inn.

The bard *had* arrived late to her two-hour show, and was only able to play for one hour of her set.

It was better than the alternative, being eaten by a grimalcat.

"Keith found me a magical door for our rooms!" Henrietta downed an entire jug of beer, slamming it down at the end of her story. The fluffy brown-haired ruler of all evil had found Brownie at the end of the show and dragged her off for lunch. "Now, I don't need to summon maids to fetch me things or wander the halls in my housecoat! Our closets are connected."

"That's perfect. Now you'll stop waking me up, coming and going every time I visit," Brownie teased her friend. The queen's suite of rooms had an office, wardrobe, private bath, lounge, entry, and a spare room for a maid or visiting family. Technically, if the queen ever took a lover, it could be used for that as well, but Henrietta and Keith were so in love she couldn't see it happening in this reign.

Keith's mother, however, had been known to have a few lovers, and no one knew who King Keith's father was.

Lady Amy sighed. "As for me, I've memorized all of the laws you sent me, and I'm standing up for my free time!"

"That's wonderful, Amy." Henrietta beamed at the elf saintess.

"Even today." Lady Amy nodded. "I've had to stand at the dungeon door as a figurehead before, praying from the beginning of the festival until the end. It was *the worst.*"

Brownie took the last bite of her garlic-and-cheese twist. She'd ordered a creamy pesto and herb pasta with baked floofpoof bird, and was almost finished with the delicious spread. Then the bard had a thought.

"Is this a ceremony to Lithnilheim required by the Dark Enchanted Forest itself? Will the forest be angry that you didn't stand there—not saying that you should!" Brownie quickly added, not trying to dampen the elf's happiness. "I'm just saying that after last night, I wouldn't want the forest upset."

"Lithnilheim does not care one *whit* about me standing there like an idiot for twelve hours while everyone celebrates late into the night," Lady Amy declared, sounding very sure of herself.

"How do you know?" Henrietta asked, curious. She grabbed a handful of nuts from a bowl on their table and started munching.

"Because he told me." Lady Amy shrugged. "I let him know when I thanked him last night, and he pretty much said that me *not* overworking myself was great, and I should have a wonderful time enjoying the festival for once. Isn't that so sweet?"

"Very." The bright smile and shining eyes of the young elf maiden made Brownie chuckle. She was talking about a dungeon boss monster who ate people, but honestly, that was very generous of the forest. The workplace regulations for Drendil were nonexistent the last time Brownie checked—though that was changing under the new leadership. Servalt and Peldeep had very guild-based economies that included most people living their jobs. Only North Sumbria and the Dark Enchanted Forest had so many benefits designed for the everyday working creature.

"Besides," Lady Amy added, "Lithnilheim will be enjoying playing with the adventuring parties today, since they'll be letting anyone in to challenge the dungeon."

That, as Brownie knew, was a part of the fun of the festival. Every few hours, adventurers would exit the dungeon and bring with them strange treasures, and show off whatever unique find they'd managed to snag. Henrietta had even mentioned her hope to compete before dinnertime.

"What about you, Brownie?" Henrietta waggled her eyebrows, glancing at the bard's ring finger. "How are things going with you and Rufus?"

"You mean aside from you hiring him to stalk me?" Brownie asked with pretend sweetness.

The queen had the grace to look bashful. "Technically, I was sending him to prove your innocence—which he *did*."

"That he did," Brownie smiled warmly and then flashed everyone her left hand. "And I'd say we are doing just fine."

"Is that?!" Henrietta leaned forward to admire the ring, while Lady Amy said, "Oh my, congratulations Brownie!"

At that point, Gerda hurried into the pub. She was wearing a white dress with beautiful magnolia-print flowers on the hem of the skirt and the same flowers woven into a crown on top of her loose flowing green hair. Brownie had never seen the troll's hair down before, and it fell like tight waves from the braids all the way down to her thighs. Henrietta was also dressed up for the day, wearing a light blue summer dress and matching bow in her hair. Brownie was wearing a red dress and vest, with her lyre harp on a strap hung over her shoulder.

The troll pulled up a chair to a chorus of welcomes. "So, what did I miss?"

"Brownie got engaged to Rufus, Lady Amy got the go-ahead from the spirit of the Dark Enchanted Forest to enjoy the festival instead of standing around praying all day, and I am happily married," Henrietta paraphrased.

"His Viciousness made a door connecting their rooms." Brownie laughed. "How about you, Gerda?"

"I'm doing alright." The troll sighed. "I don't care *how* much money it's going to cost me; I'm not taking a single step onto my dumb bridge until after the festival."

The rest of them shared a look.

Henrietta reached out and patted the troll woman on the arm. "That bad?"

"I had to reinforce *six* bridges so they wouldn't float away in the floods, and *actually* hold off a young lord from Sumbria who was determined to make it to the festival. When I told him he was going to have to wait for the repairs first, he accused me of trying to eat him or something." The troll rubbed her temple. "I barely managed to stabilize the bridge and magic him a riddle before he tried to run pass me. The bridge almost collapsed under us!"

"Wow," Henrietta commiserated. "You never use your riddle magic, so I can imagine it must have been dreadful."

"And *worse!*" Gerda dragged a hand down her green face, careful of her tusks. "He couldn't solve it!"

"What was the riddle?" Lady Amy leaned forward, intrigued.

"I was angry and gave him a harder one," the bridge troll admitted, looking sheepish.

> "What Binds the Day to the Sun,
> And Turns out Night into Space,
> What Holds the Stars in the Sky,
> What keeps the Moon in her place."

The table was quiet, though Brownie thought she knew. Lady Amy asked the question, so she answered first. "The gods?"

Gerda shook her head.

Brownie smiled, and so did Henrietta. They shared a knowing look, and both said, "Gravity."

The bard didn't want to say that it was actually pretty easy if you had any experience with gravity magic, but *she* only had that experience because overcoming gravity-based traps was a part of her assassin training.

"If everyone's done eating." Henrietta stood up. She gripped her hand and gave one excited fist pump. "Then let's go to the festival! And don't think you're off the hook Brownie, I still want to hear everything about your proposal!"

CHAPTER 117

There's Mia Now

Rufus

The only thing that made marching through the Hollow bearable was the fact that being commander general was noticeable enough for people to give me space. There were more than just elves in the Hollow today, and the rest of the forest visitors were respectful of my title.

Otherwise, it would have been impossible. As it stood, I was merely uncomfortable.

I smiled at the crowd and nodded my thanks as people parted for us.

I'd missed Brownie's performance while meeting up with the Dark Horde, and currently, there was a band of pixies playing flutes while five elven women performed a dance with flower vine whips.

The Green Oak Dungeon had a half-moon circle platform around the door where adventurers stood waiting for their turn to face the dungeon. I deliberately walked onto the platform to wait, granting me that extra separation from the crowd below. The willpower it took to ignore my notification tab *and* experience the full smell, taste, and sound of two hundred people with my [Keen Senses] was a nightmare.

"Mistress Puma." I waved at the pulsing gate. "Do you think you could identify our poisoner when she comes through?"

The beastwoman straightened. "I can."

"Then we will wait."

It was a half hour standing with the rest. Three times the gate shimmered with a bright green light and a party exited onto the platform, but Mistress Puma shook her head each time. It wasn't the party with three human mages, an elf paladin, and a ratkin sword fighter. And it wasn't the party of two wolf beastmen, a human healer, and an older elf porter. The third party, all elven adventurers from Sumbria if I judged them correctly by their cuff buttons, also had an elven porter.

I hailed one of the parties that were waiting for their turn. The leader, a preela with a greatsword at the ready, also had a porter waiting at the back of their party. "Excuse me, but are there porters for hire around here?"

"Yes, Commander General." The preela bowed politely. "There are a few still standing by the dungeon registry." The preela pointed through the crowd to where a table was set up under a shade with three Hollow elves manning it. To the left stood two elves with packs under a sign that read "Porters for Hire."

I coughed. "Thank you."

The porter who was now hiding at the back of the party looked at me with trepidation. I tried to approach the elf gently. "You're from the Hollow, yes?"

"I am already hired!" the elf squeaked, waving his hands in front of his chest and sending glances to the preela, begging for help. I sighed. This happened sometimes; whether a proud elf or a stalwart lizardkin, when faced with my title, they panicked and made assumptions. At least I knew to be patient.

"I do not need a porter," I reassured him. "I just have a question."

The elf relaxed a bit. "Alright. How can I help the commander general?"

"I'm looking for a porter named Mia?" I stabbed my thumb over my shoulder at the gate. "I'm just wondering if she's still inside?"

"She is!" The elf nodded. "She's with the Star Striker party. They have two front liners, Jerry and Mitch, and a vanguard named Paul. Their healer is a catkin named Nolan, and they have a lilith named Lily."

"Thank you," I said, expecting that to be the extent. I wasn't prepared for the elf to keep going.

"Jerry is an elf for the Yarrow clan, and he specializes in tanking. His primary focus is . . ."

The elf kept talking while I stood there, awkwardly trying to find a pause in the conversation that would let me politely escape. Porters, on top of being carriers for dungeon loot, sometimes acted as dungeon guides. They memorized floor plans and spawn times, and which creature was weak to which attack. They also kept track of the parties' strengths and weaknesses, experience points, loot division, and mana and health, often standing in as the healer if a party didn't have one, or taking care of the healer if they did.

Finally, the elf himself saved me by pointing over my shoulder. ". . . and he will buy every crinkle dewdrop you find—Ah, there's Mia now."

I spun in place, and Mistress Puma was immediately by my side, activating some skill or perk on the thread she'd picked up in the forest. It glowed faintly and lifted into the air, pointing at the party that had just come through the dungeon gate.

They were laughing and full of comradery, an elven paladin patting an elven fighter on the shoulder and saying something that made the two smile brighter. There was another elf, and the catkin and lilith, and coming in from behind was a small elf porter.

To my shock, Mia appeared to be only twelve years old. Her green skin was a softer shade, like a pastel, and her short dark-brown hair was puffier than Queen Henrietta's, if that were possible. The young girl was wearing a thigh-length green dress, with the fashionable cut of the skirt imitating a leaf, and tight leggings tucked into sturdy boots. Mia smiled at something the lilith said, pushing her wide circle-frame glasses up her nose. I couldn't see what color her eyes were, as the sun glinted off of the overly large frames.

She was easily carrying a pack four times her own size on her back.

Mistress Puma stepped forward toward the girl, and the light of the thread got brighter. The leader of the group, the paladin Jerry, immediately noticed Puma's approach. He stepped between the frowning beastwoman and the porter, a pretend smile on his face.

"Excuse me, but my porter is not available right now. We have yet to sort our loot, and I would appreciate it if you gave her some space."

"What? No—" Mistress Puma began.

Jerry cut her off, pointing toward the registry booth. "You may find your own porter over there. Good day."

I also stepped forward. With our conversation now drawing everyone's attention, I felt the stares and the sweat running down my back.

"We are not looking for a porter," I announced, calmly and only loud enough for the group or anyone with a skill to hear. "We are here to detain Mia for questioning, under orders."

Jerry frowned and shifted his weight so that he was fully blocking the young elf, who looked confused and terrified. "If you would detain a Hollow elf, I would ask that *your king* go through the proper channels. Duke Briarthorn can take her, or no one."

It was a show of rebellion against the kingdom, but I did not hold it against the elf. The entire situation was unfortunate, and I was already going to look like the villain in the eyes of the insular elves.

"Party Leader Jerry Yarrow," I announced, pulling out a magical writ and unrolling it for the elf to see the glowing signatures. "I am here on behalf of the Continental Council. Mia is coming with me."

Jerry looked between me and the elf girl, and I could tell that even as I waved the magical sheet of paper in his face, he was still probably going to stand firm.

"It's fine, Jerry," a voice piped up behind me, and I turned to see Lady Amy walking up the stairs to the platform. "I will stay with Porter Mia and make sure she has a representative."

Bronwynn, Henrietta, and Gerda were at the bottom of the stairs, with my queen waving hello and my bard holding a bag of nuts. Gerda was saying something to the queen that made the human girl laugh.

"Then I will entrust her to you. Sorry, Mia." Jerry took a step aside, and the lilith gently pushed the girl forward until she walked free of the party. The catkin man reached out for the pack when Mia unclipped her chest strap and let the bundle fall. The catkin caught the pack, and then promptly fell over, crushed under the weight of it. Jerry and another elf stepped forward to help.

"Please keep my herbs safe, Lily . . ." the girl begged, tears in her eyes, as Lady Amy took her by the arm and escorted her toward the palace.

Overhead, I spotted my missing partners in crime as two grimalcats momentarily blotted out the bright afternoon sun.

CHAPTER 118

Her Own Grimalcat

Brownie

Lady Amy followed Rufus to the palace because she was representing the young elf girl as the future duchess of the Hollow.

Queen Henrietta followed Rufus to the palace because she was the queen, and she should probably hear what the verdict was.

Momo and Slake flew to the palace because they were grimalcats, and they could go wherever they wanted. *Technically*, Slake was going to report everything back to Their Royal Highness, so he needed to be there.

Gerda and Brownie followed Rufus to the palace because they were nosy.

It wasn't every day that an international criminal who could single-handedly bring about the fall of nations was captured. Molten ash vane was one of the deadliest poisons known to kind, even if no one had been permadeathed yet, surprisingly but not surprisingly, because Madame Potts alone had prevented half of the poisonings with her predictions.

Brownie knew she probably wasn't going to see much, but she could be nearby. For moral support.

They all piled into the entry of the palace with the grand staircase that Rufus had been fighting on the night before. The doors closed behind them, blocking out the sound of the festival so severely that it was suddenly, startlingly silent.

The elf girl flinched and promptly burst into tears.

"I'm sorrrrrry," she wailed. Somehow, Brownie got the feeling that Mia had no idea what she was apologizing for and was just afraid.

"Mia." Lady Amy patted the girl's arm that was still linked with her own. "We just have a few questions for you, that's all."

"B-But I'm in t-trouble, right?" the girl sputtered through her tears.

Rufus sighed. "Porter Mia, we are here on behalf of the Continental Council to ask you about the molten ash vane."

"R-Really?" The girl rubbed her eyes with her free hand, calming down a little. "Is that all?"

Gerda choked beside Brownie. The bridge troll had no self-restraint whatsoever and was sucking on an apple fruit leather she'd acquired from somewhere.

"Got any more of those?" she whispered, accepting the snack produced and promptly sucking on the end to see how the flavor was. It was apple with a hint of strawberry. Perfection. She passed one to Henrietta as well. For a queen, Henrietta was very unassuming, and happily joined the two of them at the back of the group.

Mia fixed her glasses from where she'd knocked them askew rubbing her eyes. "I t-took over my nana's job making p-p-potions after she p-passed away last year. I've tried to make one for each delivery, but sometimes, I don't have enough . . ."

"That's what I want to ask." Rufus's eyes were scrunched closed like he had a headache during the girl's backstory reveal, but he tried to smile at the elf while speaking to her. He even handed over a kerchief. "*Why* are you making molten ash vane?"

"It's in my nana's recipe b-book." The girl accepted the cloth and blew her nose. Her face was a blotchy dark green from crying. "She told me to make what I could and leave a bag at the drop-off spot when I had ten bottles. I c-can only make molten ash vane when I have the ingredients, b-but they are rare. I have some now, from the d-dungeon. If you give me a d-day, I'll make you one?"

Rufus sighed. "Did you know"—the little girl looked up at him through her big glasses, eager to help—"that molten ash vane is an illegal poison that was banned from production and sale by all guilds across the continent?"

Mia's face blanched. "What?"

"And you're the lead felon in an international criminal investigation, with an arrest warrant from the Continental Council itself?"

"N-No—" The girl was crying again and having difficulty breathing. She looked down because Slake was winding his way around her legs. He bound over to sit in front of Rufus, facing the girl.

Brownie frowned. Poor Rufus was quest bound to retrieve the poisoner.

"There is a way," the grimalcat said. "Pick me up."

Lady Amy let Mia go so the elf girl could do as she was told, holding the large grimalcat in her small arms. She calmed a bit as she started to pet him gently. The grimalcat purred contentedly.

"You know the council is expecting the poisoner brought before them before the end of the month," Rufus stated, balling his paw into a fist before relaxing it at his side. "And Nilheim could lose our place on the council for refusing to turn her in."

"Is that true?" Henrietta whispered to Brownie.

"Mm-hmm." Brownie nodded, taking another bite of her fruit leather. A maid appeared at the top of the stairs, saw them, and hurried off.

"It's not the end of the world," Lady Amy argued. "When we explain what happened, I'm sure—"

Slake looked at Mia. "Child. What is your name?"

"Mia Underbush," she replied.

"You may call me Slake. I can take Lady Amy to represent you at the Continental Council." Slake nodded. "But you must promise me that you will never make molten ash vane again."

The grimalcat's eyes glowed a strange green, and Brownie glanced at her own grimalcat whom she'd also made a promise to. Momo was staring at a painting of the duke and duchess of the Hollow that was over the doorway behind her. They were sitting on a familiar bench, with baby Lady Amy in their arms. And a white butterfly fluttering beside some flowers.

"A-Alright." Mia nodded her head, pressing her tearstained face into Slake's furry back. The grimalcat let her.

"And you will familiarize yourself with the law so you know what you are and *are not* allowed to make," Slake continued, his eyes getting dimmer and almost back to normal.

The elf girl continued nodding, pausing only a few seconds later to blow her nose very loudly into Rufus's handkerchief.

Brownie exchanged looks with Rufus, sending a reassuring smile and subtle thumbs-up.

"Then we have an agreement." The grimalcat smiled. He looked at Rufus. "I'll take responsibility for the child. Lady Amy and I can meet you at the Summer Masquerade Council Meeting. Unless you have any complaints?"

"I have a complaint!" Duke Briarthorn stood at the top of the stairs.

CHAPTER 119

I Have Dungeon Plants

Rufus

"Duke Briarthorn." I nodded at Lady Amy's father as he descended the stairs.

"Don't you speak to me!" The duke's stern voice barely held back his anger. "What is this about Amy going to the Summer Masquerade? Absolutely not."

"Father, I'm of an age to attend—"

"No." The duke swept his hand in anger. "I've followed the law and given you leave from your responsibilities enough. You will stay here and do your duty."

"My duty is to my people," Lady Amy said, frowning.

"Then why are you standing here and not serving the festival?" her father countered, looking over them all. His anger only faltered when he saw the grimalcats, but resumed when he looked at the crowd at his door. "Is that troll the poisoner? Or the giant? Your Viciousness, please remove them from my sight."

Henrietta opened her mouth to reply, but before she could say otherwise, she was cut off by the elf girl. "Actually, it's m-me, Your Grace." She even shifted to free a hand and awkwardly wave at the duke.

"What?" That shocked the older elf, who examined the girl in confusion.

"I-I am the p-poisoner," she said, quickly returning to hugging Slake.

"Good job, Mia. That's my courage." The grimalcat nodded, approving. Slake's voice took on an echoing sound as he spoke to the duke, like he was under a spell. "The girl has promised her good behavior, and Lady Amy will be coming with me to the Summer Masquerade."

The duke drew a deep breath. I was worried that he was going to lose his temper, but instead, he released it and adopted a calmer expression. It had been a trying time for the elf, having almost died yesterday, and he was notorious for being an overprotective father.

It was the reason Lady Amy, who was of an age with the rest of us, had never joined Keith as a playmate. When Feliwyn the Dragon had visited looking for powerful children to join their Dark Lord, Duke Briarthorn had fought back tooth and nail. He'd signed more concessions to the Black Fortress than any Hollow elf had in centuries.

Ironically, that same document he'd signed was what allowed Lady Amy a four-day workweek and the freedom to do as she pleased with her spare time. King Keith had been working with the elves in a closer capacity than any ruler of the Dark Enchanted Forest before him.

And the elves hated it.

"Everybody out," the duke ordered. "I would speak with my daughter and the noble grimalcat, Slake Drakeford, alone."

The duke took a second to bow to the brown grimalcat in respect but did not afford the rest of us more than a cursory frown. I almost debated insisting proper decorum for my queen, but she was happily eating a fruit leather and didn't seem to mind.

Slake jumped from Mia's arms and walked over to the duke, looking up at the elf with disinterest. It didn't bother me one bit. Instead, I could have cheered.

"Do you have any cream?" he asked. "I would have cream and a side of fish."

"What about Mia?" Lady Amy asked, walking over to join her father at the bottom of the stairs.

The duke looked between the girl and the grimalcat. "If she is promised by you, then she may go. But don't leave the city until I give you leave."

"What about my contract?" the girl panicked, and then realized she'd questioned her lord and blushed.

"My horse has been the one picking up your poisons," Bronwynn piped up from beside the door. The minstrel spared a look at her own grimalcat, staring blankly at a wall, and continued. "After you've read up on the law, she will come and grab your delivery from your house instead."

"With that, we will be out of your hair." I nodded a polite goodbye to the duke and walked over to open the palace door. Gerda, Henrietta, Bronwynn, Mia, Momo, and myself all exited back into the crush of the festival.

Bronwynn immediately sidled up to me and linked arms. "Does that mean you can come join us?"

I stared out at the crush of people happily celebrating with candy apples and dancing and music. A mage had set up in the street, making animal bubbles for the children, and a dwarf with [Control: Size] was growing as tall as a building and giving rides.

Henrietta and Gerda were reassuring the young Mia that she was going to be alright, and even offered to walk her back to the porter area to collect her dungeon materials. Gerda insisted.

"I have to check in with my scouts," I said, already seeing Mistress Puma making her way back to me with a candy apple in her hand. "But then I should be free. What did you have in mind?"

If there was a way to love this woman more, then I found it, because she smiled at me softly and said, "Why don't we go for a walk in the gardens?"

"That is perfect." I leaned in and kissed her cheek.

It wouldn't take too long to explain to Puma what had happened. It would *have* to be quick, since I noticed her eyes were already locked on Mia. I caught the wink that Gerda gave Bronwynn as she and Henrietta dragged Mia off, waving goodbye as they blended into the crowd.

"Did I ever tell you," I asked my bard, blushing but also amused at her friend's antics, "that I have dungeon plants?"

"Really?" she asked.

"I just repotted my baby aloe vera." The plants were great for living in the dungeon, where they only needed a little bit of sunshine from the barred window. "And my new myrtle tree was in full bloom when I left on this quest . . . I can only imagine the mess my office is going to be in when I get back."

"So when you said that it would be easier if I joined you in your dungeon, you meant cleaning up flower petals?" Bronwynn teased. "Because I volunteer."

My bard wagged her eyebrows at me such that I couldn't help it: I burst into laughter.

"Alright," I agreed. "But let's clean up this mess first."

CHAPTER 120

How Do You Have 407 Notifications?

Brownie

Brownie let Donna pull them along the Great Road toward the Black Fortress while she played her instrument and sang a lively song. Tammy's Tavern.

> She smokes like a dragon, poison in the flagon
> She keeps all your change for a tip
> She won't wash the dishes, or debone the fish
> She slaps ya for given her lip
> So tonight is the night friend,
> We'll give her a fine end,
> One long overdue, gather round!
> By spell or the sword, if you're in get on board
> And we'll burn the place down to the ground,
> We'll burn the place down to the ground.

They'd left the Hollow first thing in the morning. Gerda had teleported home the previous evening, and Henrietta had taken off at a run right after breakfast. Brownie had offered her a ride, but the queen had taken one look at Donna and adamantly refused. Granted, horses made Henrietta sneeze, so she wouldn't have had a very fun ride.

The queen might not be there when Brownie and Rufus rolled in, since King Keith had plans to fly the two over to North Sumbria. They wanted to get there early to help with any last-minute wedding preparations.

Brownie had been hired to play at their wedding, and she was incredibly as one of the most brilliant minds in a hundred years. A visit to North Sumbria was like walking into a world of strange, useful inventions, from magical switch lights to self-driving carriages to rooms that lifted you into the sky between floors of her elaborate palace.

And this would be the second time in a year that Brownie was going to be able to play for the Grand Duchess . . . and hopefully, this time she wouldn't be kidnapped midset.

She and Rufus were making good time, aided by the fact that in six hours of travel, they'd *not had a single encounter*. Brownie didn't worry; she had a day or two between the Hollow and North Sumbria to figure it out.

Brownie did worry when they were approaching the turnoff for the Black Fortress. Even though she couldn't see the turnoff, she knew it was there. How? Because suddenly, her beastman stiffened and closed his eyes like he was in pain. She plucked a calming background piece as, over the course of ten minutes, Rufus slowly relaxed.

When his tail started to wag again, she asked, "Is it a perk?"

"What?" He opened his eyes, breathing deep and blinking a few times.

"The reason you hate crowds so much?" She stopped playing and set Danielle aside.

"I mean." He shrugged. "I just have a *lot* of notifications to process. It's a bit of a hassle."

"How much is a lot?" She leaned forward and grabbed Donna's reins. She could see the turnoff now, and it was less conspicuous if she pretended to be driving.

"Four hundred and seven."

Brownie's eyebrows shot up as she leaned back to stare at the beastman.

"Four hundred and seven?"

"Yes."

"*Four hundred and seven?*"

"Yes?" Rufus rubbed the back of his neck, rueful. "Why?"

"That's disgusting." Brownie crossed her arms. "No wonder you look like someone stabbed you in the kidney."

"How do you know—"

"Knife training. I've seen a lot of things. Now, *why* do you have four hundred and seven notifications?"

Rufus shrugged. "I am the right hand of the king, and in charge of the security of the Black Fortress. That means my abilities keep track of the personnel within the castle. I have notifications about the movement of the army, the well-being of the citizens, follow-ups with the patients I've mediated before, and—"

He stopped, seeing the horror that played across Brownie's face.

"And you process that many notifications . . . *every day?*" She suddenly wanted to give her beastman a very big hug.

Rufus shrugged. "Give or take."

"That's . . . I don't know what to say. Do you want a hug?"

He smiled and threw an arm around her, leaning in closer on the carriage front bench. "I would never say no to a hug from *you*."

"Tease." She poked him in the side with a finger, but then slid her hand behind his back and leaned into him. "I love you."

"I love you too."

The Black Fortress loomed ahead. It was very black and very imposing, with a moat surrounding the tall black stone walls. The bridge was wide, leaving room for two large golems to guard either side of the gateway into the castle.

And standing in the middle of the path was a familiar lizardkin, looking incredibly pleased with himself.

Rufus leaned over and whispered in her ear, "Do you think Gerda is having to pay for him standing there, or does it only count if he decides to cross the bridge?"

"Cross the bridge, I think," she replied. "He hasn't technically stepped onto the bridge yet, so she might not be charged at—Spoke too soon."

The lizardkin took a step forward to block their path. His hands were on his hips, as was his sword, and he announced with his usual grandeur, "Commander General Rufusss Triever, I challenge you to a duel!"

"Alright."

"You can't talk your way out of—What?" The lizardkin must have had no faith in Rufus's promise, since he'd obviously expected the beastman to refuse.

"I accept your challenge." Rufus hopped down from the wagon and walked over to Knolith. When he was within punching distance, the beastman raised one paw. Knolith flinched, but Rufus simply placed his hand on the lizardkin's shoulder and smiled at him. "Let's do it right now."

"You're seriousss?" General Knolith asked, eyeing Rufus suspiciously.

"Completely," Rufus confirmed. "You defeat me, and I'll step down from my position *and* not compete at the upcoming Winter Solstice Tourney."

General Knolith purposefully shrugged off Rufus's hand and took a step back. "You're making light of my abilitiesss. *Again*. But we will see who has the last laugh!"

With that, the lizardkin turned on his heel and marched toward the training grounds of the castle.

Brownie jumped down to join Rufus as he followed Knolith. The lizardkin's robes swooshed in a breeze reserved only for the swordsman.

"*That* must be a perk, right?" Brownie whispered to Rufus. "Or a passive skill?"

Donna snorted.

"Oh, that's a perk. Definitely. A waste of one, in my opinion," Rufus agreed, reaching out and taking her hand as they walked.

Behind them, news of the fight spread like mage fire. People closed up shop and gathered, and a single imp flying over the fortress saw the commotion and teleported away.

CHAPTER 121

Knolith Unclasped His Belt

Rufus

[You have attempted to use the Skill: **Examine**. You have succeeded. Six targets may be observed. **Knolith Stardancer** selected. Target is under observation. Predictive analysis: 44%. Available predictions: attack trajectory and perk activation.]

With the time it took to slowly roll up to the bridge, cross it, banter, and gather a crowd at the training yard, I'd had ample time to load [Examine]. Touching Knolith on the shoulder had even accelerated the progress by five percent.

When I was sitting beside Bronwynn on a bench outside the practice ring, people still gathering around and filling the stands, a magical portal opened up on the castle patio above. The king of the Dark Enchanted Forest and his Dark Lady jumped through the hole one after the other, landing on their feet.

"That is way better than crawling." King Keith pulled each of his robe sleeves to neaten them, and then offered his hand to his wife. They linked fingers and looked down on the crowd.

I, and everyone else, stood in respect to the king and queen of Nilheim.

"You are gathered here today," the Dark Lord announced, his voice echoing over the area, "to witness the battle for the position of commander general of the Dark Enchanted Forest."

A clamor of talking and some cheers broke out among the stands. Henrietta took up the announcing, and her voice too resounded across the crowd. "As we all know, those who come out as champion of the Winter Solstice Tourney stand as commander general of the Dark Enchanted Forest for one year. They have the right to stand for a year, and no one may force their hand."

"Rufus Triever." Keith took up the next part of the ceremony. "Do you, of your own accord, accept the challenge made by Knolith Stardancer? To forfeit unto the winner the status Commander General of the Dark Enchanted Forest?"

"I do, Your Viciousness," I stated. Bronwynn squeezed my hand in support. Henrietta looked at my opponent.

"And do you, Knolith Stardancer, hold to your duel? That should you prove the victor, you will swear fealty unto us, rightful rulers of Nilheim, as our Commander General?"

"I do, Your Viciousnesss." Knolith clasped a fist in front of his heart then let his hands drop, turning to face me with a fierce glare.

"Then it is by the power invested in us that we announce this duel officially approved." Henrietta lost her pretend serious expression for a second, her face transforming into an excited smile. "Combatants, to the ring."

Knolith unclasped his belt and shouldered off his outer robe, letting the beautiful silk garment fall to the bench behind him. He sported a tunic, but revealed that his arms and chest were clad in shining silver armor fashioned to look like dragon scales.

With that, the lizardkin leapt into the ring to thunderous cheers. I, however, let go of my bard's hand and spent the mana to pop my claws before walking into place. We stood apart, both nodding a traditional greeting.

"Let the battle . . ." Henrietta paused for dramatic effect. It worked, making the crowd suddenly draw their breath. "*BEGIN!*"

And then the cheering exploded. I pushed away my ever-blinking notification tab and sighed.

[Update: Predictive analysis: 61%. Available predictions: attack trajectory, perk activation, and team-based movements.]

Unlike usual, instead of activating his ability to create a sword made out of ice, Knolith drew a long blue blade with runes in the hilt from its sheath at his waist. The blade immediately took to his ice powers and shimmered with a frosty magical aura.

The possible attacks doubled, but I wasn't worried.

He swung the blade once in a fluid motion, shifting his feet apart and coming down into a crouch, his blade pointed at me. I let him make the first move.

"[Ice Field]." Knolith said an ability I'd never heard before as he used his free hand to touch the ground. Our previous battle had been over too quickly to properly see the new powers that Knolith had learned in that cave.

In a wave, cold ice burst from the lizardkin in a circle, encompassing the entire ring and then some. He smiled at me as I spent more mana to transform my feet more into my beast form. The toe claws would help.

"Smart," I acknowledged, taking my own stance. "Now, it's my turn to show off. [Claw Strike]."

Knolith moved his sword into a block for my oncoming paw, except I swung my entire momentum downward into the earth. The beautiful thin sheet of ice that coated the entire ring shattered. It would still be annoying, but I didn't need to worry about being knocked down if I took a single step out of line.

I dodged left to avoid the sword strike, barely missing the edge as it passed beside my right cheek.

The lizardkin retracted the sword and followed me with a side swipe, a jab, and then a full lunge. The cold emanating from the blade as it passed by me was cutting on its own. For my part, every time Knolith lunged forward, I would aim to slip under his guard and land a blow on his person.

In past bouts, I felt like the lizardkin suffered from the problem that many fighters had: trusting your abilities over your own ability. Knolith was always jumping in with a skill or perk as soon as the fight began. This put his skills on cooldown long enough to cause trouble for the swordsman. I could wait until the opportune moment when he was waiting for his skills to be ready again, and strike.

[You have attempted to use the Perk: **Force Palm**. You have failed.]

My palm hit the lizardkin in the chest, and stopped. The new armor took the blow, and I felt like it would leave a dent in *me* before it ever gave way. I pulled back my hand, shaking out the numbness.

Only to realize it wasn't numb at all—it was *freezing*.

Knolith smiled. "How do you like my new armor?"

"It's excellent." I activated my [Identify Craft] perk.

[You have attempted to use the Perk: **Identify Craft**. You have succeeded. Equipped: **Dragon Heart Scales**, a set of mithril scales sewn onto dragon hide. +1 to Elemental Magic. Durability 9/10]

"I got it in Green Oak Dungeon," he said, puffing out his chest. "With my newfound strength, defeating the dungeon was—"

The lizardkin ducked my fist to his face.

CHAPTER 122

He's a Legend

Brownie

Brownie had a front-row seat, and even *she* sometimes missed the movements of the battle.

The lizardkin was as graceful as he was deadly, and her beastman spent a lot of time stepping side to side dodging blows. It *looked* like Rufus took a hit quite a few times, but no ice appeared on him. Instead, Rufus used one as an opportunity to use his palm to strike the lizardkin on the chest.

Brownie had seen that move in Thistlecrick. Then, it had sent Knolith flying out of the ring and granted Rufus victory. This time, however, he was barely forced to take a single step back.

The lizardkin grinned.

When Rufus dipped into a sweeping kick, Knolith jumped. When Knolith almost stabbed Rufus in the thigh, Rufus redirected the sword with a shard of ice from the ring that he had picked up while in the leg sweep. The ice shard exploded into more ice, and Rufus grimaced as the shard in his hand grew just a little bigger, covering his fingers.

"Lemonade!" a voice cried out behind her. "Get your ice-cold lemonade!"

Brownie couldn't pull herself from the battle long enough to order a drink, instead concentrating as Knolith showed off his new set of armor. Well, at least new to her. She wondered if that was even *fair*.

A few seconds later, a tall glass appeared in front of her. It was handed to her by a lizardkin guard whom she'd met before. Not Sithli . . . Chikli?

"Thank you," she said, though she barely blinked away from the fray long enough to take the lemonade.

"Complimentsss of Her Viciousnesss. She's giving them out to everyone, dark blessingsss to her." The lizardkin sat down on the bench beside her. It was the bench reserved for the actual combatants, but he didn't seem to mind. Chikli ran his claws through his short gray mohawk and then said, "So you're the one who has our commander general all riled up as of late?"

"If you mean we are madly in love and swooning over each other, then yes," Brownie joked, knowing their relationship was different than that. She smiled at the slow way they'd grown together, getting closer over conversation and laughter and the journey. It might have just been a few weeks, but they'd gone so far past her desire to squish his paw beanies.

Knolith raised his sword to the sky, snow and ice and sleet summoned around the blade in a building flurry. He stuck out his free hand in time to parry a blow from Rufus.

The ice shard in Rufus's paw didn't encase him in ice like the direct attack from Knolith's ice sword last time. Instead, the ice simply grew a little every time Rufus parried a blow.

He attacked twice more, trying to stop Knolith from finishing his sword arts. The ice had already crept all the way up to the beastman's elbow. At this point, Rufus must have decided that was enough because he shouted, "[Secure]."

Knolith took a blow to the stomach where he had no armor to speak of. It must have done a number to his hit points. Brownie cheered with the crowd even as the lizardkin managed to free himself from Rufus's hold ability. Knolith brought down his sword, still all covered with swirling magical ice, and Rufus leapt back to this side of the ring.

"Go, Rufus!" she yelled, always one to enjoy a good bout. "Go for the eyes!"

Her voice carried over everyone else's, and Knolith looked past his opponent to stare at her with indignation. What could she say? She was a big, loud woman, and she loved a good knife fight.

Chikli laughed and drank some of his own lemonade. "I can see why he likesss you. Sithli likesss you too. And the kitchen ssstaff. And the Dark Lady. We're all very happy for you."

"Wow, Chikli, thank you."

The fight resumed as Knolith took a casual swing from across the ring and shards of ice shot out from the sword. They were aimed at Rufus's feet, and when he jumped high to clear the attack, the shot hit the ground and created a new field of ice. He adjusted midflight and landed on all fours, claws sinking into the ice to keep balance.

"So, wherever you end up, know that you can come back any time. I mean, it's not like you'll *never* come back." Chikli scratched behind his ear. "We just hope you will. Rufusss has been a great bosss."

Brownie finally peeled her eyes away from the fight to raise an eyebrow at the lizardkin sitting beside her on the bench.

"Why does it sound like you think Rufus is going to lose?" she asked, quickly darting her eyes back to the fight in time to see Knolith finally land a blow to Rufus's side with his next volley of sword-slash icicles. Her beastman immediately ripped off his tunic, the fabric freezing solid as she watched. He was shirtless now, wearing nothing but calf-length tights and a ring on a string around his throat.

Frowning down at his icy hand, he drew a deep breath and *yelled*, swinging his fist down and bashing his frozen hand to the ground. He must have taken damage, but he broke up another round of frosty terrain, and the ice on his arm shattered. Large chunks fell off, freeing most of his fingers and a good portion of his arm.

"Tell you what." Chikli chuckled. "I'll make a bet with you."

"What's the bet?" Brownie took a sip of her lemonade.

"If Rufusss wins, I'll buy everyone a round of drinksss at your wedding," the lizardkin stated.

"And if Knolith wins?" she asked.

"Then you've got to come watch the Winter Solstice Tourney," he said, adding, "*And* I'll ssstill buy everyone a round at your wedding."

"Well, that's not a bad deal at all," she replied as Rufus just straight up grabbed his frozen shirt and picked it up to use as a makeshift shield. Brownie was pleased to see the freeze ability was timed and no longer in effect. "Why?"

"Because the General of the East position is going to be vacant, and it's got *my* name on it!" The lizardkin thumped a fist to his chest and suddenly exuded a surprising amount of bloodlust.

Rufus glanced her way and then had to throw himself back to avoid a sword to the stomach.

"And we *all* want Rufusss to come and watch us compete," Chikli added, impassioned. "He's a *legend*."

Watching this fight, where half the ring had been shattered and destroyed or frozen, Brownie could see why other warriors of the Dark Enchanted Forest looked up to the beastman.

At this point, Knolith finally committed to an all-out attack. He blasted forward with his sword aimed straight for Rufus's heart. At the last second, Rufus turned, and the sword strike hit a barrier that Brownie didn't even know was there. The barriers in Peldeep were more obvious, with an added sheen and sparkle to let people know they were there. It was showy, and catered to the crowd.

"HOLD!" Keith's voice echoed, silencing everyone. "The battle will begin again after I set up a new barrier. Contestants may have some lemonade while they wait, but no potions."

Brownie smiled up at her beastman and offered Rufus her glass as he came over to join them. He shot a curious look at Chikli but said nothing, instead taking a long drink of her lemonade and almost finishing it entirely.

"Good fighting out there," she said. "I'm impressed."

He laughed. "I should have listened to you and gone for the eyes."

Brownie leaned forward, as if sharing a very important secret. "I like to make them think that they got me, and then jab 'em." She stuck out her index and middle finger, mimicking the attack.

Rufus leaned over and kissed her on the forehead. "And then Donna finishes them off?"

Brownie nodded. "Exactly."

He handed back her lemonade and then rejoined Knolith in the ring. The lizardkin stood with his ice sword, which had reverted back to its usual blue sheen after attacking the barrier.

Henrietta lifted her hand into the air and announced, "Contestants, are you *ready?*"

Both were in place.

The Dark Queen dropped her hand. "Then, FIGHT!"

Taking This Ssseriously

Rufus

We stood facing each other, Knolith with his sword, and me with my claws. Honestly, it was a bad matchup . . .

I missed my shirt.

The ice crunched beneath my foot as I shifted my stance lower and pushed off in a flying tackle toward the lizardkin. He wasn't expecting me to outright jump him right off the call to resume. I'd always waited for him to attack me first, since it benefited my [Examine] to see an attack. But my skill was currently at eighty-three percent, so there was no need.

This was the first time we'd gone longer than a minute fighting.

Coming down, I spent the mana to turn into my full beast form. Knolith realized that he couldn't just parry *all of me* and made the smart move to dodge.

I nicked his shirt by his left wrist, where the lower arm was unprotected. The dragon heart scales only covered his biceps, shoulders, and upper chest, so there was plenty of room left elsewhere to sink my teeth into if I so wished.

"Finally!" The lizardkin let out a genuine laugh. "You are taking this ssseriously!"

I didn't know what my beast form had to do with taking the battle seriously. If I were being honest with myself, I was hoping that the cold would be more manageable with more fur. It was, thank the gods, and it was easier to balance on the ice as well. I could have just as easily changed into my folk form and put on a pair of warm winter boots with good grip and have the same effect.

Each form had its own drawbacks, though, and even if my strength and damage and speed all remained the same in each form, I was certainly *larger* in this one.

I snapped at his wrist a second time as I dodged his blade.

The worst part about being in *this* form was that I wouldn't be able to do what Brownie suggested. Maybe I should just find an opportunity to put on a shirt instead.

"I've dreamed of this day." Knolith spun and swiped at my legs, making me jump into the air to get out of the way.

"If you wanted to fight my beast form," I said, my voice low and gravelly, "you could've just asked?"

Even as I landed, Knolith was there. But I knew he would be. A blue line that met where I was going to land told me he was going to be there, and activate a skill. I just had to deal with that in my own way.

I burned mana to land just out of reach of his blade in my folk form.

No one in the Dark Horde had ever seen my folk form before, and Knolith paused in shock.

"Change back." Knolith pulled his sword out of the ground and pointed it at me. I could see from [Examine] that he didn't have anything planned; he simply swiped his blade. I dodged easily.

"Why?" I almost skipped out of his reach as he continued swinging wildly at me with no plan or purpose. It was actually harder than it looked, because there were two or three red lines to show where his blade might attack from.

"When I defeat you," Knolith ground out, "it is going to be when you are the legendary Commander General Rufus."

"You mean when I look like this." I spent the barest bit of mana and changed just my ears. The cold of the ice beneath my bare feet was starting to burn, but I could heal that pretty quickly once this was over.

The lizardkin frowned and struck hard, his sword actually landing on the ground from the miss to my arm. "Change back!"

"Or like this?" I threw my arms and torso forward in a way that would suggest I'd change into my beast form and land on all fours again. Knolith, expecting such, hurriedly took a step to the side, his sword still pointed to the ground.

"Hah!" I snapped my clawless hand out and surprise poked him in the eyes instead.

"Gah!"

It didn't live up to my majestic image as the stoic and unyielding commander general . . . but it was worth it when Brownie let out a shout full of joy. But her exhilarating cheer turned into a concerning gasp. I turned to see her, standing up but otherwise fine.

And then I felt it.

The lizardkin hadn't been stepping to the side to let me change into beast form. He'd been *waiting*. His right hand had held the sword, but his left hand had formed his usual full ice blade in preparation for this.

He'd been baiting me.

The sword had extended and pierced into my pants at the thigh, and the ice was already encasing me. With a look of triumph, Knolith pointed his real sword at my throat while he gently leaned forward and pressed the ice blade against the skin of my thigh.

It would be really, really bad if he got ice magic into my blood.

"I yield," I said, lifting both arms.

The lizardkin didn't look like he believed me at first, or maybe that was just his squinty red eyes from my earlier jab. "Truly?"

"I *yield*," I repeated, and in that moment, I actually activated one of my most annoying perks. [Natural Poise]. The passive ability to make me look confident had made my life a thousand times easier since I'd become the commander general, but I rarely bothered to actually use the perk for its own sake. At this moment, I needed it to hide the grin that would have otherwise lit up my face and given everything away.

I knew the lizardkin could do it. Or, at least, I'd *hoped* he was strong enough, and smart enough, to take the job from me.

Because I certainly didn't want it anymore.

CHAPTER 124

Do You Wanna See My Dungeon?

Brownie

"So this is it?" King Keith offered his hand, and Rufus clasped his arm in a firm shake.

"I'll be around." Rufus let go, returning to holding Brownie's hand again. She gave it a light reassuring squeeze.

After Knolith had come out victorious, the entire Black Fortress had gone into celebration mode. It had been almost a *decade* since someone had bested their commander general, and it was the very son of their previous commander general (who definitely *wasn't* crying in the stands with fatherly pride). Knolith had finally grown powerful enough to take the position, and there was a veritable street fair going on outside.

"You know Chloe is going to just outright murder you, right?" Henrietta asked. "That you chose to step down during *her wedding*, making her miss the entire battle. I hope Brownie has ample potions on hand. Actually, here." The Dark Lady handed over two Revive potions, adding, "Just in case."

"It was a fair fight," Rufus argued. "I wouldn't just leave you to someone who wasn't powerful enough to take up my job."

"You aren't helping your case," King Keith said. But he didn't seem angry.

The two couples had stuck around to confer the Commander General title upon Knolith and settle Donna, and then had retreated to the office in the castle to file a report about it. Brownie stood as witness, and the files were already processed thanks to Henrietta. Knolith could sign his own forms later, as he was currently the star of the show outside.

"*Speaking of Chloe.*" King Keith rubbed the bridge of his nose in exasperation. "We left her with the florists. Do you think they'll be alright?"

"No." Henrietta reached out and patted her husband's arm. "We should probably get back fast. Can you summon Gimtak?"

The very imp flew in from the window. "You called for me, Your Viciousness?"

"Were you waiting outside the window this whole time?" Henrietta asked, amused.

"No." The imp shook his head, affronted. "I stayed back long enough to hear Madame Potts's Cast."

"What?!" King Keith snapped. "What did she say now?"

Gimtak opened his mouth, but the king shook his head. "No. Wait. Tulith should be here any second with the transcript."

Henrietta pulled out another potion while they waited. "Gimtak, do you have enough mana to get us back to the border, or do you need a refill?"

"I'll need one when we get there, but I'm fine for this jump, Your Viciousness," the imp reassured his queen. He eyed Brownie and Rufus. "Are all four of you coming?"

"We could bypass any encounters?" Rufus said, putting the question to Brownie.

She shook her head. "No, we still have Donna, and the week long solstice festival has only just started. We'll have plenty of time to get there before the wedding and the actual masquerade ball."

A lizardkin maid appeared in the doorway to the office, coming to a dead stop from a full-on run. Seeing them all standing there, Tulith sighed and walked up to the Dark Lord, curtsying politely.

"Perfect timing, Tulith." King Keith held out his hand, and the maid passed over a sheet of paper.

"I came as fast as I could." She frowned. "You needed to hear thisss."

Everyone leaned in to read the page.

Hello, everyone, this is Madame Potts.
The Fenrir Dungeon boss in the Hollow Gorge is bugged currently,
and only dropping rose quartz grieves. They're found on level six,
so if you want some nice grieves, now is the time to go. Or just wait
outside the dungeon to buy them.
In case anyone missed it, Peldeep came out just fine. This madame
congratulates Peregrine and Bastian on a wonderful wedding. I wish
you both a fine happily ever after.
Sumbria, you know that I know that you don't listen to anything
I say. Case in point with the capybara incident. I understand. So
instead, I'm going to tell you that you definitely should not, under
any circumstances, send your army to Orion's Cove. There are defi-
nitely no pirates docking there. Today. As we speak.

Regent Havork, I just stumbled on a contingent of Doryn loyalists while exploring your lovely countryside. I've sent you a missive with a teacup that you should have already received. Yes. That's me. Now please do the thing.

Anyone on their way to the Summer Masquerade, please note that Blackfog spies are crawling all over North Sumbria looking for something . . . or someone. Bring extra guards if you can.

Speaking of the Summer Masquerade, happy summer solstice, everyone! The seven days of celebration leading up to the masquerade ball start tomorrow! The celebrations for Necromancer Chloe and Countess Julia's wedding are in full force. This foreteller has her own invitation and will see you all at the Masque.

Oh, and if you do go to the Masque, you might get to meet some of the more elusive Valarian eligibles. Lady Amy has just confirmed attendance, and this is a rare opportunity to see the elven saintess in person. Duke Julian von Slyke will be there, and he isn't the main love interest for nothing. He's got tall, dark, and brooding down to an art, and his grumpy sunshine potential is only marred by the man's stunning purple hair. Duke Wyldon will be there, and he's still the perfect catch for anyone looking for that glasses-wearing intellectual type. Master Thomas might show up, the rogue, but he's been too busy representing Servalt on the Continental Council to do much else.

Queen Henrietta should consider bringing her sword to North Sumbria. And a Revive. Maybe four. Yes, four Revive potions should do. That way, Chloe can focus her magic elsewhere.

This is Madame Potts, over and out.

Keith let out a long sigh. "Every time. If you get kidnapped again, I'm burning it all to the ground."

"Not every time." Henrietta summoned her magical sword into her hand and stood on tippy-toes to kiss her aggrieved husband on the cheek. "This will be the second time we battle in North Sumbria."

"Every time she mentions you, there is some harrowing quest to fight evil!" Keith argued. "I would know—*I* was one of them."

"You sure you don't want the ride?" Henrietta asked Brownie, but the bard just shook her head.

"I still have a few encounters to get past, and I don't want them to happen all at once outside Grand Duchess Calisto's doorstep."

"That's probably for the best."

The royal couple bid them farewell before portaling away, leaving Rufus and Brownie in their grand office alone with a few of the bureaucratic members of the Dark Horde plying away at their desks in an alcove closer to the door.

"So." Rufus turned to her. "Do you wanna see my dungeon?"

CHAPTER 125

Happily Ever After

Rufus

I said goodbye to my proper rooms in the castle and threatened Knolith with the one thing he feared most in the entire world if he so much as touched my dungeon before I got back from the wedding to sort through it: a counseling session in that very same dungeon.

I was half joking of course, but he didn't need to know that.

We chose to stay in the inn because my dungeon was full of Blackfog spies, and because I *could*. The moment I'd stepped down as commander general, my notifications had gone from a constant flood to a reasonable trickle. I hadn't really planned what was going to happen next, but the System had filled in the blanks for me, giving me the occupation protector. It wasn't perfect, but Bronwynn and I would figure out what to call me when we had the chance.

At least it didn't choose something ridiculous like Fan Club Leader or Wagon Husband, even if it would've been more apt.

At the end of the day, I processed all of the information in my tabs. And when I was done, it finally hit me. I was in the Black Fortress, and there weren't any new notifications beating against my consciousness, screaming for my attention. The weight of the entire Dark Enchanted Forest had fallen off my shoulders.

I started shaking from the reality of what I'd done. Everything was going to change now. I collapsed into Bronwynn's arms that night and didn't let go until morning. The irony was not lost on me, though. I was practically trading my best friend for a wife . . . but I didn't mind.

I *chose* my wife, and she chose me. It was a small difference, but it meant all the world to me.

We headed out bright and early the next morning.

The first encounter happened five minutes down the road, when Bronwynn saved a crying bird from a hungry fox. It turned into a phoenix and gifted her a single phoenix feather, which was equivalent to a Resurrection potion. If [Revive] simply brought you back to life, the more impressive [Resurrection] brought you back at full hit points.

The second encounter was an overturned carriage beset by a dire wolf, which was unusual since dire wolves lived in the south. Donna spoke to the dire wolf and found out that Servalt merchants had stolen a pup, and the mother had tracked them down to get it back. It was a simple affair. Rufus secured the caravan and used his Cast Crystal to summon a Dark Horde contingent to come pick them up.

He realized that he actually *might* need that full day of counseling with Kno-lith. There were a bunch of tasks associated with the occupation, and tools for the job that still needed to be given over, including the army crystals, his badges, and a cape that Rufus had never worn and was lost somewhere in his dungeon office.

Their third encounter was Gerda, standing on her bridge with both hands on her hips.

"Perfect timing," the bridge troll said.

> "I call you in for dinner,
> But I do not eat or drink.
> Who am I, do you think?
>
> I have a face but not a mouth?
> No legs to show my progress?
> Who am I, can you guess?"

I immediately turned to Bronwynn and said, "Give me a second!"

I could tell by the self-satisfied look on my future wife's face that she'd already guessed the answer. Now that I was going to be along for the ride all the time, I wanted to get better at this.

Three guesses and fifteen minutes later, I had the answer.

"A clock?"

Bronwynn rewarded me with a kiss on the cheek.

"You've got it." Gerda relaxed her stance and stepped aside. "How about a celebratory portal to North Sumbria? I was just heading over to see if our Hero-ine of Justice brought her sword."

"That's perfect!" Bronwynn smiled at me. "We can sleep in a *real* bed tonight!"

Donna whinnied loudly.

"Yes, I bought some in the Hollow," the bard told her horse, who snorted in reply. Bronwynn raised an eyebrow. "But it's not like you're using your magic for [Haste], so why do you need the extra enchanted carrots . . . *Donna.*"

The horse stopped, having pulled us and the wagon fully onto the bridge. Donna looked over her shoulder, and I coughed a laugh into my paw. I didn't need the notification from my [Sense Lies] perk to see through her innocent act.

"Cassandra is going to be there, isn't she?" Brownie threw her arms into the air. "You can't gamble away your enchanted carrots."

Gerda interrupted, vibrant rays of aquamarine portal magic already rising about them. "Ready?"

She didn't wait for us; suddenly, we were looking up the road at the capital city of North Sumbria. The road was pretty busy, but Gerda had timed the teleport just right so we weren't portaling into someone already crossing the bridge.

Our sudden appearance turned a few heads, but when they spotted a bridge troll, most everyone accepted it and moved on.

Gerda marched ahead, choosing to walk with Donna instead of hitching a ride in the back. "Okay, let's go!"

Donna glanced at the bridge troll and sighed, starting up the road.

It was slow going as we joined the rest of the traffic. Seven days of festival and a Summer Masquerade meant a lot of people coming and going. There was another entrance for nobility, but I wasn't anyone important anymore.

"Rufus," Bronwynn said, leaning into me. "Do you want to know why the assassins are able to get past King Keith's golems?"

I suddenly stilled. "Wait, when did you figure it out?"

"Back in Peldeep." She chuckled. "So, do you want to know or not?"

". . . Tell me."

"It's in the riddle. *No foreigner with ill intent to the kingdom or its people.* You can just hire assassins who were born in Nilheim. Depending on the spell, you might be able to get in if just your parents are from the Dark Enchanted Forest."

"It can't be that easy . . ." I stopped and smiled. I wondered how long I could hold it over my king's head when I told him. If I told him.

"Now that's settled, I only have one more pressing question!" Bronwynn declared. "Do you still want to buy a house in the Dark Enchanted Forest and be a stay-at-home husband?"

"And miss out on the adventures? Never!" I wrapped my arm around her. "I'm wondering if we should invest in an upgrade?"

"What do you mean?"

"The traveling house that Tinker Tate had was pretty nice." I brought up what had been on my mind for a while now. "I like the idea of a wagon house rather than a simple canvas cover."

I accompanied this with a gentle kiss on her ear that made her blush.

"I think I'd like that too."

"And what better place to find a high-quality wagon house than in the city of innovation?" I asked. "We could add a bed and some magical lights, or a secret compartment; though we'd still want it to fit into the storage ring I gave you."

I indicated the ring on her hand, and she rubbed it. The half giantess chuckled, amusement clear in her voice. "You know, all this time, I'd been planning to thank Fergus for the ring and the tavern repair."

"Alright, you're welcome."

She guffawed at my audacity. "Really?"

I couldn't help it; I laughed aloud. Bronwynn held out for only a second longer before bursting into laughter with me.

"This is why I shipped them," Gerda whispered to the horse. I took it as a compliment.

Donna looked over her shoulder and snorted.

"I can't believe you," Bronwynn said, poking me in the side. "This is what I get for falling in love with one of my encounters!"

"Was Donna an encounter too?" I asked, innocently dragging the mare into the line of fire.

"Yes, but *technically*"—my bard waved a hand at the murder horse—"*I* saved *her*. *You* had nefarious intent!"

"True," I acknowledged. "But even so, you saved me."

And I meant it. Bronwynn could see that, and her face softened into a smile. Donna chuffed and shook her head, practically rolling her eyes at the pair of us.

"You're lucky that I love you," Bronwynn announced. "*Both* of you."

"Very lucky," I agreed.

"Now, enough of that." Bronwynn summoned Danielle into her hand, plucking a melody I'd never heard before. "Who wants to hear my new song?"

The bard sang for her beastman, as they rolled off into the sunset—technically into the city—and lived Happily Ever After.

Epilogue

The notification tab blinked.

[Quest: Survive Season Two of Dungeon Delves and Debutantes]
Welcome to the World of Valaria, an Open-World Battle Otome RPG for the ages.
Season Two features three new ikemen love interests, new dungeons, access to Servalt and Sumbria, and new crafting material. But beware the threats of revenge, for a new power rises in corruption and cruelty. And our Heroine will have even more at stake than she bargained for.
90% Scenarios Completed
96% Map Explored
87% Hidden Treasures Found
91% Characters Found
Come back to your favorite characters with even more Dungeons, Dragons, and Debutantes!

[Next Scenario: Survive the Summer Masquerade]

There wasn't much time left before the end of season two, and there was still so much to do . . . and saving the world alone was becoming more and more difficult.

The gates to the city loomed, and guards called to show any paperwork for proof of entry. With Blackfog spies afoot, security was almost double that of the Spring Ball.

The invitation was a pass into the city, a wondrous place that was so close to the comforts of home but engineered with magic instead of science.

Sigh.

"Hey, Gerda, wait up!"

About the Author

Mystic Neptune was born and raised on an island surrounded by temperate rainforests, lakes, mountains, and endless ocean. She started writing books when she was twelve, and by the age of fourteen she'd written her first novel. It was about an elven space princess whose evil stepmother messed up her trans-dimensional portal trip to university and sent her to a war-torn restricted universe instead. It was very cheesy, and the ultimately-nine-book series was lost forever on the family PC (Windows 95, anyone?) that died a very final death the summer she was sixteen.

By then, Mystic was living with her very sick single mother and her little brother, and working nights to help pay the bills. There was a little time to read during her school breaks, but not for much else—and no money to replace the home computer. So she filled notebooks with the beginnings of stories and eventually got a laptop in college. Around that time, she also met the love of her life, who read just as much as she did, and they got married shortly after a terrible accident befell her . . .

One day when Mystic was walking to the mall, an iron fence from a construction site fell on her. She suffered from amnesia so bad that she had to relearn English and re-meet all her friends and family. She even walked past her mother in the street and didn't recognize her. But it's OK! She got better!

Once she could read again, Mystic got into isekai because she was tired of picking up books only to remember she'd already finished them. Isekai was new at the time, so she didn't need to worry that her silly memory would come back halfway through a story and spoil the ending. Mystic enjoys reading light novels, webnovels, LitRPG, gamelit, and fantasy. She also loves middle grade and YA books. Her favorite authors/heroes are Patricia C. Wrede, Tamora Pierce, and Diana Wynne Jones.

In Mystic's spare time, she writes and does edit-swap date nights with her husband, Jolly Jupiter. O he of famed dwarven comedy! She also runs after her daughter, Phoebe Vaara. Phoebe is named after Saturn's moon, and Vaara means Danger in Finnish and Stranger in Greek. Phoebe is a rockstar social diva toddler who hikes mountains and has more friends than both her parents combined, so it fits.

Mystic is probably writing right now.

Podium
DISCOVER
STORIES UNBOUND
PodiumAudio.com

www.ingramcontent.com/pod-product-compliance
Lightning Source LLC
Chambersburg PA
CBHW030920120726
47906CB00002B/408